WANTON

Andrea Arven

First published in 1994 by
Nexus
332 Ladbroke Grove
London W10 5AH

Reprinted 1995

Copyright © Andrea Arven 1994

Typeset by TW Typesetting, Plymouth, Devon
Printed and bound in Great Britain by
Cox & Wyman Ltd, Reading, Berkshire

ISBN 0 352 32916 5

This book is a work of fiction.
In real life, make sure you practise safe sex.

1

The women took each of the men in turn. He had to come into the room by himself. It was dimly lit and music played softly. The women were in their party clothes, so that the room was a scented cave filled with the sly sheen and iridescent glow of fine fabric.

The men were blindfolded. That was part of the fun. Though they were all invited, though most of them were friends, they didn't actually know whose hand was on their body, whose hand stripped their clothes.

Each man lay in his turn sacrificially spread. Soft hands undid his garments. Warm hands removed them. Each man felt his flesh stroked, tantalised, aroused by the unseen women fluttering over him. Friends and neighbours, they were seeing him naked, at their mercy.

Now it was Rollo's turn. His eyes were shut behind the mask and he was peaceful. He gave himself up to the tender caresses, the erotic play of the women clustering about his increasingly naked body.

He was beautiful, a handsome golden man full of strength. It pleased him to be exposed. He liked his sex on display. He felt hands lift and stroke it. His own hands were taken and pressed to warm flesh. He felt a woman's breast and as he squeezed, the nipple jutted sweetly into his palm.

His other hand received something even more interesting. It was hard but silky in texture. His fingers slipped. He felt a hot, moist interior.

Within his mask he laughed. It was becoming fashionable again to remove all genital hair. He had in his hand a naked female pudendum. He didn't know who she was, it could be any one of the twenty or so female guests, but his hand was in her cunt and it felt good.

Now they prepared him. He heard them laughing. His cock was lifted. Fingers tickled his balls. His stomach jumped as the first cool stroke took him from root to tip.

They used a pure sable brush, broad and soft. It was dipped into the liquid silk and then painted onto his erect cock. They had made sure he was erect first, and with Rollo this was no problem. It had been easy to lie there and feel their unseen hands making his cock grow. He was warm and at ease, caressed by admiring eyes. One woman had even kissed his naked gland.

Now the brush stroked again and again the length of his cock, firm and cool, delicious, the liquid silk drying at once to form an elastic stretching membrane that enhanced rather than obscured feeling.

They painted his balls. This was the only difficult part. The sensation of the brush working around and across his testicles was so erotic he nearly came.

It wouldn't have mattered. He could have spurted under their eyes. They would have laughed with delight. They wanted to see him aroused, to see him come. It pleased him to deny them, at least for the time being.

He was finished. They took off his blindfold and stood back from him. He blinked and looked at himself. He was lying on his back. As he raised his head and looked down his body, he saw his own jutting sex glowing in green and red where they had painted him in swirls of mixed colour. In the poor light it shimmered.

The paint created an agreeable slight tension in his swollen member. It made him feel very big.

He sat up and looked around the women. They were masked, though they could see, disguised so that he could not tell who was who. He could not even tell which woman was his own wife because they all wore false hair, elaborate wigs in strange shapes.

It pleased him to pull into his arms the nearest woman. She came willingly and he kissed her, mouth to mouth. She was soft and open. His hand slid down. Other parts of her were soft and open too.

He released her and stood up.

'It's time to go through now,' said a tall woman with a husky voice.

He stood obediently while they hooded him again. This time it was a sealed unit. He could breathe, but if he spoke no one would hear and he could hear no one else. That was part of the game. Blind and deaf, he was led through to another room, to a couch.

Left to himself, he adjusted his headset to receive the sort of music he was in the mood for. He felt cut off from the room though he knew the other men were there. His naked, decorated body seemed to float. When all the men were painted as he was, the women would come and the real fun of the evening would begin.

Sandrina was the youngest woman present. She was unmarried, invited as a single, and it was her first time. She had heard about this sort of thing, of course – who hadn't? But the reality was different. If she was honest with herself, she was shocked.

She was a model, a dancer, a singer. She was anything that earned money and she was good enough at everything she did to make money. These elaborate sex-parties were a feature of the Zoo, where the ultra-rich lived. It was their latest sport.

Sandrina didn't live in the Zoo herself; she hadn't that sort of wealth, though she aimed to generate it eventually. The bubble-houses and shopping precincts set deep in the savage forest, entirely enclosed with their own micro-environment, were available only to residents and to those who were invited. She herself had an apartment in the town. She had come by taxi, by special invitation, as a friend of her agent, Mournag Hendriksen. She intended to have a good time.

So far it had more than lived up to her expectations,

though she felt her eyes were out on stalks. Personal sex for her had been something of a private experience prior to this. She was getting a big charge out of the ability to see so much cock in the raw. It might be primitive, this enjoyment of spying on the forbidden, of breaking the rules governing modest behaviour, but it sure as hell was fun. She knew even as she stared at naked man after naked man that this was nothing to what would come later. These parties involved active penetrative sex. She didn't think privacy rated very highly with these people, not among themselves. They were one family, the family of the rich. She was a poor relation, and only that for one night unless Mournag invited her again. She hoped she would. Seeing and freely handling erect private parts was so exciting that already she was having trouble controlling her breathing.

Her own cunt felt strange. She didn't know who would be in it, or how many, before this night was done.

It had been strange to begin with. The women gathered first and shed their evening cloaks. Underneath they wore little. Sandrina had been forewarned, but it had cost her something to come in such flimsy clothes. Gauze-like, her garment drifted on the slightest draught of air. She wore no underwear. She knew it was forbidden. She felt her breasts sensitised, aroused by their lack of adequate cover. Her sex was cool and moist. She was nervous, excited. It had the effect of making her juices run.

She wanted a man. Especially, she wanted one of these rich bastards. She wanted to be poked by one of the men who ran things, who owned things. There were women here every bit as powerful and rich as the men but Sandrina was no lesbian. It was cock she wanted, up her, in her, hard.

The man they had just prepared . . . she'd go out of her way to have him. Rollo Cambridge. He personally owned the majority shareholding in TransFlow, and he ran it as chief executive. He was big business, the biggest, a man afraid of nothing, a man who advised governments. He was married to the legendary Fee Cambridge. It had been quite something meeting her. The woman wasn't young

4

but she was dynamite still, the sexiest and most powerful woman Sandrina had ever met. Sandrina might have no desire for a woman but if ever a female could give her the sexual hots, this was the one. Fee Cambridge was almost terrifying with her white face, slanting green eyes, scarred cheek and sensually perfect body. She carried with her an atmosphere of hooded potency, of secret knowledge that excited and stimulated. If she had been a man, Sandrina didn't see how she could have resisted Fee Cambridge, even with younger things like herself around. She might be juicier, in fact she probably was, but she'd never exude that wanton power, that latent sexual ferocity. She'd love to, though.

Rollo's body was big but firm. His chest and shoulders were muscled, his stomach flat and firm, his thighs corded and powerful. Perhaps riding that tiger wife of his kept him fit. When she had witnessed the sexual licence of the other women, seen how they played with the naked men at their disposal, she had taken the opportunity to do what she longed to do.

She had had her sex depilated. The skin was silky-smooth and the nude appearance of her sexual parts had a surprised air that pleased her. They seemed to pout out-wards, inviting the sly, invasive hand, the male hand to cup and caress her external genitalia. So she had taken this opportunity. While Rollo had lain naked, hard erect, sprawled for them all to see, having his cock painted in glowing liquid silk, she had taken his hand, unfurled his long fingers and placed them between her legs so that her sex rested in his palm.

His hand had explored. She had squeezed her flesh so that he must have felt the moist kiss of her pussy in the centre of his palm. The dry firmness of his skin had excited her unbearably. She wanted this man to fuck her more than she had ever wanted any man in her life before.

They had painted each man in turn. Each man had had adhered to his cock a little shape, maybe a star or a cres-cent moon, a diamond or an oval. Then he was sent through to await the next part of the proceedings.

When every man had been prepared, the women clustered round. In a velvet bag was a complementary shape to match each that had been used for a man. The women each picked a shape. Sandrina found she had a square. Now she had to turn round and poke out her bottom. On one of her buttocks the shape was affixed. It was tiny, exactly the same as the man's. They were based on the patches once used as facial decoration by eighteenth-century beauties.

The women were to join the men now. The aim of the game was for the man and woman who had matching shapes to find each other. Then they would have the freedom of each other's body.

The game was played in the dark. All the women could see were glowing male sexual organs in luminous hues. The men could see nothing but they could feel. The men tended to stay in one place, lying at their ease on the furniture with cushions spread everywhere. The women would roam in the dark, feeling each man in turn, teasing at his cock, testing the little shape with their fingers. The men would feel the women, turn them round, run their hands over their buttocks, feel in their turn the shape the women wore.

No one worried too hard about finding their right partner early on. The feeling game, played in the dark, was almost the best part of the proceedings. No one could tell whose sex they felt. In the dark the difference between the smallest and largest cock was so little it couldn't be judged. The women stroked and caressed the cock and balls in their hands while the men felt round them and stroked at their buttocks, slipping sly hands in and about their vulvas.

Quite half of these Zoo women had had their sex depilated so that Sandrina was by no means easily identifiable. Indeed, she was unknown to all but one person present, her agent and friend Mournag Hendriksen. That she touched and was touched by strangers made the thrill sharper, stronger. Town morality seemed stuffier than ever. Here in the Zoo things were certainly different. She enjoyed how the men lingered in her sex, teasing her gently with avid fingers, fumbling into her welcoming orifice as they

6

pretended they aimed for her buttocks and her little marker square. Meanwhile her fingers felt the silk of their cocks, their bulging veins, their soft foreskins barely concealing the bulging gland within. All around her in the dark were soft feminine gasps, clotted breathing, tight excited laughs.

She was supposed to find the square. It was up to her and him then to couple if they wished. She was in a state of such high sexual excitement that she would have coupled with a bedpost if she hadn't had the assurance of something so much better. But secretly she was hunting the diamond.

Rollo Cambridge had the diamond patch. She had watched as it was attached to his cock. She craved to stroke his cock. She craved to have it in her.

When she found it she kept her arse away from him so that he could not detect she wasn't his assigned partner. Instead she stroked and caressed him, feeling the contours of his sex, exploring his balls with long slender fingers, creeping round between his tight hard buttocks.

He let her. He took her breasts and began to thumb her nipples. She took this as an invitation, and after sucking one finger she slid it wetly into his rear while her other hand grasped the firm column of his sex.

To one side she heard an explosion of laughter. From the general noise she deduced that one poor man, teased and aroused beyond endurance, had come to climax under the soft, never-ending assault. When his shape was matched he would want to perform again, no doubt. But then, that too was part of the fun.

She lowered her face. She began to kiss the cock in her hands. She felt him stir. The powerful body rolled slightly at what she did to it and this excited her more. The finger she had slid into his rear went in further.

This was cheating, she guessed. To bring him deliberately to climax when she wasn't his shape partner was cruel. She didn't care. This might be as close as she would ever come to fucking this man, and as second-best it wasn't bad.

7

Suddenly she wasn't playing a game any more. She released his arse and knelt between his knees. She sucked him properly. She had to make him come. Her own sex was dribbling with desire; she could feel the indecent ooze on her inner thigh. She knew she couldn't put him in her, someone would find out and protest and then she would never be invited again. But she had to make this man come with her body.

Her fingers played with his testicles. With teeth, lips and tongue she masturbated his cock. She gripped the root of it and frigged gently as she sucked and bit him. She felt his body jerk, he was thrusting suddenly and then she had it.

As he bucked hard into her mouth she swallowed him down, salty-strong, with greedy gulps that continued to suck at his climaxing cock. He pumped hard, hitting the back of her throat. She didn't gag; she was experienced at taking men this way. She loved it, eating them, eating their come, drinking their power deep into her so that some atavistic cannibal urge was satisfied along with her perverted lust.

She fell away from him. She looked wildly round the room. There were few cocks to see. Most of the women had found their shape partner and were fucking, there in the dark, in each other's presence. Sandrina found the sight of the glowing, colourful cocks, disappearing and reappearing as they went in and out of their partner's sex, beautiful, liquid art.

She found an empty cock. That was how she thought of it. Indeed, it was her long-suffering shape partner. His cock was up and hard. She turned and presented her rear. His hands cupped her buttocks, palming them. Then he ran his fingertips over her shape.

His hand went round between her thighs. She still had her back to him. His fingers rammed hard into her vagina. She groaned and spasmed on him, so close to orgasm it was a physical pain to hold it back.

He was as frantic as she. He came forward and impaled her where she knelt. She pressed her forehead into the rug, spreading her knees, the feel of the hard male sex in her exquisite.

8

She didn't know his name. She didn't know what he looked like. There had been, could be, no conversation. This was naked sex, stripped to its essentials. He was a cock with a man attached to make it work, nothing more.

He gripped her hips and began to thump into her. This was joy. She was desperate, far beyond gentle foreplay, deep into the country of climax. She went almost immediately into orgasm and she could feel her cunt round him gripping and sliding convulsively, running wet with her juices.

Moments later she lay on her front, sprawled out and exhausted. He lay, a lovely weight, on top of her. Having climaxed in his shape partner he was at liberty within the rules of the game to remove his headgear and restore himself to sight and sound, such as he could in the dark. And smell. Sandrina could smell sex.

The unknown man, his groin in wet contact with hers, placed his face against her. He opened his mouth and she opened hers. Face to face in the dark they kissed and tongued each other.

'You want it again?' he whispered. They could do as they pleased now.

'Yes,' she said languorously. 'Again.'

He rolled off her and moved her so that she lay on her back. He lifted her knees and opened her sex. She saw the hummingbird glow of his member as it swung.

'Can I do something for you?' she asked. The man had just come, after all. He would need time to recover.

'No need,' he said. 'I'm ready if you are.'

He was, too. First he bent and licked and kissed her smooth mound, running his tongue from the divide up onto the hill and back again. He bit at her clitoris, teasing it gently with his teeth. A moment later he inserted his cock into her.

He wasn't as hard as he had been, that could hardly be expected, but he was certainly firm enough to thrill her flesh. She lay lazily whilst he went in and out of her. He dropped his head and they kissed again. She stroked his back and his shoulders, feeling the muscled strength of him, the length of his hair, his neck.

They were fit, these Zoo men. It was strange, another strange thing. She had always associated big money with sagging bellies and heavy, soft flesh.

They came long and slow up the stairway to heaven, the ascending steps of joy leading to the ultimate human experience. They climaxed together with a union of melting flesh that left them panting and clinging to each other, laughing softly in each other's ears, smelling and tasting their hair, their sweat, their shared sexual pleasure.

A bell rang. 'What's that?' she asked.

He took a moment to reply. 'Your first time,' he said. There was amusement in his voice.

'There has to be a first for everyone.' She was annoyed. It was like she was admitting to virginity. These Zoo bastards sure kept themselves in good condition, but they were cocky, ego-inflated bastards, too.

'You took a while to find me.'

'Maybe I was enjoying myself.'

He laughed. 'The bell means they're going to put lights on in five minutes.'

'Do the women take their masks and wigs off?'

'No. Not yet. It's our turn to play around a little. We've only just got our senses back again.'

She couldn't help asking. 'What's it like, having your cock felt by all these women?'

'Sister, you like men feeling you?'

She laughed. 'I guess I do. It's nice to admit to it.'

Again there was that moment's thoughtful silence. She must have given herself away again. Perhaps here in the Zoo women didn't even pretend they ought to like only one man, or they ought to like sex only when they felt some softer emotion alongside it. That was certainly the case in the town. But then, this sort of party was only whispered about in the town, to be disapproved of. It wasn't that the people were any different. It was that here in the Zoo people had no shame and acted out their fantasies. In the town they repressed them and called them sin.

Light swelled soft and glowing from the corners of the room. Sandrina stayed where she was, lying on her back

10

with one knee drawn up. She could feel in herself a desire to blush. She felt exposed, so newly after sex, to have other eyes on her body. Her gauzy clothes had slipped aside. Her vulva softly throbbed. For anyone who cared to look, it was on show.

Her partner sat up and looked down at her with sardonic eyes. 'Mmm,' he said thoughtfully, 'I could tell the figure was nice. Big nipples, too. They feel very nice, lady, when they come up and speak to you. And you're young.'

'Old enough.'

'As you say, old enough.' He kissed her right breast.

He had shoulder-length hair brushed back from a wide forehead. His eyes were quite small but they were wide-spaced and bright with intelligence. He had a beaky nose and a wide, thin-lipped mouth. It added up to a very masculine man, good-looking in a rugged way. He was possibly twice her age but his body was firm and attractive and she knew he had the goods, that he could come up with the necessary.

With him bent over her she took the opportunity to look round the room. She knew who she was looking for. She saw him then, sitting up on a couch, smiling and chatting lazily.

His knees were apart, his painted sex lolling between his legs on full display. As she covertly watched him, he reached into his crotch and scratched the golden mat of hair. Lust went through her so powerfully she arched her back and felt her swollen pussy spasm again.

'Hey,' protested the man at her breast. He laughed. 'You are one greedy lady.'

She felt shame. He thought her sudden sexual charge was from him. It was pretty gross this, having one man at her while she lusted after another.

The small, keen eyes searched her face. 'No,' he said softly. 'You're getting a turn-on seeing all this. You're non-Zoo, that right?'

'That's right.' She eyed him angrily.

'You want to watch some other couple do it while I fuck your arse?' he said casually.

11

Her blood froze. The sense of what he said slowly seeped into her consciousness. Now she did blush. She was damned naïve and he knew it. Of course they all got a charge seeing each other. Indeed, this man at her body could probably see his wife right now pawing some other man or being pawed by him.

'Yes,' she said hoarsely. She did. She wanted to watch another couple at it. She wanted to have her itch serviced while she voyeuristically aroused herself. This might be her only chance, too. If Mournag didn't invite her to the Zoo again, this was a one-shot deal.

As she spoke Rollo Cambridge stretched himself full-length on his couch. The woman with him mounted him. Sandrina stared; she couldn't help it. The woman knelt either side of his hips and took his multicoloured cock in her hand. She stroked it for a moment and then she inserted it into her body. She came down over the recumbent man, pressing with her weight so that he was fully penetrating her. She began to rise and fall on him.

He lay at his ease, his arms folded behind his head. The woman was doing all the work. Her breasts bounced up and down before him. No one took any notice.

'Hey,' said a soft voice in her ear. She jumped. 'You want to watch 'em closer? I don't mind, pussycat, if it helps you to have fun. It's nice to meet someone it's new to. Only I come in the back door, see?'

She hardly heard him. She stood up and he stood with her. He came behind her and ran his hands down the length of her body, sliding them in at her groin. 'I didn't think town pussies were depilated,' he murmured.

'Yeah.' She was insulted. 'We use cutlery too.' But he was right. It was rare in the town, very rare. It had an electric effect on the men there, as well she knew.

He walked her over. Close to the couch he sat down, pulling her with him. She was blushing now. She could see the tanned skin, the springing hair, the lines of the man she wanted so crudely. She could smell his sweat, his spunk. She could see the velvet smooth texture of the woman who mounted him in contrast to his coarser, masculine skin. She could see his muscles move.

She wanted to kiss him. Even though he was being taken by another woman, she wanted to taste his mouth.

She went on her hands and knees. For a moment she shut her eyes. Fingers invaded her body. The room was full of people and she was kneeling in the middle of it, virtually naked, with fingers up inside her, stirring her sloppy, spunk-soaked pussy. Inside her mask the skin of her face was hot.

Rollo Cambridge turned his head. He had brilliant blue eyes, cold as sea-ice, and they bored into her now.

Her buttocks were separated. Her face was maybe a yard and a half away from Rollo's. She said nothing, staring into his while the periphery of her vision absorbed the thews of his neck, the width of his chest, the wisp of hair springing from his armpit.

Fingers entered her rear. She jumped and gasped slightly. A finger rolled round inside her, slippery with spunk. For a moment she was tight, then she gave a small moan and relaxed. She felt the blunt, nubby head of the cock begin to press. She groaned again, closing her eyes, feeling sweat spring on her forehead.

He was pushing hard. Her body sagged forward. She opened her eyes and looked pleadingly into space.

She looked straight into Rollo Cambridge's ice-blue stare. Very slowly, he started to smile. Her mouth fell open. The cock opened her rear and thrust right in. She panted hard, willing herself to relax. Rollo was grinning. He knew what was happening and it amused him.

The woman on him took no notice of her. Her eyes were closed and dreamily she rose up and down as if determined to enjoy the pleasure of the man beneath her for as long as possible.

The invasion in her rear was gross. She had to grit her teeth against it. She had been sucked and kissed there. She had had fingers inside her and enjoyed them. She had fucked herself with a dildo there. But she had never had a man up her and it was different, certainly different. The live pulsing flesh was cruelly exciting. She felt her pussy drip spunk as it was squeezed, almost as if she was a tube of come being compressed and emptied out.

13

She shut her eyes again at a particularly fierce thrust. She felt her face touched. Her eyelids fluttered open. Rollo had reached out one long arm and was touching her, her eyes, her lips.

She caught his finger between her teeth. He made no effort to withdraw it, as if he were uninterested in whether she would pass her pain to him or not. Instead she closed her lips, releasing her teeth. She began to suck the finger as if it were a little cock.

The thrusts were quicker now. She could feel her breasts swing. Then they too were felt. Startled she looked down, not letting the finger go from her mouth. Another man had knelt beside her and was letting her nipples brush his palms as she swayed to the blows at her rear.

Her eyes came up to Rollo's again. His smile was provocative. Gently he withdrew his finger. With sudden violence he tore her mask off. He opened his hand. She buried her burning face in it feeling its strength cup her.

The man in her came to climax. She felt the spasm of his sex as a painful pleasure. His muscle rippled and rippled in her. When he withdrew it was a blessed release.

She would have fallen but that her face was in Rollo's hand still. The man stroking her nipples sat back. He said something and people laughed. Was she being watched? Was this not normally done?

Rollo caught her under the chin and pulled gently. She came forward on her knees towards him. She saw that he wasn't young, that his knowledge was old and tired even though his body was strong yet and would be for years. He was old in experience.

Now his arm was round her shoulders. Still the woman mounted on him rose and fell. Sandrina brought her face close. She saw his lids droop, she saw the thin sensual line of his lips. A moment later she felt them under hers.

Her face was on top but he kissed her. His mouth was everything. She tasted his power, his world-weary strength, his knowledge of what she wanted from him. She felt her own youth and inexperience and eagerness and she knew she had nothing to offer him. He had everything he had ever wanted.

14

Their faces came apart and she looked into his eyes. He moved rhythmically all the time like a slow steady pump. 'I wish I had something to give you,' she whispered.

He brushed his lips on hers. This close, the coldness of his eyes was terrifying. 'I'll think of something,' he said.

He must have seen her fear. His ironical smile returned. 'I'll take that for a start,' he murmured.

'What?' She didn't understand him.

'Such desire. Such enthusiasm. Such a capacity to feel afraid. Give them to me and you can have anything you want.'

She knew that he mocked her. It was like holding a conversation with the devil. She knew further that if it lay within her power she would give him anything. Anything.

Fee Cambridge was damned angry. She and Rollo were supposed to be going out together for a quiet drink in the new place opened on Twenty-Six. They were meeting her good friend Diana and Teddy, her husband. It wasn't a big deal but then that was its charm. It wasn't business. It wasn't formal. It wasn't official. Just for once they were going to behave like a normal couple and go out casually for a drink with friends.

It was as much her fault as Rollo's, she admitted that. She had her own business life separate from his and meetings spilled into the evening, work needed doing and like him she loved to work. Sometimes they didn't see each other – bar a few exhausted hours in bed – for a week at a time. When one was free, the other was rarely. They were notables too; they were on official lists and were into embassy beanfeasts and government sprees. It was good to attend such functions, to go together, both important in their own right and quadruply so together.

She liked it when they went out together, too, both dressed up to the nines and looking really hot. She knew they made an impact as a couple. They were damned good-looking the both of them, and age wasn't harming them one bit.

But this thing with Diana and Teddy mattered to her. It

was just because it was unimportant that it was important. If they got too smart-arsed and uppity for a casual drink with old friends, then they weren't fit for anything. They'd be too smart to live. This was the reality under the game they played with their lives. This was the bedrock on which they built the crazy edifice of their wealth and charm. They needed it. Rollo should be able to figure that. He should be home with her now, getting ready.

If he wasn't going to turn up, how should she punish him? Fee thought about it carefully. Perhaps she should hire a licker. She laughed. It was a pleasing thought. There was an occasion some time ago when she had brought hired sex into the apartment. Rollo had come home and caught her at it. He had swallowed the insult of having his wife serviced by a hireling in front of his face and vented his rage on her choice of location. It should be elsewhere, he insisted, not in their home.

Fee stretched and looked out through the plastiglass wall. The vast, dark green, bifurcated leaves pressed close. The jungle outside, utterly uncontaminated by any human presence, clasped the bubble house as though it would squeeze it until it was crushed to death. It was full of beasts, little crawling carapaced things with too many segments, too many legs. There were bigger things with globular, unblinking eyes, their poisonous, slippery skins in bright, alarming colours. Yet larger were the things with scales and crests that had big dry claws to grasp their crunchy, unscreaming prey. And again, there were the furry and feathery things, stalking, fluttering, swinging through the trees, all grace and alien movement.

She remembered that last really satisfying row. She had hired the licker and had him come to the apartment because she had had a minor viral infection that made her face puffy and her eyes stream. She had wanted sex, Rollo had been busy as usual, and she hadn't wanted to go out to one of her lovers to appease her appetite because of her appearance.

Her appetite could have waited, but she didn't get a lot of free time and now, with this temporary illness, it hung unusually on her hands. It seemed hard not to fill it with something agreeable. She hadn't felt up to penetrative sex so she had dialled for a licker.

He had been a student, she remembered. They usually were, paying their way through college by supplying the rich with esoteric sexual services. He had arrived with his certificate of oral hygiene. She had removed her lower clothing before he came and wore only a loose velvet housegown that opened easily.

She had sat down and opened her legs luxuriously wide. She enjoyed displaying her sexual arena to male eyes, even insignificant ones like this unknown male student about to perform a humble sexual service for a fee. She paid more attention to her manicurist. With this boy she wouldn't even bother to ask his name.

His first task was to cleanse her. She enjoyed this. He attached the nozzle so that it was seated comfortably over her vulva and switched the appliance on.

Fee spread her arms along the back of the couch. She let her head hang back, exposing her long white throat. She closed her sore eyes. The student knelt between her open legs holding his machine.

Warm sterile water swished across her sexual parts and invaded her vagina, cleansing and sanitising her absolutely. For five full minutes the sensation went on. When it was done, the student knew that there was no way he need be afraid of what he was to suck. It was cleaner than most food.

He was quite good. He began by gently teasing her sexual lips apart and kissing the little mysteries within. He stirred her softly with his tongue. She enjoyed this, feeling her foliate flesh separated and warmed and aroused. She knew she would swell as she aroused, become a richer red. Her inner sexual cushioning would grow pulpy and soft until its rich, sugar-pink pads were exposed through the slackened opening orifice. Her clitoris would stiffen and grow a deeper pink.

He began to lick properly, beginning at her anus and working forward with long, strong licks. She shivered with

17

pleasure. This had been a good idea. Now he broke off to nibble the fleshy protrusions, to suck and stretch them until they were so sensitive that little fireworks were exploding in her pussy.

After a while he began to dart his tongue in and out of her pussy. It was at this precise moment that Rollo had come home.

The licker was doing what he was paid to do and didn't stop. Rollo came through and saw his wife there with the head of hair between her long milky thighs.

'What's this?' Rollo's voice was harsh.

Fee wasn't in the business of admitting she might be at fault. She went straight on the attack. 'I'm getting sucked. What does it look like? I didn't realise you were coming home or I'd asked you to do it for me.'

'Jesus Christ, Fee.'

'What's the matter?' She was jeering, urging him to make the conventional response.

'Not here. Not like that.' The disgust in his voice was thick.

She felt a spurt of anger. How dared he come this sanctimonious tone with her. 'Why not?' she said icily.

'Bringing some little tongue-boy home. Have you no sense of wrong and right?'

'Not so's you'd notice. And he's good. He's official, dammit. I didn't pick him up somewhere in a back alley in the town. He's certificated.'

'There are things you do at home and things you do elsewhere. I thought you knew that.'

'I don't feel well enough to go out. This is just what I want, a man at my pussy.'

All the time the lad sucked and licked at her sex. She was enjoying arguing over his head. She could feel him quivering. He was afraid. That wasn't surprising. Crossing Rollo Cambridge was only for the brave. She would pay him double and make sure he knew he was safe before he left.

Meanwhile she was angry enough to enrage Rollo as far as it was possible for her to do so.

She hadn't moved from her sprawled posture all this

18

while, except to lift and twist her head to argue with Rollo. Now he came over close. She was unable to prevent herself from feeling a thrill. Her adoration of him was unaffected by time and habit. He thrilled her as he had when she first met him. No man compared with him. Only one had even come close and he had gone away for good.

'Get rid of him,' hissed Rollo.

He was genuinely angry. He wasn't playing games. Fee smiled. 'No.' She licked her lips. 'I haven't come yet.'

'You bitch.' His voice shook. Fee saw that his lips had gone white. He was almost snarling. 'You'd do it in front of the maid.'

'I'd do it with her, sweetie. Remember? So would you.'

She had him there. Years before she had seduced their young and nubile maid, encouraging the girl to entice Rollo into her bed. The three of them had ended up together and it had been a lot of fun.

'Get out of here, boy,' roared Rollo.

Fee put out an arm with the swiftness of a snake. Her hand lay on the student's tousled head like a benefaction. 'I'm doing the hiring and firing here,' she said icily. Her cunt started to cream. The naked antagonism from Rollo was a delicious spice.

Rollo sidled round behind the kneeling figure. 'I'll attack him if he doesn't go,' he said viciously. 'Is that what you want, you bitch?'

'You'd attack a hired licker? Come on, Rollo. Be real.' She laughed. She was deliberately humiliating him.

At that moment she came. She gasped, caught almost by surprise. Her pussy pulsed hard and her head went back. Her robe fell open so that her long firm pendant breasts were visible. Her head tossed from side to side. She moaned, squirming against the boy's sucking mouth. Then she was done.

Cowering, he withdrew. 'You want cleaning, ma'am?' he enquired in a voice husky with fear. Rollo emanated violence.

'Yeah,' she said. Her breasts rose and fell. She knew Rollo was excited.

The licker attached his machine again. Warm water soothed her excited parts, washing her clean, freshening her.

Rollo said nothing. He stood for a full five minutes facing her. She smiled at him, her green eyes glittering.

Now the boy was packing up. Fee got to her feet and signed for the service he had provided. She tipped him lavishly. 'Don't be frightened,' she said casually. 'He's angry at me. He won't take it out on you. He's not that small a man.'

The boy glanced nervously over his shoulder. Rollo stood menacingly still. He licked his lips. 'Will you be OK, Ms Cambridge?'

She laughed. 'I'll be fine. You go now.'

The door to the apartment closed. They were alone. 'I want to hit you,' said Rollo. 'You slut.' His voice was tight and strained.

Fee slumped on the couch. Unaccountably, she felt ill. Her face throbbed. She closed her eyes. 'You are more than life itself to me,' she said in an exhausted voice. 'But I will not do as you say, like I was some damned lapdog or puling mistress grateful for your cock.'

'I don't want you to bring hired sex home,' he said bitingly.

She slitted her eyes at him and smiled. 'Why don't you beat me?' she whispered. She rolled over, sliding out of her housegown as she did so. She was quite naked. She drew her knees in under her so that her bottom projected upwards. 'Beat me, Rollo,' she said. 'With the whip.'

Remembering this gave her a real pleasure. There could be no way she could antagonise Rollo more simply and surely than by repeating the offence. If he came home and found a man's head between her thighs again he would be truly furious.

A man's head. Lickers came in both genders. She could hire a woman. She was perfectly happy to have a woman's soft mouth at her sexual parts. It would add a nice twist to the business. Rollo would be that much more inhibited in

20

his rage in front of a strange woman, and he would be that much more angry when she had got rid of her. That would suit her. She was spoiling for a row. The angrier he was, the greater would be her revenge.

She was at the vidi dialling when he came in. She looked coldly over her shoulder at him. He dropped his case and walked over to her, putting his hands on her shoulders. He buried his face in her hair and nuzzled her.

Bastard. They should have been with Diana an hour ago. Now it pleased him to soft-soap her.

'Could you send a female licker here, please,' she said sweetly. 'The address is . . .'

He hit the message breaker and killed the connection. He whirled her round and dropped to his knees in front of her. She looked down into his cold, blue-blazing eyes and felt the excitment take a hold of her. The adrenalin surge was better than a rush, better than the whole world. She felt mean and nasty. 'I couldn't help it,' he said. 'Don't wind me up, Fee.'

I love you, she thought and struck him hard across the face.

He didn't react as he should have done. He let his face fall forward into her lap. She grasped his hair and hauled it up. 'Something come up?' she queried. 'You couldn't call me?'

She could see the red mark coming where she had struck him. 'I was attacked,' he said strangely.

'Attacked?'

'I was in the town. I wanted to see Jacomo. He's in hospital. It's only minor but I thought it would be decent to see him in person. He collapsed at his desk, you know. I was just going to see him and come home. There was plenty of time.'

'So what happened?'

'I don't believe it myself. I saw him as planned and came out. I wasn't using the Connet as you know. I stood a moment looking for a taxi. Hell, it was a nice day. For a moment I went into the hospital grounds there and walked through this flower garden place they have. You know, the

21

sun shone, the grass was green, the birds twittered, the bees buzzed.'

'I'm not fond of nature,' said Fee coldly, 'but I kind of know what it's like.'

'I turned to come back to the taxi rank. These two women came towards me. When they got close one spoke to me. She asked me if I was Rollo Cambridge. I said yes and they jumped me.'

'You mean they tried to rape you?' Fee was heavily sarcastic.

'I mean they tried to kill me. Look.'

He stood up stiffly. He pulled his clothes apart, opening his shirt and showing Fee his side. There was a big bruise, raw and angry. His chest had marks on it too.

The women had gone for him with fists and boots. He had been kicked and punched hard. One of them had a stick. She had beaten him with it.

For a moment the surprise had been so great he had done little to defend himself. Then he had been inhibited from using his full strength by their gender. It took him only a very few seconds to realise the deadliness of their intent, but he took some severe punishment in those seconds. Then he was fighting back.

It had all been over in a very few minutes. Someone had seen and come running. The women had scrambled to their feet and fled. Rollo had been left sore and stupid-looking.

He had been taken into the hospital and examined. None of his ribs were broken. He was so angry and bemused he hadn't noticed the passage of time. Finally he had had a flaming argument with the hospital. He didn't want to report the incident to the police. He simply wanted to get away. Then he had felt ill in the taxi. The man had pulled up before arriving at the Zoo and Rollo had sat for a bit. Then he had been driven back to the town to a pharmacy. Then he had come back to the Zoo.

Fee took him to the bathroom and made him undress. The hospital had anointed his sores but she needed to see for herself. Then she stroked his hair back and asked what he wanted to do.

22

'I don't want to make you mad,' he said, 'but actually I'd like to go out for that drink.'

So they went. What it had all meant neither of them knew. Random violence certainly existed but it was rare and usually had some sort of purpose. The attack on Rollo had no purpose that either of them could figure. He carried nothing stealable, nothing that could access his wealth and resources if used by someone else. He certainly had enemies but they were business competitors who were not in the habit of punch-ups, and if they were, they wouldn't hire a couple of women.

No one had known Rollo would be where he was. His secretary knew he was going to the hospital, though not the precise time he would be there. No one, not even himself, had known he would go for that sudden spontaneous walk.

It was one of life's little mysteries. The best thing was to put it out of their heads. They would never know what the motive was, if there was anything involved that could be described as a motive. It could simply be an expression of the continuing town–Zoo antipathy. Meanwhile Rollo was sore, and Fee owed him one. She had behaved regrettably badly.

He was busy but he was bored. It had got so bad he admitted it to himself now. He felt restless and jaded. He found himself wanting to take chances, unnecessary risks with his business. TransFlow. He had built it himself, made of it a corporate empire that controlled a continent's water supply. But he had diversified very little. This was partly his own doing. He had business flair and an ability to take risks. Having established TransFlow, he had been careful to acquire a board of conservative members who would assist in its establishment and growth, men who would cut across his own crazy moves and assist him to build real wealth and security. TransFlow was Blue Chip. Its shares hardly faltered during the recurrent dips in the business cycle. Its solidity and financial worth would satisfy the most megalomaniac of empire builders, but Rollo Cambridge was in his late forties and craved a new challenge.

He took time to look at his life. It was busy and dull, predictable. The only unknown, curiously, was his crazy cat of a wife. They had been married many years now yet she still had the power to thrill him till he almost went out of his mind. Her behaviour frequently disgusted him, sometimes amused him, made him achingly proud of her but never ever bored him. She made him so mad he had hit her more than once in their long life together. She had orgasmed and laughed at him. She didn't get off on violence, it wasn't her thing, he knew that. What aroused her was arousing him. Getting him into any extreme mood gave her a real rush. Increasingly, she was the only aspect of his life that could induce any emotional fireworks at all.

These sex parties now, the latest Zoo craze. The Zoo had always, like the aristocracy of old, had its own sexual mores separate from the mass of bourgeois society. They had always stuck their noses in the air and walked their own path so far as behaviour was concerned. Modesty and innocence had never been notable Zoo virtues. But the sex parties were something else. Deliberately created to outrage decent people, they were the last gasp of a society scratching frantically at the itch of boredom. They were stuff of the sort that had made for the decline of the Roman Empire. Decadent. They were truly decadent.

He and Fee had been invited to another one now, run by their old friends Monroe and Diva Jackson. The trouble was that Zoo society was small and they were on everyone's list. He could bear to skip this latest do but Fee seemed keen. He knew why.

You could buy little patches, not decorative things like they had used at the shape-matching party, but full of a chemical that leaked slowly through the skin. These particular patches contained flavour and colour chemicals. Attached underneath a man's balls they painlessly seeped into his gonads. After some hours this had the effect of flavouring and colouring the spunk a man produced. He could then climax with milky purple and blackberry-flavoured semen. Or pink and strawberry-tasting semen. Or brown toffee-flavoured semen. The possibilities were endless.

24

The idea for the sex party was that each male guest was issued with a patch prior to the entertainment. The patch would be unidentified as to flavour. Partners were not permitted sexual congress once the patch was in place; they had to be trusted over this.

When the party commenced the idea was very simple. Each woman was given a flavour to find. The first successful woman won the prize. If, for example, you had to find the man flavoured avocado, there was only one way to go about it. In the circumstances the party was expected to last many hours.

Rollo knew that Fee adored mouthwork. Sucking was her favourite sexual perversion. She would suck men or women, she didn't care. This knowledge both revolted and excited him. She loved the taste of sex in her mouth and as she couldn't reach her own parts she reached other people's.

He admitted he got a kick out of the sex parties. He had always liked fucking in all its various forms and though Fee was enough for many men, let alone one, he had had lovers at various times just for the pleasure of the novelty. He had a feeling his horny wife was the same, though he preferred not to think about that. She had the humiliating power to make him jealous, an emotion he despised. He didn't care if she bought a perversion now and again; that couldn't threaten him and it was something he could understand, though he hated it in his home. But he had no desire to think of her really enjoying herself with another man. He worked quite hard at not letting her know this.

He had watched her at the sex parties. They didn't go deep, these public displays. She got something out of doing it in public; in another age she would have been a fabulous courtesan, but it meant little to her beyond a temporary amusing diversion.

This coming party would be something different. It was extreme even by Zoo standards. No one outside the most select Zoo circle would be invited, the Jacksons had stressed that. Rollo remembered the little town girl at the shape-matching party. His mouth twisted with amusement.

He knew about power-groupies, the women who got off on making it with famous men. It was an agreeable perk of his position in society and he wasn't above exploiting their adulation now and again. There would be no one like her at this one, though, and no blabber-mouthed gossip columnists. Town society was getting a little restive with Zoo sexual extremism as it was. They were having a swing back to conventional restrictive morality again, but it would pass, as moral fashions always did. No, his problem with this coming party was that he knew Fee would really get off on it. Twenty-four hours or so of sucking men until they came so she could taste their spunk – it might have been made to order.

Dammit, it was too much. He didn't want to be forced to watch his wife getting so much from other men. The idea was disgusting.

He couldn't back off, though. She was so damned sharp she would know why. Naturally enough, he rather liked the idea of women's mouths at his cock for a prolonged period. He didn't mind being sucked by the ladies. He just didn't want Fee there.

He would rather suffer than admit to jealousy. He was absolutely caught. He couldn't admit he was jealous, that it bothered him. So he would have to endure.

His mood could hardly have been filthier. But he smiled and nodded and went through the motions. His secretary looked at him oddly but he didn't think anyone else knew anything was wrong. Fortunately Fee was working so hard in the run up to the party she couldn't tell either.

Diva Jackson came to put on his patch. Trust her to get this extra thrill out of the business, going round all her male guests and feeling their balls before the entertainment had even got underway. She was a raddled old whore, was Diva, whose proclivities ran to very young, very dumb, muscle-bound gigolos. She liked to lead round her latest acquisition on a gold chain as though he were a pet. Which of course he was. So it was unusual to see Diva without her tame twenty-year-old at her heels. At least she had the decency to arrive at fiddling with his balls without her paid bedpartner present.

'Hey, baby,' she said almost absently as she came into the apartment. Her lizard eyes flicked round. Fee wasn't there. 'How's Rollo?'

'Bored.'

Diva tittered. 'Occupational pursuit of the great and the bad, baby. Aren't we all bored?'

'Surely not you.' Rollo grinned. The old bag had something going for her. She was always sharp, always witty, nearly always cruel.

'Oh, me. I always have the enduring problem of how to help Monroe get it up. I'm so looking forward to the party. Monroe says we should have boys as well as girls to do the tasting. What do you think, Rollo? Do you want a boy sucking you off? Monroe says it's fun.'

'Is it fun, Diva?' asked Rollo blandly.

She tittered again. 'You know me, baby. I love 'em any way they come, but especially I love 'em firm and smooth. My latest pussy-prick came into the world forty-five years after I did. Sigismund, I think his name is. He don't have much between the ears, Rollo, but he has it lower down. Between the thighs. Know what I mean? He'll suck you if you want him to. He does anything I say.' She licked her lips and looked up into Rollo's face, watching like a hawk for the first sign of repugnance. Nothing could make her laugh more than making sexually sophisticated men gag at her outrages.

'You like to watch, huh?' His tone was mild.

She cackled at the insult. 'At my age, baby, sometimes that's all I can do.' She brought her haggard face close, standing on tiptoe to reach up to Rollo's height. 'Even my mouth is dry these days,' she whispered horribly. 'No juices, darling. Sigi has to lubricate me now all the time, even before I can get to work on Monroe. But then, Monroe likes it from a boy so he doesn't mind second-hand sex-juice in me. It gives him a charge.'

He couldn't control it. His eyes flickered in revulsion. She stood back and screeched delightedly. 'Wait till it's your turn,' she shrieked. 'Wait till Fee gets like me.'

27

'That's enough!' She had gone too far.

She stopped dead. Far from mocking his sudden exposure of real emotion, Rollo saw her naked hunger, her envy for something genuine.

'You know, baby,' she whispered. 'Fee is so fucking lucky. If I'd had a man like you I guess I'd never have gone with anyone else ever.'

There was a long silence. Then she shrugged. 'Gonna let me finger you, baby? That's what I came for. Give an old friend a thrill, huh?'

'Sure. Come in here.' Rollo led her into the main living room. One wall was all plastiglass so that the jungle beat against the house in living colour and life. He removed his lower clothing, smiling faintly while he did so. Then he lay down.

Her lizard eyes went up and down his lower body. 'Mmm. Yummy,' she said. 'You know, you're nearly as well made as Sigi, and that's saying something. That guy is so well hung he's art. Now, do you want me to wash my hands?'

'For Christ's sake . . .'

'Sorry, baby. Going too far gets to be a habit. Here, let me lift your lovely dingo. Sweetie! How nice. You're responding. Ol' Diva doesn't expect gorgeous juicy men like you to get anything off her crabby old claws.'

'Stop it, Diva,' Rollo protested, half-laughing. She was so awful it wasn't true.

'Baby, baby,' she crooned. 'If you knew how I loved to feel a man swell in my hands. Regrettably, it's a rare pleasure.'

Her hands were a dry rustle on his cock. 'Fit the patch,' said Rollo. He looked out at the jungle.

He felt his balls delicately lifted and stirred. If he didn't look at her, it was a pleasant thing. She had skill, ancient skill, and he resented her talents and her ugliness going so inappropriately together. But his body responded and in a way he was glad. It was the best compliment he could pay her.

'It doesn't hurt,' she whispered.

28

'I know.' He was impatient. He wished she'd get done and go.

'Of course, some men like it to hurt.'

'I know.'

'It takes time, baby.'

'Yes.' She was frankly stroking him now.

'You and Fee, no fucky-fucky. Promise?'

'We know the party rules.'

'Baby, let me kiss it. Just once.'

'Oh Christ, Diva. Don't do this.' Don't ever beg, he pleaded silently. Don't ever get reduced to begging.

Then he screamed and sat up indignantly. 'You bit me, you bitch,' he shouted.

She rocked back on her heels, screeching with laughter. 'Didn't you know, Rollo? If I can't kiss, I bite. I thought you knew.'

She was still laughing as she went out of the door.

The party became a kind of nightmare. He didn't want to go. He didn't like having his spunk interfered with. He wasn't in the mood for witty, barbed conversation. He wanted to fuck his own wife in his own home in the ways that he and she enjoyed.

He had hardly seen her in this last while. Her computer business was expanding into business networking and problem-solving algorithms. She now made maps of how company employees communicated to get the job done; their real communication that is, not the formal hierarchy. She could depict this as a vector diagram. Having reflected the way the real company worked, the passage of information could be speeded and eased where it most mattered. Further, where problems occurred, they could be traced by means of a program to their source, and a particular defaulting employee could be identified.

These skills and services were in ever greater demand. Fee had more work than she could handle. More and more businesses found that far from her being too expensive, it cost them too much to manage without what she could do for them.

29

Now she had cleared the decks for this indecent party. Rollo felt a futile anger. Couldn't she see that her priorities were wrong?

Of course she couldn't. All she could see was a glut of oral gratification. She was happily looking forward to it.

Again the women and the men were masked. Since the men were otherwise entirely naked, they wore elaborate headdresses and confections that expressed whatever aspect of their personality they felt like exaggerating. There were judges' wigs, mortar boards, Roman helmets, puffed and powdered hairdos of all kinds. The women retained their clothes, but wore little black satin masks that enhanced their seductive attractiveness.

It went on and on. They ate. They drank. They sucked.

Rollo discovered he was mango-flavoured. He had the strong feeling that Diva had fixed things since her own husband, Monroe, ludicrously had the flavour of a banana. Her tame thing, the young man she kept as her sexual pet, was durian. This was so extreme that Rollo knew she must have had the flavours made specially.

He was annoyed about this. There had been an agreement not to talk about this one outside the circle of invited guests. They all knew they were at the limits of acceptable social behaviour, and many of them led some kind of quasi-official or public life. They didn't need publicity about this, especially in the current climate of opinion outside the Zoo.

But if Diva had had the patches made specially instead of just buying what was available, which was normally described coyly as enhancing the marital experience, then the supplier would know that this was a special occasion. A social occasion. And the news would be out.

The terrible thing was that he enjoyed it. His mind and body revolted against each other. He really enjoyed lying back and having lips on his cock, drawing it up, playing with it. He liked the wet warmth of the mouth caverns applied to his sexual member. While they sucked, most of the women played with his balls, fingered him and titillated his arse. These were skilled sexual sophisticates. They were

30

enjoying themselves, and in the process they were giving him one hell of a lot of enjoyment.

He had a kind of extra kick. He and Fee were leaders in their society. Even the exclusive Zoo acknowledged that some of its members were greater than others, and he and Fee were up there at the top. They lent a cachet to an occasion simply by being present. Thus he knew, as the ladies came to him one after another, after sensitively-managed intervals so that his performance would be gratifyingly electric, that these women wanted to sleep with him. He had power, he had authority, he had status even in this powerful and status-ridden world. And he was good-looking. It wasn't vanity, it was common sense. He was a beautiful man, he could hardly help knowing it. So for some of the party guests, getting access to Rollo Cambridge's body was the best thing about the whole business.

He knew it and it soured him. What the hell else was there for him in life? He had it all. He had everything. He was a man who enjoyed living on the edge, and his edges were so far out there was little left outside them. The very breadth of his experience had become a cage.

The party began to get out of hand as time went on. Not all the men were sexual athletes. One had protested laughingly that he couldn't manage any more. He was spunked out. He'd shot his load for good and would need days of rest. The women had taken this as a challenge. They combined to bring him off one more time. They would make him spunk in the open and then they would all get a taste. They wanted to see him arc.

Rollo went to one of the bathrooms. He took off his black hangman's hood. Wearily he pushed his bright hair back and looked into his blue, cold eyes. He washed his face and his cock. Then he went to the bedroom and found his clothes. He dressed. He had come all in black. Now he slid stealthily out of the apartment. He could hear them shouting and screeching with laughter in the main room.

He had looked in as he passed. His wife Fee was masturbating the man with her breasts.

He decided to get drunk.

31

2

Sandrina had a two-week spot singing at the Black Cat Casino in Level Verges on the west side of town. She had herself listed in a multi-skill agency because she hated doing the same thing for long. Fortunately her skills were diverse enough for her to earn her living in a variety of ways. The drawback was that she made no progress in any one of her spheres of competency, but then she was still young. She was in her early twenties. She had a long way to go yet, and if ever she concentrated her energies, she felt with youth's happy optimism that she would go far.

She was singing *Blue Lovin' Gone Bad*, giving it all she had, when she saw him.

He sat at the bar nursing his drink. Through the smoke-hazed air she saw him bright, though that was her fancy. He wore all black and sat very still. He appeared to be alone. She didn't know what happy coincidence had brought him here but she was sure as hell going to get what she could out of it. It was OK for her to floorwalk as she sang if she had the confidence, and so she stepped elegantly down off the raised staging now and began to circulate among the customers resting in the bar after losing their money in the next room.

She sang and shimmied a little and stroked a couple of heads and made the customers smirk and feel flattered. Slowly she worked her way to the bar. Rollo was slumped against it but he was watching her from under hooded eyes. He recognised her, she was sure. The implicit flattery in this was lovely. If he remembered her, she was halfway there.

She had moved onto her next number by the time she reached him. It was the classic old weepy, *Full Heart, Empty Bed*.

The words were banal, the melody treacly, yet it never failed to stir. It had that rare unpredictable combination of schmaltz and truth that hit below the emotional belt. Now she stood directly in front of Rollo and sang with a soft, sad throatiness:

> The sun has lost its heat.
> The music's lost its beat.
> Even the fire is cool.
> Lover, without you it must be said:
> I'm all pain. Full heart, empty bed.

The number shivered to its close. She faced Rollo, touching the button that turned off her throat mike. 'May I join you for a drink afterwards?' she asked.

He nodded. She flipped the button back on and began to walk between the clapping crowded tables, smiling and saying her thank-yous. Her heart blazed in triumph.

Before she took him home she knew that he was profoundly drunk, as drunk as she had ever seen any man. That he could still walk was a mystery to her. He could certainly barely speak. It was a marvel to her that she did this. She wanted him so badly that his condition didn't matter. This was true of no other man in her life, ever. Her obsession left her no room for pride. She knew he would not have come with her had he not been close to insensibility. Her pride could bear the insult. She could bear anything, to have this man.

It wasn't that she expected him to perform. He would be incapable, of course, and anyway she had enough pride in herself to want a man capable of knowing what he was doing when he was at her body. No, she was trying to create a relationship. She wanted him to feel grateful to her. It was important not to humiliate him, not to make herself connected with a bad memory. She wanted him back here, fully alert, at some future time. Then they could fuck.

He smelt a bit. She guessed it had taken him more than a day to get into this state. She wondered if he normally behaved like this, went on periodic binges. She hoped not. It diminished him. He had a godlike status for her. She didn't want to think of him like this, stupid, probably sick, a ruin of a man.

The taxi driver had been offensive. 'You know what you're doing, sister?' he asked as they helped the staggering Rollo out of the vehicle.

'Thanks for the ride,' she snapped, settling the bill.

The man sniggered. 'It's more'n you'll get from lover-boy here.'

Once inside she settled him on her couch. He sat there, his eyes open, blazing quietly in his useless body.

She knelt in front of him and looked into his face. 'Can I get you anything?' she asked. 'Coffee? Would you like some coffee?'

'Rye,' he said. Something close to a smile crossed his face. His eyes held hers.

It was deliberate. He was in this state on purpose. She understood now. He was drinking himself stupid as an escape, as an answer to something. She fetched whisky, wondering what the hell had done this to him.

His hand was slack and limp-wristed as he tried to take the glass. The smile became more pronounced. 'Why don't you help me drink it?' he whispered, articulating each word with slow husky care. 'Hold my hand for me, huh?' His head rolled slightly and for a moment his eyes went out of focus.

'Why are you doing this?' she asked, horrified.

'You want me to go?' His voice was a slow, triumphant croak.

She put her hand round his, steadying the glass. She lifted carefully, feeling his jerky help as he tried to control his muscles. The glass clattered against his teeth. She held it like he was a baby. His head tilted back and he let go. She tipped the spirit into his mouth and he swallowed convulsively.

'Good girl,' he said after several long seconds. 'Now, again. And again.'

He took two glasses this way. She wondered if she was killing him. There was a limit to what the body could cope with. Was he committing suicide in front of her, with her assistance?

He began to slide with farcical slowness sideways. He couldn't control himself. She caught him and for a moment he rested there, in her arms. Still those blue eyes blazed with disconcerting intelligence.

She touched his face, stroking it gently. His mouth opened. Stale whisky fumes wafted up. 'Open your dress,' he whispered. His lips drew back over his teeth a little. She didn't know whether he was grinning or snarling.

She laid him gently down so that his head rested on the arm of the couch and was supported. She put a cushion under his shoulders. She was sure he was conscious of all she did, and that he was laughing at her. Even so she undid the front of her dress. It was stiff and strapless, the dress she had worn to perform in. Her breasts were naked underneath. She had a wide-shouldered, full-breasted figure and she could feel them hang heavy, between her and the drunken man.

One unsteady hand came up. He reached into her bosom. His hand was dry and cold. He clasped clumsily at her left breast.

She put her hand under his and supported it. She pressed his hand against her, rubbing herself so that her nipple would be felt swelling in his palm.

His eyelids drooped and closed. His mouth relaxed. His hand against her skin began to warm. She felt rather than saw his body grow slack and peaceful. But she knelt there, her breast in his hand, long after she knew he was asleep.

She reckoned he owed her. She took her payment by stripping his helpless body. She washed his clothes and put them to dry; that was her excuse. The truth was she wanted to see him. When she had done so – without wasting the opportunity to touch his sleeping sex – she covered him on the couch where he lay, and left him to sleep it off.

She woke the next morning and instantly recalled what had happened. Then she realised what had woken her and she

35

felt a leap of pleasure. He was grinding coffee beans. He was on his feet and thinking again.

She felt a momentary qualm. He must be feeling terrible. No one could be that drunk and not suffer viciously. She reached for her bag and found her pocket mirror. It wouldn't do to have gummy eyes or hair too messed up. She wanted to look good, smell nice. She debated going to the bathroom.

She had left her bedroom door open in case he was sick in the night or woke up disoriented and unable to find the bathroom. Now he came silently through it and stood there, watching her.

Her heart turned over. He had found his clothes and wore them with an elegant ease. She felt a spurt of anger. He had no right to look so gorgeous after such a session. By rights he should be on all fours, hardly able to open his eyes.

'How do you feel?' she asked uncertainly.

He smiled. 'There's no justice in the world, is there?'

'You mean you're OK?' She was incredulous.

'I'm sorry to disappoint you.'

'No. I mean, of course I'm glad . . .'

'The hell you are.'

She stopped. He was smiling still but it came to her in full force that he was a tricksy, complex man, infinitely wiser and more sophisticated than herself. He would win any games. She must stop herself being so naïve.

There was one game she could play, though, if he really felt OK. She thrust back the covers and stood up and stretched.

The late morning sun slanted through the greenery she had by her window. The soft, warm, dappled light would flatter her, she knew. Not that she needed the flattery. Her tall body with its deep breasts and narrow waist was one to be proud of. Her hair was a coppery brown and would pick up the sunlight behind her as threads of red-gold. Her naked pussy was slyly innocent.

'I can hear coffee brewing,' she said.

'That's in the kitchen. What's brewing in here, I wonder?'

36

She walked towards him and stopped in front of him. She had deep blue smoky eyes and now she used them, looking at him from under her thick lashes. 'I washed your clothes for you,' she said. 'They stank. How long had you been drinking?'

'Not too long,' he said. His eyes went slowly down her body and up again. 'Not long enough to forget.' Very gently, he touched her breast.

He was difficult to talk to, capable of alarming silences she felt impelled to fill. 'Do you want anything to eat?' she asked desperately. She knew her nipples were erect.

'I'm not inhuman,' he said gently. 'I've injected a dextrose solution directly into my vein. I'm sorry I'm not cross-eyed with pain but I do assure you I don't do this often. I just don't feel the need to pay off some moral debt by gratuitous suffering, that's all. I wanted to go on a drunken binge: I did it. I have no intention of paying for it if I can avoid it. It's very irritating, isn't it? But then, those who know me better know that I rarely pay the price for the occasional folly I commit. Face it, sweetheart. I'm a bastard. You'll never get any satisfaction with me.'

'There's only one sort of satisfaction I want,' she said coldly.

He moved so fast she was unprepared. He spun her round and propelled her sharply towards the bed. She fell across it and felt him pushing at her. 'No,' she cried out. But he was at her. Her body had done its work too well. He was fully erect and one savage thrust took him into her from behind. He began to thrust powerfully, slamming into her body. One hand held her hip, the other held her by a fistful of hair, pushing her face down into her bedding so that it was hard to breathe.

Moments later he was done. With contemptuous strength he rolled her over so that she was bent back facing him, red-faced and gasping. His wet cock pressed against her naked mound. 'I think you're playing in too big a league, darling,' he said. He still gripped her hair cruelly tightly. 'You come to the Zoo and let naughty men poke you up the arse in full sight of the company. We all knew

37

each other. You were the only one paying entrance money. You want me so bad you'll take me drunk. Don't you have any goddamn pride at all? The moment you see I can stand up, you put on the full display and very fucking pretty it is. So now I've fucked you. You've got what you wanted. OK? OK?' He shook her hard and then he let go. He stood up, backing away from her, fixing his clothes.

She sat up, struggling to control her tears. She saw how cold he was and she knew he was right. She had had no pride. She was out of her depth.

'You bastard.' She was shaking. 'That was cruel.'

He smiled. When he spoke his voice was soft. 'You've got that wrong, little sister,' he said. 'It's only cruel when you don't want it.'

'Carlissa?'

'Ms Cambridge. How are you?'

'Fine. Is Rollo there?'

'I'm afraid not, Ms Cambridge.'

'You expecting him?'

'Nothing specific. His schedule's slack just now. He sometimes uses those times to . . .'

'I know.' Fee was impatient. She liked and respected Rollo's personal secretary. The black face was intelligent as well as beautiful under the shaven skull. But she knew that if Rollo had a day's gap in his appointments he sometimes took off, grabbed himself a little private life.

She knew nothing of his schedule for the past week. She had barely seen him. Once upon a time they had aligned their business life on a daily basis so they could share the occasional meal together, have some social life in common. That discipline had slipped.

Everything had slipped, she thought savagely, breaking the vidi connection with Carlissa. She did not lower herself by asking Carlissa to have Rollo call her when he next deigned to come into his office. When a wife had to make appointments with her own husband via his secretary, things had come to a pretty pass.

She tried to remember what day she had seen him last. Two days ago? Three?

She missed him. Literally, she missed him like a thorn in the flesh, because he was sore to live with just now. He was moody, inclined to criticise her, no fun at all.

She couldn't do without him, though. At the moment there was a void in her life because she hadn't seen him for a couple of days, and that void would grow and make itself more and more noticeable till she would have trouble thinking about her own business. Damn the man. Damn herself, for caring. But she did care. She could no more wish not to care than she could wish not to have an itch for sex. Rollo had given her too much pleasure, too much happiness down all the years, for her to want to do without him. He had never let her down, never been a disappointment, even when he had most infuriated her.

She could bear to know where he was, who he was with. What turned him on these days? She knew he was sickened by the Zoo parties, yet surely he knew them for what they were, an antidote to boredom.

Fee thought briefly about life in the town and dismissed it. She was not much prone to giving thought to other people's lives. Other people, those beyond her immediate circle, were dull. Their lives were dull and insignificant. They were satisfied with so little. Fee despised the narrow, the conventional, the routine.

Surely Rollo wasn't down in the town. What could it offer that the Zoo couldn't do better? But the Zoo was a tight society and she would have heard if he had been somewhere, done something, done someone. There were those sufficiently jealous of her position to enjoy telling tales on her husband.

Fee smiled. She liked it when people were jealous of her. It was right that they should be so. She was the cream.

She took a moment to go to the hangar and check the Connet was *in situ*. It was their supercar, their turbo dream-machine that could spin them at speeds of 300 mph plus to anywhere in the world connected by the super highways, the starlanes that crisscrossed the surface of the planet.

The Connet was home where it should be. Rollo was local, within taxi distance at the most.

Fee stood in her kitchen naked. Her long white body glowed slightly. She was experimenting with a new cosmetic, a body powder made of tiny quartz crystals that picked up and amplified the tiniest amount of light. Her white, naked body shimmered slightly in the dim room.

She admired herself. She was truly beautiful. Suddenly she thought she would like to be painted.

The whole thing came into her mind at one go. A new fashion. A nude fashion. The Zoo was reaching more and more into the outrageous as the town became less and less tolerant.

She could have herself painted all over with flexible body-paint, or even with liquid silk like they had used for the men's cocks in that party recently. Then she could enter society wearing nothing else. Not one damned stitch.

She amused herself with the idea. She did some work, and in the intervals of her mental involvement, she played again with the naughtiness of the idea.

She would like to share it with Rollo. She would like to tease him and pretend she would really do it. She would like to make him angry so they could fight. Then they would fuck. Then she would be painted so that she could parade just for him, just for his private gloating satisfaction.

And life would go on.

Rollo didn't come back.

Carlissa vidied her at work.

'Ms Cambridge?'

'Carlissa.' Fee felt herself become smooth and dangerous. So Rollo had come crawling back, had he? Not to her, not to his wife. He had appeared at work and told his secretary to contact her.

Damn him. Rage began to grow in Fee. She smiled widely at Carlissa, slitting her eyes, preparing herself for Rollo's face appearing on the screen.

'I tried your home. Mr Cambridge isn't there. Could you

40

tell me where he is, ma'am? He's missed two appointments yesterday and one already today. He has a big one this afternoon. If he isn't going to show I'll have to cancel. It's a minister of state, ma'am.'

It took Fee a moment to readjust her ideas. 'Scramble,' she said suddenly.

The vidi screen blurred and cleared. Now they could not be listened in on. Their digitalised communication tangled like the threads of a cotton ball with a thousand other conversations. Only her decoder could make sense of it and give her the message clearly.

'Now,' said Fee. 'Which minister?'

'Jamesis Condorvan, Ms Cambridge.'

'This is the rights issue, is it?'

'Yes, ma'am. It isn't like Mr Cambridge to play games when so much is at stake.'

'He's not here, Carlissa. He's not at home. I haven't seen him for days.'

'What am I going to say to Mr Condorvan?'

It was a naked plea for help. Fee thought rapidly. 'Fax me the data,' she said. 'I'll vidi-confer with you for a verbal thirty minutes before the meeting. Have you Rollo's memory tapes of any previous meetings?'

'Yes, ma'am. The meeting's at three.'

'Duration?'

'Forty minutes.'

'Place?'

'The Chrissa Rooms, Zoo-Central.'

'Book me a vidi booth so I can do the confer with you from there. Book me a beauty go-over for the same period. Is the hospitality arranged?'

'Yes, ma'am.'

'OK. Begin the info transfer now, here. I'll need a profile of Condorvan, too. A digest. I know a little but it's superficial. Socio, not psych.'

'Will do. Thanks, Ms Cambridge.'

Fee opened a locked cupboard. She would be receiving information concerning the business expansion almost instantly. It would contain market forecasts, business projec-

41

tions, several finance vectors, the report of the city analysts who would handle the venture, a summing up of Trans-Flow's current position and a digest of its past. She would also be getting background material on the various import-ant people whose influence Rollo needed.

Like Jamesis Condorvan himself. Rollo would have commissioned a psychological profile so he could make his pitch for the minister's help in the most acceptable manner.

Fee had five hours before the meeting where she aimed to take Rollo's place. It would take her a fortnight to ab-sorb the information pouring out of her fax. The last half hour must be spent simply talking herself into the feel of the thing with Carlissa and Rollo's team who had put the package together.

She would take four pills. It would not be pleasant. They would stop all the surface of her mind from working, all conscious thought. But if she set herself to speed-read for four hours, she would have most of what she needed in her subconscious, retrievable at will for a brief period. In real time she needed headings so she could access the deep thought where the mass of information would lie.

The effects would wear off quickly. After the burst of enhanced neural activity, though, she would pay the price in the shape of an overwhelming, sickening fatigue. But the need was driving. People like Condorvan couldn't be stood up. At the moment he was neutral, but if he went away feeling Rollo had insulted him, he would screw the deal. She couldn't let that happen.

Meanwhile Rollo had vanished. Fee suppressed the thought. Business first. She would handle the personal problems later.

The Chrissa Rooms were mercifully close to Fee's own of-fice complex. She cancelled her own appointments and went over feeling spaced out. The Qwik-Pilz did this. She had a nascent mental buzz, but she forced herself to ignore it.

The pills were not entirely safe, but she was playing for high stakes, taking risks. Her blood sang. One pill took effect for one hour. She was free of them now. Her mind bulged with what it had received. It wouldn't scramble for another four hours. When it did, she would be very, very tired.

She'd get over it. She entered the Chrissa Rooms and checked in at the desk. They recognised her, which gave her ego a small lift, and directed her to the booth.

The bank of screens was on already. The small room was warm and clean. The beautician stood ready, her earplugs switched on. Fee would be talking private business and there must be no leaks.

Fee had remembered her scanner. She checked the booth for listeners and watchers and found it clean. She stripped and settled. She would be voice only during the confer since she was being physically prepared for the meet. She could see Rollo's employees, though, their faces tight and anxious as they prepared her briefing. She hoped Carlissa had the sense to control leaks. It mustn't be known Rollo had gone AWOL. Not yet. Not till she had had time to think about it, plan the announcement. She needed to ensure she could temporarily fill his place.

She was a director; she couldn't have accessed the information otherwise, even though she was Rollo's wife. As it was, she had maximum clearance. Just as well.

The beautician began with her hair. Fee lay as comfortably as she could. The team began to talk, to explain what Rollo had been going for, what he hoped to achieve, as best they understood. TransFlow controlled the water supply of a continent. The pipework went everywhere, to every home, carrying water hundreds of miles from wet uplands to dry southern areas. The technology was simple, but the maintenance was expensive. There had to be access, but the pipes had to be guarded. The water was treated as it flowed and was recycled, and it provided an easy way to attack a complex society.

Rollo aimed to cover these costs and expand the business at a stroke. The first generation fibre-optics that carried the continent's communications needed replacing. Rollo wanted to raise a rights issue to capitalise new

43

ducting on TransFlow's pipework. The ducts would carry the replacement fibre-optics, going everywhere, to everyone. They carried TV, vidi, business communications, digitalised entertainment, the lot.

TransFlow would charge for supplying the convenient routes for all this, for maintaining them and for guarding them from interference. The profit would cover their own costs in maintenance work and security.

The drawback was that unprecedented control would go into the hands of one mega-business. TransFlow would be able to hold the nation to ransom, controlling its water and its communications. It was a state within a state, almost.

Rollo headed TransFlow. He was TransFlow, whatever the board thought. He had to persuade the government that the company was safe in his hands. If he succeeded and won the sole franchise for carrying fibre-optics, he would be king in the land. Profits would quadruple.

The meeting with Condorvan was a vital step, one of many. But each one must succeed. No underling could take Rollo's place.

Fee lay listening to the team, allowing her newly-acquired knowledge to well up through her mind and be used. Occasionally she interjected a remark. The team began to relax. Fee sounded good. It might work. No one else could replace Rollo and not insult the minister. It had to be Fee, whose status equalled her husband's.

The beautician worked. Fee had read Condorvan's profile. He liked boys.

Her hair was bound tight to her head. Over it a male wig was fixed, the flopping hair in the style affected by the young studs such as those employed by Diva Jackson.

She had her breasts bound tightly to her body. This was as far as she would go. Her eyes were made up, her nails painted in natural. Then she stood up and was dressed in a dull gold, heavy jacket that obscured her luscious contours. Trousers in the same dull gold were cinched at the waist but hung loosely, defeminising her shape.

Fee's voice was naturally low. She had her lips reddened.

She was aiming for the androgynous look. She would be a beautiful man–woman.

At three minutes to three she left the booth and went through to the hospitality room. She scanned it. Then she settled in a chair and waited.

She had no aides. She had no paperwork. There was nothing in the room but food, drink and herself. Rollo had ordered no entertainment, no background, and she had to assume he knew what he was about. She hadn't interfered.

The door bleeped. Fee ordered it to open with the remote control. Jamesis Condorvan came in.

She had never met him. He was a government mogul of recent making but his power was real. He had talent and he was very aware of it. If he made a mistake this early in his career, he was scuppered.

His profile had suggested he was a risk-taker. He was unlikely to play safe. He would calculate the odds, though. She had to make them in her favour.

He entered the room and stood for a moment, looking for Rollo. Fee sat just long enough for his eyes to find and absorb who she was not. She came to her feet in a flowing movement and walked across the room. She wore flat shoes. She stopped when she was just a little too close to Condorvan for social ease. She had been giving him eye contact as she moved but now she drooped her neck a little. It was willowy, graceful as a swan's, as white, as firm. 'I have to apologise,' she said huskily, looking at Condorvan's feet.

'You do?'

She lifted her face and stood back. She gazed sombrely into the minister's face. It was mid-brown in tone, the colour accentuated by his blond hair.

'Rollo took sick less than half an hour ago. It was too late to cancel you. We felt the disruption very keenly. Are you prepared to meet with me instead, Mr Condorvan? I am Fee Cambridge, a director of TransFlow.'

'Are you briefed?' His voice was hard. He was angry.

'I am, sir. Would you like to continue or could we reschedule? You must realise our regrets are sincere.'

He broke the lock her gaze had imposed on him. He walked across the room restlessly and looked at the food laid out on the table. 'We'll continue,' he said irritably. He looked at his watch. 'You have thirty-eight minutes.'

'Do you wish to scan?'

'Haven't you?'

'Of course. But I don't expect you to accept my probity automatically.'

His heavy head swung round. 'Then why am I here? Are you going to persuade me?' He grinned unpleasantly.

Fee shrugged. 'Our proposition is good. Solid. It looks forward and anticipates the future, which will be easier if we are successful in this. You are our future's guardian. We think of profit first, communal good second, though the two walk hand in hand in a healthy economy. You have different priorities but I believe we have common ground on this occasion.'

Condorvan cocked his head to one side. 'Sounds good,' he murmured. 'A shade familiar, though.'

'Westlake, the campaign of '79,' said Fee and grinned. She had taken his own words and used them. And improved them.

He narrowed his eyes. 'Am I to be manipulated by cheap tricks, Ms Cambridge?'

'I hope not, or you'll reject us. There are other potential franchisees. Frankly we thought you had more weight than that.'

'I assume money isn't the problem,' he murmured.

'No. We are Blue Chip. Finance is no problem.'

'Why should one corporation have so much power?'

'Carrying water and communications? Because it's safer.'

'To guard, you mean. *Sed quis custodiet ipsos custodes.*'

Fee smiled. 'I don't mean that at all. I mean it's easier for you to keep a check on us. That's what you get in return. We hold all that power, but we hold it under licence from you. You can keep as close an eye on us as the enabling legislation chooses to ask for. By giving so much to us, you can control it so much more easily. And our record is good, Mr Condorvan. We have never used our water monopoly to gain political clout. We stay out of the political arena entirely. You know that.'

'May I sit down? Your hospitality lacks grace, Ms Cambridge.'

'Sit, sir, and be fed. Allow me to wait on you.'

'I have been approached by Continental Communications who have suggested that if you have the monopoly of carrying communications as you do with carrying water, they will lie a little uneasy in your powerful grasp. You will be able to call all the shots.'

'I would suggest that ConComm look to the roads. Road-makers don't control vehicle manufacture though they exist to transport it. TransFlow is no more than a carrying company. The more we carry, the better we fulfil our corporate function.'

Fee presented Condorvan with a plate of food. She poured champagne into a tulip glass. He chewed and swallowed. 'Can you make a return on your investment before ConComm don't need you any more?' he asked cruelly.

'Laser communications are thirty years off, whatever ConComm tell you. We'll have recovered our outlay in ten.' Fee sat opposite and sipped champagne herself. She opened her legs and deliberately put one ankle on her other knee, a graceless, boyish pose. Her dark gold suit shifted and settled. It was made entirely of feathers.

'What if a future board of TransFlow lacked the integrity of the current one?' Condorvan's eyes were dancing. He was relaxing.

'There would need to be a ministerial watchdog,' murmured Fee. 'Someone astute. Incorruptible. Wise.' She watched the bribe take effect. All these damned politicians were the same.

'I don't see,' said Condorvan politely, 'how you know more about ConComm's research than they do themselves.'

'They know,' said Fee. 'They're in problems with their carbon fibre chip technology. They have an unacceptable loss in quality control and they don't know why yet. They are concentrating more and more of their research facility towards solving it. Several of their decoders have failed lately, with important information being lost. Their share price is dropping and the market is becoming uneasy.'

Condorvan watched her silently. Fee quoted figures illustrating her point. They were accurate figures. She knew Condorvan would be recording her. He would check her data later and find she was right.

'If ConComm are so flawed, why do you want to be tied up with them?' he asked.

'They'll solve it. Then they'll go ahead with their laser programme, only slowly. It will cost them to get over this current hiccup. Using us as a carrier will cut their second-generation installation costs to an absolute minimum. We estimate that TransFlow will come close to saving their corporate arses. They'll return to profitability much quicker, and get their shareholders off their back. They'll be at you cap-in-hand otherwise within two years, looking for government funds to bale them out. I think you know this already.'

Fee refilled his champagne glass. Her mind was rocketing through dense forests of facts and figures. And an unexpected side-effect of the pills was beginning to manifest itself. She wanted to slide the gold feathers down and off her long slim haunches and turn her back. She would bend over the table and split her legs wide. Condorvan would approach her and take out his fat cock. He would smear it with pâté and slide it into her arse. He liked boys. She would invite him to bugger her while her face and hands were thrashing in the broken meats and despoiled food on the table. His heavy hips would thunder . . .

'Are you worried about your husband?'

Her judgment was starting to slip. Thank God his allotted time was almost over. She would say something, do something strange soon and blow the whole thing.

'He is receiving medical attention. He is angry not to be meeting you.'

'He doesn't delegate well?'

'He does. That's the point.'

48

It took him a moment to get the compliment. He wasn't work to delegate. He was first-rate in importance.

Champagne. She would fill a glass and dip his cock into it. She would lift the bubble-clad member to her lips and suck the cool misting of alcohol until it was clean. She would dip it again . . .

'I hadn't realised you were so active at TransFlow.'

She would smear her breasts with roulade and he would lick them clean. *No.* He didn't like women.

Inside her head, Fee rode on electric pulses. She sped through last year's accounts for TransFlow. The numbers bubbled in her mind.

Ask me, she pleaded, looking at Condorvan. *Ask me. I know so much. Let it come out so that I can be free, my mind my own once more.*

He was preparing to leave. Watch him, her mind said desperately. He'll have a tricky one. For when I'm off guard.

'Your hospitality is positively spartan.' He was smiling. 'I had expected something lusher.'

His voice was light and challenging. He was watching her with amusement, his head slightly to one side. He was commenting on her, not the food. She knew she had a hot reputation.

'It was our understanding that you were busy, that serious work had to be done. We want you to take us seriously, Mr Condorvan. We believe we'll be good for you.' *May I suck your cock, sir? Would you like the market analysed?*

He was leaving. Thank God. 'Your finance vectors,' he said casually. 'A shade conservative, I thought.'

There. The stinger. She agreed. They were damned conservative. If they carried ConComm's fibre-optics their profits would be astronomical, within five years, not ten. 'It's a bull market at the moment,' she said, trying not to put her hand between her legs, exhaustion tugging at her consciousness. *Rollo. Where are you? I can't hold out much longer.* 'We think it's nearing its peak. We project a three year down-turn with a percentage business loss that'll slice our profits and slow our programme. We are a cautious company, Mr Condorvan. We don't aim to buck the business cycle. We ride it.'

Ride it!

'You see the coming downturn as the result of the business cycle, and not of government policy?'

The hell we do, thought Fee. She smiled. *Grimaced?* The coming downturn. What had he given away? Her remarks had been waffle because he had spotted massaged figures.

My forehead sweats silver balls. Oh, fuck me, sweet man and burn my mind free of figures. Let my thoughts wing . . .

She shrugged. 'Stock overprices. The market lifts. Indicators are ignored. Confidence gets high. Everyone's happy. A few go mad and exploit the situation. The bubble bursts. The market plummets. Things overvalued become undervalued. Gradually investors enter the arena again, lured by the thoughts of easy profits.'

His smile was sinister. He had overrun his time. 'You think we should prevent it?'

'It winnows out weak companies. On average, over time, the value of stock is realistic. Not in the short term, though. So allowing the market to find its own level forces companies to plan long term, if they are to survive. As we do. We can ride out a bear market.'

The flattery was complete. Her shallow words were what he wanted to hear. He didn't believe her but it was the government line, the government excuse. He believed she had told him that the government of which he was a member was successfully conning the corporate sector.

Balls. But he was on her side now. He believed he knew better than her and he believed the government had fooled TransFlow. Therefore the government could control TransFlow. He would advise they be granted the franchise to carry ConCom's replacement fibre-optic system.

She had done it. He was shaking her hand, smiling at her, allowing his eyes to admire her slim, boyish appearance.

'It's been an enormous pleasure meeting you, Ms Cambridge. I'm so sorry about your husband.'

50

Her eyes let him know he was a hell of a man. 'I trust we'll meet again,' she said huskily. 'If there's anything you want further clarity on . . .?'

'Of course.'

Baby, suck me. I want the government to diddle my clit.

He was gone. Fee folded slowly, crumpling to the floor. Her body was shutting down. Her mind skydived, freefalling towards ground zero.

She was aware of tears falling down her cheeks. She fumbled for the vidi.

'Carlissa.'

'How'd it go, Ms Cambridge?'

'Suckertime.'

'You're in clear, Ms Cambridge. Scramble.' Carlissa was aghast.

Fee giggled weakly. 'I need to be debriefed.' She gave a fat snort. 'He didn't take 'em off.'

'You're in clear. I'm breaking the transmission. Someone'll be over to debrief. Please stay there, Ms Cambridge.'

She lay on the floor on her back. Gold feathers lay loose where she plucked herself. Her mind slid down a long, long slope. Like a bear market. Down down down.

They'd better get here quick or there'd be nothing to debrief. Her recorder would give the bones, but the feel of the thing, what mattered, had to come from her subjective impressions.

I invited the minister to bugger me, but he said there wasn't time, it wasn't on his schedule. Fie upon your schedule, I cried. Am I not a pretty boy with my rosy arsehole proffered . . .?

'Fee. Ms Cambridge. Fee, wake up. What's wrong?'

'Qwik-Pilz after-effects,' she slurred. 'Take me home.'

It was Roddy Dupique. He was one of Rollo's top men. They had met at every TransFlow social gathering for over three years.

Her mind sparked. A brief ripple of lucidity washed over her. Good ol' Roddy. Finance Director. Young for the job. Maybe ten years her junior. Figuring figures took quick brains, these days. It was a job for the young.

51

He got her to her feet, gold feathers fluttering. She stood like a drunken canary, leaning against him. She began to slide down his front, pulling on his jacket as he tried to support her.

'Roddy.'

'Yes.'

'Get the beautician,' she mumbled.

'You mean that?'

She made an enormous effort. 'Fix the wig. Fancy make-up. I mustn't be recognised like this.'

I can't help myself, her brain whimpered.

Roddy took control. The beautician was bribed into silence. Fee looked like any slightly drunk Zoo lady, walking stiff-legged out of the Chrissa Rooms. Her feathers fluttered in her wake.

Roddy pushed her into a taxi and took her home. He held her while she accessed her doorlock and he took her in.

No Rollo. No live-in maid.

'Can I get you anything?'

A smooth young man, all social smarminess, admiring the boss's wife. Now he looked anxious. His tie was awry. His hair was mussed. Fee liked him better this way.

'It'll go,' she said thickly. 'Take the information. I'm begging. Then I can let go.' *And fly.*

'OK. What do you say?'

'Took the watchdog bribe. Likes easy money. Prickly. Homo but bi. Astute, saw fudged figures. I blamed coming downturn. He agreed as fact. That's on tape.'

She said everything, not orderly as she should but in a rattle as she tried to get it out before the coming collapse.

Black, vast, a Kraken in her mind. It was heaving.

Fee began to whimper. Her green eyes pleaded. The face over hers wavered and faded. 'Don't leave me alone,' she begged.

Someone wiped her nose. Her clothes were taken off. She felt herself sinking. Then she floated in warm water.

She came round again. She was naked in the bath. In his shirt sleeves Roddy sat by her.

'Don't leave me,' she said clearly.

'Can I get a woman friend for you? It isn't right that I'm here.'

Good-looking smug little bastard. 'No,' Fee murmured. 'You're doing a grand job.'

She was hot when she clambered out. She wouldn't let him dress her. He held her naked against his clothed body for a moment, then fetched her some hot black coffee.

It was no good. He carried her through to her bedroom. As he laid her down, her eyes fixed his and told him to stay.

It was night-time. His body was roused. This was not the sort of offer he was going to turn down.

His mouth closed hard over hers and he kissed her fiercely. 'I love my job,' he said. 'I'm worth more than you pay me and other companies know that. But working with you is more than enough compensation. God, I want to get inside you.'

He was doing it. He was pushing his body. Fee moaned and opened her legs.

'You gorgeous bitch,' he said. 'You gorgeous, classy bitch. I want to fuck you. I've always wanted to fuck you. You're so beautiful.'

Fee shivered and shuddered. His jerking hips filled her pussy. Her mind flooded. This was the perfect way to stay awake.

He had his hands in her black hair, dragging her head back. He kissed her throat as he pushed his cock into her again and again. 'Sweet charity,' he mumbled. His body shook. Fee felt hers lift as she came nearer to orgasm. She took him with her pussy muscles and screwed down on his swollen sex. He shouted and she felt his tears on her face.

She was at peace afterwards. 'Roddy,' she said huskily.

He was asleep. He woke slowly. She had no sense of time. 'Roddy.'

'Yes.' He woke.

'Your body is young and beautiful. You've used it to help me.'

'If Mr Cambridge catches me in bed with you . . .'

Fee stroked his hair back from his face. 'Carnal desire,' she said softly.

'You shouldn't be so . . .'

'What? What shouldn't I be?'

'Beautiful. Fierce. Carnal. Clever. How can I resist you? You could be business death to me. But I can't resist you. What man could?'

Fee laughed. 'Jamesis Condorvan. He likes boys.'

'You were brilliant.'

'What happened at the end? I was flaked by then.'

'You were OK. You handled it. You did the business.'

'Thank God.' Her eyes bore into his. 'I want to fuck.'

He held her tightly. She felt his cock firm.

She pushed him onto his back and moved down his body. She put the light on, the light in the bed.

The membrane they lay on glowed. Roddy was a dark shape in the starshine of the bed's surface. Fee hung over him, witch-lit. Her mouth drifted over his chest. She kissed the hollows in his neck. She licked his armpits. She sucked his hard nipples. She licked each rib. She kissed his stomach where it sucked in. She dribbled saliva into his navel and sucked it out again.

Her breasts massaged his cock. She took it under her chin and held it. She allowed her hair to abrade it. She kissed it.

He lay on his back, his arms spread, his legs apart.

Slowly, carefully, Fee began to caress his cock with her mouth. She kissed it. Her tongue fondled it. Her teeth teased it.

She caught the foreskin and pulled it gently. She sucked the throbbing veins. She began to take him all the way with her mouth. She felt his stomach flutter. She took his balls into her mouth and sucked the furry globes. She held his cock in her mouth and tickled the tip with her tongue.

She engulfed him. She sucked steadily, holding the root of his cock and working her hand in concert with her sucking mouth. He sobbed drily and came, spunking into her mouth.

Fee rolled him over. She opened his furred cheeks and

54

laid her full mouth between them. She let the spunk dribble out. She put her tongue in and played with his slippery cleft. Then her tongue entered his rear.

He was holding his breath, rigid. Fee smiled and slid a spunk-soaked finger into his rear. Roddy whimpered. She made him roll over so he lay on her finger, driving it further in.

She kissed his slack cock. Dreamily she kissed it and nibbled it. Gradually his taut body relaxed. He became sleepy. She released his tender arse and kissed his cock. It began to grow again.

When it was big enough she drew herself gently up the bed. She got herself astride his body and she lifted herself.

Light blazed in a soft radiance all around him. He looked up at her. The light caught her under her chin and made sockets of her eyes.

Her long pendulous breasts swung. She lowered herself and opened her pussy. His cock lifted. She took the tip of his cock and sat on it. It pressed against her damp pussy. It began to slide in. Fee laughed softly in her throat and pressed down. Roddy gave a quiet groan. His cock slid into her.

She was hot velvet, tight, elastic, alive. His cock went on into her. He felt her thighs on his hips. As he rose up he saw the column of his cock dark between their bodies. Light gleamed on its satin-wet surface. She came down on him and he gasped at the tight sweet pleasure of it.

Now she leaned slightly forward. Her breasts swayed. He lifted his head and caught one, sucking the nipple into his mouth. She held her upper body stiff while she shivered quickly on his cock, exciting him unbearably.

She bent low over him. Her breasts fell, one on either side of his face. She rubbed him like that. Then she curled her upper body and found his mouth with hers.

He tasted her, salty. She had sucked him a short time ago. He was being taken by Fee Cambridge.

Tiger wife. They called her the tiger wife. She was the queen of cock. Rollo was envied, admired, for keeping her ferocious appetite satisfied.

It was rumoured she took lovers because she was greedy. Cruel. To torment Rollo.

He was her lover now, his young body dominated and controlled by her experience, her expertise.

Their mouths wound together. She was doing something with her cunt-muscles. He couldn't control himself. He'd never been fucked like this. Her cunt was alive and writhing. His mouth went wide under hers as he reached climax.

She hit hard with her sex, driving down ferociously. He bucked upwards, shuddering in release. It was what he had wanted, a fierce taking at the end. She rode him violently as he spunked up into her, a great roaring in his ears as he shouted with the blinding joy of being screwed by her.

Now he was gasping, flat on the bed, released from her glorious body. He took her hair and held her while he moved on the bed. He wiped his wet cock in her breasts, moaning in the aftermath of pleasure. Then he nuzzled into them, taking a nipple into his mouth to suck. He held her to him and went to sleep.

He woke in daylight and stared down at the sleeping woman. She had stuffed her fist into her mouth. Her black hair was all dishevelled. She smelt of stale sweat and spunk.

He thought he had never seen so desirable a woman. Her body was long and slim-waisted, but the flare of her hips and the fullness of her breasts were voluptuous. One breast was caught with the nipple bent under the soft, creamy, blue-veined flesh. The other nipple pointed down, brushing the bed membrane. It was plummy, dark in colour and soft. Soft and long.

Everything about her invited him. Teased him. Messy, vulnerable in sleep, smeared with love-making, she was all invitation. He wanted to bite her. He wanted to suck her. She invited indulgence, the grosser the better.

He knew how to behave with women. Usually, the morning after hot sex, he would be tactful while they got themselves sorted out, cleaned off cosmetics, washed used body parts. He would be polite, undemanding, until he knew what they felt like. He wouldn't take liberties till he was very sure of his ground.

Not Fee Cambridge, though. She had the soul of a panther dressed in a woman's body, with a woman's cunt. With a panther you didn't ask. You grabbed, taking your chance with the claws. Or you left the magnificent beast alone altogether.

No half measures with Fee. She was a woman who needed grabbing, who needed mastery. Her skin was porcelain, delicately perfect, but under its blue-white veined glaze she was coarse and powerful. Excess. She invited excess. He reached over her and opened the cheeks of her arse. He pushed his head in and kissed her bottom.

He felt her wake up. Her hands came sleepily over his body. His cock was hard. He sucked her arse and kissed it. He rolled over her body and brought himself behind her. His excitement mounted. He tucked his body into the curve of hers as they both lay on their side. He put an arm round her and held her breast.

He began to work his cock into her backside. It was hard. He pushed hard, hurting himself. He kept at it.

The orifice was wet with his saliva. He pushed and he began to get inside her.

He felt her stiffen and then force herself to relax. He had not spoken to her since waking up. He had just forced himself into her.

She was incredibly tight on him. He made himself keep going, not come too quickly. She was very hot. Her arse was like an elastic bandage. He strained in her.

He tried to keep it going but when she began to wriggle on him he couldn't resist. She was fire, delicious fire.

He drew out of her when he was done. He had a look at his handiwork. Her puckered rear was soft and open. His spunk was grey and frothy. He put his face against one of her smooth cheeks. He bit it.

Afterwards he hung over her on his elbows, looking into her face. The green eyes were narrowed against the light. Her pale skin was clear apart from the slender jagged scar over one cheek. The bones of her face were like wings. White on black. White skin, blue-black hair. No kindness in her. She was a predator through and through.

'It's the only way,' he said shakily.

'What is?'

'Get in first. Take what you want.'

'Are you talking about business?'

'I'm talking about you, Fee Cambridge. You scare me to death. I want you unbearably.' He dropped his face suddenly into her full, warm bosom.

She took his hair and dragged his face off her. She made him lie on his side and she lay facing him, their faces very close.

'You do right to be afraid,' she whispered softly. 'I eat delectable little boys like you.'

'I'm in my thirties, damn you. I'm no boy.'

She kissed him, hot slow kisses while her hand remained tangled painfully in his hair.

'For the time being,' she said between kisses, 'you can have me. However you like. No comebacks. Nothing outside of this, us two, on the bed, naked. But when it's over, it's over. You understand?'

His response was to mount her frenetically. His body was on top and he held her wrists so she could barely move. He was physically stronger than her and he made sure she knew it. He took her hard and fast and then he lay on her and slept.

His dreams were velvet, tiger-striped. He fell into mantraps and was shot in the balls by bitch women hunters. He was the tiger. Or they were.

3

She wore a skin-tight all-over bodysuit. It looked sprayed on. It was black and covered every part of her up to and including her neck. Only her white face showed with its green-eyed glare, and her cascade of black hair.

Her black fingers looked incredibly long. She was toying with a laser light pencil. She took no notes, though.

The board was meeting. The managing director had vanished into thin air. The board had to decide what to do.

Simeon Grey was chairing. He looked inimically at Fee. 'This must be a very distressing time for you,' he said in his gravelly voice. He didn't sound as though he believed his own words.

Pompous old fart, thought Fee. She eased herself within her tight black sheath, her second skin. Roddy had made love to her five times in the night. Her cunt felt alive and glowing. She could feel her swollen vulva pressing against her clothes. 'We are here to discuss how TransFlow will manage the current crisis,' she said. Her tone was repressive and cold. Her private affairs, her personal emotions were nothing to do with the board, she said silently.

'We'll have to bring the police in.' This was Weiner Lutz.

'We can't,' said Roddy. 'The publicity.'

'The man's missing!' Weiner's eyes slid to check out Fee. They were talking about her husband. He thought her the most cold-blooded woman he had ever met.

Salazar tapped the tabletop with her red-painted nails. 'The rights issue,' she said. 'It can't be done.'

'What can't be?' snapped Simeon.

'Notifying the police we've lost our managing director

and continuing with the rights issue. One or the other,' said Salazar. 'Not both.'

'Have you completed the audit?' Simeon's voice was sly. He tried so hard not to look at Fee that everyone else did. Roddy flushed slightly. If Rollo had made off with Trans-Flow's family jewels, his position screwing the boss's wife would be an uncomfortable one. Sex was one thing. Financial fraud was another. Perhaps he ought to stay clear.

'Almost.' Salazar was contemptuous. She made little attempt to conceal her view that TransFlow's board was divided into those who knew what they were at, who guided the company, and those who lent it gravitas and tone but were otherwise useless. She put herself into the former category, whereas Simeon Grey was purely ornamental. 'But we'll need outside auditors. You must understand that. When this thing goes public they aren't going to take our word for it that the cupboard is still full.'

'And is it?' Simeon was enjoying his malice.

Salazar leaned back and smiled at Fee. The two women were about the same age. Sal wore shorts and overtunic made from fine metal links. She tinkled slightly as she moved, and the rise and fall of her breasts produced a fascinating rippling sheen.

She liked women. Fee knew this, having read the security file on her. Only women, too. She didn't like men in her bed at all. Now she said softly: 'All present and correct, sir. The managing director has not had his hand in the till. Or if he has, he's too damn clever for me.'

'And me,' said Roddy. 'There's no evidence of fraud, Simeon. There'll be no scandal.'

'A managing director gone AWOL is scandalous enough, even without the possibility of fraud,' said Simeon.

'I agree,' said Fee. Her husky voice was quiet but they all instantly stilled, listening to her. 'We can get someone private to look for Rollo.'

Weiner said: 'You can't keep something like this secret. It'll be worse in the long run. We ought to jump the press and control the information by getting in first.'

'I disagree,' said Roddy mildly. Under the table he was erect. Fee's calm in this discussion concerning the disappearance of her husband aroused him painfully. He had fucked her all night. A weaker woman would have been embarrassed. Tearful. Frightened. Worried.

Fee missed her husband's cock. Roddy wasn't sure about anything else. The woman was an enigma.

He remembered peeling her clothes off her. He remembered her weeping and pleading with him to stay. He would never see her like that again, but by Christ, he would love to! He wanted Fee to beg from him.

His mind began to turn over fantasies where her white body strained as she pleaded for release. He would like to see her rump red-wealed. He would like to wield the lash.

Jessie Canlan, a motherly woman in her fifties who headed the powerful investments department, could feel the antipathies flowing around the table. She sensed Roddy Dupique's sexual hunger and guessed that it was based in fact rather than fantasy. Simeon lusted just as hotly for Fee only he would never succeed, she thought tiredly. Consequently he hated Fee and was jealous of Rollo.

Weiner was a fool, always had been. She could ignore him. Sal deserved respect. Thank goodness Rollo hadn't defaulted. Not that she, Jessie, would believe it for a moment even if Sal had found inconsistencies. Rollo headed TransFlow for the power. He was wealthy enough for money to be completely incidental to him now. He could live, as they said, off the income of his income.

She respected Rollo Cambridge. He was a businessman because he loved it. He had the courage to take chances and yet he had the flair to pick a winner. He had the guts to push through his view.

Did Roddy predate or postdate the disappearance? she wondered. Fee's indiscretions were notorious, though she doubted anyone else suspected this latest affair yet. Jessie didn't think Rollo would disappear because Fee had his finance director in her bed. He was perfectly capable of dealing with a little problem like that. Indeed, Jessie suspected their marriage thrived on conflict, betrayal, lust and possession. Fee paraded her lovers as a form of extreme foreplay, to arouse her husband and tease him to sexual fury.

Jessie admired her for it. It wasn't her way; she was comfortably married herself, and was and had always been the model of matrimonial virtue. But Rollo Cambridge was man enough to stir even her respectable breast. He had cruel, beautiful good looks. He was undoubtedly a passionate man. He was powerful and he was wealthy. Women fell over in line for him, fools that they were, and he became bored with them.

No man could get bored with Fee. Disgusted, furious, revolted, maddened – all those, yes. But not bored. Fee handled her magnificent husband just right.

'Can we be sure of the calibre of a private firm of investigators?' she asked mildly. 'They won't have the resources of the police, nor will they have their authority to question people.'

'They'll be able to pay for information,' said Fee. She smiled at the board. 'If they are authorised to bribe and have funds available, that is.'

Simeon stiffened dangerously. He was realist enough to feel no compunction about bribing, which he considered a legitimate business tool. What got him going was Fee's subtext. She wasn't willing to finance personally the search for her husband. Simeon believed it was the board's duty to find its managing director, and was perfectly willing to authorise the funds. But he felt Fee should have offered. She wasn't behaving as a wife should. It was probably her whorish behaviour that had driven her husband away in the first place. No decent man would stand for it.

'You see,' said Fee prettily, reading Simeon like a book, 'if I paid for the agency to find Rollo, I would consider any information I received as belonging to me personally. I might sell it on to TransFlow, or there again, I might not. But today we are talking as a business. This board needs to know what has happened. So this board will have to pay for it.'

Roddy grinned. Weiner nodded like an anxious puppy. Sal yawned. She thought the point obvious. Fee was here in her capacity as a board member, not as Rollo's wife. Simeon was a fool.

Cal Ostermann, the research director, stared at Simeon. Why didn't the chair take a vote? The discussion was all but over. He had work to do, even if no one else did.

Brady of public relations pushed the point. 'If Simeon takes the vote and we agree to get private help to find Rollo,' he said, 'we must have a story we all agree on. We can't keep this down indefinitely. Rollo has public engagements and he's missing them.'

'Will he be gone long?' asked Weiner fatuously.

'A cover story,' mused Fee. 'I've already told Jamesis Condorvan he was sick. Shall we have him in a nursing home?'

'Bad for the rights issue,' objected Sal. 'They like health on the board.'

'An accident,' said Roddy. 'A broken leg or something. He could be handling things from his bed of pain. We could set up a smoker to lend verisimilitude.'

'A smoker?' Simeon was lost.

'A stooge,' said Roddy patiently. 'Someone pretending to be Rollo, so that communications go backwards and forwards. Perhaps Ms Cambridge wouldn't mind visiting occasionally.'

'I do so want to help,' said Fee. She smiled.

'I don't see why it's called a smoker,' said Simeon.

'No smoke without fire,' said Jessie. 'Only in this case there is. Perhaps the chair would take the vote.'

They agreed to have a private firm investigate Rollo's disappearance, reporting back to the board through the head of security. Brady, their top PR man, would fix the cover story and organise the details, informing the financial press in a casual way.

Fee's home was a series of connected glass domes shrouded in raw jungle. The polarisation of the plastiglass was set so that as you rambled from one room to another and thence to another, looking out into the green alien world, you could not see back into another room.

The rooms interconnected like a warren. There were work-stations, sitting rooms, studies, bedrooms, kitchens, libraries, rest rooms, bathrooms – so many that the bubble house was like frogspawn in a stagnant jungly pool.

There were games rooms, a gymnasium, two swimming pools – the house grew all the time as they added more bubbles.

The air circulated softly, cleaning dust and biological debris out of the air. Dirt eaters in the carpets kept the floors clean. A maid came in several times a week for other cleaning, but there was little of it.

Fee loved her rambling halls. She loved the claustrophobic jungle that swathed her home in tendrils and creepers. Fat, bifurcated leaves pressed like vacant faces against her walls. She could switch the walls to matt – most bubble dwellers did – and the jungle would disappear. But Fee loved to see it, as she loved to see the filigreed natural light fall through the canopy in slanting bars to pierce the green cathedral gloom below.

Occasionally there was the jewelled flash of a parrot. Tiny orange monkeys swung through the trees. Huge sleepy snakes preyed on them. Iridescent crunchy things lived in the leaf mould.

'When I die,' said Fee to the detective who was interviewing her, 'I want it to be out there. I want to moulder and grow maggoty, being eaten by a whole city of crawling squirming wriggling things.'

Maslow tried not to sweat. He knew this was the most important assignment his agency had ever received. These people were at the top of society. He was both fascinated and excited to be interviewing Fee Cambridge. He had come to her apartment in the Zoo determined not to be overawed. She was just a woman. She was just a wife with a missing husband. He must hang on to that.

He had seen her on the screen when the news reported some social or business event involving TransFlow. He knew her for a beautiful woman but he was disconcerted by her in the flesh.

She was raw. Not raw with emotion. Just raw. He felt he teetered on a mountain edge.

She was filthy, too. Filthy in her thoughts, that is. Filthy in what she said. Decent folk didn't talk about dying. Nor did they talk about breaking the law by entering the jungle which was forbidden to all. Nor did they mention such grotesqueries as rotting flesh.

He had worked in the Zoo before. He thought he knew these people, vain, rich, overindulged, shameless.

Fee Cambridge was something else. She was all those things, certainly. But she was something else as well.

'So what do you want to ask me?' she said suddenly.

Maslow thought he would skip his prepared intro about how upset she must be feeling. 'When did you last see Mr Cambridge?' he asked crisply.

'Ten days ago.'

'Has he ever disappeared before?'

'Not in this sense. I don't always know where he is. A day or so might go by without us seeing each other if we can't align our schedules. This is different.'

'But you would always see each other at night.'

'No,' said Fee coolly.

'You mean he sometimes spends nights away?'

'Or I do.'

Jesus, thought Maslow. The sexual mores of Zoo people were notorious, but he would have expected some shame, some hesitation.

'Has Mr Cambridge a mistress?'

'Possibly.'

'You don't know?'

'I don't check up on my husband.' Fee was contemptuous.

'Do you mind if he has a mistress?'

'I don't tell the man what to put on,' said Fee coarsely.

'Do you have a lover?'

'Sometimes.'

'Like now?'

'I do.'

'Does Mr Cambridge know about him?'

'Them.'

Maslow swallowed. 'Them.'

'I have no idea. I mean, I doubt he knows which individuals are concerned. I hardly know myself. Men can be so forgettable.' Fee smiled. 'But he knows that in general I will probably be having sex with other people from time to time.'

Maslow persevered as impassively as he was able. 'Anyone in particular?'

'No.'

'It would be a help if you were frank with me, Ms Cambridge.'

'I'm being frank.'

'I've been told you are having an affair with another member of the TransFlow board.'

'I go to bed with Roddy Dupique, yes, if it's any of your business.'

'I think it must be, if I am to understand what has happened to Mr Cambridge.'

Fee sat down. She took a long pull at her iced gin and took time to place the glass carefully back in its wet ring. 'Mr Maslow,' she said softly. 'You are barking up the wrong tree. Down in the town where no doubt you usually work, a husband or a wife screwing around might make some difference. With Rollo and me it does not. If he eats salad, I might eat fish. Another night we might both eat steak together. Do you understand me?'

Maslow blinked. 'You mean it's normal for you both to play around.'

'That is correct. This with Roddy, now. It postdates Rollo's disappearance. Moreover, Roddy Dupique is not someone in particular. I am like Autolycus in the Shakespeare play, Mr Maslow. I snap up unconsidered trifles. I eat pretty men. I gobble boys in my bed, Mr Maslow, because I like it. I have a healthy appetite. I even like the girlies for a nice soft change.'

Maslow burned with the insult. 'Right,' he said, licking his lips. 'I won't pursue the sexual angle. I had that wrong.'

'No,' said Fee. 'You could be right. Maybe Rollo has gone off after a woman. He struck me as restless, lately. Bored. Maybe he has some little town plaything he is indulging himself with and he is too lazy to come back.'

'Do you believe that?'

Fee considered. 'No. I think he would come back.'

'What do you really believe, Ms Cambridge?'

Fee took another slug of gin. Again she set her glass back precisely in the same position. She looked Maslow in the eye. The guy wasn't entirely stupid. 'I think he's in trouble,' she said calmly. 'I think something's wrong.'

There was a long silence. Maslow made no move to go. Finally Fee said: 'Do I take it you have a theory, Mr Maslow?'

He was beginning to get the measure of her, if only slightly. At the least, he knew he could say what was in his mind. This woman didn't know the meaning of the word squeamish.

'Townsfolk . . .' he began.

'Of which you are one.'

'Of which I am one.' Christ, she was quick. 'Don't like the Zoo.'

Fee smiled, remaining silent.

'I guess they never did. You are rich and exclusive.'

'Mmm,' agreed Fee warmly.

'Townsfolk don't like your morals either.'

'My my.'

'There is an appearance,' said Maslow carefully, 'of things getting more extreme.'

'Is that right?' Fee was dulcet.

Maslow got crosser. 'There are rumours of sex parties. No doubt things are exaggerated.'

'Oh, I don't think so.'

'We're going the other way, you might say.'

'We go both ways,' said Fee helpfully.

'The town is getting more strait-laced.'

'I'm so sorry.'

'I doubt you are sorry at all. My point is that the latent antagonism between the town and the Zoo has never been stronger.'

'Are you suggesting my husband is the victim of town jealousy?'

'Disapproval, not jealousy. Yes, I am. There are ugly

67

rumours about new groups forming to cleanse society of people like . . .'

'Me,' said Fee. 'I wonder you dare come here, Mr Maslow. Do you wear a chastity belt, in case women like me attack decent, ordinary men like you?'

As she taunted him, Fee suddenly remembered the strange mugging Rollo had experienced when he had visited the hospital.

Maslow got his temper in check. 'This isn't meant to be personal.'

Fee stood up. For a minute she looked down at the seated man. 'I want my husband back,' she said. She resumed the restless pacing that had characterised the earlier part of the interview. 'Intact,' she added. 'In one piece. If he has gone voluntarily and intends to stay away, I want proof.' She swung round to face Maslow. 'There was a town girl at a recent sex party here. I thought she had the hots for Rollo but maybe she got angry when he didn't want her. Maybe she's sicked some nasty friends onto him.'

'How do I find her?'

'Mournag Hendriksen brought her. Mournag's Zoo. I'll give you her listing. And Rollo was mugged recently.'

Maslow had grey eyes. They narrowed at this news. 'Tell me,' he said softly.

Fee told him.

It took Maslow a while to find Sandrina. She had stopped work for a week or two to go to the coast for a music festival. It was a strange investigation where money was no object but time and discretion were of the essence.

He would have to go to the coast. He couldn't wait until the girl decided to come home. He had booked a flight when an idea came to him.

He vidied Fee Cambridge. Her answer machine took the call and she got back to him on his portable.

'I need to go to the coast,' he said directly.

Fee was bewildered. 'You don't need my authority. Hasn't this been explained?'

'Do you have a Connet?'

Fee understood. Long distances could be as easily driven as they could be flown, if you could afford a Connet car. They were ground rockets, really, marvellous machines that used a neural web as their computer mind. Driving was programming. You told the car where you wanted to go and when you wanted to arrive. Then the car took you on the super highways that flew across the old cities, across the plain, through the hills, all over the world. The cars contained a highway map of the world. In theory you could program the North Pole and go to sleep while the car took you there.

If Maslow wanted to get to the coast in a hurry, a Connet was his best bet.

'I have to come along,' she said drily. The cars responded to their owners alone. Thus they were unstealable: though, years before, pirates had lived in the old cities and hacked into the cars' computers as they went by, disabling them. The occupants had then been ransomed back to their loved ones.

'I know,' said Maslow. 'Do you mind?'

'The question is, can I spare the time?'

'And can you?'

'I guess I can. I'll expect you in an hour.'

Having programmed the car with the destination given her by Maslow, Fee settled to work solidly for the duration of the journey. In retaliation, Maslow went to sleep.

On their arrival they booked into a hotel. It was one of the best. Fee stayed there naturally as befitted her position in life and her wealth. Maslow, who was on expenses, had the excuse that everywhere cheaper was fully booked during the festival. He only expected to stay one night. Sandrina couldn't be that hard to find.

He bribed a boy at the central booking agency. A rapid computer search showed what tickets Sandrina had purchased, which events she aimed to attend. She was not performing. She was in town purely as a spectator.

He had a publicity still of the girl. He needed to find her early on, because late at night the unlisted fringe events took over. By then, Sandrina could be in any bar or square or on the beach with thousands of other people watching free entertainment. He'd never find her.

She had a ticket for a blues combo. Maslow bought a ticket and got there early. He found himself a seat near the door and settled down to drink slowly, watching every person who entered.

She came in around nine thirty. She was one of a group of people, evidently friends.

Maslow approved. The girl had looks and she moved like the dancer she was. She was young, she was pretty and she looked fresh. Of course, after a day in the company of Fee Cambridge, she looked a little insipid as any woman did, but Maslow could allow for that. At least he wouldn't have to check he still had his balls attached after being in the company of Sandrina. That was the effect Fee had on him.

He rarely went in for elaborate charades, pretend characters. He let Sandrina settle and begin to enjoy the music. She ordered food and drink. Her group planned to stay a while. That was good.

He let her go to the ladies room and waited for her when she emerged. The bar was hot and crowded now. It was the interval, the band were having a break, and conversation was loud and thick as cigar smoke.

He touched her arm as she went by. 'Sandrina,' he murmured.

She looked startled, as well she might. 'Yes?'

'My name is Maslow. I'd very much like to speak to you in private for a few minutes.'

She looked across at her friends and frowned. 'What about?'

'Someone you met recently. I'm a private investigator. The thing is, I'd prefer it to be somewhere quiet.'

There was a roar as the combo took the stand again.

'Who are we talking about?'

'Here's my card. Could you meet me afterwards for ten minutes? At the Connaught in the bar.'

'The Connaught?' She was incredulous. One drink in the Connaught bar equalled an overnight stay in a lesser hotel.

70

'I'll walk you over when you're done here. Then I'll bring you back to your friends, wherever you are going on to. I wish you would.'

Suddenly Sandrina's blood quickened. She hadn't slept with a man since Rollo Cambridge's humiliating treatment of her. She tended to keep her sex life and her friends separate. Most of them wouldn't approve of her longings to indulge. She had told none of them about going to the sex party in the Zoo. Mostly they reckoned such things were filthy.

She was out of step. Morality irked her. She wanted to sleep around, play with different men, but it would upset people she cared about if they knew that she did so.

The music tonight had got into her blood and roused her up. All of her friends were nice, celibate souls going back to their shared bedrooms – shared with pals of the same sex, that is. She herself was sharing a room with Helen and Suzanna. It wasn't a bedroom, it was a girls' dormitory.

This man, this detective. He was tall, not fat, kind of nice-looking in a rugged way. She could go with him to the Connaught and find out what its ultra-posh bar was like at first hand. She could answer his questions if they were OK, and see where things led. Her friends wouldn't know if she screwed him before joining them again.

Maslow couldn't read Sandrina's mind but he felt her sudden shift of interest. He was mildly astonished. He was maybe twenty years older than the girl. Yet her interest in him was as a male, he was sure.

'OK,' said Sandrina. 'This finishes around eleven. We'll go for a drink then. But I don't promise to answer any questions, though I will if I can.'

'There won't be a problem,' Maslow assured her. Actually, there would. He doubted if she had any information to give him. Fee had said she fancied Rollo Cambridge at a sex party. The girl might have spoken about what occurred there, and so brought down the New Moralists' wrath on Rollo's powerful head. That mugging incident was damned queer. The women must have recognised Rollo and just attacked him on impulse. If Sandrina belonged to

71

the organisation and had been ordered to find out more about him, or the sex parties, then she would be unlikely to tell him, Maslow, of her spying activities. Besides, she didn't seem to be that sort of girl. Frankly, he had felt himself appraised as a possible sexual partner. But if she hadn't been sent to the party to spy on what the rich folks was gettin' up to, then she would have no information to give.

Maybe he had better find out just what had taken place at this pary. He had time to find Fee and ask her before the interview with Sandrina.

Maslow went back to the hotel.

Fee was in her room, working. She admitted Maslow and asked him to sit down. Then she offered him a drink.

He took whisky. He had had several beers already and didn't like to feel bloated.

'I've found the girl,' he said.

'Has she got anything to say?'

'I'm bringing her here for a drink later on.'

Fee smiled.

'I came for some information,' said Maslow. 'About that party she attended. You said she had the hots for your husband. How did you know that?'

He was amused, though he didn't show it. He knew of no other woman he could ask such a question so baldly. He was getting used to Fee Cambridge. She wasn't all bad. Her coarseness was the product of a kind of ruthless honesty. Allied to her desire for glut, for excess, it made her what she was.

Amazing.

'Do you understand these parties?' said Fee after a momentary silence.

'Nope. I mean, I understand sex.' Maslow looked blandly at Fee. 'I guess that's what you all do.'

'They are games. Elaborate scenarios. We play parts.'

'Like acting?'

'No. We tend to be anonymous. At this particular party, the women were all in disguise. Our heads and faces, that is. Our bodies were almost naked.'

Maslow was silent. A nerve began to jump under his left eye.

'We painted the sexual parts of the men. I mean, we women together took each man in turn and handled his private parts so that we could paint them with liquid silk.'

Maslow felt his cock harden. It was a delicious idea.

'The men were given a shape. A little shape, a diamond or a star or a square or whatever, was affixed to their penis. They tended to be erect at this stage.'

Maslow kept absolutely still.

'The men had to wear blind and deaf helmets. They were all in a room. We women had shapes which were picked by chance. We had to find our shape partner in the dark and make it with him. The penises glowed, of course.'

'Of course.' Maslow swallowed drily.

'After we had found and used our shape partners, the men could take off their helmets and the lights were put on. It was playtime. I remember that Rollo was lying on a couch. Melanie was mounting him, I think. Astride him, I mean. Then this girl took the centre of the floor. Her man took her arse.' Fee smiled. 'It created quite a stir. That was strong, even by Zoo standards. I mean, this thing was kneeling in the middle of a lit room. We were all around. The guy had her up her rear. Colthorpe Archer, I think it was. He likes the back door.'

'You said she wanted Rollo,' said Maslow. His voice was remarkably calm considering how he was feeling.

'All the time she was being buggered in public,' said Fee slowly, 'she stared at Rollo. She was only a foot or so away from him where Melanie was doing the business. He was just lying on his back, you see. Well, he couldn't fail to notice her. I mean, she was hungry and it showed. So after a while he reached out and touched her face.'

Abruptly Fee fell silent.

'And then?' prompted Maslow gently.

'Then nothing. He tore off her mask. Then he kissed her as soon as she could move. I mean, he had Melanie taking him so he was pinned to the couch. But as soon as Colthorpe finished in her, the girl crawled over to Rollo like a pet dog. She didn't even wipe herself. I mean, she had this guy's spunk dribbling . . .'

'OK,' said Maslow sharply. 'So they made it then?'

'No. Rollo wasn't interested. Amused, maybe. No more. But we all knew the girl was desperate for him. She made no attempt to hide it.'

Fee sipped her drink and watched Maslow with amusement. He was aware of her scrutiny and intent on giving away as little of his feelings as possible. He found himself revolted and aroused in about equal parts. He had a hunger suddenly so fierce he could hardly cope with it, to get between Fee's thighs and give it to her.

She let that finance director in there. And countless others. Somehow Maslow didn't think he would be welcome, nor did he think he would be too pleased with himself if he did succeed. She wasn't his client, that was TransFlow, but it might fall to him to tell her Rollo was dead. It would be better if there was no sex between them.

Anyway, he had no desire to be a notch on her gun.

He finished his drink. 'Thank you very much,' he said. 'I should have asked you about all this much earlier. Having seen the girl, I have to admit I'm surprised.'

'You mean, she doesn't look the sort of female who'd show herself like that, who'd do such things?' Fee smiled.

'No, she doesn't.' Maslow was standing up, ready to go.

'Perhaps good little town girls and naughty old Zoo women are just sisters under the skin,' said Fee softly.

Maslow looked at Fee and grinned unwillingly. 'Damn you,' he said helplessly.

Fee grinned broadly back and for a moment they shared the jest, friends almost.

Then he left.

He was thoughtful as he walked Sandrina through the crowded festival streets to the imposing mass of the Connaught Hotel, lit like an ocean liner. On the other side of the road was the sea, vast and black, still its own master despite man's technological genius.

74

Sandrina said nothing. Indeed, conversation would have been difficult with the street noise so loud.

Maslow felt he had received something of a revelation concerning the girl. Not for one moment did he doubt Fee's account of the terrible party. This slender and seemingly innocent girl had joined in so lasciviously that she had mildly startled the Zoo sophisticates she had ventured among.

He could be honest with Fee. He could approach her directly if he had something to ask. Whatever her feelings were concerning her missing husband, she had them under control.

Sandrina would be different. They were both town, and she was not rich and beyond the reach of the opinion of others. She had her pride, her self-respect, and she would protect those if Maslow questioned her too closely.

He felt a moment's impatience. He was checking an unimportant lead. This girl couldn't be working for a New Morality group. If she was, she was playing a deep game.

He took her arm as they went through the doors into the palatial lobby of the famous hotel. He guided her into the bar.

He had chosen it because it was divided into separate booths, each a mini island of privacy. Once installed, they could dial the kind of music they liked and then call up the bar for the drinks they required. Otherwise they would be left alone, entirely alone.

He, Maslow, stayed on whisky. Sandrina was drinking wine. He ordered some snack food to go with the drinks. Then he let Sandrina choose the music.

'This is very nice,' she said uncertainly. The treated air was softly spiced, warm and alive.

He laughed. 'I'm on expenses. You have whatever you want and enjoy it.'

She looked at him more closely. 'Why am I here, Mr Maslow? What is this all about?'

He looked down and swirled his drink. Then he turned his head and looked at her, smiling ruefully. 'I hadn't expected you to be so nice.'

'What?' She was half-laughing, incredulous.

'I'm looking for someone. They said he'd been seen with this dancer. But you are lovely. What sort of dancing do you do?'

'Light classical. Some ballet. Musicals. Whatever I can get. What do you mean about someone being seen with me?'

Maslow took a deep breath. 'I mean Rollo Cambridge,' he said.

She flushed a deep, vivid red. Her hand trembled so that her wine slopped over the rim. She stared at the mess. Maslow reached over and used his large, warm hand to take hers from the glass. With his other hand he wiped the table with his napkin. He set her glass back on the clean surface. Then he released her hand.

He knew how to handle the interview now. 'Did you want him very badly?' he asked gently. The horny little bitch had behaved so atrociously he had to give her some let out, some way of preserving face.

'How do you know all this?' asked Sandrina in a stifled voice.

'I'm sorry.' Maslow sounded sincere. 'I'd spare you this if I could. Please don't think I'm prying.'

She raised a flaming face. 'Did he tell you?'

'He knew your name, did he?'

'He must have. I mean, I was billed under my own name, I always am. Though I still don't know whether he was in the place by chance.' She took a deep breath. 'He never said and I never asked.'

Maslow felt his blood pound. Jackpot. The girl wasn't talking about the party. This was some other occasion.

'He just turned up?' he said casually.

'I saw him at the bar. I was singing, you see. I came down among the crowd and went over to him. I was still singing, I mean. They call it floorwalking when you go out among the customers. I asked him to buy me a drink afterwards.'

'Which he did.'

'Yes. I was flattered.' Sandrina stared miserably at her drink.

For a moment Maslow felt a flash of irritation. She was so bowled over by this character that she could talk of him like this to another man. She so took for granted Rollo's preeminence in male terms that she didn't need to explain it. The great Rollo Cambridge had consented to have a drink with a dancer-singer in some bar. She was grateful.

Condescending bastard, thought Maslow. But he kept his voice gentle and kind. The girl was confessing. All he had to do was to lead her gently along.

'Then what?'

'He came back to my place.' The girl's voice sank lower. 'He was really drunk.'

'Drunk?'

'Almost incapable of standing. He could speak but he couldn't do much else. He made me, he made me . . .' Her voice faltered.

Maslow felt his cock stir again. He was getting too many vicarious thrills off this case. He could do with some live action soon.

'He made me hold the glass to his mouth so he could drink more. He was doing it deliberately.'

'Did he tell you why he wanted to be so drunk?'

'No. He held me in contempt, I think.' She kept looking at her glass.

'Do you know why?'

'I wanted him so nakedly. I let it show. I didn't care what state he was in. I guess he's used to women like me, throwing themselves at him. Having no pride.'

Maslow reached over and stroked her long coppery hair back. She lifted her face and looked at him, her eyes luminous with misery.

Silly cow, thought Maslow. What did she think she would get? 'You're beautiful,' he said gently. 'So beautiful.'

She smiled tremulously. 'I'm a fool.'

'No.' Maslow spoke very seriously. 'You weren't the fool.'

Sandrina looked back at her drink. 'He fell asleep on the couch and I went to bed. But he was up before me in the morning. He had injected himself with a dextrose solution, he said. He appeared to be feeling fine.'

'And then?' prompted Maslow.

'He ravished me.'

'What?'

'I wanted him to take me to bed. I got up, naked, to tempt him. He took me, laughing at me because I desired him so much. He called me names. I was nothing, less than nothing, because I wanted him so badly. Then he left.'

She finished her drink and gave Maslow a look of bright-eyed defiance. Her story was out. She had confessed.

'You poor thing,' he said earnestly. He leant in towards her and kissed her mouth.

Shallow. Romantic. Oversexed. A power groupie. Most men would hold her in contempt. But she had the body of an angel and the mind of a virgin harlot. Maslow decided to treat himself to a screw. He needed to fix dates on this unfortunate meeting and he needed to check there had been nothing afterwards, no subsequent meeting. But if Rollo Cambridge was slumming it in the town, boozing and whoring, then TransFlow's managing director was bored with his job and bored with his life.

A man who is bored with Fee Cambridge is definitely in terminal *ennui*, thought Maslow darkly. He ran his tongue round Sandrina's mouth and wondered what kissing Fee would be like. He put his hand round Sandrina's throat and moved her head away from his. He gazed intently into her eyes.

'I want to go to bed with you,' he said. He touched his lips onto hers and rubbed their noses together. 'Very much indeed.'

He saw her ego pick itself up with a delightful wriggle.

'After what I've told you?' she asked.

This is pure melodrama, thought Maslow. I must remember this little girly let herself be arse-fucked in a room full of people.

'You're so beautiful,' he repeated. He hoped she wouldn't carry this shrinking violet stuff into the bedroom. He actually felt like a good hard fuck. He had been teased too much by dirty talk from women. He wanted action.

They had another drink. Sandrina put dates on her

meeting with Rollo. It had taken place about two days after his disappearance.

Initially then, Rollo had intended to go away, to go on a spree. The best bet was that he was holed up in a house of pleasure somewhere with twenty doting women pawing him.

How did a man like Rollo Cambridge kick over the traces? He did what he liked anyway, at the least of times.

What the hell was there left for such a man?

Maslow began to get irritated. The girl liked it. He was hungry for it. Yet they had to act out this charade. He had to be avuncular, comforting, ego-building. She had to be remorseful, sincere, tantalising. All he wanted to do was get his cock between her cool thighs and work himself to peace inside her deep, tight pussy.

She had breasts like Fee Cambridge, he noted. They were long and full, cones of desire. He reached in and undid Sandrina's blouse. The flesh was deliciously heavy in his palm and he saw the girl's eyes dilate slightly as he touched her nipples.

She really did like it, then.

'Is nobody waiting for you to come back?' he whispered, kissing her throat, her upper breasts.

'They don't do it,' she said, her head back, her eyes closed.

'Don't do it?'

'Sex. It's out of fashion. You know that. You're town like me.'

'Some of us buck the trend,' said Maslow. He licked a nipple.

Sandrina giggled. 'Don't let the New Moralists hear you.'

Maslow slid a hand up inside Sandrina's thigh. He looked into her face as he felt for her fleece, to tickle it. Her eyes narrowed expectantly. He gasped slightly. She was depilated.

A slow joy filled him. She really was a horny bitch. She was red hot for it. The little-girl hypocritical stuff was falling away as he roused her. She wanted it as badly as he did.

79

His finger felt the dampness of her aroused sexual parts. 'You ever come across the New Moralists in the flesh?' he murmured.

She wriggled so that his finger slid deeper into her vulva. 'Only tub-thumping. Street corner stuff. Outside the bars I work when I'm singing, sometimes.'

Keeping his finger in her sex, Maslow bent his head to kiss her exposed breasts again. 'How about,' he said slyly, 'we make it right here in the Connaught bar?'

Sandrina giggled. 'Here?'

He released her pussy and pushed up her skirt with both hands. Then he swung her across his lap so that she was sitting astride him, facing him. He reached under her and opened his trousers so his erect penis was freed. He worked the crotch of her panties to one side and began to edge his pole into position.

She moved on him to help him, incidentally rubbing her hanging breasts into his face. He bit them as his cock sank upwards into the well of her sex. Then he grasped her hips and began to fuck her, hard.

Afterwards he took her to his room. The vast curtains were open and the view of the black night sparkling with lights on the nearby ocean and on the street below was beautiful. She pulled off her clothes lustfully and stood waiting for him.

'So how did Rollo Cambridge take you then?' Maslow looked at her as he said this, grinning slyly.

'Like this.' She spun round and threw herself onto the bed, buckling at the knees so that she half-knelt on the floor, sprawling forward onto the bed. Her arms were wide. Her sweet, pale, rounded rump beckoned.

Maslow grabbed her hips and lifted her. He shoved his hard cock into her wet slack pussy, still full of his juice. He slid in easily. He took her quickly because he was still very randy, and he watched their reflection in the black glass of the window as he did it.

She was imagining he was Rollo. He knew she was. He could tell when a woman fantasised in bed. The bitch was doing it now.

He pulled out of her when he was finished and sat on the bed panting. She lifted her head with her hair all tousled and gave him a raunchy look. He took a fistful of hair and yanked her so that she got to her feet and then fell over his knees. He held her there, bent over, and began to smack her bottom.

'This,' he grunted between smacks, 'is for throwing yourself at that Zoo cowboy who isn't worth a hair of your head.'

Sandrina wriggled and screamed. She was red-faced, spunk dribbling down her legs, her breasts flopping and heavy, her hair all over the place.

Maslow cheered up and smacked harder. His palm striking the plump young flesh was delightful. He'd like to do this to that Zoo bitch, Fee Cambridge. He'd really like to smack some manners into that one.

Sandrina was sobbing. Her bottom was cherry red. There were vivid palm-prints on it.

Maslow grabbed her by her hips and lifted her so that her bottom came up, leaving her bent double at the waist. He buried his face in her buttocks and pushed till he could get at the delicious fruit within. He found her little arse and licked it.

The heat of her flaming cheeks was in his face. He prodded her rear with his tongue. He could smell their combined juices. He slid his hand round and round her pussy. He drove his thumb into it and stirred the sexy, sticky gloop he found there. He let the girl slip back across his knees and he put a finger in her bottom.

She squealed. Maslow pushed his finger further in. The thumb of the same hand was up her pussy. He tried to press finger and thumb together through the membrane inside her.

Sandrina wriggled and squirmed, held by his finger and thumb, penetrating her arse and her cunt. Maslow felt a shock of pure lust run through him. He worked her back off his lap till she was kneeling by him, her arse lewdly cocked so he didn't have to let her go.

'Suck me,' he said hoarsely.

He worked his fingers. Her mouth closed over his erect cock. It didn't seem to matter how often he had it, he kept coming back for more. He pinned the girl with his hand and jerked his hips as he eased his throbbing member in her mouth. She was good at this. She had done it before. Maslow groaned and felt himself near to coming.

Christ, she was hot. These Zoo bitches weren't all display. They could come up with the goods.

The words filtered through Maslow's brain. As the tide rose unbearably in his cock, he remembered it wasn't Fee who was serving him. No, it was Rollo's reject, Rollo's groupie, fastened like a limpet to his private parts.

He came with a grunt. His visual field began to restore itself. He saw the door to his room was open.

He hadn't locked it. A woman leaned on the frame grinning as she watched his sexual antics. She wore a green silk robe that shimmered as she shook with silent laughter.

Maslow extracted his fingers from Sandrina's body. With his other hand he stroked the girl's hair as she laid her face in his groin, panting after her endeavours. He looked at Fee watching him. The he took Sandrina's face between his two hands, keeping it turned away from the door. He lifted the girl, feeling breasts brush his knees, his thighs, his chest as he did so.

All the time he looked at Fee. Then he raised Sandrina sufficiently so that her face was opposite his. He kissed her on the mouth, a long, slow exploratory kiss, tasting himself in the girl. Her arms wound round his neck.

When he finished, Fee had gone.

4

They left early the next morning, Fee claiming she needed to get into her office. Even in this electronic age, some things needed to be done in person.

Neither of them referred to the previous evening's display. Fee did however ask with douce politeness whether the trip had been worthwhile.

'You're a member of the board, Ms Cambridge,' said Maslow.

'I am.'

'I'm meant to be reporting to your head of security, Jermyn Ames.'

'Who reports to the board.'

'If you say so.'

'I didn't have to provide this lift, Mr Maslow.'

He considered. She was right. He'd used her precisely because she was a member of the board, and the board were employing him through their head of security. Moreover, it wouldn't be nice for her to have all this stuff in front of a bunch of pompous bastards. This way she'd be prepared.

'Your husband went to see this girl, Sandrina. She's a dancer, a singer.'

'He went to see her?' Fee sounded incredulous.

'It may have been coincidence. She was singing at the Black Cat in Level Verges. He appeared at the bar. She made the connection. I mean, she spoke to him first, on her own admission.'

'Then what?' Fee sounded faintly bored.

'He was dead drunk. She took him home with her. He

could barely stand up. She fed him more whisky on his command. Then he passed out on her couch.'

With another woman he would have been kinder. With Fee Cambridge he openly stared.

She blushed. She turned a faint rosy red, her pale face suffused with colour. It came to him that she was angry rather than ashamed. She was angry because Rollo had been mindlessly drunk. She would have preferred him to be sober, to have fucked the girl. That would have been normal, understandable.

'In the morning he got it up her and left,' said Maslow callously.

Now she was white. When it was too late it occurred to him that his spite was childish and he had exposed himself.

Fee turned to look at him. The car vibrated gently as it rode its cushion of air, hurtling back to his own town. To home. All the padded comfort could not quite dispel the sense of speed, of adventure. It was a wonderful machine.

Fee's eyes were ice-green. They glittered in the gloom of the car.

Maslow felt himself tremble. The rushing was inside him now. He could see the veins of his own eyeballs.

He felt about fourteen. His balls ached. 'I want to kiss you,' he said feebly. There were tears of shame at the corners of his eyes.

She lay back. She pulled up her skirt. She wore no panties. She lay with her eyes wide open, unemotional. Her knees were up and wide apart.

Maslow knelt humbly. He put his face down. His tears were wiped on her inner thighs. He kissed her lips. He tongued them apart. They were spiced and musky. His mouth trembled as he pressed it harder to her flesh. His tongue touched her sex.

She didn't move. He began to kiss her properly. Her sex swelled as he aroused her. Her lips were fatter, crisp, wet watermelon flesh. His tongue probed the valleys and sank into the pit.

She was tropic. The blood thundered in his ears like the

roar of surf. Her cunt was dark spice, hot and heady. His tongue dipped deeply into it. He ran it round and felt the faint ripple of her vaginal muscles.

He groaned and sucked hard. The flesh drew into his mouth and expanded. He prodded again with his tongue and then sucked.

He found her clitoris. It was hard. He pushed his chin into her cunt and concentrated on her clit. He found he could bite it quite forcefully. She quivered and when he moved his face again, his chin was wet.

He licked hard with his tongue flattened like a spade. He went right back to her arse and licked round to her clit, allowing his tongue to curve and wrap itself over every part of the delicate shaping of her sex. He returned to her hole at last and began systematically to suck and lick and probe her until she came.

He felt the coming of her. She arched her back slightly and pushed into his face. Her pussy throbbed and there was a gush of thin, honeyed fluid. He sucked her climax as though he was drinking nectar. Which he was.

He licked her gently once or twice to clean her. Then he withdrew his face.

Fee sat up and pulled her skirt down. 'You want to watch a movie?' she asked. 'Me,' she yawned, revealing a pink mouth like a cat's, 'I'm going to nap.'

Try as he might, Maslow could not find out what had happened to Rollo when he had left Sandrina's apartment. He questioned the neighbours. He talked to people on the street. He went into shops. He tirelessly contacted every taxi that covered the area.

When all this failed he went to the hospital. The man Rollo had come to see had been discharged, but Maslow prowled about and inspected the little gardens where Rollo had been attacked.

All this got him nowhere. He now felt he had to approach the problem from the other end.

He could find no trace of Rollo and so he couldn't follow him. But he could make some surmises about where

Rollo might be and begin to check them out until, by elimination, he tracked the missing man down.

He met with Jermyn Ames to talk over his progress, or rather his lack of it.

'I don't think he's dead any more,' he said. 'I would have found him by now, unless he took off and left the town altogether and went out into the wild. And he's not in hospital. I've had all of them checked.'

'What if he isn't in under his own name?' asked Ames. He was a heavy-built, jowly man, police-trained.

'I don't see why he'd do that.'

'If the man wants to hide . . .'

'He wouldn't choose a hospital,' argued Maslow. 'If he was hurt, he would use his own name. He'd have to, to pay for treatment. He can't access funds without being himself. Unless he has some other name and account to step into. But I've had photographs shown around and he is a distinctive man.'

'And Ms Cambridge is quite sure he's accessed no personal funds since the evening he was seen in the Black Cat by that singer girl?'

'So she says. I can hardly go over her head and get at their bank accounts. He's used no TransFlow accounts. Your own Ms Salazar is keeping herself wide awake for that. But a man like Rollo Cambridge could have funds anywhere, under any amount of names. He could have accounts his wife knows nothing about. His tax affairs will be labyrinthine. His career is littered with company formations. Some of them may be still active. I have to say there is no evidence either way. He could get money if he wanted it. The thing is,' said Maslow, 'if this is organised, he could have an entire second life to step into. But it is hard to see why he would do such a thing. He can get free of Trans-Flow if it bores him. He can leave his wife. God knows, they don't keep each other on a short rein. He could find no freer life than the one he had, really.'

'This dancer he met with,' observed Ames. 'That hardly sounds like an organised abandonment of one life for another.'

'No,' agreed Maslow. 'The guy went off on a bender. The girl admits to making the play for him. He fucked her and walked out. In the bar at the Black Cat he used his own name and credit. Up to that point he wasn't covering anything up. I think he intended to come back. Something prevented him. If it was an accident, he would have been using his own name and we'd know all about it.'

'Maybe,' said Ames, 'he left the girl's place feeling pretty disgusting. I know he'd given himself a shot and appeared to her not be hung over, but the truth of it is he'd have had some reaction to the toxic effects of the booze. And he did treat the girl bad.'

'You're not suggesting suicide?' Maslow was aghast.

Ames laughed. 'If you'd ever met him you'd know how impossible that is. Rollo Cambridge might take out the world for letting him down, but he wouldn't take his own sweet self out of it. He reckons he is far too precious for that. This is a man who thinks well of himself.'

'What did you mean, then?'

'Nothing much. I was thinking aloud. Let's say he feels a little disgusted with himself, and he isn't used to spoiling his self-esteem. He leaves the girl's, and . . . what?'

'He does something quixotic,' said Maslow slowly. 'Something happens, something by chance, but his response is odd.'

'He goes off with someone,' said Ames.

Maslow looked sober. 'I won't find him if he's down deep in suburbia having an adolescent love affair with some chance-met bimbo. Mind you, he'll get bored and surface of his own accord when the screen palls as entertainment, and he's sick of drinking himself stupid.'

'Do you believe that's what's happened?' Ames had small, deep-set eyes. He stared at Maslow.

'No.' Maslow shook his head. 'I think he may have been recognised.'

'You think he was snatched? There's been no ransom demand.'

'Maybe the snatch went wrong. Maybe he was killed.'

The two men looked at each other.

87

'So what next?' asked Ames.

'It'll be expensive. I'll need an army of helpers. But I think we ought to check every house of pleasure, every hotel, and see if he's been seen.'

Ames was restless. 'The news will leak. Someone will tell the press.'

'It'll take me a long time alone or with one or two helpers whose silence I can guarantee.'

Ames sighed. 'I'll speak to the board, but I don't think they'll go for the blanket approach. Not yet, anyway. Are you watching the girl, by the way?'

'Sandrina? Oh yes.' Maslow grinned. 'I don't think she was lying, but I'm not taking any chances. If she's in contact with him we'll know pretty soon.'

'What about your other idea, that the New Moralists or someone might have got their hands on him?'

'There's all sorts of screwy groups about, but if any of them had him, wouldn't they be crowing about it?' asked Maslow.

He went back to see Fee. He made the appointment formally through her secretary, and saw her in the office. He didn't even want to think about what had occurred in the Connet coming back from the coast, nor did he want the slightest chance that things might repeat themselves. He felt deeply humiliated about the whole thing.

She wore a navy blue velvet creation that looked as though it had been sprayed onto her. Her body was perfect. Her thigh-high suede boots were a deep maroon colour. On each of her wrists was a solid gold bangle, heavy as a manacle.

'Can you tell me if any of your friends have houses up in the country park?' asked Maslow.

'I guess so. Some of them do. The more social ones.' Fee smiled.

'Look, if Mr Cambridge wanted to vanish for a while, for whatever reason, the easiest way for him to do it would be to hole up in someone's house. Let's say a big house with a swimming pool and leisure facilities so he can keep himself amused. Or a second house, so no one but the friend knows he is there. Let's say the friend is bankrolling him. I can't trace him in those circumstances.'

Fee looked at him stonily.

'If you give me a list of possibles, of friends who might offer Rollo such a service if he asked it of them, I could discreetly check out their places. Watch for a while. Of course,' added Maslow quietly, 'the obvious person to hide him is you.'

'Now why would I do that?'

'I don't know why he's disappeared, Ms Cambridge. If I did I might be able to answer your question.'

'I'll mail you the list tonight,' said Fee.

'Thank you so much.'

Diana said: 'How are you, honey?'

'Fine,' replied Fee heartily.

'How's that sweet man of yours?'

'Resting up, Diana. He's been feeling the strain.' Fee found it curiously unpleasant to lie to her closest friend.

'Hasn't TransFlow got some big deal coming up?'

'That's it. He's buried himself away to work on it. He's cancelled all appointments.'

'He won't be going to the Starling party, then.'

'No. No. I guess not.'

'Will you?'

'I don't know, Diana.'

There was silence. 'Everything OK, honeychile?' Diana's voice was soft. The two women went back a long way.

'Sure. Things are great. Of course I'll be at the party. Work's been a bit hectic, that's all. Teddy OK?'

'He sure is. I still love the schmuck, yeah?'

'Yeah,' said Fee and laughed.

Diana and Teddy didn't attend the sex parties because, quite against the stream of current Zoo behaviour, they were entirely faithful to one another. Fee had paid little attention to the details of the Starling party, but after this conversation with Diana she assumed it was an ordinary social event. The Starlings aspired to be society leaders, and were given to lavish and expensive hospitality. Their last party had been in aid of charity. They had had their main salon done over to represent a casino. The roulette and blackjack tables were manned by professional croupiers. Everything the players lost and everything they won went to charity. It had been a most expensive evening, but the height of vulgarity in the Zoo was to admit that one could feel the financial pinch.

Fee decided to quell any gossip Rollo's prolonged absence might cause by attending the party. Moreover, she decided to take Roddy. As finance director he was now pulling in enough money to make it into the Zoo and buy himself a bubble house. But the Zoo was fussy. A man or woman had to show a five-year income before being allowed to join the most exclusive club in the world. Roddy could come as a guest; anyone could come into the Zoo if they were invited, and it would do him good to see what he probably aspired to.

Fee would not admit to a growing anger with regard to Rollo. She did not believe him to be dead. She was sure he would have been found if that was the case. Nor did she believe him to be hurt. Again, his whereabouts would have surfaced by now.

No, she believed that either he was in hiding under his own name, using a friend as Maslow had suggested, or that he had stepped into another personality and was deliberately keeping away from her.

Either of these two ideas made her increasingly angry. Left a grass widow, she could only be foolish. TransFlow was as much in the lurch as she was, but their corporate pride was not her concern. Her personal pride was.

There was no rule that said Rollo had to continue wanting her. If he didn't, however, he should have the decency to let her know where she stood. Their marriage had had its ups and downs but in her view, that had only added to the excitement. She liked excitement. Rollo going missing was not exciting. It was sordid. And boring.

So she would go to the party, and Roddy better not have any other plans. He would be her escort.

For a moment she thought about Maslow. He was rough and unpolished and she guessed his mind was small. But he was a real man for all that, full of the masculine juices she so adored. It would be fun to take him to a sex party and feel him quivering with bourgeois disapproval.

This Starling party. She had better decide what to wear.

The Castel d'Amour was famous for its floorshow. Here, the most gorgeous girls flaunted their lovely bodies to the most exciting music. Erotic ballet, cancan, even stripping, were all raised to new levels of art and ingenuity. New singers were forever being discovered at the Castel. Its cabaret was sharper, spicier. When Sandrina was told by Mournag, her agent, that she had a booking, she was delighted.

'It's to strip,' said Mournag flatly.

'Oh. Not to sing.'

'No. But you'll be given a lot of leeway. You get to solo dance. That's it, really. It's just that you take your clothes off while you do it.'

'Who decides the music?'

'They want you along. They'll talk it over with you. They might want to try someone out, see, same as they are trying you out.'

'When do I go?'

Mournag told her. 'Get this right, honey, and you'll fly. You have the talent.'

'I wish it wasn't stripping.'

'What do you care? Just imagine Rollo Cambridge is out there in the audience. Do it for him, sweetheart. You'll have them drooling.'

Sandrina blushed. Mournag didn't realise how genuine her feeling for Rollo was. That he was a bastard, that her emotion meant nothing to him, was beside the point. She loved him. She craved for him. He wasn't even in the news right now.

She wondered vaguely why Maslow had been questioning her. It had been a relief to confess the horribleness of what had happened, and she had enjoyed Maslow's sexual attentions afterwards. The man was properly humble. He was screwing a woman who had been screwed by Rollo Cambridge, even if it was lousy at the time.

Maslow had been fine. It was good to find a man who was a little greedy for sex, as she was. They were so rare in the town these days. She didn't want to pick up barflies – she wasn't that desperate – but her own good friends were all curiously sexless. She could only suppose they didn't get the urge like she did, or that they sublimated it somehow.

Maybe there was something wrong with her. If there was, it was wrong with those crazy Zoo women as well. They had gone at sex ferociously, gluttonously, and she had felt at one with them.

Sandrina shuddered delicately. All that wonderful erect maleness, all those painted cocks, that glow-in-the-dark hide-and-seek where women fumbled with cock-flesh and fondled men's balls. It was like the best of fantasies come true.

She'd love to go again. She wished Mournag wasn't her entry. She didn't want anyone who knew her from her town life to know her in the life she craved, up there in the Zoo.

Meanwhile she had her career to consider. It might be a strip, but she would make it the best of strips, a complete work of art. First of all she needed to know her music.

Fee bought a dress made of scales. Each tiny, overlapping scale was treated holographically. The dress was dull silver in repose. When Fee moved the scales rippled sensuously and exploded into deep blues and glowing, iridescent greens. It was a short tight dress fitting her like a glove, so that it emphasised her wonderful deep-breasted body.

She looked at herself in the mirror. She looked marvellous. Fantastic. Her hair glowed blue-black with the deep velvet softness of a pansy petal. On her white face no cosmetic showed, though her lips were subtly heightened in colour by the application of an enzyme. She drew attention to her eyes by her use of a belladonna derivative that made her pupils enlarge within their startling ice-green irises.

Rollo should see her. He should be here. She needed him. He tended to wear a deep royal blue to major parties like this. It emphasised his piercing, brilliant blue eyes and his tanned, glowing skin. His blond hair, overlong for the fashion of the times, was his glory, his golden crown.

They were superb together. Damn him. He should be here.

Fee picked up a broad platinum collar and fixed it around her neck. Then she clipped a platinum vambrace onto each arm. The white metal glowed, accentuating the iridescent dress, her pure blue-white skin.

She stared at herself some more in the mirror. Not flawless. She was never flawless because she had that mark, that diamond trickle over her winged cheekbone where so long ago a bullet had scarred her perfect face, and she had not troubled to have it repaired.

She was so beautiful it hurt her to look at herself. She wanted to have sex with herself. What use was any of it, what use was anything without Rollo?

She couldn't breathe. He was her space, her freedom, and he was gone.

The Castel d'Amour suggested with charming diffidence that Sandrina might like to strip to this particular piece of music composed and performed by a nobody that they, the Castel d'Amour, thought might be rather exciting, a real find.

After hearing it Sandrina was inclined to agree. The boy looked about eighteen. He had wisps of unsatisfactory hair sprouting oddly on his face but his music made your heart stammer and he played it like an angel.

It occurred to her that he might want something better than a stripper performing to it.

However, he was pleasant to her. He played his piece several times and then gave her a recording of it. They arranged a rehearsal schedule and she took the music away to choreograph her piece.

The style of the music made several approaches out of the question. Nothing vulgar fitted it. She soon saw what

93

she must do. She must act out a little playlet. She would be a girl imploring her lover to take her. She would plead, expose her body, seek to entice him, to stir him, to arouse him to consummate the act with her. She would play so vividly to this recalcitrant lover that the audience would all but see him. And they would pity her and know her lover for a blind fool.

Next she had to decide on her costume. Something white, lacy, virginal. Like a lily, white and lovely. Her dance would be ballet, a ballet of love. And proffered sex.

She had a week to put her package together and show it to the floorshow managers at the Castel. She found her costume partly in antique shops and partly from her own resources. She demonstrated it to Mournag and sensed that her agent wasn't impressed. She didn't care. She needed the big stage, the ambience of the theatre to get it across. Working through it in a small room killed it stone dead.

The composer, Andreaz, rehearsed the piece live with her. He seemed interested, but she couldn't bring herself to ask for his opinion up front. She was committed now and she had to believe in her own work, in what she had done.

She came on the appointed afternoon and was shown to a dressing room. There were several other girls there and they were putting on feathers and frou-frou for a vigorous, lusty cancan-derived dance. They eyed Sandrina's demure, simple, lacy clothes with ill-concealed disdain. The bodice of the sleeveless dress was loose and shapeless. The skirt dropped gently from her hips to below knee level. It was made of broderie anglaise and was, in fact, an ancient petticoat or underslip.

Sandrina ignored them. She bound up her hair and twisted the artificial white flowers into it.

Her feet were bare. It was hard to dance without ballet shoes, but it was necessary. She would manage.

She was called and came to wait in the wings. All the upcoming acts were being checked one by one to make sure they met the required standard. She could still be dropped even at this late stage if they felt she did not make the grade.

She stayed offstage as Andreaz began. He was immersed in the piece as always. His booking was assured, which was what he deserved. The music was wonderful.

Now she fluttered onto the stage backwards as if she had left a garden or some other people behind. She turned and saw her lover. She reached out to him and smiled, dancing happily because he was there.

He didn't respond. She began to tease him, showing a leg, a pretty arm, her throat.

She became more urgent. She reached out longing arms. Still no response. She became sensuous, she began to promise things. Her dancing became a little wanton, a little suggestive. She had to peer over her shoulder to see if he responded.

Not enough.

Now she began to plead using her bodily charms. She arched her body suggestively, curving herself invitingly, stroking her own flesh, offering, pleading.

The music stammered and twisted through complicated, halting melodies. Sandrina lifted her skirts high and twirled, showing all her legs, her lacy drawers, her naked waist. Then she flung the dress from her and bent to the floor as if to cover her breasts.

Under the dress she wore a short camisole. Now she danced undoing the buttons it had down its front. Then she spread her arms wide again so that her breasts were revealed.

She danced like this, in her loose drawers and open shift, making her body more and more explicit. Then she flung the camisole from her and held her own breasts out to the unseen and obdurate lover. She stroked her breasts, caressed them, tried to lick her own nipple.

It was all unavailing. She began to lower her drawers. She danced and teased and finally shed them. She was now entirely naked.

The dance lifted in tempo. She danced magnificently, doing great leaps and turns but always revolving so that she returned to the unmoved lover. She offered her breasts, her belly, she opened her legs and finally she cartwheeled rapidly round the stage. She slowed, held the final cartwheel upside down with her legs wide apart, came down and right over until she lay on her back with her head towards the unseen lover. She arched her back. She lifted one leg. Now the audience were looking straight at her sex. She slipped a flower from her hair and laid it on her vulva. She lifted her arms and made them supplicate and the music finished.

Mournag said. 'I was impressed. That was very good. They're pleased with you.'

'I wanted something original,' said Sandrina. She was cleaning the stage make-up off her face.

'I think you've got it.'

The night of Sandrina's performance debut at the Castel d'Amour was the night of the Starling party. Roddy turned up promptly and gasped when he saw Fee. He thanked his merciful stars he had chosen the most subfusc of costumes. Fee needed a foil, not a competitor. His dull black clothes were the perfect counterpoint.

He had wanted to screw her first but he saw that that was impossible. She offered him a drink though, and he sat and sipped it while she said goodbye to the maid who had served her as she dressed.

She came over to him afterwards. He felt the air around her tingle. The hairs on his arms rose up. She was terrifying.

'Put your hand up my skirt,' she said calmly.

He set down his drink and obeyed.

'Right up.'

He put it right up.

'Touch my clitoris.'

He found the little piece of flesh and began gently to manipulate it.

Fee stood over him. He was sitting on her couch, leaning forward to her where she stood before him, his hand inside her skirt causing coruscations of colour.

She rested her hands lightly on his shoulders for balance. 'Keep going,' she said huskily.

He felt her breathing change as she became aroused. Her chest rose and fell. Her vulva became moist.

'That's it,' she whispered. 'That's enough.'

He swallowed and began to remove his hand.

'No.' She touched his shoulder. 'Dip your finger into my pussy.'

He did so.

'Now take it out and dab the inside of my wrist with it. Here, I'll move the bracelet.'

She made him anoint her at wrists and throat. The woman wore her own sex juices as perfume. Roddy felt dizzy with her. She was gross. She was too much. How could he handle such a creature? She was altogether too much for him.

They left for the party. 'Who are these people?' he asked.

'Bankers. It's an old family, old money. The bank's OK, though.'

'Which bank?'

'Sorry, I forgot you were finance.' Fee named it. It was one of the larger of the independents. 'They are venture capitalists mostly. Rollo and I used them a little in our early days but we don't have much call for them now in their working capacity.'

I bet you don't, thought Roddy. The Cambridges stank of wealth, though they hadn't been born to it.

He realised he had a lot to learn. He should have realised who these Starling people were. The name hadn't registered properly with him. He must be careful not to expose his ignorance tonight. He wasn't used to brushing shoulders like this with the mighty in the land. If he aimed to play in this league he must do more homework.

'Are you married?' Fee asked casually on the way over.

'Yes.'

'She know you're with me?'

'No. She thinks I'm at a business occasion.'

Fee smiled, catlike. 'Perhaps you are.'

Roddy swallowed the insult. He would remember it, though.

* * *

97

Sandrina said: 'Maslow.'

'Yeah.' They were talking on the vidi.

'I'm performing at the Castel d'Amour tonight.'

'Hey. How about that. Well done.'

'I want you to come.'

'Me?'

'I want you to see my act.'

'Well, I'd love to see your act . . .'

'Please.'

'OK,' said Maslow slowly. He didn't really have the time. He was making no progress on this TransFlow account. 'Look,' he said suddenly. 'Would you be mad if I brought someone?'

'Who?'

'A journalist. I really need to see her concerning a case I'm working on. If I can talk to her tonight, it won't matter me taking the time off.'

'This isn't anything to do with Rollo Cambridge, is it?'

'No, honey. That was wrapped up some time ago,' lied Maslow easily.

'You have to see her tonight?'

'I do. But I can watch your act and when she's gone, I'll have a clear conscience. I'll be able to pay some attention to you.' Maslow hesitated. 'Like you deserve.'

'OK,' said Sandrina slowly, 'I'll be able to join you after my performance.'

'I'm looking forward to it already.'

He had had to get special permission to contact this woman. Her name was Richelle Matthews and she was a feature writer. For the past year, she had made it her speciality to investigate the strange new groups developing in the town, aspects of the new moral culture beginning to prevail at grass roots level.

Some of them were very strange indeed. The sexual life of the town was changing. On the one hand were groups exploring esoteric and extreme forms of obsessional behaviour. On the other hand there were groups arguing that all non-procreational sex was wrong. Each believed passionately that they had the rights of it, that they had found the primrose path to true human pleasure. Whether that pleasure was pleasure in excess, pleasure in obsession or pleasure in denial, seemed to the outsider to make very little difference. Each group was sure it had found the Way.

The TransFlow board was naturally wary of any contact with the press, but Maslow had persuaded them that this was necessary.

He had already contacted Richelle and now he vidied her to ask if she would join him at the Castel d'Amour.

'As my guest,' he added smoothly. 'I have a friend performing and she asked me to come. I hope you won't mind.'

'Not at all. But I would like to know the client you're working for.'

'I can't tell you, Ms Matthews. They want to retain anonymity and you are a journalist.'

'Well, well. We'll see. What time will you come by, Mr Maslow?'

And so it was arranged.

As soon as Fee was welcomed into the Starling party she knew she had made a terrible mistake. This was a sex party. Diana had merely been asking Fee if she was going as a matter of information. The implication that she was going herself with Teddy had been a figment of Fee's imagination.

It was a sex party and it was going to be very very hot.

Fee wasn't in the mood. No, that wasn't quite right. Fee was always in the mood for sex, always hungry, but she wasn't in the mood for elaborate spicy games with her friends and social peers. It would have been different if Rollo had been there, but he wasn't. Rollo was missing. It was unbelievable, but Rollo was missing and she felt that she didn't understand anything any more, that she didn't know anything.

Roddy was with her because she had to have a man, and because she had to have sex. Sex was as necessary as eating and drinking, more so. It was an affirmation of life. It held away all the bad things in life like old age, disease, pain, failure. It anaesthetised her mind, it was a trip, it was the permanent rush.

She was using Roddy like an animated dildo, and she was beginning to let it show. That crack she had made – that he had no choice over being with her because he was an employee, and she was demanding his social and sexual attentions with no right of refusal on his side – he had picked up on it. The man wasn't stupid, intellectually or emotionally. As she, Fee Cambridge, went more and more out of balance without Rollo, so she behaved worse and worse.

Damn, damn, damn. She didn't want to be at this party and how the hell was she supposed to get out of it now?

The scales of her dress flashed aquamarine fire. Fee felt cold and dangerous inside.

The Castel d'Amour was full of people out to enjoy themselves. The vast rococo emporium glittered like a spangled wedding cake, impossibly, ludicrously, comically over-decorated. Balconies and boxes filled with parties of merrymakers clung to the ornate sides of the auditorium as though Spanish galleons had sailed into the walls and stuck, leaving their poops behind them. Waiters rushed to and fro serving people seated on the stairs, at tables, in the raked seats, on the balconies, as if in a warren or a termite hill, all passages and chambers humming with insect life.

The vastness was starry with pinpricked light. The only solid glow, so bright it seemed to phosphoresce, was the stage. The Castel d'Amour was famed for its cabaret, and the fame was justified. You might come to eat, to drink, to make merry, even to make love, but also you came to be entertained and to have your senses ravished by the entertainment.

Maslow sat with Richelle Matthews. The journalist was a tall woman with luscious auburn hair and deep hazel eyes. She wore something formal and silky in black so that her hair had a burnished coppery look, and her eyes were soft dark wells in her pale, freckled face. Once seated, she took from her bag a bracelet or necklet, Maslow couldn't tell which, of amber beads. She played constantly with these beads, holding them between her fingers and working them sensuously. The movements were not obtrusive – she toyed with the thing in her lap virtually out of sight – but Maslow found it fascinating.

As the hardened resin was moved between those cool fingers, so he imagined himself being touched. She fondled the amber casually, and he thought how he would like to be the recipient of her casual attentions. How nice to lie reading the paper, watching the screen, having this tall, exciting red-headed woman touch him, press him, roll his flesh between her fingers.

He shook himself free of the sexual fantasy. He had work to do.

'You have made bizarre sexual groups your speciality,' he began.

'They don't think of themselves as bizarre.'

'They don't? I'd have thought that was one of the pleasures.'

'Pleasure doesn't figure very largely in their vocabulary. They certainly get pleasure,' Richelle smiled, 'but it comes from complex causes and in complex ways. It's altogether a tortuous business.'

Maslow looked at her. He, or rather TransFlow, was paying for her time. A consultancy fee. 'Like religion,' he suggested.

'Very like religion. These are sexual sects as opposed to religious sects. They see themselves as religious. They are fanatical. Fervent. Schismatic. Obsessional.'

'Are they fun?' Maslow couldn't help grinning.

Richelle met his eyes directly. 'They are limiting,' she said. 'They are fun as far as they go. But they exclude. They are built on exclusion. My personal opinion, if you care about that, is that they exclude too much.'

This was delicious. Maslow found he had to remind himself he was working. 'Are they evangelical?' he asked.

'Absolutely not. They don't only exclude behaviours that don't fall within their rigid brief, they exclude people.

101

They don't want to have a common appeal. They don't want mass membership. These people thrive on being special. They are the elect. The ones who know. They are in on the secret.'

Maslow's eyes went to the stage. A woman was singing. She was probably very good, for the Castel had a high standard, but he was engrossed in Richelle.

'The impression given to outsiders,' he said carefully, 'is that they are mostly female sects.'

'I think that's fair. They mostly are.'

'Why do you think that is?'

Richelle looked mischievous. 'Women are growing up still,' she murmured. 'We stood a couple of thousand years of patriarchal society. We're still recovering genetically. I guess we've reached the secret society stage. For men it flourished in medieval times. For us, the time is now.'

The beads rolled softly and silently through her long fingers.

'Does it matter?' asked Maslow.

'Who can say? It offends those of us who feel too mature for such behaviour. Live and let live, I suppose. It's cultural baggage, isn't it? We all need to carry a little luggage around with us, to tell us who we are, to confirm our status.'

'You're very cynical.'

'I don't think so.'

Maslow wanted to take her to bed so badly it hurt. 'And are they man-haters?' he asked.

'Often. Not always.'

'Why?'

'Fear. Envy. The human need to hate.'

'Which groups principally hate men? For whom are we the enemy, really the enemy?'

Richelle was silent.

'Don't you know? I thought you were the expert.'

'I do know. I am the expert.'

'Then why don't you answer my question?' Maslow's tone was soft, unbullying. He was probing, but she was an expert in that as well, and would be able to defend herself easily if it came to the point.

'I wish I knew, Mr Maslow, why you require this information.'

'I can't tell you. You know that.'

'The information you seek is information I have. Yet I feel I need to know how you intend to use it.'

'You're not selling me arms. I don't have to supply an end-user certificate.'

'Maybe I am. Maybe you do.'

'I'm paying,' said Maslow patiently, 'a fat consultancy fee.' Christ, he wanted her body.

'You see, these women are, in my opinion, foolish women. Pathetic women. Even dangerous women. But I don't want to turn the guns on them.'

'You've made it your journalistic ambition to expose them.'

'To defuse them. No, not exactly. I examine them. I analyse them. I ponder on their role in society. Perhaps I warn society that it exerts pressures which result in sects such as these.'

'Such as what?' Maslow was beginning to show his frustration.

'The Sisters of Pain,' said Richelle. 'The New Moralists. Bound and Free. Latex Libido. The Virgin Queens.'

'Hold on,' said Maslow. 'Are these all man-haters?'

'No. The first two are.'

'The New Moralists. I've heard of them. I thought they were against sex of any kind.'

'Except for procreation. So they are. They think once is quite enough in our lifetimes. Two or three times if you don't score a bull first off.'

'Why do they hate men? It's sex they hate.'

Richelle looked at Maslow from under her lashes. 'I guess they equate the two. If you only screw a man once in your life, you aren't likely to enjoy the experience too much. They feel men have seduced women into believing, quite falsely, that they want sex frequently. Men have conned women and women have been suckers. Looked at another way, you could say they want men and sex but they are afraid. They won't admit to fear so it has to be hate.'

'Do they hate men enough to be violent?'

'I believe they do.'

'Enough to attack particular men?' Maslow persisted.

'I think that could be true.'

'What men might be singled out for attack?'

'Men associated with sex,' said Richelle promptly.

Maslow sat back. He felt he had his answer. Someone had taken Rollo Cambridge out of circulation, he was sure. It could be Rollo himself but he was checking on that. It wasn't a criminal gang because they would have asked for ransom money. So it had to be an enemy.

He must check up more thoroughly on old business enemies, and on lovers his hellcat of a wife might have had. But his favourite hypothesis at the moment was that the mugging of Rollo Cambridge at the time of his hospital visit had been fortuitous. Two members of the New Moralists had recognised Rollo and attacked him on the off-chance. Subsequently they had followed up the attack by snatching him.

The mechanics of it were unclear. He had failed to find a link between Sandrina and any such group, yet she appeared to be the last person to see Rollo on the loose. Could a second serendipitous meeting have triggered the snatch? Had the snatch been planned, and Rollo watched? Had he gone deliberately to the town to drink himself stupid or had he been invited with malice aforethought?

Why Rollo Cambridge? Perhaps that was the easiest question to answer. He was good-looking, a sexual force in himself. He was powerful, and if there was such a thing remaining as a sexual imbalance at the top of society, Rollo would epitomise the male aspect of that domination. He was Zoo. Mainstream life in the town was becoming more staid, more prudish. In their way, the extreme sects were part and parcel of that movement, that change in morality. As the generality of town society became more proper, less sexually active, so the fringe became more tightly focused, odder.

In the Zoo, however, sex raged. The Zoo sex parties were notorious. Maslow found it hard to give them proper credence. But the town loved them because they gave it the excuse it needed to hate. It focused the town's jealousy of Zoofolk and justified its disapproval. Zoofolk were decadent. It was time they fell from grace.

Had Rollo Cambridge fallen already? If so, he would be Lucifer, the best and the brightest of the angels, most beautiful in his sin.

'Is this your girl?' asked Richelle.

Maslow jerked back to attention. The act was changing. A very young man was playing some music that sounded intriguing. A pretty little thing was dancing backwards onto the stage looking pure and fragile.

Yes, it was Sandrina. Maslow settled to watch.

Richelle watched him covertly, her beads flowing between her fingers. A man had been attacked. She could work out that much from the drift of his questions. A man had been attacked by women and she had heard nothing of it.

Zoo. He must be Zoo. They would have the influence to keep any sordid little story out of the papers. They would have the money to employ someone of Maslow's calibre. She wasn't coming cheap herself.

Somebody in the Zoo felt under threat. Or was under threat. Richelle turned her eyes to the stage.

She hoped the retribution that would fall on the women silly enough to tackle so dangerous an enemy would be limited. The Zoo, with a flick of its powerful finger, could order a sledgehammer to crush a beetle. The New Moralists and their ilk were pathetic women, sex-starved, fearful and foolish. They wouldn't be able to handle the wrath of the Zoo if one of its members was hurt. Richelle was woman enough, town enough, to dislike the hegemony of the Zoo. The arrogant bastards were riding for a fall the way they behaved, as if no one and nothing but themselves mattered. She could bear to see them brought down a peg or two. They deserved to have their knuckles rapped.

Yet here she was, in the business of aiding the enemy. Richelle watched Maslow watching the girl on stage. No. He wasn't the enemy. He was a man doing his job. Nor was the Zoo the enemy. They were a privileged élite, nothing more, nothing less. All societies had them.

The enemy was within. The enemy was the beast called Fear, lurking inside everyone. People were generally OK when they weren't afraid.

Maslow's girlfriend was showing her pussy to an enthusiastic audience. Richelle listened to the applause and wondered how much longer sex would be overt and on show, as it was here tonight. This kind of thing was going out of fashion. She wouldn't be surprised if the Castel d'Amour didn't drop strip acts in the near future.

Sex was about to go underground. She could feel it coming. Society would become one of nods and winks, saucy allusions, suggestiveness with a hypocritical veneer of propriety.

Who cared? Did it matter? The cycle was endless, from prudishness to prurience, from propriety to promiscuity.

Maslow was looking at her. 'Would you like to do this again sometime?' he was asking. 'Not in the company's time?'

'Watch your girlfriend take her clothes off, you mean?' asked Richelle innocently.

'She's not my girlfriend, she's research.' Maslow grinned broadly.

'I think that's worse.'

Maslow looked at her. He leaned forward and spoke softly. 'I'd like to touch your breasts,' he said.

Something flickered as he spoke, at the periphery of his vision. There was a faint hiss from the tables around them. He looked up and for a moment felt nothing but a blank astonishment.

Fee kissed Anita Starling on the cheek. She introduced Roddy. She could sense his wariness.

'The game is moo-cows,' said Anita merrily.

'Moo-cows?'

'Darling, don't be dense.'

Diva Jackson hove into view. 'Fee,' she shrieked. 'Is darling Rollo here?'

'He's taking the cure, honey,' said Fee easily.

'Cure for what?' Diva's eyes raked Roddy. He felt undressed.

'Women.'

'If you turn Rollo onto boys I swear I'm going to have a sex change,' said Diva. She winked broadly at Roddy, who felt his toes curl. This terrible old woman gave the lie to the story that witches didn't exist.

'I thought you already had,' said Fee and those within hearing began to laugh as the joke penetrated.

'We milk the men, baby,' said Anita. 'We measure their output. Best of three. It's time we ladies had a league table here.'

Damn, damn, damn, thought Fee wearily.

'We all dress up as dairymaids, Fee,' said Diva maliciously. 'The men wear cowsuits and go about on all fours. Of course, they haven't exactly got udders. But they can be milked all the same, can't they?' She nudged Roddy who felt sick. Fee had made it clear he wasn't a free agent in this business. How far was he supposed to go in order to keep his job?

'We milk the men,' Anita said, 'into these dinky little glass containers. They are all properly calibrated, you see. Then we find out which guy is the spunkiest.'

'Then what?' asked Fee, sounding bored.

'He gets his reward.'

'Which is?'

'Whatever he fancies from whomever he fancies it. The rest of us get to watch.'

Some new arrivals interrupted this. Roddy stood stiffly, the blood thumping in his ears. There was no way he was going to fail to make a fool of himself. He could feel it coming.

The game was being explained to the new arrivals. The man roared with laughter and his voice boomed out. 'You mean I have to crawl around on all fours inside a pantomime cow and have my dipstick pulled by the ladies till I spout?'

'That's it.' Anita's voice was amused.

107

Fee met Roddy's eyes. He looked miserable enough for her to feel a lash of spite. Weakness always brought out the worst in her. Maybe she should give way to cruelty and make him stay.

Maybe not.

So how to get out of this while saving face? The one thing never to show was disgust. That was the game they were really playing. They were pushing each other to see how far they would go. No doubt they would all be relieved when someone cried *enough!* and they could stop these stupid parties, but no one wanted to be the one who did. It would involve losing caste.

No feigning illness. That had been done, and wouldn't be believed even if the illness was unfeigned. There must be some other way.

Dammit, she was Fee Cambridge and she did as she pleased. No one, not even Zoofolk, told her what to do.

'Anita,' she called, pitching her voice up so that it carried well.

'Fee, honey?'

'My therapist says non-penetrative sex is bad for me. I guess I'll give this one a body-swerve and go home and make it with Roddy here.'

There was a moment's stunned silence. Fee Cambridge was backing down.

Diva Jackson said: 'Isn't the baby boy up to it, darling?' She fluttered vast false eyelashes at Roddy, who felt himself turn white.

Fee picked up one of the dinky little glass dishes Anita had displayed so proudly. 'Diva,' she said sadly, 'you can't put a quart into a pint pot, no how, honey. Ain't you learned that yet?' She looked at Diva's latest pet, barely of age and with a massive musculature. 'Perhaps not,' she added softly.

There was a roar of laughter. Fee put her arm in Roddy's and kissed Anita goodbye.

Maslow stared. The woman coming between the tables towards him was Fee Cambridge. A sigh went up from those she passed. She radiated a cold, fabulous beauty. Her dress gleamed like the scales of a dragon, in iridescent blues and greens. Some nothing male was accompanying her. She screamed Zoo, and here she was slumming in the Castel d'Amour.

Richelle felt annoyed at Maslow's sudden switch of attention. The guy had been making his pitch, and now he stopped to look at someone else.

He was staring so hard she had to turn round and look, she couldn't help herself.

Jesus, she thought. That's Fee Cambridge. Richelle had seen her on the screen, and at one or two public functions that she had covered in her journalistic career. Fee with her raven's wing hair, white, high-cheekboned face and slim, full-breasted height would be striking anywhere. Here, dressed to kill, she was a peacock among sparrows.

She was stopping by their table. The waiter leading her and her escort stopped also when he saw that she did so.

Fee smiled down into Maslow's upturned face. He hadn't known whether to greet her or not. She might not relish a private investigator claiming acquaintance. Yet here she was, stopping.

'Maslow,' she said huskily. He saw the devilment in her eyes. Damn the cow. He stood up and kissed her on the lips.

She didn't respond but when he drew back he saw she was amused. 'This is Roddy Dupique,' she said, introducing her companion.

The lover. TransFlow's finance director. Conceivably the man who had done away with Rollo Cambridge, though Fee denied it.

'Richelle Matthews,' said Maslow.

Richelle stood up. The woman was as beautiful in the flesh as she looked on screen. More so.

Fee looked at her, eyes narrowed. 'Richelle Matthews,' she murmured. 'Is it your columns that I've read with such pleasure?'

Roddy, Maslow and Richelle felt a simultaneous admiration for Fee. That the beautiful body contained a razor-sharp mind was well-known. Experiencing her quickness in action was something else.

Sandrina arrived, wondering what the hell was going on. She saw Fee and blinked, recognising her.

Richelle was amused. She didn't know what was going on, but the arrival of Maslow's stripper girlfriend was not going to help. Moreover, the girlfriend looked cross. No doubt she had come over high from performing, ready to receive praise. Instead she was being effortlessly upstaged by the first lady of the Zoo. Perhaps the cream of the joke was that Maslow had been pitching to go to bed with herself just as all this happened.

'Sandrina,' said Maslow, pulling himself together. How could he be so callow? Damn the Zoo bitch for turning him into a gauche adolescent.

Fee looked with apparent interest at Sandrina. 'We were at a party together recently, honey,' she cooed. According to Maslow, Rollo had balled this chick just before he disappeared. 'Do you remember? I don't think we were introduced.'

Roddy was getting sick of Fee calling the shots. 'We caught your act,' he said to Sandrina. 'You were beautiful.'

'Thank you.' She looked confused.

'I like a girl who knows how to take her clothes off gracefully,' said Fee.

Richelle choked.

'Really beautiful,' said Roddy, so that Sandrina would know he wanted to get closer to what she had been showing off on stage.

Sandrina looked at Maslow. As did Richelle, with raised eyebrows and her head slightly to one side. And Fee.

'Fee Cambridge,' said Maslow after clearing his throat, 'was my girlfriend when I was thirteen. Not many people know that.'

Fee said: 'He broke it off. He preferred Kerrin Jay. She was a very early developer.' She nodded at Maslow thoughtfully.

'You didn't come on so bad, Fee.' His voice was mild.

Richelle was having trouble not laughing out loud. She

didn't believe this for an instant. The pair of them were making it up as they went along.

Why? What were they hiding? Was it anything to do with Maslow's mysterious client?

Perhaps she should fuck Maslow and find out. She would quite like to; he had a nice body, and the equipment up top to guide it. Why would Fee Cambridge know a private investigator? She couldn't pass up the chance for a good story.

'Were you really born in the town?' asked Sandrina naïvely. Why wasn't Fee with Rollo? The man she had with her was nice, but not a patch on her own husband. No wonder Rollo got drunk and was so bitter. It must be terrible being married to Fee.

Roddy felt a spasm of raw jealousy. Fee and this man were flirting under his eyes. He had wanted to get inside her all evening and she had been holding out on him.

Maybe it did give his ego a big rush to be seen out in her company. But he wasn't concerned much about his ego. What he wanted was to cover this woman, to insert his penis into her glorious, frightening hole and pump till his cock burst.

Fee moved slightly. Deep starbursts of ocean colour rippled from her dress. There was an 'aaah' of admiration from the tables round them. Fee said in her husky voice: 'The next act is starting. We'd better sit down, Roddy. Dammit, I'm hungry too. What would you recommend?' She looked at Maslow who had insultingly sat down. 'Piranha,' he said. 'They serve it with the teeth.'

'Vagina dentata,' said Richelle, unable to control herself.

Fee winked at her and they moved on.

Sandrina said: 'What was all that about?'

She and Maslow were alone at their table. Richelle had left immediately after Fee and Roddy.

Maslow leaned towards her. He took her chin in his hand and drew her face towards his. He kissed her. 'Take me home,' he said. 'Your pussy is beautiful. Now I want to get inside it.'

5

They left him to his own devices for two days. He lay on his front, spread-eagled naked on the floor, chained at each wrist and each ankle. At first he was sick from the knockout they had injected into him. Later he was thirsty and furious. Then he was thirsty, just thirsty. Very thirsty.

He wet himself. He starved. He was cold. The worst, though, far beyond anything, was the thirst.

On the second day they came into the room. They were present before he was aware of them. He had entered a stage of somnolence, dazed and dozing.

When he realised they were there, he wearily lifted his face. He didn't smell good. His eyes were gummy, and he had difficulty seeing. The red smears at his bloodied wrists, where he had futilely strained against his manacles, seemed to be the only colour in the room.

'I need a drink,' he croaked.

They watched him without speaking. They kept their hands folded neatly in front of them. They seemed indifferent to the smell. Rollo's head dropped. 'A drink,' he said. His voice rasped in his throat which burned and tortured him.

They went away and Rollo lay with his eyes open, staring blindly at the wall.

Some time passed. There was noise and he knew he had company again.

Suddenly he jerked with horrible painfulness and gasped. They were hosing him. Water ran over and around his body, washing him clean.

It was bitterly cold and his body reacted violently, pulling in on his ankles and wrists. But his face was down lapping, licking the floor, his cracked lips and parched tongue desperate for the liquid.

The hose went on for a long time. Then it stopped. He was freezing, but he was quite clean.

Someone took a handful of his wet hair and jerked his face up. Water was poured into his open mouth. He swallowed painfully. They gave him more. Then they left him again.

He was dirty when they came back. He couldn't help it. They hosed him again and gave him clean water to drink. He was starving.

They removed the manacles and lifted him to his feet. He hung limp between them, without strength. His tortured limbs wouldn't work. With his arms around their necks he was helped from the room.

By the time they arrived at his next room, he had regained the use of his legs, though it hurt abominably after so long chained on the floor, immobile.

This room was warm. It had a bed in it. They sat Rollo on the bed and he lifted his head to look around.

There was food on a plate, and milk.

He restrained himself and looked up at his captors from red-rimmed eyes. He was shivering uncontrollably. 'Why?' he said.

'You'll see.'

These were the first words any of them had spoken to him.

Rollo began to eat.

There was a bathroom attached to his room. He could perform his necessary functions in a clean and decent manner. He found he was grateful for this. There was salve for his bleeding wrists and ankles, and Newskin to spray over the clean wounds. There was depilatory for his face.

Showered, with his hair washed, his body cleaned, and food in his belly, Rollo began to take stock.

They were all women. That was curious. He assumed he was being held for ransom. TransFlow must be going spare.

113

Rollo smiled a tight smile. It could hardly have come at a worse time. His captors must be asking for a great deal of money, since he hadn't already been released.

Perhaps it had been agreed. Perhaps he was being tidied up for release.

He remembered himself in that room, on the floor. One of the torture-induced fantasies he had had was that many people had watched him. His mind skittered away. It was unbearable, knowing himself to have been reduced to that.

Rollo stood up and, despite the pain, began to do some simple exercises to restore his body after the abuse it had received.

He was fed again. His aching muscles felt better. He became bored.

This emotion was so qualitatively different from the boredom he had felt before his captivity that he was almost amused. Then the girl came to visit him and he wasn't bored at all.

Like himself she was naked. She was dumb, unable to say a word. She was beautiful.

He thought she was maybe eighteen years of age. Her body was slim and small-breasted. She had pale hair, a silvery sheet hanging straight to well below her shoulders. At her groin she was depilated, making her look even younger, even more vulnerable. Her breasts were tipped fawn. He tried to speak to her but she shook her head. She couldn't even seem to communicate yes or no. He had no means of talking to her.

She curled onto the bed with him, her slender body pressed against his male hardness.

He became aroused. He did nothing about it but when she realised his penis was erect, she touched it.

Rollo lay on his back. The dumb girl hung over him, exploring with soft fingers his stiff cock, his balls. She went all over his body, feeling his muscles, investigating his armpits, the cleft of his arse, his features.

Rollo tried to kiss her but she withdrew, apparently shocked. Afterwards, however, she kissed his chest. She licked his nipples hesitantly, as if she had never done it before to a man. She pressed his belly and made his cock bounce slightly. He began to need sex quite badly.

She sat up and fiddled with his cock till he had to shut his eyes and grit his teeth. She pulled at him then and when he put his arms around her, she wriggled delightedly.

He came on top of her and she opened her legs. Rollo began to work his sex into her. She was very tight but surprisingly slippery. He started to fuck, keeping it as gentle as possible.

As the slippery, sliding, tight velvet caress on his cock worked its usual magic, he felt some of the recent horrors retreat and diminish.

He began to move to climax. She had teased him greatly with her exploration of his body, and he was ready to come quickly. Also the whole situation felt odd, and he was anxious to service his need since he felt off-guard and vulnerable like this. The girl was very odd. Part of him didn't think this was a good idea.

For the moment he forgot all these doubts and fears. He was just about to come. He was cresting the wave, about to surf into ecstasy. As he let go, grunting slightly as he foamed into the girl, he felt a stab of pain.

He cried out, jerking sharply out of control, his spunk jetting messily over the girl's thighs even as his body slammed down onto the bed.

The pain stopped. He lay quivering. After a moment he opened his eyes.

The girl lay beside him, grinning broadly. Rollo felt the sweat greasy on his forehead. 'Did you do that?' he asked huskily. There were shockwaves going through his body. The pain had been in his pelvis at the moment of climax.

'No,' she answered calmly. 'Your orgasm did it.'

'You can talk.'

'I can do many things.'

'Was that deliberate?'

'Was what?'

'Hurting me.'

She turned to look at him, her pale eyes dancing. If he reached out he could strangle her with one hand. Her throat was slender and vulnerable.

'The pain is your friend,' she said. 'Don't fight it.'

He licked his lips – they were still cracked from his ordeal – and looked down at the bed. He was resting on his elbows. She was on her back looking up into his face, while hers was alive with mischief.

'What's going on?' he said.

'I don't think I'll answer that.'

'I could make you.' Rollo kept his voice even. He was very angry.

'Try.' She smiled impudently, little dimples appearing in her cheeks.

Rollo reached over and took her throat as he had imagined he might.

He felt her Adam's apple wobbling, soft and vulnerable, under his hand. He felt the pulse in the throat. The silk of her hair brushed the back of his hand. Her skin was warm and smooth.

He squeezed.

Her head went back. Her lips parted and her tongue tip showed. She smiled, eyes closed and Rollo gasped and collapsed.

His shoulder had caught fire. The pain had been like a hot poker boring into muscle and tendon. He lay with that shoulder down on the bed, biting his lip as he got over the shock of the pain.

He realised the girl was stroking him. She bent over his body and kissed his good shoulder. He hunched himself, not responding.

'Don't be cross with me,' she murmured. 'You started being nasty to me first. I had to defend myself.'

'How do you do it?' asked Rollo dully.

'That's my secret.' She seemed delighted. She stroked his hair.

With an effort Rollo rolled over. 'Tell me what this is all about,' he asked in a level voice. His shoulder throbbed.

Her fingers played across his chest. 'Don't hurt me unless I ask you to. I didn't want you to press my throat, so I stopped you.'

'How did you stop me?'

'With my mind.'

116

'You can't do that.'

'Yes, I can.' She grinned. 'Like this.'

Rollo groaned and grasped his leg. It felt as though it had been struck by a hammer. When he opened his eyes the girl was smiling at him. 'You are good looking,' she confided. 'Much prettier than the last one they gave me.'

'The last one?'

'The last one I had to play with. My name is Melissa, by the way. What's yours?'

'Why did you hurt me during the sex?' asked Rollo carefully.

Melissa smiled. 'I like fucky-fucky when you get hurt. Don't you?'

'You were hurt as well?'

'Not that time. You were hurt. I liked that.'

Rollo stared at Melissa unseeingly. Somewhere he had strayed into a nightmare. He jumped slightly. Her hand was winding softly, sweetly, about his limp sex.

'I'd like to do it again,' she said, snuggling into him. 'Let's see if you can.'

Fee was reading Richelle Matthew's column over breakfast. Richelle had a story to tell the readers.

A man, known as Mr X for the purposes of the article, had been taken before a kangaroo court, tried, found guilty, been sentenced and had that sentence carried out in extraordinary circumstances.

Mr X ran a feelie bar in Hedgeways, a moderately unsavoury district on the extreme southern fringe of the town. A feelie bar was what it sounded like. The customers, and they were of both sexes, went into the bar and ordered what food and drink they required. All the orders were taken by waiters and waitresses who had one thing in common. It was extremely easy to gain access to their private parts. While ordering food, and the customer was encouraged to linger over this process, he or she could feel their waiter or waitress, or both, as much as they pleased. Women stroked the sexual organs of the waiter taking their order. Men slid their hands up the short skirts of waitresses

117

who seemed not to have heard of panties. The waitresses, good juicy girls with plump soft pussies, would rotate their hips and smile as they made a note of the food and drink. They seemed to be able to write only very slowly. The waiters also had this mild writing disability, mysteriously coupled with a facility in sexual erection that the female clients of the feelie bar found very appetising.

Once upon a time, feelie bars had been almost respectable, naughty and amusing places to go when one wanted a saucy novelty. Passing time had turned them sordid. The changing town morality meant that they were now viewed with downright disapproval. There was a feeling in the air that soon they would lose their licences – respectable people didn't want them existing any more.

Mr X, it seemed, was a victim of the changing times. Unknown women had snatched him and taken him prisoner. Bound and blindfolded, he had appeared before an unseen judge. He had been accused of promoting loose and lewd immoral practices, and making a profit on them. He had been allowed to speak, but his claim that he wasn't breaking the law was not admitted as evidence. He was breaking moral law, said the judge. The jury found him guilty. He was sentenced to a public flogging.

This was carried out immediately. The women stripped him and removed his blindfold. Quite naked, he found himself surrounded by hooded women with whips. These women wore floor-length white shapeless robes. They surrounded the helpless man and whipped him till his flesh burned. At the same time, presumably to taunt him, a group of hooded women watched. These women wore no white robes. They wore no robes at all. Their luscious young, full, bodies were entirely naked. They paraded slowly up and down, watching the chastisement of the feelie bar manager, holding their breasts out to him and touching their sexual parts as though to torment him for his exploitation of the sexual desires of humanity.

The sobbing, naked man was dumped at night in front of the civic hall. To complete his humiliation, the women chained him to railings and there he was found the following morning by early strollers.

There was a message painted on the ground where Mr X was chained. *Be warned*, it said simply.

Mr X was now in hospital. This was because the women had done one other thing to him, the worst of all.

They had prised back his foreskin and fitted a disc with a hole in the centre over his penis. The foreskin had been placed over the disc and the whole thing had been sealed with Newskin.

Mr X could still use his penis for natural body functions such as expelling waste. But the projecting disc, a kind of penis frill, made one thing unpleasant and another impossible.

If Mr X became erect, the disc cut painfully into his flesh. There was no way, furthermore, that Mr X could insert his cock into the vagina of a woman. The disc made it impossible. For that matter, he couldn't insert his sexual organ into any constricted space. The women had effectively fitted him with a chastity belt.

It required a hospital operation to remove it and left the poor man sore and uncomfortable.

Fee put down the paper and thought about this chilling tale. As usual, she felt nothing but contempt for the bourgeois morality of the town. It didn't concern her and she considered she need take no notice of it. But Rollo was missing. That was a fact.

Could these people have him? They had taken Mr X, dealt with him immediately and released him to a fanfare. Rollo had been missing for over two weeks, nearly three now. There was no word.

Had they practised their horrible plan on Rollo, to have it go wrong? Was he dead?

Fee sat and shuddered, feeling sick. She had to have Rollo back. She had to know he was alive. Even if he rejected her, that was OK. She would always have the hope that she might win him back. But she couldn't reach him from beyond the grave. He would be truly lost to her if he was dead and that was something she could not contemplate.

She needed action. She had to do something. The waiting was driving her mad.

She had put her own business virtually on hold, delegating urgent work but taking on nothing new. She had to visit a hospital every day to maintain the fiction of Rollo being bed-ridden. TransFlow was continuing with the run-up to its rights issue and was simultaneously engaged in wooing ConComm to its point of view, that they needed TransFlow as carriers which would free ConComm's capital to be moved from installation to research. ConComm knew perfectly well that whatever their short-term problems, in the long term, they ought not to be in TransFlow's pocket. Yet they were finding it hard to resist the courtship and promised financial easement. That it would cost them more in the long run seemed less and less important.

Fee was underworked and over-worried. She vidied Maslow.

An answering machine took her call, promising to page him and get back to her. It was an hour before he did.

'Can you scramble?' asked Fee.

'Yes.'

They did so.

'Are you any nearer to finding Rollo?'

'I'm reporting to Jermyn Ames, Ms Cambridge. You know that.'

'You were with that journalist lady last night.'

'Richelle Matthews. Yes.'

'Did you see her piece today?'

'I did.'

'Jesus, Maslow, get a move on.'

'Look, lady,' said Maslow tightly. 'I have to find this guy without telling anyone he's lost. That's my remit. I could find him in a couple of days if I was allowed to do it my way. But you have a company to protect, a reputation to keep, and you want all this *sub rosa* in case this man's disappearance affects profitability and the way you run your business. You want speed and publicity, you get the police. It'll cost you nothing, your taxes have already paid for it. But me, I come expensive. I'm working on this the best way I know how, and I'm moving as fast as I can given that I'm not allowed to use helpers in any meaningful way. I can tell you that I've had every house on the list you gave me watched to see if someone is living quietly in the country park, keeping out of sight. They all report negative. No one is there except folks that ought to be there. We've broken and entered most of these places in case your husband is lurking in the basement or the attic. No deal. He's not there. It's not that he's not there because my people were looking for Rollo Cambridge – that's information I can't hand out. They were looking for anyone and they found no one.'

'You've tried houses of pleasure?'

'How come this man needs houses of pleasure? He's living in a brothel up there in the Zoo.'

'You bastard,' shouted Fee.

'What was he doing before he went off on that drinking spree? You were mighty cagey about that, lady. What was the last thing you did before he got so sick of the whole business he took himself off and got stewed?'

Fee swallowed. 'We were at a party. He walked out of it. I haven't seen him since.'

'A sex party.'

'Yes.'

'What particular little wrinkle did you sweethearts come up with?'

Fee licked her lips. 'Uh, that is, we, er, put sex patches on. You know?'

Maslow thought for a moment. 'Oh yes,' he said coldly. 'Men wear them. They add colour and flavour.'

'That's right. It was a game. We, er, had to identify the flavours the men had.'

There was a long silence while Maslow stared steadily out of the screen at Fee. Then he said quietly: 'I don't think he's holed up in a house of pleasure.'

'No,' said Fee dully.

'Because,' went on Maslow, ignoring her, 'that's what he was trying to get away from. You disgusted him. He got drunk. This dancer girl took him home and offered herself.

He shafted her all right but it was contemptuous. Almost cruel. Then he vanished.'

'She was the stripper you were watching last night.'

'I was interviewing Richelle Matthews last night. Where and how I do it is my business.'

'You make it sound like he got converted. I don't see Rollo doing a road to Damascus, Maslow.'

'Frankly, neither do I, though I've had the religious organisations checked out for novices. I think that would be too simple a solution for such a complex man.'

'So what do you think?'

'Like you, I didn't find Richelle's piece comfortable reading.'

Fee broke the connection. She walked over to the plastiglass wall and rested her head against the cool smoothness of it.

Maslow was town. She had to hang onto that. He saw things through town eyes. He saw Rollo's motivation in getting drunk primarily in sexual terms because that's what shocked him about Zoo behaviour.

He accused her, Fee Cambridge, of disgusting her husband so much that he ran away from her. *You disgusted him. He got drunk.* To Maslow, that was a simple equation.

The thing is, it was wrong. Rollo was bored. The sex parties were extreme, but they weren't enough to trigger his abandonment of home and job. Rollo was bored and Rollo got drunk. That was the equation that mattered.

Rollo wasn't in the process of becoming a monk right now. Either he had found something very very interesting, so interesting he was prepared to let TransFlow go soak its corporate head, or he was being held against his will.

Rollo might be bored with TransFlow, but he held a majority stake in it with Fee and she didn't see him throwing that away and lousing up the rights issue because he had a touch of middle-age blues.

He was being held against his will. Or he was dead, but this was less likely because it was hard to hide a dead body for any length of time.

He was being held against his will. She was sure of it.

Fee reached out for the vidi again. It was time she took a hand in this business.

Sandrina woke late, stretched, and remembered.

She lay quietly, feeling her body warm under the bed-clothes. The performance had gone well. Mournag was hopeful of more bookings. She should be feeling good.

She remembered the strange scene at the table when she had joined Maslow. Instead of receiving his admiration and attention, she had found him seated with that journalist woman and being chatted up by Fee Cambridge.

His attention had only come back to her when both women had left them. He had then swept her up, taken her back to her place and comprehensively fucked her.

There had been plenty of it. He had taken her three ways before leaving her. Her body felt dull and heavy in the aftermath of their vigorous activity. Yet she was curiously unsatisfied. It had been as though his attention was elsewhere, as all the while he competently brought herself and himself to climax.

He had fallen on her as soon as they had arrived, pulling her clothes apart, kissing her breasts and sucking her nipples as his hands fumbled up her skirt and into her panties. She remembered writhing against a wall as he knelt to eat her body, kissing her naked mound and licking it while his fingers pushed between her sticky lips and drove up into her hot eager hole. She had nearly come like that, with him kneeling there, licking and sucking what he could get at, but he had lifted her and shaken his clothes apart till his hard cock had slid into her ruptured flesh. She had felt herself divide as he thrust forcefully up. She had felt her flesh cleave and then close again, tight round the intruder as it pumped up and down.

He had held her up, jammed against the wall, her legs round his waist and both of them still dressed. His greediness had excited her and she remembered straining upwards, her head tossing from side to side in ecstasy as he approached his violent climax.

He had leant against her panting afterwards, his head

123

driven into her breast, jamming her hard against the wall. When finally she had slid down and off him, he had turned away and fixed his clothes.

She made him a drink which he took through to her bedroom without asking. He had stripped quickly and lain there, watching her.

He had come for the sex and, insultingly, he had let it be known that there was nothing else he wanted. He didn't talk to her. He didn't develop their relationship. He didn't spend any time doing anything that wasn't directly related to screwing.

The second time he had her he made her kneel and push her face into the bedclothes. He knelt behind her and poked his hard cock into her soft, open hole again. Having got it in, he slid a finger carefully into her arse.

She had squealed and wriggled. He ignored this and pressed down within her rear passage as though determined to feel his own cock bloating her sexual entrance. He had removed his finger and then dealt expertly with his own need, making sure she matched his climax by reaching under and tickling her clitoris.

It had been a cold, knowledgeable performance.

Afterwards, she had lain and slowly licked his cock. Even this had produced no warmth in him. He simply lay there, silent in her bed, letting her service him as he had serviced her.

It was like being a prostitute. She had felt part of a business transaction.

She had licked and kissed him, kissing his hard muscular belly, his calloused hands, his silk-clad cock, till it was full again.

She was quite prepared to suck him to climax. It was as though that would make him beholden to her. But he had turned round in the bed and fastened his powerful mouth like a limpet over her sweetly throbbing pussy. She had sucked him and been sucked in her turn.

He owed her nothing, therefore. After their joint explosion of pleasure he had showered and left, barely bothering to brush her lips with his own.

Not very nice, thought Sandrina, and shuddered. But very good sex. The man knew how to move. He could do things that made her cry out with lust.

She should accept that's how it was. She could have romance, sexless romance, from among her acquaintance in the town. But sex was out for nice young people these days, virtually off the agenda. Maslow was older, twice her age, and could give her romanceless sex.

She should be grateful. Her need for sex was real. She must learn to separate mushy emotion from the essential act.

Maslow could give her the essential act with all its physical trimmings. No emotional trimmings, though.

That was what she wanted, of course. Her heart belonged to that bastard, Rollo Cambridge.

Maslow would do for fucking.

Her vidi sounded. Leaving her sending screen off, Sandrina answered it. Her heart leapt. Perhaps Maslow was calling her.

The white, exotically scarred face with its starling-black hair was instantly recognisable. 'Fee Cambridge,' the woman said coldly. 'I'd like to see you. Can I call by?'

'Me? You mean me, Sandrina? When?' Sandrina knew she was gabbling.

'An hour?'

'Yes. OK. What's it about?'

'I'll tell you when I arrive.'

Fee cut the connection. Sandrina stared at the blank screen. What could Fee Cambridge want with her? She climbed out of bed and went to the bathroom.

Fee said: 'I have a document I want you to sign.'

Sandrina stared at her. She was on home ground and she felt helplessly at a loss.

'A document?'

'Yes. This meeting is pointless unless you sign.'

Sandrina took it and began to read the words. It took her two goes before the sense began to sink in.

The colour drained from her face. 'I don't understand,' she whispered.

Fee flicked imaginary fluff off her clothes. She was dressed entirely in white and looked fearful. Only her scarlet mouth gave colour, her green eyes curiously drained. 'It's simple enough language,' she observed. 'You agree not to reveal anything of the conversation that we are about to have.'

'This document talks about forfeiting all my goods.' Sandrina gazed blankly at Fee.

Fee looked insultingly round the apartment. 'That is insignificant, of course. The point is, Jose Armitting is a good friend of mine. At the moment he's inclined to give you a contract. You step out of line and I'll tell him not to. Dancers are ten a penny, sweetheart. He'll kill your career.'

Sandrina knew who Jose Armitting was. He was the floorshow manager at the Castel d'Amour.

'That's blackmail.'

'Yes. Blackmail. If you reveal anything of what I am about to say, I will destroy you as a performer. I have the power. I have the connections.'

Sandrina stared at Fee with her mouth open. 'Why?'

'I'm going to ask you to do something. I'm not blackmailing you to do it, you will have free will. But I have to impart some information that is, shall we say, dynamite, in order to make my request. I have to know that that information remains secure, whether you help me or not.'

'I wouldn't help you if you were the last person on Earth,' said Sandrina.

Fee smiled. 'Pussycat. What claws. Sign the document now, like a good girly.'

'No.'

'Say goodbye to your agent.'

'What?'

'Mournag knows I'm here. We go way back. I could give her ten times what she makes off you in commission in perpetuity and never feel it. And she would be helping an old pal. No one will want to be your agent after I've finished with you.'

Tears of rage sprang to Sandrina's eyes. 'Why are you doing this to me?'

126

'I've told you. I want to ask you to do something for me. You don't have to do it. I'll leave you alone. If you say no you'll still get your contract and you'll still have your agent. But if you speak out I'll crush you. Totally.'

'There are laws against this,' said Sandrina hotly.

'Are there?' Fee wasn't interested. 'I was guest speaker with the Police Federation last year. The Home Secretary, sweetheart, shares my bed.'

'This isn't fair.' Sandrina was reduced almost to a wail.

'No,' Fee agreed. 'Now, can we get on?'

Sandrina signed with a shaking hand.

For the first time, Fee smiled. Strangely, the girl found this more chilling than her previous manner. 'What you have signed,' she said, 'will stand up in a court of law. You might argue that you signed under duress, but you'll find that mysteriously you won't be able to prove it. I'll have discredited you long before a court appearance anyway. Moreover, if you decide I wouldn't be vindictive enough to carry out the threats I have made today, you would be wrong. I am a completely ruthless woman. It is one of the things my husband loves about me.' She paused meaningfully.

Sandrina knew genuine fear.

'Rollo,' said Fee, 'needs your help.'

This was so unexpected that Sandrina found she couldn't keep up. Fee was battering her emotionally. She felt exhausted. 'My help?'

'Yes. He's in trouble. He needs help.'

'From me?'

'I know how you feel about him,' said Fee.

The silence stretched. 'I don't see how,' said Sandrina bravely.

'You'd do anything for him. Anything at all.'

Sandrina remembered her sweating face close to Rollo at the party. She remembered her tingling arse – there had been a man at her there – and there had been a stray hand at her breast. But her world had been Rollo Cambridge; his eyes burned her, she could ignore the woman fastened on his penis. For that moment she had had his attention.

127

I wish I could give you something. Anything, she had said. Or words to that effect.

How could Fee have known without Rollo telling her? Sandrina's face burned. 'What is it you want?' she said in a small voice.

Fee sighed. 'I want you to be converted to the New Morality. I want you to spill all about the Zoo party you attended. I want you to say you renounce sex absolutely. I want you to join the sect.'

'Why? They're horrible. You of all people . . .'

'Because they might have Rollo in their clutches.'

'*What?*'

'Because Rollo left your apartment three weeks ago, the morning after you brought him back here drunk, and he hasn't been seen since.'

'I . . . I . . .'

'I think you care about him, though I know he treated you badly. He was pretty fed up at something else; you just set yourself up to get knocked down at the wrong moment. If those bitches have got him and you find out, we can get him out. He would be very very grateful. So would I.'

Sandrina drew herself up. 'I wouldn't need a reward for helping Mr Cambridge.'

'Not even his body in your arms?'

'How can you! He's your husband.'

'He's one hell of a man. No one, least of all me, owns Rollo Cambridge. You get him in bed with him paying attention and lady, all other men will seem pallid by comparison. That's your lookout, of course. Getting what you want has always been the most dangerous thing there is.'

Sandrina stood up and began to walk about, too agitated to sit still. 'Why did you threaten me? Why all that heavy stuff? You must have known I'd want to help.'

'I told you.' Fee was patient. 'I'm not blackmailing you to do this. You can refuse and I'll step out of your life, no harm done. You probably will get that contract from Jose, he was impressed with you last night. The point is, you now hold privileged and valuable information. Rollo Cambridge, head of TransFlow, is missing. Lost. AWOL.

Ducky, the papers would pay plenty for that. Why do you think it isn't being splashed across the headlines? We have to keep the search for him a secret. Rollo is not a private man. He has a public capacity, a business capacity. Millions rest on his behaviour. You could half the worth of TransFlow by sinking its share value just by using the vidi after I've gone.'

'Why do you tell me this?'

'Because you might have the brain to work it out for yourself after I've gone. I'm blackmailing you to keep quiet. Nothing more. If you do blab, I'll ruin you. Totally. No holds barred. You'll sink, sister, without trace.'

Sandrina stared. 'You're horrible.'

Fee smiled. 'I'm fighting for my man. I'm trying to protect his business interests. Is that so awful? What would you do, in my place?'

Sandrina turned away. 'You want me to infiltrate the New Moralists and find out if they are holding Rollo captive?'

'Yes. I wouldn't expect you to get him out. If you located him and passed that information on, I'd arrange the rest.'

'You think they'd accept me?'

'With your background, yes. Camp up your stripper activities. Tell them about coming to the Zoo. Lie about it if you like. Exaggerate it. Anything that you think will help. They'll want salacious details and hot confessions so be prepared. Bewail your own filth. Agree to anything. And keep your eyes open.'

'What if they don't have him?'

'I'll get you out painlessly. We'll have to have a means of contacting each other. If Rollo turns up elsewhere, I'll need to be able to let you know.'

Sandrina's hand flew to her mouth. 'What if he's dead?'

Fee looked steadily at Sandrina. Her green eyes glowed. It seemed to Sandrina that the scar on her cheek quivered and writhed with a secret life of its own. 'That is not a possibility I can accept at this stage,' she said in a small deadly voice.

'You really care about him, don't you?' Sandrina felt almost shy.

'My feelings are my own concern. What I can promise you is access to Rollo if you help me like this. He is never, perhaps, a kind man, but he is not always as brusque sexually as he was with you. You would enjoy the experience.' Fee smiled.

Sandrina felt sick and excited. 'How do I set about this?' she whispered unsteadily. 'How will I communicate with you?'

'Let's take a little trip,' said Fee. 'I promise it won't hurt.'

In pursuance of her plan, Fee had to contact Maslow again. She knew the man lusted after her and she knew she had humiliated him. He was man enough to spit back. She liked that. Just as well, since it made this next part of the business easier.

'Ms Cambridge,' he said when he got back to her in answer to her call. 'I have to tell you I'm very busy. I am working for TransFlow, you know. Not you.'

'I appreciate that. I think you got some things wrong. I have to help. Is there any time you can drop by today? Or tonight. Please.'

She sounded contrite. She sounded weak. This was the combination she guessed would most appeal to his ego.

'I can't promise.'

You arrogant bastard, thought Fee. 'I'm begging,' she said huskily. 'As soon as you can.'

'Can't you tell me now?'

'No. I'll have to explain. It's tenuous. It may add up to nothing at all.'

'I'll see what I can do.' Maslow killed the connection.

Fee knew he would come. She could make him come. He could not refuse her, however much he disliked her.

It was very late when he arrived. Fee admitted him to her apartment and took him into a small, neutral sitting room. She wore a loose shirt and baggy shorts. She had bare feet. The clothes were graceless and unfeminine. They

130

made her look young and defenceless. This was precisely the effect she had set out to achieve.

Her luxurious hair was bound back in a pony tail. Her face was clear of make up. She looked tired and anxious.

She offered Maslow a drink almost absently.

'It's about me and Rollo,' she said. 'I think you've got us wrong. You are on the wrong track here and I can't have you wasting time when I know that I can help.'

'What do you mean?'

'This sex thing. It bugs you. You think of it quite differently from how Rollo and I think of it.'

Maslow looked sour. 'Zoofolk and townfolk are brothers under the skin. You can't deny that.'

'We've done what we want for so long. Mr Maslow, can you imagine what it is like to be able to do anything? Anything at all. Anything nonviolent, that is. I'm not talking about attacking people or killing them.'

'Perhaps I can't. So what?'

Fee leant towards him, her face serious. 'People like Rollo and I don't end up running TransFlow and my company without taking risks. Without exploring our own potential. Without having a craving for excitement. This isn't confined to our business life. It spills over into everything. You think me gross, Mr Maslow, and maybe I am. But Rollo is no different from me. We are two of a kind.'

Maslow swallowed. Fee's lashes were very black and thick. She was looking down now and they lay soft on her white skin.

She slipped to the floor and knelt at his feet. One hand lay gently on his knee. 'You have fantasies, desires,' she said huskily. 'Sure, Zoo and town are no different under the skin. But we act out our fantasies. You don't. That's the only difference.'

'Why are you telling me this?'

'Rollo isn't disgusted with the prevailing sexual mores of the Zoo. That's not what has sent him off balance. That is town-think and it is making you think wrong. We are Zoo, Mr Maslow. Zoo through and through. If we feel like doing something, we do it. Can't you see that?'

131

'I guess so. You're more self-indulgent.'

'That's it.' Fee nodded. 'If you were Zoo, you'd do what you wanted to do right now. It's being town that holds you back.'

Maslow stared at her. 'You know what I want to do,' he said jerkily.

'Do it,' hissed Fee.

He undid the front of his trousers. He drew out his erect cock. 'Suck me,' he said hoarsely.

Fee's tongue tip came out. She touched the end of Maslow's cock. It jumped slightly. She licked it delicately, curling her tongue round the straining foreskin. Her hand came up and she teased the tight sheath of skin back. She dabbed her tongue tip on the eye. Then she licked it. Her lips closed slowly over the bulging head. Inside her mouth she touched the end with her tongue again. She pressed her lips tight and then allowed them to slide up and off until she could kiss the end of Maslow's cock. Her hand came out and she caught the stem to steady it. She closed her lips over the cock again so that they pressed where the foreskin was attached.

She sucked.

Maslow's breath came raggedly. Fee released his cock with her hand, but not with her mouth. She put both hands behind her head and released her hair.

The black cascade of warm silk surrounded Maslow's sex. He eased his breeks down and felt her hair on his thighs, on the base of his belly. She pushed her head down so that his cock sank deeply into her mouth. Her tongue made a python dance around it and she sucked again, deeply.

Maslow let his head go back over the back of the couch he sat on, yielding to the carnal caress. His arms spread along the couch. His knees opened wide, the woman crouched between them, bent to her task.

He closed his eyes and gave himself up to the delights of her mouth. Her tongue wandered snakily all over his gently pulsing cock. He felt himself drawn up, focused, so that his developing need to orgasm was teased into a thread and Fee was the spinner.

Her fingers were in his balls. She held the base of his cock so she could draw down on it as she sucked the fat end of his erection. Her mouth was an orchestra, deep sucks, lesser ones, the weaving tongue, the gentle rasp of her teeth.

Maslow felt himself sob as his orgasm mounted. He lifted his hips slightly. She was frigging him expertly and sucking in time so that his cock was stretched and squeezed. A moment later he burst into her mouth.

She sucked and swallowed each spasmodic pulse of spunk. He felt that as he ejected it, so she drew it from him. He relaxed back shakily, his belly trembling.

His cock felt marvellous. His belly was one dull glow of pleasure. For a moment his mind ran in neutral, downhill, easily.

Fee came up between his legs. She had undone her shirt and within it Maslow saw her wonderful breasts hanging free.

Fee took his face between her hands. She pressed into him so that her breasts were crushed against his chest. She twisted her head slightly and kissed his mouth.

She had swallowed his spunk but her mouth still tasted of sex. She kissed him expertly, movingly, so that his arms came round her and he caught her under the loose abundance of her hair.

He held her away to look into her face. He had no idea what he would see. What he saw astonished him.

The tears were like diamonds. They glittered as they streaked her white face. Her green eyes were huge, her lashes tear-wet and endearingly sticky. 'Can you understand?' she pleaded, her lower lip trembling. 'I love Rollo. You must find him for me. But I need you like this, too. Help me. Help me to get through this awful period. Please.'

Maslow kissed her. She twisted under him and he came down onto the floor, on top of her.

Their union was long and slow. He had no idea a woman could offer such deep velvet pleasure. Every move she made was warm and alive and gentle. Her body was like silk under his, strong and long and sweetly tender. It

133

seemed to him she took up the mess in himself, his doubts, his failures, his problems, and sorted it all into life and strength by the slow contortions of her knowledgeable, experienced body.

When he was done he stroked her hair back. 'How can you be like this,' he said helplessly, 'when you are like that, so often?'

Her lips brushed his. 'It's a defence,' she said, her voice low and humming. 'Men lust for me. I keep them away. This is what I'm really like.'

'I don't see how you can do those other things.'

'They are part of this. Don't you realise that? The one is the obverse of the other. Together they make a whole.'

Maslow shook his head in confusion and touched her lips.

'Live out your fantasies,' whispered Fee. 'That is what I offer. You can do anything you like with me. Anything. Anything at all.'

'Don't,' groaned Maslow. 'I might take you up on it.'

'I want you to.' Fee was sweetly fierce. 'I'm begging you to.'

She took pity on him then and released him. She refilled his drink and sat beside him, touching him, smiling.

He was deeply happy.

Fee laughed. 'I can't understand those New Moralists,' she said. 'When this is such a joy, such sweet pleasure. How can this be bad?'

'Not everyone makes love like an angel. Like you.'

'They don't make love at all?'

'So it seems.'

'How do women join them? How do they get their membership?'

'That journalist, Richelle Matthews, she told me.'

So Maslow told Fee. Fee told Sandrina. And so Sandrina was able to join the New Moralists.

Having got what she wanted, Fee found it tempting to drop Maslow, who bored her when he wasn't inside her cunt. She decided that it would be wiser to string him along, however. She might need inside information again, and seducing Maslow a second time would be tedious and timewasting. For the sake of a few fucks now and again she could keep him dangling at her beck and call.

She didn't expect him to come up with anything original, despite her offer to do whatever he wanted. His repertoire, his sexual imagination, would be limited. He wasn't bad in bed, though. Sex with him wouldn't be that much of a penance.

6

'Do you enjoy sex?'

'I have enjoyed it,' said Sandrina, her head hung with shame.

'Do you like men?'

'I have liked them.'

'What then has changed?'

'I have been badly treated. The sex was not enjoyable. I do not like men any longer. I am afraid of them.'

Her interlocutor considered. She was a graceful woman of middle age. Her face was kindly, her manner austere but not forbidding. 'There is nothing, of course, to fear,' she said calmly. 'That can be readily dealt with. However, if one man has driven you to us, you labour under a misapprehension.'

'All men,' whispered Sandrina. 'I realised he was all men. He had the characteristics that men share. I had blinded myself before, been blinded by my own lust, my own needs. Now I see what men really are.'

The woman smiled. 'And what are they?'

'Arrogant. Cruel. Greedy. Uncaring. They used my body as goods. As a toy, a plaything. I offered them a little of my soul each time I made love. They couldn't see that. They can't understand. Men are like beasts, the wild beasts of the jungle. They take by instinct, without thought for what they take.'

The woman said: 'I want you to spend some time with some other young women who have not been with us very long. You will learn there of our philosophy of life. Of the ascension of the senses. How the senses can be served and pleased but kept in their place. We will teach you to free the mind so that you dominate your body, instead of it dominating you. It is a long lesson and can be wearisome.'

'Let me start, then,' said Sandrina fiercely. 'Too much time has been wasted already.'

'There is a process of exorcism. This can be painful.'

'Exorcism?'

'We exorcise the ghosts of your past lovers and the shadows of the future ones.'

'There will be no future ones.' Sandrina's eyes blazed.

'That is correct.' The woman nodded gently. 'Though they already have a hold over you, it is a hold we will break.'

They took her clothes away and burned them. They led her naked into a room full of naked women. Sandrina started and shivered when she saw them. She knew immediately that what had happened to them must happen to her. Seated in their midst, she felt the scissors enter her hair. As the blades slices away her glory, salt tears ran down her cheeks and she thought of Rollo, beautiful, strong, animal in his strength.

Where was he?

They washed her all over and shaved her head smooth. They rubbed an inhibitory cream into her scalp so that her hair wouldn't regrow quickly. They took away the hair in her armpits and the soft down she had allowed to return in her groin.

This was strange. Women held her body open and felt about her flesh, her private parts. Women fingered her and touched her body. Women changed her appearance.

She didn't want to see herself. Her hairless scalp and hairless pudendum loomed in her mind. She didn't want a visual picture to complement this.

They scraped her skin with bone scrapers when she was soft and lathered. It was as if every part of her old life was being removed.

Next her sex was examined. Sandrina, who had no lesbian leanings, found this the worst of all, worse even than having her hair removed. She felt the women's intrusive fingers like slugs crawling over her vulva, into her vagina. It was all done so publicly. The naked, hairless girls crowded round and stared. Their eyes as much as the fingers invaded her and shamed her.

She felt fingers up inside her. She cried out and writhed.

'Don't be afraid. We have to know. We have to check you out.'

'I said I had had men,' cried Sandrina. She was frightened and lonely. 'You could have believed me.'

'We do believe you. But we must measure you for your man-hater, check you are able to receive it.'

'My man-hater? What's that?'

'You'll see soon enough. Don't worry. There's nothing to worry about now. You are safe. Everything bad is behind you.'

When the older women left, the shaven girls clustered round Sandrina. She felt they stifled her. They seemed to her to be inexpressibly ugly, with small piggy eyes and fat, flopping flesh.

They were fascinated by her long, lean, dancer's body. She lay on her pallet quivering with a misery so deep she couldn't hide it, not even for Rollo, whom she loved and who was her reason for being here.

Fee had promised him to her when this was done. Curiously, she didn't doubt Fee's ability to make her husband fuck with her, though he hadn't liked her when she was attractive. Now, hairless, she was grotesque.

'Aren't your breasts big,' said one girl.

Sandrina stared at her. The girl grinned. 'My name is Sansa,' she said. 'We all felt frightened at first.'

'We have a game,' said another. 'Want to join in?'

'Game?' said Sandrina in a dull voice.

'Who has the longest lips. Look!' the girl laughed. She opened her legs and reached into her sex. She drew down her labia and tugged them till they hung low, flaps of flesh. 'See? Are yours that big?'

'Let's look,' said another girl.

Sandrina lay rigid and terrified. The women earlier had

been bad enough. Now these girls pulled and poked her private parts so that she felt sick. She jumped suddenly. One of them was in her arse. 'Stop it,' she said in a terrified squeak. 'I've come here to escape this.'

'No,' said Sansa. 'You've come here to learn to do without men. Women are good. We understand. We are kind. You don't need men, you've got us.'

She bent her head. Her mouth closed over Sandrina's damp, excited sex-flesh.

'No!' cried Sandrina.

Hands caught her wrists. Her legs were grabbed and held open. Sansa licked and sucked at her sex. Another girl fumbled in, and Sandrina began to shudder as her arse was invaded at the same time as her pussy was licked.

Her eyes remained closed until she came to orgasm.

The following day she entered a feelie suit for her first lecture on the hegemony of the senses.

She knew about feelie suits. They formed the basis of standard sexual jokes. Feelie suits were bought by people and used as a substitute for sex. That is, they offered sex without the necessity of a human partner.

Inside the suit with all the connections made, Sandrina tried to relax and listen to what she was being told about appetite, pleasure receptor sites, emotion and muscle complementarity, aesthetics, the pleasure of exhaustion and mind control.

The subject moved on. Sex was described, and how it fitted into all aspects of human pleasure, excitement, titillation, power, physical effort and emotional satisfaction.

The quiet female voice explained that this was an illusion. Sex might do this for men, but for women it failed.

Sandrina, naked in the suit, began to feel a certain stimulation. Parts of her body were touched. She was urged to relax. The suit was monitoring her pulse.

She had no sense of connection with the outside world. Dark, contained in the womb of the suit, Sandrina found it easier to relax and allow the complicated machine that gloved her to have its way.

139

Her mood was manipulated. Her senses swam, urged this way and that till she was all liquid compliance. Probes touched her, entered her. She felt herself brought up the steep slope of sex and knocked back down again. It was Sisyphean. She was taken up and allowed to fall back down again and again. She wept tears of exhaustion. She had no control over her bodily sensations.

At last she was taken up and allowed to go over. Her orgasm came as a sweet relief. She lay trembling in the enveloping dark and made no move to release herself when the lecture ended.

They came for her and took her limp and tremblng body out. She was half-carried to a large bathing pool, and in it she lazed, half-asleep, the warm scented water soft on her skin.

She ate and rested in a garden. After this they brought her her man-hater.

It was a dildo. To her intense embarrassment, they pressed the greased plastic tube into her flesh. It was large and she felt distended, not least because she was not sexually aroused and receptive.

She lay on her back with her legs open and her knees drawn up. She felt scarlet with shame. Her face burned. The girls stared curiously.

The woman fitting the dildo was one of the older women again. She wore a long white robe. Only the class of younger women, the novices like Sandrina, had to go naked all the time.

'Good,' she said presently, having forced the alien object into Sandrina's reluctant flesh. 'Does that hurt?'

'It's very uncomfortable,' gasped Sandrina.

'Hmm. I'll try it again. Hold on.'

Blessedly, the thing was removed. Sandrina lay with her muscles relaxing. The last thing she had expected from the New Moralists was this constant harping on sex.

She jumped. The woman had thrust stubby fingers into Sandrina. 'I'm just greasing you, dearie,' she said cheerfully.

Mentally Sandrina squirmed. She kept getting women's

fingers stuffed in her vagina. Why was it OK for women and not for men? If Rollo had been doing this, or even Maslow, that would have been different. It would have been fun. These women were sex mad. It was just that they did it with each other instead of men.

She disliked being touched, being looked at. She must remember she was doing this for Rollo. She stood this beastly business because he was worth it. This toad-like crone who paddled in her pussy and pretended she wasn't getting a charge out of it was paving the way for the most fabulous man in the world to put his fat sex into her willing cunt, and once he was there he would screw her to blinding glory.

'Lovely,' crowed the toad-woman. 'You are nicely juicy now. Look, girls.' She actually held up her fingers and showed the other girls how wet and slimy they were from Sandrina's sexual juices.

It wasn't the woman's fingers. It was fantasising about Rollo inside her that had made her feel sexy.

The gross dildo pressed back inside her yielding flesh. It made Sandrina gasp, it was so big. The inflated thing lay like an airship up her pussy.

She whimpered.

'Now we strap it into place,' said toad-face. 'This might hurt.'

Sandrina yelped. Her body flinched upwards but they were there, restraining her.

The pain began to ebb. Anaesthetic was sprayed onto her throbbing vulva.

'What did you do? she whispered.

'I sealed part of your labia over the man-hater so that it can't come out,' said toad-woman. 'Here. Look in this mirror. You'll see.'

They held a mirror between her legs. Someone lifted her head. Sandrina felt dizzy.

Her labia had been brought together and a metal stud put through. The stud was sealed. She couldn't open it. Her sex was stuffed with an artificial penis and she had no power to empty it.

141

She was at the mercy of her new friends, if friends they were.

She forgot the eager, watching eyes. She didn't notice the sly glances of amusement. 'How long does this stay in?' she asked huskily.

'We remove it for cleansing,' said the toad-woman. 'Otherwise it stays in till you learn to hate men.'

That night she couldn't sleep. The thing in her bulged and seemed to pant, so that her soft sex was squeezed and crushed and bruised. She cried to herself, rolling in her bed in an effort to release the inexorable pressure.

They came to her, then. They came to her soft and gentle and loving. They stroked her brow and kissed her. They stroked her breasts and soothed her. They touched her trembling thighs and eased them.

Sandrina dozed and dreamed of Rollo. He came towards her naked, his sex vast and visibly pulsing. He smiled a cruel, golden smile, his blue eyes blazing. The torpedo in his groin was red and glowing.

He was going to put it in her. He was going to split her. Her body shivered and shrank: she couldn't bear this, he would kill her.

She woke, sweating and afraid. They kissed her and held her and told her she was safe. There were no men here.

Fee put in azure contact lenses. She colourwashed her hair a pale peachy colour. She took Instan tablets and allowed her white skin to darken to a pale coffee colour. She covered her scar till it didn't show. Then she smiled to herself and dyed her pussy fleece the same colour as the hair on her head.

She put on short breeks and an overshirt such as the poorer townsfolk wore. Then she covered everything with a hooded cloak so that her cheap clothes and vulgar coiffure were hidden.

She left her bubble house and went on the moving walkways to the taxi rank at the Zoo gate. Here, she engaged a taxi to take her to the town. Only after she had paid off the taxi did she slip into an unlit alley and remove the cloak, folding it small and tucking it into her bag.

Now she swaggered out and began to walk along the street. She turned with confidence, threading her way through a maze of small streets till she came to a main thoroughfare again.

There were plenty of cars about, electric ones computer-aided, nothing to equal the superb rocketbeast she had herself, back home in the Zoo. Connets were for the élite. Not even all Zoo dwellers could afford them. It was like having a private rocket in your garage, a million credits' worth of mechanised streamlined glory.

Fee undid the fastening of her loose overshirt. She reached in and hooked one long, cone-shaped breast out. She let it lie on view, projecting from her shirt.

She swayed her hips. She licked her reddened lips. She looked like all the other prostitutes now.

The joke was, prostitution was increasing. It worked inversely with the prevailing moral climate. As the town became more propriety conscious, so more and more people went to buy what they needed since they couldn't get it any other way.

Nice people. Respectable people. People who wanted to fuck but didn't want their friends and neighbours to know they wanted to fuck.

There was a uniform to wear, so that the public knew who had sex for sale. The women exposed one breast if they were heterosexual, two if they were bisexual. Male prostitutes exposed one cheek of their arse if they were hetero, two if they were bi. Those who only went with their own sex had to explain to customers individually. It was no different from explaining what kinks you did or didn't do.

Fee liked women, but she was in the mood for men. She wanted fat men, ugly men, panting, gasping men who had to have help climaxing.

She wanted weak men. She wanted men who gave her money for sex. It amused her to know that there were men who had made it with Fee Cambridge, socialite queen, for a few credits and not even known that they had done so.

These men came out of the dark and squatted over her

143

body, puffing and panting in their anxiety to release their sexual need. It amused Fee to satisfy them and then send them on their way.

Her first customer stopped. He touched her breast. Fee stood there, one hand on her hip, letting the stranger paw her.

He was a big man, heavy-built. Just what she wanted. 'How d'you like it, lover?' she said in a bored voice.

'Back door. That OK with you?'

'Yeah, yeah. Usual fee.'

He passed over the greasy notes. Fee smiled and took his hand. They went into the nearest hotel – this part of town was littered with them – and took a room for twenty minutes.

Fee stripped rapidly and turned, letting the man look at her. He had cold eyes, and he assessed her magnificent body indifferently. Then she turned and splayed her legs. She bent forward over the bed and waited.

He didn't use any grease – she suspected he would have liked it to hurt – but she had prepared her body thoroughly. Her anus was softened and relaxed, her rear passage slithery and open. His big cock slid in without difficulty and with no preliminary pawing of her. All he wanted to do was poke.

He thumped away as if he were uninterested in any conceivable refinement of the act. She felt him squirt, and he hung over her for a few moments till his penis became slack. Then he slid it out.

Fee turned round. He was red-faced, panting a little. He looked mulish now.

'Quite a bull,' she observed. 'Baby, you're big there. A real man.'

'Yeah.' The word was a grunt, but he straightened up. He began to look a little smug. 'You ain't so bad, lady. Why d'you do this?'

'For men like you.' Fee smiled.

'Yeah yeah. And the dough.'

'Gotta live.'

'Sure you do. See you again, sweetheart. That's a nice arse.'

144

She was back on the street in ten minutes. Fee crowed quietly to herself. Maybe they should make this a Zoo game. All the women could come down and see how many tricks they could turn in an hour, how much they could earn. The men could watch them and count the customers.

Fee tittered to herself. It was a neat idea. The only problem with making it a Zoo game was that she would lose her private kink.

She liked slutting like this now and again. She liked the degradation of her body, its smearing in low-grade slime.

Another man stopped and touched her breast. He was small and quivering with tension. 'How's it for you, brother?' asked Fee.

'Dirty,' he whispered. 'I want it dirty. Will you do filthy things for me?'

'You've come to the right lady,' said Fee. 'But it'll cost you.'

'I can pay, see. I can pay whatever you want. But it must be dirty.'

They went into the hotel. Fee felt that curious humming in her that blanked through and quieted her restless brain. Her restless spirit. She dared not analyse why she did this because she might not like herself. She might have to stop it. All she knew was that she had to have this relief sometimes. It blinded her mind. It gagged her thoughts. It blanked her emotions.

It gave her peace – for a time. If you never went into the abyss, how could you know the glory of climbing out of it?

She took lipstick and had the little man rub the red glossy wax round her pouting sex. Then she crouched over his face and kissed him with her cunt. He rolled his face in her pendulous breasts till they in their turn were smeared with red wax. Fee took his cock in her breasts and rolled and squeezed it till it too was smeared. Then she reddened her lips and kissed and sucked his fragile member till it was soldier-stiff and alert.

She held up a dildo and painted the wax colour on it. Then she strapped the dildo on and made the man bend over. She entered his arse and very gently rogered it while

145

he stuttered and wept. When she was done, she kissed it. She made him lie on the bed on his back. She put his smeary cock inside her hot squeezing pussy. She reached under him and slid the dildo back into his rear. She made him have her that way, his arse bulging, his cock pumping flutily in her writhing slithery hole.

When he was done and was grey with exhaustion, she beat him. She smacked his arse till he cried. She told him he was scum, filth, a dirty, wicked boy. She held his flaccid cock and beat it with a little springy rod. Then she held his balls and rotated and caressed them, all the time gently, carefully whipping his strengthening cock.

He came awkwardly, as if he was ashamed at his jetting spunk. Fee took him into the bathroom and cleansed him, bowing meekly at his feet and servicing him as though he were her lord and master.

He went out with a swagger.

She had spent three-quarters of an hour on him, but he had paid four times the previous customer's price. Now she went back on the street. She was getting tired. Maybe one trick more and she would go home and sleep in deep oblivion.

Rollo. Come home. I can't do without you.

There was a noise along the street. At first Fee took no notice. Her mind was spaced out, ranging inside itself in the void of her emotions. She stood faintly swaying, her exposed breast cool in the night air.

The noise came closer, and vaguely she began to take notice. The prostitutes round her of both sexes were muttering and drawing back. There were stifled exclamations of annoyance, some of humour.

The customers had melted away. Fee saw that a rout, a troupe, a gaggle of people, mostly women, were coming along the street.

Traffic had been brought to a halt. The women and their few male hangers-on were shouting. They carried banners.

Fee felt contempt, whatever the precise interest group they represented. This wasn't how you got things done. This wasn't how things were changed. You put your point

146

of view, you served your interest by indirect means, by flattery, by subterfuge. It was children who shouted. It was children who gathered into groups and wailed. There were more effective ways for adults. Ways that were more cunning, more fun.

She saw the banners, heard the words. *Clean the streets. Street trash out. Ban bought sex.*

Fee began to sway backwards, her eyes narrowing with amusement. What these townfolk got up to! How they told each other off. Zoo folk got bored and did various things that might or might not be in bad taste, but at least they didn't go round telling each other what to do in their private time, with their private lives. That was one of the many differences between the town and the Zoo. The Zoo enabled. The town disallowed.

Suddenly she realised there was a personal threat. The marching women were striking out as they passed. Some of the prostitutes were struck and thrown down. There were clubs. People were being hit.

Fee looked round for a doorway to shrink into. Behind her, the yellow rectangles of dull, welcoming light had all vanished. The hotels had slammed their doors and barred them. She had no escape.

Fee tucked her breast in, slid her cloak on, slung it back over her shoulders and stood forward. She was just in time.

'Street trash out,' screamed a woman. She advanced on Fee, her face distorted with rage, a baton whirling.

Fee stepped into the weapon, deflected it with the tiny club that had appeared in her hand, and struck the woman smartly in the throat.

The woman stopped as if she had hit a brick wall and sat down. Several of those with her stumbled over her, unable to get out of the way in time. Someone saw Fee and shouted. Three or four began to advance menacingly. Fee dropped into a defensive crouch, whirled sharply and put one booted high-heeled foot up so that it scythed round on her advancing attackers.

Someone was raked in the stomach. They fell back, momentarily nonplussed. They hadn't expected resistance.

147

Fee stood waiting, in perfect balance. A small smile played around her lips. She felt very good, very alive.

A man pushed forward. 'I'll get the bitch,' he snarled. The main crowd surged on past, too caught in its own momentum to stop for this local difficulty.

'Whore,' said the man softly, advancing on Fee. 'Bitch filth.'

Fee jumped and kicked him in the stomach. She hit the ground on one hand, her elbow and her falling legs giving immediately. She sprang up and flung her right arm straight out in front of her. The hand which held the little club made contact with the man's face as he rushed towards her, having hauled himself to his feet.

His arms were longer than hers and he had a grip on her before her blow struck home. Knocked almost senseless, his hands loosened. Fee struck his left wrist with her club and the arm fell uselessly away. The man sat down again, releasing her. He looked dopey.

Fee leapt over him. Swirling her cloak around her, she thrust into the densest part of the crowd. Moments later her attackers had lost sight of her and she could no longer be told apart from their own kind.

Fee worked her way across the crowd. She felt as though she were swimming in sewage. Her nose wrinkled in disgust. The people were hot and excited, their eyes blazing frenziedly as they chanted their repetitive slogans. When she could, she got free of them and the first side street she saw, she vanished along.

At her back the noise and lights from the torches dwindled. She heard crashing noises as windows were broken and property was smashed. This was Hedgeways, where the feelie bar manager had been snatched.

After a while she rested, squatting in a quiet residential doorway. She fixed the little club back in her hair where it looked like an ornament. She never came down here unarmed. It was just a habit, a trick she had picked up years before when she used to go to the old city where things were really anarchic, and no law and order prevailed.

The town wasn't usually like this. It was a boring, staid

place, extremely concerned with law and order. Even Hedgeways, despite its notoriety, was merely noisy. There was never any trouble.

Fee could hear sirens now. Belatedly, the police were responding. She suspected they didn't hurry themselves. They didn't mind if the good town citizenry got its jollies from attacking the social fringe. No doubt they felt they should allow an hour or two's fun and indulgence before they intervened to protect property.

She began to walk back to the more steady, residential areas where the solid citizens carried out their solid lives. Eventually Fee took a taxi. She came back to the Zoo, to her bubble house and went to bathe. She would destroy the clothes she had worn.

All her pleasures were being taken from her, one by one. She missed her husband. Nobody understood. Nobody knew. She was alone in her loneliness. She could tell none of her friends because of the TransFlow rights issue. It was scheduled to occur in less than two weeks' time.

It was on this subject, that Simeon Grey, chairman of the board, called her the next day.

Fee dutifully scrambled.

'We need to have a launch party, Ms Cambridge,' said Simeon, as though he were the first man on the planet to come up with such an idea.

Fee felt bad. Taking pills to make her sleep did this to her.

'I know,' she said sourly.

'Our friend the smoker, will he be able to present himself as your husband?'

Fee visited the clinic daily as part of the fabrication that Rollo was resting. 'No,' she said simply. 'Rollo will be expected to give a speech. To talk to people. No one can do that but himself. And since the market is uneasy over his prolonged rest cure, the investment managers will be keener than usual to see that he is OK. One can hardly blame them. I would expect Jessie Conlan to do no less when she is acting on TransFlow's behalf. A sick executive, where that executive virtually runs the company,' she added rudely, 'is a significant thing.'

'We all do our bit, Ms Cambridge,' said Simeon, bristling.

Fee remained aggravatingly silent.

Simeon contorted his face into a smile. 'I do appreciate the strain you are under, Ms Cambridge,' he said with unction dripping from his voice.

Fee stayed silent.

'I feel, by virtue of my age and the long relationship I have enjoyed with you and your husband, the freedom to say that I would understand any need you had for comfort. Please believe I am always here. I hope I am a discreet man. You would find me very reliable.'

Fee gaped mentally. Was he offering her connubial comforts, or just a shoulder to lean on? It hardly bore thinking about.

She arranged her features into a sad smile. 'I'm finding Roddy Dupique very comforting,' she said huskily. 'He relieves the strain wonderfully. At his age, he's pretty reliable, too. However, I very much appreciate your offer. If anything ever happens to you, I'm sure Ms Grey would find Roddy just the job. You might tell her that. He comes with my recommendation.'

She broke the vidi connection just as the purple flush began to spread over Simeon's features. Pompous fart. He deserved that. How dare he elevate their business relationship into one of friendship.

She would tell Rollo to dump him when he came home. The man was a deadweight. His directional fees made a hole in the profits. They could be used to plump up the Christmas bonus. The staff would like that.

The man in the white overshirt and short white breeks was putting up posters all over his part of the town. They were quite small posters, little more than handbills, but he was spreading them all over so that everyone would see them.

In each corner of the town there were men doing likewise. The posters read: *Sex is vice. Let's break the habit. Rally Saturday 15th, Sunshine Park. Forward with morality.*

Tony was doing Flowers, a mixed commercial and residential area close to the University. He was pleased to have such a good patch. The sisters had been kind to him. He knew that here, students would see his posters and it was particularly advantageous to get at the young. They had to be turned from their wicked, vice-ridden ways. They had to know the purity of celibacy, how clean and easy life became once you had conquered the itch.

Men were such weak vessels – he knew he would never be allowed to join the sisters in morality. But that was right, it was as it should be. All down the ages, women had been the moral guardians of mankind. For him it was enough just to serve, just to aid the cause.

Tony whistled as he fixed posters to every available surface. No policeman stopped him. He knew they wouldn't, even though technically he was committing an offence. The police sympathised. They knew the sisters had the rights of it. Filth had to be rooted out. Sex had to be crushed. Then society would have a chance to become orderly again. Some moral advancement could be made. They didn't even have to go through the squalid business of having sex to get babies. That could all be done without copulation now.

Tony paused and lifted his head. To his left, a hill rose up and was crowned as if with white icing with the glittering Institute of Science. What did they know? thought Tony contemptuously. There was too much of their sort of knowledge already. What was needed was different. People needed to know their natures. They needed to quell the beast within.

He turned his head. The plazas stretched away, fluffy with trees and bushes. Beyond them, filling the far distance, hills rose, one behind the other in a seemingly endless succession till they melted, blue-hazed, into the sky.

Those hills were covered with trees. With rainforest. With jungle. Into that jungle mankind was forbidden to go. Animals were not kept in reservations these days. People were. At last, man had learnt to subjugate only his local environment, leaving the mass of the planet to get on without him, doing its job of keeping itself harmoniously in balance to support life as humanity wanted it.

151

The jungle hid the Zoo. That was exclusive too. Only the very rich, society's élite, lived there in their sprawling bubble houses. They kept everyone else out, though they came and went freely. To Tony's way of thinking, they behaved no better than the beasts they lived among. They were filth. They rutted like animals. They did it in public. They practically swung from the trees sucking their own sex organs – or they would have done if they could.

Tony imagined them, walking their private precincts, their sexes exposed. He hadn't invented this for himself. The sisters had told him. They had said how in the Zoo, the women hiked up their skirts and walked about with their naked pudenda on show. Any man could stop and poke one, like he might stop at a drinking fountain and enjoy a cooling draught.

Tony found that thinking of this filth made him grow hot and sweaty. It was said that the men walked about with their drooping penises on the outside. If a woman wanted a man, she touched his penis. He would let her fondle him then, there on the street, and they would lie down and do it in front of everyone, anyone.

That was the Zoo for you, thought Tony. The place ought to be bombed. It ought to be flattened. It was a virus and it had infected the town.

He was a doctor. He was a garbage man actually, but he saw himself as a doctor. The town was sick. He was helping to heal it.

The source of the infection was the Zoo, though. Eventually the Zoo would have to be cauterised.

Tony felt his blood thump faster. Perhaps he would be there when they breached the barricades, when they broke down the Zoo gate and began the business of cleaning out the Augean stables. He would enjoy that. The sisters of the New Morality had told him and the other male helpers that when they did clean out the Zoo, the women would have to be lined up and whipped for their sins. Naked. In public. Men would whip them until they knew they had done wrong, till they begged for punishment. Till they mended their ways.

Tony licked his lips and hurried on, sticking up his posters. He wanted to get the most put up. There was a prize for the man who posted the most. He didn't care about the prize, but he did want the sisters' approbation, their praise.

Here was a pretty alleyway. A fountain played. Geraniums made bright red splashes. A café had seats out on the pavement.

The café was closed and without customers. Tony turned to come back the way he had come, to regain the main throughfare, when he saw three men.

'Good morning, brothers,' he said cheerfully, attempting to move past.

'Good morning, brother,' said one. Another put up a friendly hand. Tony turned, puzzled, and smelled the sweet, dizzying smell.

His posters tumbled from his suddenly slack hands. In an instant his slack body was placed in a car. Two men got in so that he sat propped between them, the third got in the front passenger seat. The driver drove sedately away.

Jermyn Ames faced the board. Simeon Grey was speaking. 'We have to hold the launch party for the rights issue. The chief executive is missing. You have had this man Maslow on the business for two weeks. He has come up with nothing.'

'He's making progress,' said Ames. 'It's slow work. He can't go public, we've forbidden that. He's limited as to how he can use manpower because he can't explain who the missing person is. He has eliminated many possibilities already. It doesn't look like progress, but it is.'

'You speak as his apologist,' snapped Simeon.

'I know the man's been working,' said Ames patiently.

Jessie Conlan said: 'Is Rollo dead, Jermyn? Is that Maslow's opinion?'

'It's a possibility,' said Ames. He didn't look at Fee. 'The balance is that the body would have turned up by now. That suggests he is alive.'

'Is it so hard to dispose of a body?' asked Simeon.

The board hissed in shock. Fee sat calmly. She was being punished for the vidi call, she knew that.

Ames faced him directly. 'You can mince them up fine and dig them in, but even then the parks and gardens people would notice. We have very refined sewage, water and rubbish disposal systems, Mr Grey. They would pick up on anything big and organic like a body.'

'What about the city?' asked Salazar.

Ames turned to her in relief. 'You could dispose of a thousand people in the city,' he said. 'The thing is, the riffraff down there don't let anyone in. They are more exclusive than the Zoo.'

Fee smiled at the weak joke. She liked Ames. She considered his job at the moment next to impossible.

'They wouldn't let any townee come among them to dispose of a corpse,' said Ames bluntly. 'About five years ago someone tried it. The city simply spewed it back and it was discovered on the edge of the town in full view.'

'What if city people are responsible for Rollo's disappearance?' asked Roddy.

'It's possible,' said Ames. 'But very improbable. They operate completely outside the law. They aren't interested in the town. If they had snatched Mr Cambridge, it would have been for one reason only. To ransom him. We've heard nothing.'

'They could have bungled the snatch,' said Simeon maliciously.

'They are experts in crime,' said Ames, his voice sober. 'They wouldn't have bungled it. He would be too valuable to them alive. Even if they had killed him accidentally, they could have sent us a bit of him, to con us into paying to get him back.'

'I'd pay, even to get his dead body back,' said Fee. 'They'd know that.'

There was an ugly silence.

'He could just be in someone's house,' said Simeon obstinately.

'He could,' agreed Ames. 'But alive, not dead. The public health monitors would have picked up on him if his

154

body was just mouldering somewhere. I'm sorry, Ms Cambridge.' He turned to look at Fee.

'I understand.'

Simeon tapped on the table. He liked to grow one nail extra long and he used it for this irritating habit. 'The girl,' he said. 'Maslow was having her watched. She's disappeared.'

'Sandrina.' Ames spoke reluctantly. 'Yes, she has.'

'Isn't that suspicious in itself?' asked Jessie. 'Girls don't generally disappear.'

'Yes, it is. It's possible the same people have her.'

'That's what Maslow thinks, isn't it?' said Fee. 'That one of these weird groups has Rollo.'

'Yes, it is. And I agree with him, though we have absolutely no proof.'

'Why aren't they boasting about their plum?' asked Salazar.

'I don't know. There's a big rally planned for next Saturday. It's possible Mr Cambridge is the star attraction. They might be keeping him under wraps till then.'

Suddenly Fee's cool deserted her. 'No!' she shouted. The board, accustomed to her calm, turned as one with astonished faces. 'I won't have him paraded publicly, humiliated in front of those town bastards.'

Ames was from the town. So were Roddy, Wiener Lutz and Brady of public relations, who although he wasn't a member of the board was being allowed to sit in on this one.

Fee was standing, her eyes flashing, her hands trembling. 'I won't have it,' she snarled. 'He is no prize animal, no slave won by conquest. I won't have him paraded so the masses can see him and laugh.'

Jessie said: 'Fee, tell the police. Damn TransFlow. It's your right as his wife. They can lay on an operation and if he does appear, they'll lift him. What can we do? What can Maslow do?'

Fee swallowed. 'I wanted him to have his business intact and undamaged,' she said in a small voice. 'It's the least he'd expect me to do.'

'I know, darling,' said Jessie. 'But time is passing. There are other priorities.'

Ames shifted on his feet. 'I think Ms Conlan is right. I think it's time we called in the police. I think TransFlow ought to do it. From the top. Go through the Home Secretary. He'll understand the ramifications. He'll see the need for secrecy.'

'We'll lose the ConComm franchise,' observed Simeon Grey.

'Not necessarily. If it's handled with discretion, I don't think that need be the outcome.' This was Roddy. 'Our economic position doesn't rest on Rollo Cambridge. The Home Secretary will understand that. You know him, don't you, Fee?'

'Yes.' Fee sat down. 'I could talk to him.'

'Perhaps Ms Cambridge doesn't agree with Mr Dupique that TransFlow is healthy without Mr Cambridge. That our future is assured.' Simeon's voice was silky.

'Damn you to hell,' said Fee. 'If all TransFlow had was you, that would certainly be my opinion.'

Simeon stiffened in shock. Jessie saw that the chairman was useless and stepped in. 'Emotions are running high,' she observed dryly. 'I vote that last exchange be deleted from the record. I suggest we take a vote on approaching the police formally.'

So it was agreed.

Tony sat in a bare room and wondered why the roof had fallen in on his head. Lights shone in his eyes, and he felt nauseous and dazzled. His brain scurried feebly over what had happened to him.

He had been attacked. Why? Because he was helping the sisters. These men were bad. They were working for the opposition, the forces of evil.

He, Tony, had been selected. In its way it was an honour. He was a martyr.

Briefly he imagined himself with Sister Elysia. He would explain that the men had hurt him, but he hadn't said anything. He was reliable. He would do anything for the sisters.

Did he have anything to say? His mind scrabbled for gobbets of information that might satisfy his captors.

He didn't want to be hurt.

The lights were adjusted. People were in the room. Tony felt fear grip him so that his bowels and bladder felt weak.

A cup of coffee appeared on the table. Gratefully he reached for it. Was it drugged? Would it make him speak?

Tony's hands shook. The coffee slopped. He had to eat and drink, didn't he? Refusal was pointless.

The big man said: 'There's no need to act so damn frightened. We aren't going to hurt you.'

The lean man with grey eyes said nothing. He just watched Tony shakily drinking his coffee.

'Sorry about the snatch,' said the big man. 'We didn't think you'd cooperate if we held a conversation on the street.'

'Cooperate?' squeaked Tony.

'These New Moralists, they decent people?'

The question was laconic. Tony couldn't see any harm in it. 'Of course,' he said indignantly. 'They're the best. They believe in clean living. Sex promotes violence, disordered senses, over-indulgence, laziness at work . . .' His voice died away. He had been anxious to proselytise, expecting to be cut short. But no one had interrupted. The men had sat there as if they were prepared to listen to him all day. It made it curiously difficult to carry on.

'They let you join? I mean, you're a man.'

'They let men help,' said Tony stiffly. 'One can't blame them for being wary about men. I mean, we can be beasts, animals, always on about sex and, er, that.' Again his voice tailed away. Big men, muscular men always made him feel he was at a disadvantage.

'That must be real nice,' said the big man.

'It's worthwhile.'

'I see that. You like the ladies?'

'What do you mean? I admire them. I revere them.'

'You helping at the rally on Saturday?'

Tony smiled self-importantly. 'I'm an usher. I help with crowd control. If there's trouble, I'm a guard. The sisters

157

have to be kept safe. Virtue is always under threat from vice.'

'You just stroll about in the crowd, clapping and cheering where it's appropriate, keeping your eyes peeled for any trouble?'

'That's right,' said Tony uncertainly. He couldn't quite put his finger on the aspect of this speech that didn't feel right.

'They're just having speakers, are they?'

Tony wondered why the lean man never spoke. He just sat there watching Tony, letting the big man do all the talking.

'There'll be singing. We can all join in. I'll be handing out song sheets.'

'Fireworks?'

'Fireworks? Oh, I see what you mean. Probably. I'm not certain.'

'And emotional fireworks, too. Got anything to wow the crowd? Anything special?'

Tony licked his lips and looked from one man to the other. 'Why am I here?' he asked nervously.

The grey-eyed man said: 'Tony, we can't spell it out. You understand.'

'I do?'

'It's our job to know what's going on. We can't help that. We don't want to hassle the sisters and put them on the spot. If they are planning a big finale though, we need to know. We can't have those fancy Zoo bastards leaning on their government pals and saying we aren't in control, that the sisters have to be stopped. If we have it on record we knew what was going to happen before it happened, then we can be seen to be doing our job, yeah? We're keeping the lid on. The sisters are acting within the law.'

'You're the police,' said Tony with relief.

'We didn't say that,' said the big man. 'You can't say it.'

'You understand,' said the lean man again, in tones of relief. He visibly relaxed. 'You're a good guy, Tony. This is helping a lot.'

'You're protecting the sisters,' said the big man solemnly.

'I see,' said Tony. He thought he did. He wasn't being hurt. The questions were fine. These men were officials or policemen or something. It was all alright.

'So what's the big deal, Tony?' asked the big man. 'The main event. The show stopper.'

'I'm not sure.' Tony was serious, man to man. 'They definitely have something planned. We've been told we'll enjoy it.'

'You've no idea what it is? We were sure you would, being on the inside, like.'

Tony felt the implication. He was small beer. He struggled to make them think better of him. 'It's something to do with the pets, I think.'

'The pets?'

'They have these men. They used to be tigers. You know, out for what they could get. Now they've seen the error of their ways. They're tame. The sisters call them pets. I think some of them might speak on Saturday. If they are rich enough, maybe they'll make donations to encourage the crowd. The sisters need funds. And, and . . .' Tony stammered.

'What is it, Tony?' The lean man's voice was soft.

'There's a suggestion men ought to volunteer to be castrated.' Tony could not help sounding deeply unhappy. 'You know, if thine eye offend, pluck it out, and all that. Maybe someone will actually go that far, I mean make that commitment, next Saturday.'

The big man could not quite keep all the emotion out of his voice. 'You mean, some guy might offer to be castrated because the sisters think sex is bad?'

'No. I mean do it. Actually do it. On the platform. I know one of the sisters is a surgeon. I mean, if a man went through with it in public, before a crowd, it would have an impact, wouldn't it?' said Tony. His eyes were unhappy and he seemed to be pleading with the two men. 'Wouldn't it?' he repeated.

Maslow vidied Fee. 'I need to see you,' he said.

'I need to see you too. Today?'

'Can I come over now?'

'Of course.'

When he arrived, he asked Fee directly: 'Have you been to the police yet?'

'This afternoon. I've an appointment with the Home Secretary.'

'Do you need to do it this way? Can't you just go to your local trooper?'

'It's the financial angle,' said Fee wearily.

'Why you?' asked Maslow curiously. 'Why not your chairman or someone from the board?'

'Simeon's an ass. And I have something the Home Secretary wants.'

Maslow's face showed disgust. 'Oh no, Fee, not that.'

She was tense and unhappy, and not looking forward to the afternoon. Maslow's pinpricking, moralising smallness seemed the final straw. 'Why not?' she hissed. 'I'm fighting for my husband and for his business. Why can't I use any means I have at my disposal?'

'You don't need sex.' Maslow was outraged. 'They'll all jump to help anyway. You just like putting out.'

Fee struck him. The accumulated tensions of the past month suddenly snapped. She hit Maslow with all her force across his face.

He stood aghast, his head ringing from the blow. Then anger shook him. He reached over and grabbed Fee's hair, forcing her to her knees. As she went down she straight-armed him in the groin and he doubled over. She twisted under him and elbowed him in the face.

Maslow punched her in the kidneys and wrapped one of her arms back. He came round on top of her till he was sitting astride her body. She lay face down under him, her arms bent up and back.

'I use my sex,' she sobbed. 'You use your strength. So tell me the difference.'

He turned her over and caught her up, holding her close. His face stung. 'They're going to produce tame men on Saturday,' he mumbled. 'They might offer money, express their support for the cause. They might go further.'

'Rollo isn't tame. What do you mean, go further?'

'There's a whisper they are going to have a public castration. It might not be true. You know how rumour exaggerates.'

Fee was stone in his arms. He felt her body so rigid that she might have been a statue. Slowly he released her, holding her and looking at her.

Her face was livid. It was a white flame. She was terrifying, repulsive, and yet he found himself aching to arouse such a feeling in a woman on his account.

That bastard, Rollo Cambridge. This woman would go through fire for him. He would never understand the Zoo. She'd fuck anything that moved and cuckold her husband up hill and down dale, but here in his arms he had the evidence that she would kill for Rollo.

'It doesn't have to be true,' he whispered. 'But you must tell the police. They will stop anything happening.'

She jerked suddenly. 'Sandrina. She's on the inside. I put her there.'

'The inside?'

'She's joined the New Moralists. You told me how it was done. I told her. I promised her Rollo. She's desperate to fuck with him. She's with them now.'

Maslow was pierced by jealousy. He didn't go much on Sandrina, who had made the running, and he thought Fee a slut, a beautiful overused slut. But both these women would do anything to have Rollo Cambridge.

He couldn't understand it. He wasn't a vain man, but he couldn't see that Rollo had that much more than himself. A touch of glamour maybe. Money, certainly. But that was it.

He released Fee and sat down. 'I've been wasting my time looking for that girl,' he said.

'She's got a skinspeaker. An implant. She'll activate it as soon as she gets word of Rollo – if she does. I'm carrying a pager. If she uses it, I'll come running and see what's happening.'

Sandrina had consented to having a tiny microphone implanted in the hollow of her shoulder. If she pressed it,

161

it would record. If it recorded, Fee had monitoring equipment that would pick it up. Fee's equipment would automatically page her and she could come and listen to the tapes. If Rollo turned up elsewhere, and Fee wanted Sandrina to abort and get free, she could activate a pulse in the skin-speaker that Sandrina would be able to feel through her skin. For an hour the implant would pulse, and Sandrina would not be able to help feeling the irritating click in her shoulder muscle. She would know then to escape. If she didn't turn up within twenty-four hours, Fee would send help.

'You got me to tell you how,' he said queerly.

'Oh, dear God,' cried Fee. 'Is that all you can think about? Have you never done business over a meal? Didn't I see you entertaining Richelle Matthews when you were interviewing her? So I mix business and sex. So what? Can't you think and chew gum? Is it doing two things at once that freaks you out?'

Maslow stared. 'You equate sex and cocktail snacks.'

Fee gripped his balls. 'Too right I do,' she said. 'Who played fucky in his hotel room, with TransFlow picking up the tab? Mr Clean, as I recall it.'

Maslow fell over backwards laughing. 'You're the most terrible woman I've ever met. You whore like you clean your teeth. You make love like an anaconda. I'd hate to be your enemy, sweetheart. Do you tear out hearts and eat them, if the boyfriend won't play?'

Fee moved on top of him. 'I made it with you because I needed to control you,' she said. 'Maybe you're more fun this way. I'm getting to like you, small man.'

'You're giving me nightmares. Succubus.'

'Compliments, compliments,' said Fee softly. Her mouth closed over his. He felt the soft velvet heaven of her embrace. Her mouth was nectar. He wanted to drown with her. He felt her hands move on his body. He couldn't help responding. Was it like this with prostitutes? They did everything. You couldn't help yourself. What you thought of them made no difference. Their hands, full of skill and experience, their mouths trained to entice, their cunts soft and welcoming – how could these delights be resisted?

162

Fee had his shirt and trousers open now. Her lips caressed his chest, his groin. She laid her long, rich breasts against him. A nipple entered his mouth. He sucked and felt his balls caressed and stirred. His cock was softly abraded in her wonderful hair. Her tongue probed his anus. A hand fluttered delicately over his cock. She kissed his mouth with her vulva, honeyed musk.

His senses were so ravished he hardly knew when she took his cock into her body. He entered heaven having the urge to climax tended, explored, developed, brought on, enlarged and then held for a long, delicious moment of utter sexual bliss before he fell over the edge in explosions of pleasure that shook and racked his body.

He was so utterly at peace afterwards that he slept. Fee washed and changed. When it was time for her to leave, she woke him up.

'I don't have time for this,' he said. 'There's so much to do.'

Fee was dressed in dull, perfect black all over, except for a crisp stiff white frill in a vee shape, exposing her from throat to waist and narrowly missing exposing all her bosom. Her hair was slicked tight to her head and bound back. She wore no jewellery except for two heavy rock-crystal bracelets, one on each wrist. They were icy green, the colour of her eyes.

'We're on the same side,' said Fee. 'It's something to remember.'

'No more freelancing,' said Maslow. 'This Sandrina business . . .'

'Is a fact. So use it. I have to go. Keep in touch, huh?'

Being Fee Cambridge, this last might have been an order. But Fee made it a plea, her husky voice caressing and tender.

Bitch, thought Maslow. Marvellous, wonderful bitch.

7

Sandrina screamed. 'No, no, no.' She scrabbled across the floor, her rear lifting and seeming to push her. She flung away the girls who tried to soothe her. The thing in her was driving her mad. She couldn't get away from it. When she hit the wall she tried to climb it.

They tranquillised her. She was sobbing as she was led to her bed. All her body was the great slug in her pussy, pushing outwards, pressing up against her soft parts.

They were breaking the metal seal. She felt the enormous thing begin to be expelled from her body. Tears of relief ran down her face. It was gone. It was out.

She lay dopily, the aftermath of shock washing over her. She seemed to be alone. Even that was bliss.

Now someone sat on her bed. She was too drowsy to open heavy-lidded eyes.

Her belly was stroked. She felt her breasts lifted and examined. Someone ran a large, warm hand down her side, down her flanks.

A man.

Sandrina opened her eyes. A tall, bronzed man with attractive rugged features was caressing her naked body.

'Who are you?' she whispered.

'Your reward. For the pain you've undergone.' He stroked her naked mound, his palm cupping its rounded silken shape.

'No,' she said hoarsely. 'We aren't supposed to have men.'

He bent over her and lightly kissed her lips. 'I belong,' he said. 'You can have me.'

'I don't understand.'

His fingers slid into her pussy. 'You mustn't suffer any permanent damage,' he said. 'I have to make sure the man-hater doesn't do too much.'

'I don't want you in me,' she whimpered.

'That's all right.' His voice was kind. 'Here, stroke my penis while we talk.'

She found her hand lifted and placed over his sex. He was springy, part erect. She felt the satin column, spongy and soft, with developing resilience. She felt the soft crisp genital hair. As the cock grew in her grasp, she felt his balls nestling against the back of her hand.

He moved his hips gently so that he masturbated himself idly in her loose clasp. He stroked her naked skull and kissed her brow, her eyelids.

After a while he released himself from her hand and climbed astride her. He began to massage her, working her muscles where they were tired from frenzy she had endured.

She drowsed, allowing his hands to work all over her body. He turned her over and did her back and her neck muscles. Then he turned her back.

She woke up to find a warmth and wonderful easement at her pussy. A delicious glow pervaded all her lower body. It was some time before she identified the source.

The man – she didn't know his name – was kissing her pussy. Very slowly and gently he was sucking her. Her vulva was warm and wet. Her pussy felt soft and relaxed.

She was aroused. She woke up fully. Her pussy felt wonderful and quite happy to have a man insert his sex. The man's tongue was marvellous, softly marvellous.

The tiredness had worn off. So had the fear. She felt able to think again.

Was this a test? Was she being tempted? It was hard to imagine she was allowed such succulent delights in a sect that denied the right to engage in sex. This was sex. She was engaging in it, albeit passively.

It would be reassuring, having this man inside her. She was frightened they had damaged her pussy. She needed it for Rollo Cambridge. She had to have him. She loved him. She craved sexual congress with him, needed him to pay her attention, to do to her what this man was doing.

She wanted to be roused, played with, enticed, seduced by Rollo. She wanted him to make an effort with her, to please her. If her pussy was destroyed by these madwomen, it would all be for nothing.

She wanted sex. If she took it, as it was offered to her now, would she lose her chance to help Rollo? Was she being put through some sort of initiation test?

'Leave me,' she said feebly.

He broke off. 'You don't mean that,' he said softly.

'Leave me,' she said again. She was perilously close to orgasm. There was a hunger in her belly now.

'Let me take you all the way.' His hands were on her body, warm, kind.

'It's wrong,' she sobbed. 'You tempt me.'

'Please,' he whispered. 'You are so very beautiful.'

'No.' Her voice was sharp. She sat up.

He knelt back and smiled. Two women came in.

'That was very good,' said one to Sandrina. 'My dear, you did well.'

Sandrina gazed at her blankly. The man stood up. His cock jutted out.

'Men,' said the woman who had spoken to Sandrina, 'can't help it. We understand that. See, having aroused him, we will allow him to be satisfied.' She pressed a wrist buzzer. A girl came in. The girl was fat and squat, her baldness accentuating her large ears and small eyes and mouth. The flesh wobbled in rings on her hips. Her stomach was pleated. Sandrina looked, amazed, on the solid dimpled thighs, the heavy buttocks, the drooping swinging breasts.

'Sister Jessamine will service the man's need,' said the woman. 'Sister Jessamine is an advanced student and implacable in her dislike of penetration. She will submit because I ask her to. Won't you, sister?'

'Yes, Sister Grace. For you, I submit eagerly. The man is a pet and will not harm me. What he does is nothing.'

Jessamine turned round and bent over. She planted her feet firmly apart. She reached behind her and opened the plump quivering cheeks of her arse.

The man advanced with his cock sticking out in front of him. He slid it into the pink fissure in Sister Jessamine's flesh. He began to pump rapidly, standing before them all, quite unconcerned.

Sister Jessamine absorbed the jolts her body received. When the man was done, he pulled his wet, softening penis out of her. She stood up and beamed.

'Was I good, Sister Grace? Was that the right thing to do?'

'You were wonderful, dear Jessamine. You will have your reward at the next meal time.'

The girl smiled smugly and waddled out. The man looked back over his shoulder at Sandrina and smiled. Then he too was gone.

'You meant him to tempt me,' said Sandrina. She was shocked at what she had seen. These people were worse than the Zoo. Seeing sex so blatant made her embarrassed.

'We have to test your commitment. You have had much to do with men, by your own account. We must be sure that your rejection of them and their works is sincere.'

'I think,' said Sandrina slowly, 'I need practice. I nearly gave way.'

Grace watched her. 'Do you have many men?' asked Sandrina.

'A few. We call them our pets. They are tame, my dear. They do as we say.'

'Why? Is it in their interests?'

'You are thinking sloppily. Is denial of sex bad for men?'

'No.' Sandrina corrected herself instantly. 'Rejecting sex calms fears. Soothes desires. Controls temper and indulgence.' She was reciting learned lessons. 'Denial of sex brings freedom and mental peace. It brings relief.'

'Good girl,' said Grace. 'Now, how about your own desires? The man was with you for some time.'

Sandrina was sufficiently nauseated by the act she was putting on to have killed her own urge. She smiled at

Grace. 'Dear sister,' she said. 'I need nothing. I am becoming liberated.'

Rollo stood against the wall, his fingers attempting to embed themselves in its unyielding surface. Melissa stood before him with another girl, who might have been her twin.

'Go away,' said Rollo.

'We want you to love us,' said the Melissa-twin.

'I can't,' said Rollo. 'You hurt me.'

'The pain helps,' explained Melissa, as if Rollo was a child.

'No,' said Rollo. 'It doesn't help at all.'

'He's pretty,' said Melissa-twin. 'You've been too strong.'

'I don't think so.' Melissa was sulking.

Melissa-twin advanced on Rollo. He turned his head away and closed his eyes. She touched his chest, feeling his smooth skin and his muscles. She ran her small, warm palm over his glistening skin. 'He is pretty,' she repeated.

'See if you can make him stand,' said Melissa.

The muscles round Rollo's mouth stood out as he clenched himself. All his post-adolescent life he had encouraged his sexual response to women. His personal good looks, his charisma, his aura of hard-headed success had all helped him to have what he wanted. Even the latent cruelty in his make-up had proved an added sexual attraction.

Now he had to resist. He was lonely. He was bored. He was frightened. He had enough confidence in his potency to believe he could seduce a woman to help him, even as he pleasured his body with hers. Part of his problem was that he had become too successful in manipulating women to his will. They offered no challenge any more. There was no thrill except for the basic thrill of satisfying his itch.

These women wanted him. His common sense told him to give way to them, and to attempt to win them over. He could make marvellous things happen for them sexually, he knew this.

He would be hurt, though. That cruel little girl, Melissa, had it in her power to double his powerful body over with pain. She enjoyed doing it. She particularly liked doing it as part of the sexual act.

Rollo was frightened. He was ashamed. He desperately wanted to be free. He had entered some ghastly nightmare world where pleasure was turned on its head.

Being vulnerable was a new experience for him. He was used to having the upper hand. Melissa had made him cry with pain once and he didn't enjoy the memory or the thought that she might do it again.

Melissa-twin stroked his skin, his sex. She kissed him. He tried to push himself back into the wall but there was no escape.

The soft advances continued. She kissed his neck, his face. She stroked his hair. She dropped to her knees and kissed his cock.

Slowly his head came round. Across the room, his prison cell, he met the eyes of Melissa. She was smiling. She always smiled. Below him, he could see the silken head of the girl who sucked him. He felt her hands against his thighs, her hair brushing his belly. Her mouth shrouded his cock. Her coffin mouth. Her mouth of death.

'Melissa,' he said.

'Yes.'

'Do you know who I am?'

Her wide spaced, pale eyes gazed with blank cheerfulness. 'Does it matter?' she asked.

'I'm quite important,' said Rollo with some difficulty. His cock had grown in Melissa-twin's mouth. He couldn't help it. 'I have some money. I have a business. Would you like some money, Melissa?'

'What for?' She drifted over to Melissa-twin. She faced Rollo. 'Kiss me,' she said.

He bent his golden head. If he failed to kiss her she would hurt him.

They took him to the bed and made him lie down. He was between them, on his back.

The two girls looked at each other over his body. They were up on their elbows. They leant over him and kissed each other on the mouth.

Rollo lay stiff. They kissed, sitting up to get closer to each other but keeping his body between them. Their breasts mingled so that he was oppressed by the desire to feel in among those softnesses, those abundances of full flesh. The girls had honey-coloured skin, caramel nipples.

He wondered if they were sisters. They looked like clones. It was normal speech to address a woman as sister, a man as brother. It didn't indicate any relationship deeper than that of belonging to humanity. But these girls were so alike.

Their thighs rubbed against him. He felt their hair brush him. Melissa twisted and lay with her legs apart. The cleft of her sex was moist, glistening. Melissa-twin held back her hair and kissed Melissa on this cleft, on her sex.

One of her hands stole out. She kissed Melissa's sex and clasped Rollo's cock. She began very gently to masturbate him. He watched the girls more or less across his chest indulging in sex. At the same time, his own sex was aroused.

Melissa-twin sat up, not releasing Rollo's cock. She reached down into the bag she had brought with her into the room. Rollo had forgotten it. From it she took a large dildo. She held it up and pressed a button. A skin of spikes appeared, quills, all over the surface of the artefact.

Rollo stared into Melissa's sex. He saw a bubble form and slowly pop. The girl was drooling with excitement, drooling her sex juices.

Melissa-twin gave the thing to Rollo. She turned away and bent her head over his hard penis. She began to suck him.

Rollo's body trembled. He knew he had the urge to come, despite the pain it had caused before. The girl sucking him was good, very good, and he was hungry for orgasm after so much arousal.

Before him were two damp pussies. Melissa-twin had her rear to him, raised up as she bent to mouth his sex. He could see the dark-tipped leaves of her sex, the rich pink interior bursting juicily through.

Melissa lay partly across him, legs splayed wide. She too

170

had her adorable sex fully on show. Her vulva was snail-shiny from her own juices. Rollo slid the dildo in.

He liked doing this to women. He liked seeing the plastic object split their flesh and open it. He liked seeing the fatness of the artificial penis slide into the deep, hot interior of a willing woman. He loved the way the flesh clove to and caressed the invader.

He slid it in, Melissa lifting her hips slightly to allow it deeper ingress. When it was fully in, he turned it and pushed so that she could feel it distending her inner sex. Then he pressed the button.

At the end of the thing he could see the little hedgehog skin of spikes. They vanished into her body. She gave a gasp of delight, her skin going red and then white. Rollo moved the thing for her. Her whole body came alive, stimulating him in turn, since much of her weight was on him. She writhed and squirmed, crying out and flailing her arms. Melissa-twin stopped sucking Rollo and climbed off the bed. She caught Melissa under her head and kissed her, upside down, on the lips. Then she put a nipple into her mouth.

Rollo held the dildo in the bucking orgasmic girl. He watched as they kissed, as the one sucked the nipple of the other. Melissa started to shout, and he felt his hand grow wet.

He pressed the button. The spikes retracted. Melissa went limp, her eyes unfocused.

Melissa-twin reached into the bag. She drew out a tube, a bristling tube. It was a sheath, and she slid it over Rollo's sex.

Now his penis resembled the spiky dildo. Melissa-twin was arranging herself astride him. She reached under herself and opened her sex. She began to sit down, down on Rollo's sex, down on the bristling thing his sex had become.

He saw her tender flesh pricked as the thing that was partly his own body and partly a weapon slid in. She strained, arching her back, holding her breasts, and Rollo could smell the sweat on her as it rolled from her armpits and her forehead, from between her breasts.

171

The thing was in. He cautiously moved and Melissa-twin cried out and rolled her head.

Suddenly a black fury overcame him. He had very little sensation inside the prickly sheath, but the two girls would hardly care about that. He fucked sharply upwards with a powerful surge of his hips.

Melissa-twin moaned. Rollo fucked harder, in short, savage bursts. Spittle accumulated at the corners of Melissa-twin's mouth.

Rollo gripped her hips. He began to fuck hard upwards, slamming into the frail body with the monstrous thing they had dressed him in. Melissa was screaming and the girl he impaled was shaking like a rag doll.

The pain he had been expecting all along began. He winced. When they first snatched him, they had kept him unconscious. During that time they must have implanted the tiny painmakers in his flesh. He had come round in a stupor on the floor of his first prison. They must have known he was at their mercy.

Rollo slammed violently upwards and fell off the bed. Melissa-twin came off his body, taking the dreadful sheath with her. Rollo continued to writhe as the pain coursed through his body. He rolled across to the far wall and came back again. He hit the bed hard and punched Melissa on the jaw. She rolled off the bed and the pain stopped.

Rollo knelt on all fours quivering. Sweat poured off him. His body shook. Melissa-twin was cowering in the corner. Rollo dragged himself to his feet. He went over to her and felt between her legs. He dragged the filthy little toy out of her. The adrenalin surging through him blanked the pain. He picked the girl up and bit her breasts. Then he sucked her nipples powerfully. He slung her onto his body so that her legs came around his waist. He was up and furiously erect. He sat her on his hard pole and, bracing her against the wall, began to take her properly.

At first she squirmed, as if to fight away from him. As he pounded upwards she began to respond. Panting, gulping air, his chest heaving, Rollo brought himself to his long deferred climax.

He stopped, his face in her shoulder, panting still. Gradually he let her slip down. She stood between him and the wall, his powerful body big beside her frailness.

'You shouldn't have done that,' she said in her little girl whine.

'Why not, dammit?' growled Rollo.

'Melissa . . .'

Rollo turned and went over to the girl he had knocked out. She was sitting holding her sore jaw. Rollo grabbed her and picked her up and sat her on the bed.

'Not with me, sister,' he said, breathing hard. 'You get some other sucker. All you'll get with me is a busted jaw and all I'll get is a heart attack. See? You push me and I'll die before I play your pretty games.' He thrust his face in close. 'I am not your plaything,' he snarled. 'Nobody owns me. Nobody ever will.'

It was a beautiful room. The ceiling was moulded, plastered in rococo perfection, the vine leaves clustered playfully.

Dark wood panelling made up part of the walls. No plastiglass here; this was an ancient building lovingly restored. There were vast dark bookcases containing texts now hardly worth preserving on disc. This was purely ornamental.

Pictures hung on the walls. The carpet, an authentic old carpet from pre dirt-digester days, was patterned in dull reds and greens. It was like being in a museum.

Fee didn't like it, but then she didn't have to live with it. It was what the minister liked that mattered. Or it was what he decided he ought to appear to like, to create the image of himself he wished to project.

Fee didn't care. 'Weston,' she said warmly. 'I want you to know how much I appreciate this time you have given up to me. I wouldn't have pestered you if it hadn't been serious. You must believe that.'

The minister's eyes flickered to Fee's companion. She wore no cosmetics. Her hair was lank and straight. Her figure was flat. She looked about sixteen.

'It's a pleasure to see you,' he said, politely, but his eyes were on the girl.

'I could have gone to my local captain of police,' said Fee. 'I should have done. But the situation is out of hand. We need your help directly from the top.'

The girl walked across to the minister's desk and removed her clothes. She folded them neatly. Her body was pale and thin. She had the tiniest tuft of hair at her sex.

'You'd better explain,' said Weston, removing his tie.

'Rollo vanished a month ago,' said Fee.

The minister stopped in the act of removing his trousers. The girl was folding his clothes as he took them off.

'Do I hear you right?' asked Weston.

'You do. He was bored. He went on a bender in the town. He vanished. A girl he vaguely knew was the last to admit to seeing him. We've had her checked out very thoroughly.'

Weston took off his shirt and gave it to the girl who folded it and hung it over the back of a chair.

'Go on,' he said.

'We called in a firm of private investigators. By "we" I mean the TransFlow board. We set up someone in a clinic, resting, whom I visited daily. We let our investigator search discreetly. He's come up with nothing. Nothing at all. He has some ideas but no proof.'

'What are his ideas?' The Minister was stretching his length on a couch. The girl bent over his body.

'He thinks one of these new anti-sex groups has him. They won't be interested in his ransom potential. They will be interested in him as a sexual male, as a Zoo man. There's a bit of antipathy between the town and the Zoo right now. Maybe you know this.'

'Those parties, Fee. Stories have been leaking out. I don't think you are always very wise.'

The girl had stroked the minister's sex until it was erect. Now she was mounting his body. Fee watched sombrely.

'There is a faint suggestion that this big rally planned for Saturday – you'll know about it from your people – will have something special to display. It might be men, men they have captured and worked on all this time.'

'Spoils of war, huh?'

'The suggestion is that these men will espouse the no-sex cause. They might offer substantial donations. They might volunteer to be castrated.'

The minister was silent. The girl bobbed up and down on his sex.

'The thing is,' he said at last, 'we aren't entirely against these new moral groups. It holds the crime rate down. Domestic violence has decreased. Maybe they have a point. There is too much sexual excitement around. It does lead people to do strange things.'

Fee watched the nymphet taking the minister to climax. The girl was a find. She was actually nineteen but she looked three or four years younger. That was how Weston liked them. Very very young.

'We are not suggesting you stop the rally. We want a police operation to rescue any men from being displayed. Even if it's apparently against their will. Preferably before they can be recognised, before they speak.'

'I understand,' said Weston, reddening as he approached his climax. He did understand. Public humiliation was something he was very alive to.

'There is the TransFlow rights issue,' said Fee. 'The ConComm franchise.'

'You don't want the company revealing its chief executive is missing.'

'If TransFlow shares are affected and we lose value before this critical rights issue,' said Fee, 'we might try to regain our relative position by inducing a bear market. The signs are already there and I think we have the financial muscle. It would be our only way out as a corporation.'

The minister considered the blackmail as the girl held him just short of orgasm. 'We've two sensitive by-elections coming up,' he said. 'A falling market would be bad news.'

'For all of us,' said Fee. 'I think it's to be avoided.'

'If TransFlow's problems adversely affected the markets,' said Weston, 'their position as franchisee might be in doubt.'

Wily old bastard, thought Fee affectionately, watching

175

the minister achieve orgasm. Long ago, a psych profile had revealed that the minister liked underage sex, preferably simulated underage sex since he had his ministerial position to protect, in the presence of his mature women friends. Fee had never had congress with Weston. Neither of them wanted it. But once or twice before, she had supplied his particular kink, watching him fuck a girly while they chatted.

'The best thing,' said Fee, 'is for a successful share flotation to emphasise the market's strength and that of the underlying economy. TransFlow would raise the capital it needs. The ConComm franchise would be assured, and we would enter the rest of the decade secure in wise financing and development.'

'All of which rests on getting Rollo home safe and sound with no one the wiser.'

'Which may or may not depend on a police operation next Saturday,' agreed Fee. 'The board wants the police in on it now anyway. As do I.'

Weston sat up, naked and happy. The girl showed him her pussy, wet with his spunk. He nodded absently.

'OK,' he said. 'I'll lay it on. I'll set things rolling right away. You'll get someone to see you pretty soon. Later today, I should imagine, so hold yourself available.'

'I will.' Fee stood up gratefully. Weston shrugged himself into his shirt and did up the buttons. The girl knelt at his limp cock and kissed it, licking it clean with her long pink tongue.

'Have this investigator chappie ready too. He'll have to spill all.'

'Certainly. He'll cooperate absolutely.'

Weston smoothed his tie. The girl still licked his sex. 'A word of advice, Fee.'

'Yes?'

'Cool these parties down. Too much sex, my girl. Too much sex too much in the open. OK?'

'Yes,' said Fee meekly. She watched the girl dress while Weston got busy on the vidi. Then they left. As the door closed behind them the girl removed the soundblockers in her ears. 'Was that all right, ma'am?' she lisped.

176

'You've earned your fee. Don't worry about that.'

Fee wondered why she was so tired as she headed for home. It could simply be Rollo's absence. Each day that passed with him gone made the balancing act of her life that much harder to sustain.

They bathed him. They oiled his golden skin. Then they placed a neck collar on him and led him, chained, into a long hall. Here he was fastened like Samson between two pillars, standing chained and naked.

His punishment began. The girls ran past him whipping him as they ran. The little spiteful flicks accumulated till Rollo's body was one big ache. They concentrated on his buttocks, on his penis. He felt red raw with pain.

All the time they whipped him, others of them lay on couches in Roman decadence. He saw the girls kiss each other on the breasts, the mouth, between their legs. He saw girls with artificial penises strapped to their hips walking around penetrating their sisters, their sister cult members.

They stopped whipping him. Through pain-dulled eyes he saw there were other men subjected to similar chastisements. The chained men hung and groaned, or cried out.

Now someone was behind him. He felt hands at his stinging buttocks. He felt his burning cheeks opened and then he gasped. Something cold and hard was being inserted into his anus.

They left it there. He didn't know what it was. Later a man was led by him, shambling, his head down. From his rear something projected. Rollo could only guess it was the same for himself.

It was like a tail, a feathery tail. A metal rod poked into his arse. From it sprang a riot of colourful feathers. The thing was risible, grotesque. It waggled comically as the man walked.

That night they put him in a cage with straw on the floor. Rollo lay in its foulness with women watching him, giggling, pointing. They came and went. It occurred to him that he was in a clubhouse, a place of entertainment. These women had lives outside they returned to periodically. This was playtime.

He was fed raw vegetables and plain water from tin plates on the floor. Some of the women delighted in pressing their naked buttocks against the bars in a gesture of derision.

The next day he was chained to the pillars again, as were the other men. He thought there were about six of them altogether, but it was hard to count. He never had a moment for private conversation.

He felt he understood now. It was the male suffering and degradation that triggered these women's sexual urges. The more he and his brothers suffered, the greater the women's pleasure.

They put his tail back on. They kept flicking at his cock to make him jump and jerk and shake his feathers.

They painted his cock with Ever-Up. This was a herb-based preparation that induced priapism. He was constantly erect, his cock painful and itchy.

He felt foul, despite having been hosed like a farm animal that morning. His invaded anus, his irritated erect prick, his sore wrists, his aching legs all combined to reduce him to a nadir of despair he had never believed he was capable of.

He wanted to be home with his wife.

He hung there. A woman bent over and reversed onto his jutting sex. She was laughing as she forced him to fill her. Another woman crouched at her feet. This woman put her fingers into the first woman's anus, before Rollo's horrified eyes. 'I can feel him,' she crowed. 'I can feel him in you.'

'Let me,' called another. 'I want to feel him in Marsa.' She came over and sank her fingers into the bent woman's anus, to feel Rollo's cock lying next door, in her pussy.

He could feel them too. He could feel their prodding fingers pressing on his cock where it lay, loaded in Marsa, like a bullet in a gun.

He didn't want it to go off, he thought dully. He didn't think he could control it.

The woman fingering Marsa pressed up against him. She was wearing a silky green toga-like garment. It was very short. When she moved, it could be seen that she wore nothing underneath.

She was a tall woman. Even so, she had to strain to put her face into his. Rollo pulled back, but movement was difficult. And futile.

Her lips were on his face, in his hair. 'Rollo,' she breathed. 'I'm a friend. I'm going to get you out of here.'

Maslow, Jermyn Ames and Fee spent the afternoon with a quiet policeman who asked persistent and detailed questions, recording their answers. They told him everything, including the kidnapping of Tony and how Ames and Maslow had interrogated him. Fee told him about Sandrina.

'Why did she agree to do this?' he asked.

'She has a sexual thing for Rollo,' said Fee coldly. 'She'll expect a reward.'

'A sexual reward?'

'That's right.'

Watching Fee, Maslow marvelled. She didn't care. She really didn't give a damn about other people's opinions. Heaven only knew what this policeman must be thinking of her.

'This sexual thing dates from her going to a party in the Zoo; then Mr Cambridge came across her, possibly by chance, singing in a casino in Level Verges.'

'That's her story,' said Maslow. 'Her behaviour is consistent with it.'

'Is she promiscuous?' asked the policeman.

'That's a value judgment,' said Fee.

'Then make it,' observed the policeman icily.

Fee shrugged. 'She was happy to copulate in public before strangers,' she said. 'She has or had a thing going with our friend Maslow here. She wants my husband so badly she could eat him. I guess you could say she's promiscuous.'

Jermyn Ames looked at Maslow uneasily. 'Is that right, about you and the dancer? You didn't tell me.'

'It makes no difference,' said Maslow. He was furious with Fee. 'I've had her too,' he said brutally. 'It doesn't alter the investigation.'

The policeman turned neutral eyes on Fee. 'Do you confirm that, Ms Cambridge?'

'That I've had sex with Maslow here or that it's made no difference to the investigation?'

'Let's take them in turn.' The policeman's name was Guedo Sandar. He hadn't mentioned his rank.

'Certainly I've had it with Maslow. If we're talking value judgments, I'm definitely promiscuous.'

Ames covered his eyes. The terrible thing was, the more time he spent in Fee Cambridge's company, the better he liked her. She was a brilliant harlot, her mind as promiscuous and as active as her body. She had the rare quality of forcing judgments about her to be on her own terms.

'And certainly it's made a difference to the investigation. I seduced him in order to extract the information he held on how I was to get Sandrina into this moralist sect. I didn't want him to realise he was being pumped so I sort of mixed it in.' Fee smiled blandly.

They were in Maslow's offices. Sandar stood up. 'I'll be in touch,' he said. He turned to Fee. 'You'll let me know if the girl makes contact.'

'Of course.'

He watched her for a moment. 'Don't play games with me,' he said.

Fee was genuinely startled. 'I'm not.'

'If I'm to get your husband and any other poor bastard these women are holding out, I'll need your fullest, frankest assistance.'

'It's yours,' said Fee stiffly.

'No private clever games on the side. You won't know the details of our operation and you could easily screw it up.'

'I understand.' Fee was furious.

Sandar watched her. 'We have no assurance that your husband is with these women. We will be pursuing other avenues.'

'I'm not stupid.'

For a moment, Maslow thought Sandar was going to smile. There was the slightest tightening of the muscles around his mouth. 'I didn't think you were, Ms Cambridge,' he said softly and left them.

Tony said: 'Sister, the men asked me questions.'

'Tell us the questions, little brother.'

'About Saturday. What you had planned. They said they were policemen. They were sympathetic. But the Zoo has a lot of influence and they have to look good. They didn't want to interfere.'

'So what did you say, little brother?' The sister's voice was caressing.

'I said I didn't know. There were rumours about pets. About donations, public confessions.'

'And?'

'Castrations,' whispered Tony.

The sister said softly. 'You've been a bad boy, Tony.'

'No, sister.'

'You've said things, Tony brother.'

'Please, sister. They said they wanted to help.'

'What shall we do, Tony?'

Tony began to sob.

The sister clapped her hands. 'I know,' she said. 'I think we need a little operation.'

Tony lifted his face. He was dead white and tear-streaked. 'No,' he whimpered. 'I'm not ready yet. I will be, I promise. But not yet.'

'Just a little operation,' said the sister gaily. 'You can have a starring role on Saturday.'

Tony stopped blubbering. 'On the platform?' he whispered.

'On the platform. With the others.'

Rollo lost track of time. Days were passing. Days had passed. Weeks. His life before this was becoming remote. TransFlow. Fee. The Zoo.

The woman who had whispered in his ear came to him again. That night when he was in his cage, she joined in a game of poking him through the bars with pointed sticks. Backing away from one group of tormentors, he found

181

himself caught and held against the side of his cage by another. Something was thrust into his rear while he struggled helplessly.

Afterwards, lying on his filthy straw, he cleared it out. The thin plastic tube had a slip of paper rolled tightly inside it. *Your cage will be unlocked tonight*, it said.

There was a timelock on the cage. Instead of releasing at the usual morning hour, Rollo found himself free at midnight.

He slid from his cage. He was alarmed at how frightened he was, how weak he felt. He seemed to have as little courage as he had strength.

The cages were underground somewhere, in old stone passages. Rollo could do nothing to release the other inmates, and was reluctant to stir them up. He flitted past on bare feet, a shadow in the gloom.

There appeared to be no electronic surveillance, which he thought odd. He went on, feeling his way, desperate to find an exit.

Some women walked past, laughing loudly. Rollo shrank into deeper shadow and waited.

He went on. The stone was cold and gritty under his feet. The soles had hardened all this long time without shoes. Just as well.

He came to a large metal door. It appeared to be bolted rather than locked. With the sweat standing out on his brow, and his body shivering in the dank cold of the cellarlike tunnels, Rollo began to ease back the bolts.

It took a long time. They squeaked and he tried to lubricate them with spittle. At last he swung the door open.

He slid through it into total darkness. He couldn't see anything. It was warm, a lapping warmth that beat against his cold flesh. He shivered nervously and began to edge away from the door.

He heard a soft moaning noise. His flesh began to creep. It was such a little noise, there, in the dark.

He had the sense of being in a large area, high roofed. He stood still, listening for the little noise.

It came again. His flesh crawled with nervous anticipation. It was a horrible noise, the sound of something suffering.

He moved sideways again. The darkness was impenetrable and little lights flashed on his retina as his brain invented images.

The wall he touched was soft. Warm. Yielding. *Alive.*

He could not contain his grunt of shock. He felt a terrific buffet and he fell forward. He went over an edge into space. He never knew whether his voice worked, but every nerve in his body screamed. He hit something thick and muffling. He began to sink.

Lights sprang on everywhere. He was in a pit, in some thick pink gooey stuff that offered no purchase but was too sticky for him to swim in.

He was sinking. Drowning. Around him, around the edges of the pit, stood the women.

He had long ago realised that there were only twenty or so, usually less at any one moment as they came and went. Now almost all of them were gathered. This was spectacular entertainment.

The woman who had pretended to be his friend, Felicia, was there, clapping her hands.

They were playing with him. The monstrous, horrible witches were playing with him. There was no escape. They had deliberately raised his hopes to lead him to walk into this filth.

He was drowning in it. His chest heaved as he struggled to keep his head above the sucking, sticky surface. The faces loomed over him, gleeful, full of malice.

Rollo's head went back in an effort to keep his face out of the stuff. 'Help me,' he roared, in a final despairing plea.

A rope landed by him. Convulsively he pulled an arm free and grabbed it.

'You have to beg,' called someone.

Rollo got a second hand on the rope. He saw one of the women was standing with a knife. 'Beg,' she shouted.

'Help me,' said Rollo hoarsely. The rope was attached to a winch. They were winching him in, if the knife-woman would let them.

'Beg harder,' she snarled.

His arm muscles strained. His chin was in the stuff. 'I'm begging you to save my life,' he said. The words were muffled at the end, as some of the pink stuff went into his mouth.

The rope pulled him. He lifted his head up as he came onto his stomach.

'Keep begging,' insisted the knife-woman. The winch stopped and Rollo, almost lying flat in the pink stuff, immediately began to sink.

'Please, sister, please help me,' begged Rollo. The tears in his eyes were for his shame, not his danger.

'Keep it up.'

Rollo kept it up. The winch worked, the rope pulled him and he moved towards the edge of the pit. He saw as he begged, as he was pulled, that one of the women sat in a chair grand enough to be called a throne. Her legs were apart. Between them Melissa knelt. Or was it Melissa-twin? The girl kissed and sucked her sister-mistress, the cult queen, while Rollo chose between drowning or begging for his life. Death or humiliation. Rollo paid the price for life.

Now he lay on the edge of the pit, exhausted. Using the rope to steady him, he began to climb out. He couldn't stand, he could only lie there, covered in muck, trembling and shamed.

He lifted his head to look into the face of his chief torturer. Her face was blazing. As he looked bitterly at her, her breasts flushed, and little noises issued from her mouth. His degradation was her triumph. She was in climax.

The following day Rollo was forced to parade up and down the hall with his tail feathers in place, which wobbled amusingly as he walked. If he stopped or tried to deviate from the allowed path, the sisters corrected him by activating the painmakers implanted in his body.

He knew things now. They were lesbians. They were man-haters. There were about twenty of them in total. They occupied a small area in a large building. They had some rooms, the hall, a swimming pool and gymnasium and the cellarage underneath. It must be an old building.

He saw no daylight.

There were about six male prisoners in total, but there was never an opportunity to speak. The others seemed in as bad a condition as Rollo.

Then one man went over. He begged to be allowed to help the women. He offered his strength for their entertainment.

The women enjoyed his mental capitulation. They rewarded him by removing four of his five implants, his painmakers.

They weren't entirely lesbian, and they clothed him and fed him till he felt better. Then they made him perform.

He was eager. He showed them what a man could do with his cock. They liked to see him spunk, and they encouraged him to lay on performances for them.

He obliged. The other men, dirty, exhausted, kept like brutes, watched.

Peto became the sect servant. He liked to lie among the women when they took their ease. They enjoyed him playing with their sex before they took pleasure from each other. He would tease and tantalise their vulvas while they chatted. They would then consummate their lust with each other, with Peto encouraging them and applauding.

It was Peto who came up with the idea of armed combat. 'Gladiators,' he said, clapping his hands gleefully. 'Why don't you make them fight each other?'

The cult queen asked: 'To what end, Peto? For what purpose?'

'To the death,' said Peto. 'Let them fight to the death. The one who wins could be rewarded. It would be entertaining to watch.'

Rollo, listening dumbly with the other prisoners, played his last card. 'Queen,' he called.

She lifted her head and looked past Peto, past the reclining women, to Rollo, chained with his tail feathers bobbing cheerfully from his impaled anus. 'I hear you,' she said.

'I am a wealthy man. A very wealthy man. I run a vast business empire. I live in the Zoo. I own a Connet. You could ransom me for untold wealth.'

The queen laughed. 'You are unhinged,' she said. 'No one important is missing. There is no search for someone lost from the Zoo. You were picked up as street scum, sour with drink. No one looks for you, Rollo-from-nowhere. This is a delusion.' She tittered. 'One would almost think you were not enjoying your time as our visitor.'

'All visits,' said Rollo, 'have a natural ending. I feel I have outstayed my welcome.'

'I'm so sorry you feel that,' said the queen. 'We must allow you to be the first to play Peto's game. What would be your preferred choice of weapon? Sword? Trident and net? That lovely spiked ball on the end of a chain? Think on these things, Rollo Zooman. We are impatient for our treat.'

Rollo stared at her across the laughing women, and the quisling Peto.

For the first time he thought seriously about death.

8

'There's a journalist on the line,' said Fee's personal assistant. She was sitting blankly in her office, trying to work.

Her kneejerk response was to deny her presence. Then she remembered wearily their vulnerability. She had better make sure that who ever it was had no clue as to what was going on.

'Put him on,' she said.

'Her, ma'am. It's a Richelle Matthews.'

Fee's interest sharpened. When the vidi screen lit up, she watched it alertly.

'Ms Cambridge?'

'Ms Matthews. We met at the Castel d'Amour not long ago. How can I help you?'

'I'm very gratified to get through to you so easily,' said Richelle. Fee felt a trickle of ice down her spine. It was hard to behave as if things were normal. She would have had her PA get details at any other time. Richelle was so smart she was already smelling a rat.

She kept quiet. Better to let the other woman lead.

'May I ask for a personal meeting?' asked Richelle.

'For what purpose?'

'I don't feel I can say anything over the vidi.'

Fee considered. 'You expect me to take you on trust?'

'That's what I'm asking.' Richelle was calm.

She had a right to be. She was a top lady in her field, that of investigative journalism, as was Fee in hers. Fee might have the wealth and the social position, but in terms of their achievements, they were equals.

'At my home?' asked Fee with raised eyebrows.

'Or mine. We need guaranteed privacy.'

'You're attempting to blackmail me.'

Richelle smiled. 'I don't think so,' she said gently.

'Is it personal or business?' asked Fee.

'Personal mostly,' said Richelle. 'For you, that is. It's business for me.'

She came that evening. Her first action was to use a scanner to sweep the apartment.

'We're bugged,' she observed to Fee.

'Did you expect otherwise?'

'Of course not. Switch it off for the moment and scan yourself. I want you to be sure I'm not bugging you.'

'My my,' said Fee mildly.

'You'll see why in a minute,' said Richelle.

Fee made them both a drink and the woman sat down warily. Richelle began.

'I've been interviewed by a private investigator called Maslow concerning the cult female groups that have sprung up in the town in recent times.'

'You're considered the expert,' murmured Fee.

'Not without cause. I've made it my special study, and I've related their extremism to the growing sexual prudery of the mass of the town population. This isn't restricted to our town. This is a continent-wide thing.'

There weren't many towns nowadays, but each one was huge. It was hard sometimes not to develop a city-state mentality. Yet life went on elsewhere on the planet in much the same way.

'You see a dichotomy,' said Fee easily. 'The weirdos can't be accommodated in mainstream society anymore, because it's too proper, too narrow-minded, sexually speaking. So they get even more extreme and make little cult groups all over the place.'

'That's my thesis,' said Richelle. 'I see them as the product of the decline in public sexual activity among the generality of people, not its cause.'

'Correct me if I'm wrong,' said Fee maliciously, 'but you see the town's increasing disapproval of sex for pleasure fired in part by the Zoo's naughtiness in these matters, don't you?'

'I do not believe that the Zoo has ever before been so extreme and so overt about its sexual activity.'

'Is this what brings you here today, Ms Matthews?'

'Call me Richelle. I'm no enemy to you or the Zoo. I analyse and draw conclusions. I don't judge.'

Fee stayed politely silent. She could feel the bite was coming.

'I've been interviewed by the police now,' said Richelle. 'Same subject. What they want to know is whether any of these groups is dangerous to men.'

'Are they?' asked Fee.

'In my opinion, yes. And dangerous to the Zoo, as well.'

Fee thought about the demonstration she had become involved in. Richelle was right. There was a smell of violence in the air.

'It occurred to me,' said Richelle, 'that Maslow's refusal to reveal his client, and the refusal of the police to say what it was all about, were because someone was being protected. Some big name. Someone is under threat.'

Fee was impassive.

'A man, obviously,' said Richelle. 'I thought about it a bit. Maslow knew you. I thought that was surprising.'

'School,' murmured Fee. 'I have very humble origins, you know.'

'I do know. More humble than Maslow's, actually. And not the same school. You shared no years in education together.'

Fee stayed silent.

'I was taxed to know how a man like Maslow might be on nodding acquaintance with Fee Cambridge, the first lady of the Zoo. An acquaintanceship, moreover, they both lied about.'

'Maybe you are investing this with a significance it lacks,' said Fee.

'Maybe indeed. We shall see. I decided to check up on the whereabouts of your husband, Rollo Cambridge, chief executive of TransFlow.'

'It wouldn't be difficult. Rollo is a public man.'

'It was very difficult. He hadn't been seen in public for a month. He'd dropped right out of view.'

'He's in a clinic,' said Fee. 'Ligamental damage. I visit him daily. Your research is a little on the weak side, Ms Matthews.'

'If something awful has happened to Rollo Cambridge,' said Richelle, 'I wondered why it wasn't in the public domain. Executives have heart trouble. Their marriages collapse. They get caught with their hands in the till. They fiddle tax. It all comes out. But nothing was coming out about Rollo Cambridge, nothing at all. Not from his business, not from his wife, not from his friends and colleagues and associates, not from any governmental source. The whole shooting match was as tight-lipped or as ignorant as could be.'

'Perhaps because there is nothing to hide,' said Fee.

'TransFlow is about to make a very sensitive, very important market move. I refer to the new rights issue. The financial sector believes TransFlow is going for the Con-Comm franchise, which would be very hot news and would boost TransFlow's shares just as the new issue was launched. That's one side of the equation. The other side is that you know a private investigator, a very senior one. He interviewed me concerning the danger to men from extreme female cults. The police have interviewed me along the same lines, including how to infiltrate such a group. Your husband has dropped out of sight. You know what I think, Ms Cambridge? I think you're in deep trouble. Deep, deep trouble. And everyone is so concerned with saving TransFlow's ass that your husband is going to the wall.'

Fee sat tight, a roaring in her ears. 'Are you going to print this made-up filth?' she asked eventually.

'Can you give me any proof that Rollo Cambridge is safe and well at this particular moment?'

'I don't think I need do that.'

'It would bring my house of cards tumbling down. Surely you would want that. It costs you nothing.'

Fee stood up. She went over to the vidi. She called the clinic.

'Patch me through to Mr Cambridge's suite,' she said.

'Tell him I have a journalist with me who doesn't believe he is suffering from strained ligaments.'

They saw the blond man with bright blue eyes lying on a bed, apparently flicking through company documents.

'Is this important, Fee?' his voice came impatiently. 'I'm due for a physio session.'

'It's not important, honey,' said Fee. 'I'll be over later.' She cut the connection and turned to face Richelle. 'I think you'd better leave,' she said.

'A voice synthesiser,' said Richelle softly. 'A smoker. Why all the secrecy? Is the ransom so large you can't pay? I didn't think these groups were interested in money. They aren't criminal in that sense. They aren't extortionists. What the hell is going on?'

'Get out,' said Fee. 'You've had what you came for.'

Richelle stood up and walked over to the vidi. She dialled the clinic, her long fingers reaching under the machine.

They saw again the receptionist listen, nod and smile. Then they saw the blond man with the bright blue eyes lying on his bed, flicking through documents. 'Is this important, Fee?' he said again, impatiently. 'I'm due for a physio session.'

'Neat,' she observed. 'You cut it in manually after the clinic number has been dialled. You never get through to the clinic, of course.' She looked at Fee.

Fee looked as though she was carved in ice.

'You poor woman,' said Richelle softly. 'What the hell have they made you do?'

Very slowly, very slightly at first, Fee began to quiver. Her face worked. Suddenly she bowed her head. Her shoulders shook. She made no noise as she sat there, crying, crying for her lost husband.

She gave in to her grief. Everything in her turbulent nature rebelled at her inaction over the loss of Rollo. It was totally alien to her character to sit back and do nothing. The strain of the past month on her focused and came to a dreadful climax.

It was some time before she became aware that Richelle was holding her, stroking her hair back, helping her wipe

191

her eyes. She lifted her ravaged face and looked into the face of the woman who had penetrated her secret and, she believed, held Rollo's life in her hands. She looked and was astonished.

There was no doubting the expression on Richelle's face. It held both compassion and yearning.

All of a sudden Fee gave way completely. All her barriers dropped. She faced Richelle nakedly. 'I can't make it without him,' she said hoarsely.

'I understand. I'm willing to help you get him back, if it lies within my power.'

'Why?' said Fee.

'Don't you know?'

For a long moment, Richelle held Fee's gaze. Then she leant in towards her. She wiped the last traces of tears from Fee's face. Slowly she took her face between her two hands. She leant into Fee. She kissed her on the lips.

Fee liked women. She felt no repulsion. Richelle was a beautiful woman, strong and sexy. She was not accustomed to being in anyone's power, but for the moment it was a release. She had had too much to bear. She felt as though Richelle had lifted the responsibility from her shoulders.

She began to respond to the embrace. Richelle put her arms around her and drew Fee into her. The women clung to one another, kissing each other deeply, exploring their mouths and tongues and lips.

As fear left her, so desire came in its train. Richelle held her by the nape of her neck, under her hair, kissing her face, her eyelids, her jaw, her cheekbones. Her other hand sought to release Fee's clothing and touch her breast.

Fee's breathing came harder. She didn't usually submit and let another take the lead. Now it seemed good to let Richelle do as she pleased. She lay in the journalist's arms and allowed her clothes to be opened.

She lay right back feeling Richelle's lips on her breasts. This was a wanton luxury. Her body became soft and open. Richelle took a nipple into her mouth and sucked and stretched it, lengthening it till she could tongue it and kiss it and suck it to her heart's desire.

Fee's clothes fell away from her. She felt Richelle's hair on her belly and thighs. A moment later she felt fingers questing between her legs. She moaned slightly and opened them further.

She had to clench her fists, the sensation in her vulva was so exquisite. Richelle was kissing her clitoris and at the same time was delicately plucking her sex-flesh and teasing it to erection. Her fingers sought softly. Then they were sharp as she used her nails to scrape at Fee's tenderised flesh.

Fee felt herself warm and wet. Richelle had taken tresses of her own coppery auburn hair and was tenderly rubbing the entrance to Fee's bottom, the entrance to her womb, with the silky material. Fee felt her orifices enlarge. Now there were lips at her anus, delicately kissing her there. Now there were lips at her pussy, kissing and licking and sucking it till she quivered inside, and felt her stomach tighten as her orgasm grew to fruition.

Richelle scratched Fee's arse with a long red fingernail. At the same time she progressed in nibbling bites along the edge of Fee's labia. Her free hand was flat on Fee's belly, pressing so that the skin drew tight over Fee's sexual mound, which in turn stimulated her sensitive clitoris.

Fee bucked slightly as she approached orgasm. She felt Richelle's teeth butting at her pussy entrance. The finger at her rear penetrated her and pressed against the membranes between her cunt and her arse. Richelle's tongue snaked into her vagina. The pressure on her belly increased. A thumb touched her clitoris and Fee exploded into climax.

Richelle lapped lazily at Fee, enjoying the nectar of orgasm. 'You are the most beautiful woman I've ever made love to,' she said.

'You like women?' asked Fee drowsily.

'Special women. Beautiful women. Like you.'

'What about men?'

'They don't appeal.'

Fee sat up. Richelle had her blouse undone, and her rounded rich breasts were jutting out. Fee bent her head and kissed their creamy plump curves. 'Come to bed,' she begged. 'I want to return the favour.'

193

'You owe me nothing,' Richelle was positive. 'The pleasure was mine.'

Fee kissed her tenderly on the lips. 'I want to make love with you,' she said huskily.

'Then we shall,' said Richelle, and they moved into the bedroom.

Fee explored Richelle's sweet, rich body at a leisurely pace. Suddenly there seemed to be all the time in the world. Her rounded belly, the warm column of her thighs, her full, soft breasts, her mysterious woman's smell. Fee opened the long thighs and looked with delight on the mysteries within. She put her velvet mouth to Richelle's divine rift and kissed and sucked till the musk ran sweet for her.

They stroked each other's mounds and kissed each other's breasts, their breaths mingling, their hair confused in a tangle of black and copper silk, their eyes and minds only for each other.

For the first time since she knew he was missing, Fee forgot Rollo. She was in a different country and it had rare, rich fruits. The wine of the country ran down her chin and she was intoxicated.

The door's buzzer sounded. Fee stirred warm limbs, soft and muddled in with Richelle's. 'Damn,' she said softly.

Richelle laughed. 'You'd better see to it,' she said.

Fee slid into a robe and went to her door. 'Who is it?' she asked languorously.

'Guedo Sandar.'

'Can you come back? It isn't convenient.'

'Let me in, Ms Cambridge.' His voice was hard.

Fee sighed and released the door. Sandar slid in.

His eyes took in the love-drugged woman at once. The disarray of her clothes, her tumbled hair, her pale face and sleep-soft eyes, all told their own tale. She smelt of sex, too. Sandar felt the hairs rise on the back of his neck. Fee was warm, liquid desire incarnate.

She leant on the wall. 'What is it?' she murmured. Her lips curved at the thought of what lay next door. Of who lay next door, waiting for her.

'What's going on?' he said abruptly. 'Who's here?'

'None of your goddam business.' Fee pushed hair out of her eyes. Her robe slipped and Sandar could see the curve of one long, fascinating breast.

'Your husband's missing and you're having sex with someone. It is my business,' he said. 'Is it Dupique?'

'Perhaps you ought to know,' said Fee. She led Sandar to her bedroom door and motioned him through.

The voluptuous nakedness of the woman on the bed distracted him. He was an ascetic man, not given to much carnal indulgence, though he savoured what he did have. He saw the profusion of copper hair. He saw the long, white body richly full at hip and breast. The heavy fall of the ripe breasts distracted him as well. He couldn't tell the precise colour of the nipples in the low, seductive lighting.

He could tell the colour of the sexual fleece though. It was a dark, rich red.

His blood pounded. He turned to look at Fee striving to keep his face neutral. The images evoked by the two women twisting and turning together as they pleasured their sexual zones was strong. It made him groan inside. 'Richelle Matthews,' he said. 'I think I should have known this before.'

Richelle stirred and pulled the cover over her body. Fee moved out of the room, drawing Sandar after her. She sat down on a couch careless of her slipping robe. 'This didn't exist before, Mr Policeman,' she said. 'If I have to account for my personal sex life, I would time this aspect of it from around six this evening. Do you want to know how often we've made each other come to climax?'

'She's a journalist.'

'She's one smart lady. She's guessed most of what has happened. She doesn't know any details because I've told her nothing.'

'I can vouch for that,' said Richelle. She stood naked, leaning on the doorframe, like a Rubens' painting. She looked marvellous.

Sandar looked from one woman to the other. They were ignoring him, their eyes on each other. Fee's robe slipped further. There was a powerful sexual tension in the air.

195

'You mustn't tell her anything,' he said to Fee. His breathing was laboured.

'I might be able to help,' said Richelle. 'I know a lot about these groups you are so interested in.'

'Why should you help?' Sandar was brutal. 'Your loyalties lie elsewhere.'

'Personal reasons,' said Richelle, her gaze never wavering.

'You're screwing the man's wife.' His voice was full of loathing. 'Why help get him back?'

'The wife wants it.' Richelle's voice was soft. 'And I want the wife.'

Fee stood up. She swayed across to Richelle. Her robe slipped off her shoulders and fell to the floor.

Sandar, watching, saw the two naked women meet and press their bodies together. He saw their lips join. He heard them kiss, saw them wind tightly together, their arms going around each other.

His heart thudded dully. His forehead was greasy. He let himself out of the apartment.

He was aware he wanted to stay.

To strengthen her ability to resist men, Sandrina was taken to the hall of temptation. In her imagination, she had assumed it to be some kind of reverse harem. She would walk through the men laying at their elegant ease, tempting her with soft music, ripe fruit, knowledgeable hands and strong, sweet bodies. They would try to seduce her with soft delights; she would resist, knowing that to resist gave its own sharp pleasure, its strong reward.

It was nothing like that at all. The pets were all lined up like meat. They had been arranged to lie back on tables, their legs bent at the knees on the edge of the table so that their feet hung down.

Over their bodies at chest level, screens were fixed. Sandrina had no way of seeing their faces. This disconcerted her seriously. She felt she was seeing most of the pets belonging to the organisation, and here they all were without her being able to tell if Rollo Cambridge was among them.

She was one of five girls all in the hall together. Her problem was to identify Rollo solely from his lower body. The men, of course, were naked.

She found she didn't like seeing men this way. It reduced them to their sex organs, nothing more. On every side she saw naked nestling penises in their individual clouds of hair. If this was supposed to tempt her, it was way off beam.

Perhaps it was meant to disgust her. It certainly came nearer to arousing that emotion than any other.

The other girls didn't seem to be so squeamish. They were squealing with delight, perfectly happy to touch the pets. Indeed, they made a point of playing with the male sex organs laid out on the slab for them. They picked them up. They tickled them. One girl daringly kissed the cock she held. In fact, the girls blatantly attempted to arouse the men.

Sandrina felt frantic. There were at least seven blond men. Two of these looked too weedy to be Rollo. She didn't know his body well, but she had examined him that night in her apartment when he was unconscious with drink. She had stripped him and considered him naked. He had a flat, muscled belly. His thighs were strong with visible thews. His waist was neat and firm.

If she touched the possible men here in this dreadful hall, would she be able to tell if it was Rollo she was touching? Would the magic somehow survive the appalling conditions so that she would feel the thrill of his flesh?

She went over to one man, the most likely, she thought. Sister Jessamine was pulling on his cock like it was made of particularly tough elastic.

'Not that way,' said Sandrina, suddenly impatient. She took the abused organ from Jessamine's clumsy hands. She stroked it gently, lifting it and squeezing it. She cradled the man's testicles and fondled them. As his cock began to swell, she moved the foreskin back a little. She caressed the man and began carefully to masturbate him.

Jessamine was sulky. 'Anyone would think you enjoyed it,' she said.

'I don't enjoy cleaning my apartment,' snapped Sandrina. 'That doesn't stop me from doing it properly.' She let go of the cock she held. Was it Rollo's? She had better feel some of the others.

She remembered all that time ago in the Zoo party. She remembered the men having their cocks painted with liquid silk. She remembered the hot thrill she had had watching the men, so unselfconscious in their nakedness. She had yearned to make free with their sex.

Now she could, but the thrill was gone. She wondered why that was. Was it something to do with those powerful and rich Zoo men displaying themselves for pleasure, as against these submissive, obedient and doglike pets, who served the New Moralists so eagerly, so much to their own disadvantage? The one was a turn-on, the other a turn-off.

Looking round at these men, it was plain they didn't mind their humiliating position one bit. Maybe they found this blind testing of their sex exciting. A perk of the job. Most of them were erect now, and the girls giggled and played with them freely.

Sandrina chose another golden-haired male and began to play with his swollen organ. Her memory told her Rollo was special, but then this man was very nice. How much had she seen Rollo's sex? Never erect. It had been inside a woman at the party when he had kissed her. He had been slack in his drunkenness when she stripped him on her couch. The following morning, when he had taken her with that swift and brutal rapacity, she hadn't even see the golden ravager. He had put it in and yanked it out as soon as it had released its load.

She burned at the memory. Curious how desperately she wanted Rollo considering how badly he had treated her. Having him was what she wanted. The conditions didn't matter. Suffering all that she was suffering now would earn her access to Rollo. She didn't doubt Fee's word on the matter.

Would he want her? Would he be kind? Would he be cold?

She became aware that the male she handled was very close to orgasm. Whatever this hall was supposed to do to

198

make her hate men, it certainly didn't include failing to make them come. The other girls were laughing hard as they took their men over the top.

Who was this man, this anonymous man. Was he handsome? Was he brave? Was he exciting? Unlikely.

Was he a prisoner? If he was a prisoner, how did the sisters enforce this sort of passive behaviour?

Suddenly Sandrina felt cold. She had no idea what was happening to the other end of the man with whom she toyed sexually. He could be strapped to the bench he lay on, for all she knew. He could be hooded and gagged. He could be threatened ... No. If these men were being seriously threatened, not any amount of tickling play would bring about the response they were showing.

'Go on,' said Lirinda. 'Take him all the way.'

'Why are we pleasuring them?' asked Sandrina. The cock in her hand was hot and bulging with excitement.

'It's part of their reward.'

'Reward?'

'For what they're giving up.' Lirinda looked at Sandrina as though she were lacking slightly in her wits.

'Because they're pets, you mean?'

'No, silly. Because of what's happening on Saturday. At the rally.'

Sandrina bent over the man she held and stroked gently. She smiled at Lirinda. 'Saturday?' she said. 'What's so special?'

'All the pets here have agreed to be fitted with discs.'

Sandrina's smile grew wider, more dreamy. 'Discs?' she said softly, though she knew what they were.

Lirinda chuckled. 'Penis discs. Clamped round their cocks. Right here,' she added playfully, touching Sandrina's man where the foreskin joined the stem of his cock. 'So they'll have no more hand-fucky like we're giving them today, and no more pussy-fucky. They're taking a vow, see. No more naughties.'

Sandrina moved her hand sharply. The man's hips jerked and he shot creamy spunk from his urgent climaxing sex.

* * *

For two days he had a room to himself with bathroom attached, good food and peace. Rollo found it almost worse. The women's enjoyment came from treating their human toys with malice aforethought. They liked to see their prisoners suffer. Their pleasure was in sadism.

Now he was well-treated. He had the sensation of being fattened up for the slaughter so strongly that sometimes it seemed to him he could smell burning flesh.

They fed him lavishly, at regular times. On the second day Rollo struck his leg so sharply the calf bled. This happened only some ten minutes before a meal.

He asked the female who brought his food for antiseptic salve and Newskin. She was eager to help. This concern for his body was even more alarming.

She came back with the products he had requested. He cleansed the wound and sprayed Newskin over it, sealing it and promoting the rapid growth of his own natural skin.

He had failed to find any surveillance operating in these old rooms and corridors. He suspected the cult lacked money for a serious level of property investment, and that these premises were so antiquated they came cheap. No one would interfere with a tenant willing to accept so little. The women could do as they pleased.

Rollo lay on the bed and willed himself to relax. He practised what psychological techniques he knew, which were pitifully few. One of his hands gripped a metal spoon tightly. He had no knife and fork, only this blunt thing.

He drew a sharp breath and stabbed himself in the shoulder. He stabbed himself again. Then he tore into his grazed and broken flesh with the spoon. With his teeth clenched so hard his gums hurt, his eyes squeezing against a weakness of tears, he dug his fingers into the agony of the wound and scrabbled.

Sweat stood out on his forehead, while his body shuddered convulsively. He pried into raw and bloody flesh till he felt the little silicon wafer. He pulled the bloody thing out and pressed a prepared pad to his self-inflicted wound.

After a moment or two he walked shakily into the bath-

200

room. Here he washed the wound. He applied salve and then he sprayed the bleeding mess with Newskin.

Within an hour the pain had reduced to a dull bruised ache. Rollo had managed to free himself of three more implants in that time. The actual wound sites were the least of his worries. The whole of his body, tensed in the knowledge of the pain, felt on fire. His muscles burned. Yet he was cold. He had blankets on the bed and he huddled in them shivering, bowed down by his sense of failure.

He had dealt with his left shoulder, his right hip, his left and his right legs. It was dealing with his hip, the implant that had caused his pain during congress, that had left him so weak. Now he could not bring himself to take out the implant in his right arm. He needed to use his left and it felt clumsy and weak. His wholy body was in shock. He knew he had to get the last painmaker out but he couldn't do it, he couldn't bring himself to do it.

He lay in the bed racked with pain and felt a mental torture that was worse. He had failed. He was a coward. He couldn't stand the pace.

The next day his misery was interrupted. One of the sisters came to see him. All the sisters carried the little triggers by which they could control their large, strong, male prisoners. They wore tiny pads fixed to their bodies somewhere, anywhere that pleased them, and they pressed the pad in the appropriate section to trigger the nearest painmaker. It was also possible to tune the painmakers to respond to one frequency only. Rollo suspected they had done this because none of the sisters seemed to be afraid of being alone with any of the men.

'My name is Jye,' she said. She wore a floorlength apricot robe. Rollo noticed how she had the dead eyes of the sisters. It was a thing they shared in common. What woke them up, bringing sparks to their eyes and a flush to their skin, was pain. Pain inflicted on other sentient beings.

'I bring you these things,' said Jye. She handed them over to Rollo.

He had been given a pair of leather briefs. There were two wide straps designed to go across his chest from shoulder to hip. There were also leather gaiters for his lower legs and a close-fitting leather helmet for his head, with a brilliant red plume as a crest.

'I'd like to spank your backside,' he said softly.

The pain in his arm was a spear of fire. As he jerked and held himself against a repeat, he realised it was as well he had one painmaker left. Had he failed to react just then Jye would have had him investigated.

'Kiss my feet,' said Jye.

'Damn you,' said Rollo. This time the pain was so fierce he actually went up into the air in his convulsive reaction.

'Kiss my feet,' said Jye.

He rolled off the bed and crawled, whimpering, across the floor. He bent down as she lifted the hem of her garment, and kissed her feet.

'Now bend over the bed,' said Jye.

Rollo obeyed.

Jye took one of the leather chest straps. She struck Rollo sharply with it across his buttocks. She struck him again and again till the soreness filled him.

She stopped and he held himself, quivering, against the bed, waiting for whatever humiliation she next saw fit to impose. When it came, it could hardly have been worse.

She took a fistful of his blond hair and yanked his head back. She smiled down into his blue eyes. She pulled him back, away from the bed, and reached a hand down his front.

His cock, with a mind of its own, leapt to life.

Jye squatted by Rollo. He could smell her perfume as she must have been able to smell his sweat. Even this close, there was nothing he could do to her. She had command of him because she commanded his pain.

Now it seemed to please her that she commanded his sex. Her long sensitive fingers played with him. For a lesbian, she showed much knowledge of a man's needs in masturbation. She gazed dreamily into Rollo's eyes and there, kneeling on the floor, took him to climax.

She stood up and surveyed the man she had cowed, beaten and milked. Everything about her body language expressed her contempt for him. She turned on her heel and left the room.

Rollo faced the bed, still kneeling on the floor. When he turned his head and lifted it, he was smiling.

Sandrina felt frantic. Saturday was two days away. She still had no idea whether Rollo was one of the pets or not.

That night, she crept out of her dormitory and made her way to the pets' quarters. Most of them lived on the outside, she knew that. Some of the senior sisters lived on the outside too, broadcasting their message, engaging in the necessary propaganda war to cause their way of thinking to prevail.

Sandrina thought ruefully of her own position. She remembered her silent frenzy to get a man without admitting to her weakness for sex. She relived her humiliation at the hands of Rollo Cambridge. She thought on the different standards operating in the Zoo and the town.

Perhaps these women were right. It would be nice to have the itch cured, to settle down to her preferred life as a singer and dancer. Sex did cause such problems, so many jealousies, such agony in the emotions.

For all that, she needed to do this job now. If she didn't, she was sure Fee Cambridge would ruin her chances at the Castel d'Amour. The woman was a bitch, a sex-mad bitch, cold as charity and only happy when she was getting her claws into some poor man.

Sandrina giggled to herself. It would be good to get Fee stuck in this situation. She would like to think of her with a man-hater up her pussy, held in place by metal studs.

Sandrina let her fingers steal between her thighs. She had a matching pair of holes in her labia where the stud had fastened her. She knew that many of the sisters wore studs voluntarily. They could put them in and remove them at will. The sisters liked the feeling it gave them, of being in control of their own bodies.

Sandrina wriggled slightly. She might like to wear studs. The idea had become pleasing to her.

She had arrived at the pets' quarters. She stopped for a

moment to arrange the piece of cloth she was wearing as a hood. She activated the little communicator implant she had consented to having under her skin. She flung open the door and said in a loud, deep voice: 'Rollo Cambridge. If you are here, speak now. Quickly.'

The pets rolled over and woke from sleep in various states of confusion and dismay. 'Rollo,' said Sandrina desperately. 'You must speak.'

Fee heard the cry. Her sensing equipment had been activated, which in its turn had activated her pager. She hung her head and despaired. She felt caged and unable to go out. The press were besieging her vidi lines. Some fool Zooperson, some witless clown, had given an interview to the gutter press in the town. They had spilled all, even stuff Fee didn't know. It was all written down for anyone to read, their names and what they had done with each other, in explicit detail. A fair amount of it was simple fabrication, but even Fee found it hard to identify where truth ended and falsehood began.

The story made salacious reading. It concerned corporate heads, media barons, screen stars, a scattering of high government members, and the very very rich.

Half a dozen saucy parties between friends had been turned into what sounded like a massive and continuous sex-romp. The press implied that people in the Zoo hardly knew who their spouses were any more. It claimed they did it in the street, in shopping malls, on the moving walkways, everywhere. Hanging from the ceiling, thought Fee gloomily. This was publicity the Zoo could do without.

Her own name was mentioned, but because she was primarily a business woman and only secondarily a socialite, she received less attention than the screen stars and politicians.

It was inflammatory stuff, thought Fee, remembering that protest march. She shivered. *Rollo*, she thought. *Rollo*.

Richelle vidied her. 'Can I come into the Zoo and talk to you?' she asked urgently.

'Please, darling,' said Fee.

Richelle was admitted into the Zoo, Fee having issued the necessary instruction. She arrived some twenty minutes later, having travelled the moving walkways rather than take a taxi. This had given her time to calm herself.

Fee opened her house door and let Richelle in. The two women clung passionately to each other. Then Fee found Richelle's face from among her tumbling hair, smoothed it back, and kissed her full on the mouth.

It was a long seductive kiss, the soft, full mouths of the women pressing close while their tongues explored. They kissed with passion and knowledge.

Almost greedily, Fee kissed Richelle on her creamy throat while her hands fumbled with the other woman's clothes. A moment later she had exposed one rich ripe breast. Eagerly she bent her head so that her black hair fell all about the white flesh. She touched the point of the chestnut pink nipple with her tongue tip. Richelle moaned softly. Fee ran her tongue round the nipple till it shone wetly, and then she took it into her pursed lips and sucked gently. Her other hand went down and lifted the hem of Richelle's dress. She felt up the smooth thigh till she came to the crotch of her panties. She ran her nail along this so that the pressure was translated through the silky garment to tantalise Richelle's sex.

The nipple in her mouth lengthened and danced with Fee's pointed tongue. Fee rubbed Richelle's vulva through her panties more firmly. Richelle began to gasp and shudder. Her body quivered as intense emotion shook her. Fee sucked deeply so that the whole breast-tip went into her mouth, dragging the sumptuous flesh and stretching the skin. She scratched at Richelle's clitoris.

She had the response she sought. She felt Richelle's panties grow damp. The woman trembled as Fee controlled her climax.

At last she relaxed. She smiled weakly. 'I've only just got in the door,' she said.

'That's the best time,' murmured Fee, admiring the line of the exposed breast.

'I must talk to you,' said Richelle, suddenly remembering why she had come.

'Take some clothes off, darling.' Fee's voice was husky. 'You are so good to look at.'

She made Richelle lie down. She removed her damp panties and kissed them. Then she threw them to one side. She pulled up Richelle's skirt so that she could look on the long, pink, wriggling divide of her sex. Meanwhile Richelle adjusted her upper garment so that both her breasts spilled out.

Fee examined her with satisfaction. Richelle smiled. 'You give me such a feeling of freedom,' she confessed. 'With you, anything can be said, can be done. I've never felt so free from judgment. In the town, it's like a cloud now. It settles on you and blinds you. I feel suffocated and unnatural, permanently on guard.'

'You've had other lovers,' said Fee. She kissed Richelle on her inner thigh.

'Yes. But I've had to be so careful. So circumspect.'

'But I thought women were all the thing now.' Fee looked sly. 'Isn't that the point? It's men who are rejected.'

'It's sex for fun that's rejected. It's like the temperance movement. Drink leads to criminal behaviour, a lack of seriousness, an incapacity for hard work. For drink read sex.'

'I work very hard,' said Fee, and kissed Richelle's pussy.

'I know,' said Richelle softly. 'But the anti-sex movement has become confused with being anti-men; most of its adherents are women and men still want sex as much as ever. To reject men and still want sex, that's the most wicked thing of all.'

'So wicked,' agreed Fee, nibbling Richelle's clitoris.

'Mind you,' went on Richelle almost desperately, as the soft assault on her senses took more and more effect, 'human nature doesn't change, so I bet those women get up to all sorts of things behind closed doors.'

Fee stopped. 'The women in these extremist groups, you mean.'

Richelle realised what she had said. Fee believed she had a husband in the clutches of one of the extremist groups. She looked at her curiously. 'Despite all this,' she said, gesturing at the two of them and their intimate contact, 'you really care for a man?'

Fee sat back, robbing the move of hostility by sliding a finger inside Richelle's moist cunt. 'You haven't met Rollo,' she said. 'I like men anyway, I'm not ashamed to admit it, but Rollo is something special.'

'He's very good-looking,' Richelle sounded dubious.

'He's arrogant,' said Fee. 'He's strong. He's cruel. He's clever. He's fierce. He has an aura of power. I can orgasm just being in his company, knowing I can touch his panther-sleek body whenever I feel like it. He's my private playing field.'

'He puts it about,' said Richelle brutally.

'So do I. That doesn't stop me belonging to him nor him belonging to me.' Fee smiled, catlike. 'We've even shared our lovers before now.'

Richelle stared.

'Shared them,' emphasised Fee, 'simultaneously.'

'I came to tell you,' said Richelle abruptly. 'I've heard rumours.'

'What kind of rumours?'

'The New Moralists, they have this rally planned for Saturday, the day after tomorrow.'

'I know about this,' said Fee. Her face was hard.

'They are going to parade men for show, men prepared to have their sexual ability interfered with. For the cause,' added Richelle bitterly.

'Castration,' said Fee, spitting the word out.

Richelle was startled. 'As extreme as that? They just stuck a disc on that guy they snatched, the feelie bar manager, remember?'

'I remember,' said Fee.

'These men are supposed to be volunteers. Could Rollo be brainwashed into acting as though he was doing what he wanted to do?'

'No,' snapped Fee.

'They call them their pets. These men come and go.'

Fee thought of Tony, whom Ames and Maslow had picked up. He would be one of the pets.

207

'But men have disappeared recently in the town,' Richelle went on. 'Single men without many connections. Men about whom nobody cares very much. Drunks. No-goods.'

'What are you suggesting?'

'That they might have been snatched as playthings. There are rumours that the women have these men prisoner, to play with, to humiliate.'

Fee was white. 'What sort of credence do you give to such rumours?'

'Normally I'd reject them as salacious nonsense. There's an element of wish-fulfilment in such a rumour that screams fantasy and fabrication. Women want to harm men, have them under their thumb, and then rumours to that effect start up. It's a catharsis, really.'

'Not when it's true.'

'It might be true,' conceded Richelle. 'It is a fact that men have vanished. Someone must be holding them unless they have all gone to another town, but even then, by this time, they would have turned up on the computers.'

'Do you know,' asked Fee carefully, 'who might be holding these men? Which specific group and where?'

'I don't know anything. But the rumours are supposed to emanate from a group calling themselves the Sisters of Pain.'

'Sado-masochism,' said Fee flatly.

'Mostly sadism,' said Richelle. 'The masochistic tendency is very limited.'

Fee moaned faintly. Then, with an obvious effort, she pulled herself together. 'Can I get inside?' she asked. 'Tell me how to infiltrate them.'

'Darling.' Richelle put a hand on Fee's arm. 'With your looks, you are far too well-known.'

'I could disguise myself,' said Fee desperately.

'There's another solution.'

'We could bust them. Send in the police.' Fee was eager.

'It's your choice,' said Richelle.

'I don't understand. Do you have some other suggestion?'

'I could join the Sisters of Pain,' said Richelle.

'You,' said Fee stupidly. 'But you must be their enemy. You expose these groups.'

'I write about them and I discuss what trends in society bring them about,' corrected Richelle. 'I've never explicitly attacked them. How do you think I get my material?'

'Tell me.' Fee was grim.

'I have friends. People prepared to talk to me. Connections.'

'Why? Why do they do it?'

'Some are disgruntled. Some are rejected. Some are frightened. Some want to put their point of view across. All sorts of reasons. Some I pay.'

Fee considered. Information had a quality, and it seemed to her that Richelle's lacked quality control.

'I cross-check,' added Richelle, uncannily reading Fee's mind. 'I'm an experienced journalist, you know.'

'I still don't see how you could join these people.'

'I have a friend, an ex-lover,' said Richelle. 'She is a member.'

'She would get you in?'

'Yes. She owes me a favour and she's wanting out herself. That isn't easy, apparently. The Sisters have ways of controlling their members. She wants me to help her escape. I've said I can do this best from the inside.'

'They wouldn't object to having you?'

Richelle smiled. 'I think they would. I would have to be disguised but then, I am not so distinctive as you, and my face is not generally known. It's my name that is recognised, not me.'

Fee said: 'You don't even care about Rollo.'

'I care about you.'

'When would you do this?'

'Immediately, if you say so.'

Fee considered. Then she vidied Sandar. It took fifteen minutes or so before he called her back, and he looked alien and unkind.

'You have a scrambler?' asked Fee.

'Of course.'

Fee stopped to scramble. Then she said: 'I have been told that another group in the town might have male prisoners.'

'Who?'

'They call themselves the Sisters of Pain.'

'Who tells you this?'

Fee looked across the room. Richelle nodded. 'Richelle Matthews,' she said.

Sandar's face tightened. He knew from Fee's action that Richelle was there with her. 'I'll make a note of what you say,' he said.

'That's all?' Fee was incredulous.

'Lady, Saturday is a big deal. Let's sort that one out before we start busting women going about their legitimate affairs.'

'You can't think and chew gum,' said Fee sarcastically.

'What?'

'Do two things at once, you ignorant . . .'

'Listen!' The command was rapped out. 'Thanks to the kinky goings on you Zoo sluts have been getting up to with your tame gigolos, we have a powder keg situation here. The local troopers are frightened of serious trouble if the mood turns ugly on Saturday, which it might well do because of the unnecessarily heavy policing there's going to be. That is all thanks to you and your roaming drunken husband. These ladies just want to get on with talking about what they believe in, no harm in that. But we are going to have to act like they are criminals, in case someone has the head of TransFlow in their pocket. They are already angry about what you have been getting up to in the Zoo, and I have to say that most decent people are pretty affronted too. Now you propose to make things worse. You want us simultaneously to bust another freaky bunch just to rub salt in the wound.'

'You shit,' said Fee breathlessly. 'You narrow-minded judgmental pig.'

Sandar broke the connection.

Fee wheeled round and looked at Richelle. She was so blazingly furious that Richelle felt a momentary fear. 'You're prepared to do this?' asked Fee.

'Yes.'

'Go to it, sister.'

The first thing Richelle did was to have all her hair cut.

Fee quelled her anxiety the only way she knew how. Deprived of Richelle, she turned to Roddy.

He was eager. Fee's strong charms were proving much to his taste. He could hardly get out of his mind the long white body, cleverly agile, and the strange things she did with it, the way she pleased herself so ferociously on his willing flesh.

He came into the bubble house full of anticipation. It was evening and the lights were all low, the bubble house shrouded in gloom.

He saw her then and he gasped.

In the dimness, she was pale and glowing. Ghost powder all over her body made of her a white, shimmering creature, something from the depths of the imagination. As she came closer he saw she wore a band about her body. It began at her neck and then wound round and round her, going down her body leaving gaps of white shining flesh, till it met one thigh. Here it curled on down to her foot.

The strange garment was intensely erotic. It revealed all the intimate places that he might wish to explore, yet its snaking progress down her body was exciting.

'Roddy,' she whispered, swaying towards him.

He caught her and kissed her, pressing one breast cruelly hard. She moaned faintly and he knew she was intensely excited.

They went through to a bedroom. The bed had posts at all four corners. Fee handed thongs to Roddy. 'Bind me,' she said. 'Bind me to the bed.'

He felt dizzy. She lay on her back but he made her roll over. He tied one wrist to one corner, her other wrist to the other corner.

Next he tied the ankle of the leg that was naked, leaving the leg with the curious webbing free.

He felt excitement. She was at his mercy. He worked the cheeks of her arse apart and fumbled into her rear.

She arched hard, shooting her bottom up into the air as hard as she could. She had the free leg tucked under her but she could do nothing with the other. Roddy laughed. Then he saw, in the small pool of light beside the bed, that Fee had provided things.

A dildo. More than one, in differing sizes. A whip. A rubberised bat. There were more things, things that for the moment he had no time to examine and identify.

He picked up a dildo thoughtfully. Then he put it down. He chose a larger one. There was cream in a pot, and he smoothed it over the thing till it was glossy and plump. Then he began to work it between Fee's buttocks.

She wriggled and cried out. He picked up the bat and smacked her. She subsided, and let him thrust the engine into her.

It slid in, despite her resistance. He found the sight of the stretched, caramel flesh of her anus entrancing as the mighty tool bulged from it. Fee was gasping piteously. Callously, Roddy moved the thing in and out a few times. Then he felt round and under Fee.

Her pussy was dripping. The whory bitch was hot for sex. Roddy picked up the whip and gently stroked her pulpy vulva with its thongs. He pulled the tongs tight and admired how the pink crisp flesh was twisted and distorted. Then he slid a couple of fingers into the hot interior of the bound woman.

The dildo felt very good. It bulged down, its hard presence a mere membrane away. Roddy began to consider entering Fee with the dildo inside her rear. It would be nice to fight for space in there.

He stripped and untied her leg. Using the whip, he made her kneel with her rear up. He enjoyed flicking the multiple thongs of the whip. He enjoyed the noise they made as they stung her gleaming body.

He considered further. Then he tied one ankle and passed the rope under the bed and round and up to the other ankle. Now she couldn't draw them together. By tying another rope to the one that bound her ankles, he could attach it to the head of the bed. This meant that not only could she not open her ankles any further, she couldn't push them down the bed to stop kneeling.

The dildo wavered about gratifyingly. Kneeling on the bed himself now, Roddy felt again in Fee's cunt.

It was wonderful. It was like sinking his fingers deep into the ripe flesh of a warm peach. Moist tight satin lined Fee's inner sex. Roddy's cock was up hard.

Abruptly he stopped. Instead of his cock, he took the whip into his hand. He reversed it and began to thrust the leather-bound handle into the palpitating aperture in front of him.

Fee began to writhe and squirm. 'Don't do it,' she begged. 'Please, it's too much. Stop it, I'm begging you.'

Roddy laughed. He drew back slightly to get a better view of the artefacts wobbling in Fee's body. He reached under her and touched her clitoris.

She cried out and jerked sharply, so that the bonds bit into her flesh. Roddy took the paddle and beat her buttocks sharply. The flesh between the strange bond-garment she wore gaped and turned red. Roddy bent his head and bit it.

She tasted so good he tried to lick her round where the handle of the whip disappeared inside her. As he did this, he fingered her clitoris. She began to buck and heave so strongly he couldn't keep the sexy flesh in his mouth. He was enjoying tasting the dribble of sexual juices that squeezed out round the fat hand of the whip.

He moved away from Fee and stood up. He grasped his cock in his hand and pointed it at Fee. He began to frig himself. Fee twisted her face and saw what he was doing. Her face went red as she tried to expel the things in her. Roddy felt himself mount the stairway to heaven. A moment later he was at the top, shooting his spunk over the helpless body of the woman tied in front of him.

He stood breathlessly. Fee lay as inert as he had bound her. He reached over for a knife and cut the garment she had tied around herself.

Pink and white, indented by deep weals, her bottom flesh revealed itself. Still the dildo quivered obscenely, sticking out from between her buttocks. The pink rift of her sex was similarly held apart, the thongs of the whip lying on the bed where they hung down from her pussy.

Roddy removed the whip handle.

Fee sobbed with relief. Roddy dropped his head and applied his mouth. Her orgasm came jerkily, out of control.

He laughed. He took off more bindings and now he tied Fee round her thighs just above the back of the knee, doubling her over so that her knees came under her chin and the rope went around her back. He pulled it as tight as he dared. Her position now was gross. Her breasts were crushed by her doubled posture. Her rear stuck up, emphasising the obscenity of the thing sticking out of her arse. She could hardly move.

Roddy picked up the whip. He laid the thongs across the sensitively erect flesh of her vulva. He tweaked the labia so they stood out. He spat on Fee's clitoris and rubbed his saliva into it. As he did this he saw her muscles work galvanically. He whipped them.

Fee moaned. He whipped her quivering sex again. He could see her juices running. He whipped her again, and now the muscular contractions of her continuing orgasm were so great that the dildo in her arse popped suddenly out. Roddy whipped harder, now catching her anus with a lick of a thong. He whipped again and then, unable to wait any longer, he plunged his hard, erect cock into the foaming heat of her sex.

Fee felt his balls thudding against her thighs. She felt the power of his erection, how desperate he was. Her awkward position left her little room to manoeuvre, but it magnified every movement of Roddy's. She wept and cried out as he bloomed inside her.

A moment later she felt his teeth. He had pulled his cock out and was biting her pulsing sex. Gradually her tremors ceased. She felt him lap her, lick her, and even when he bit her clitoris she felt nothing but an increasing glow of peace.

He released her and let her roll on her back. He stroked her breasts and kissed her nipples. She lay, dazed and passive.

'I have some news,' he said tentatively.

'Good or bad?' Fee's voice was slurred.

'Bad, I guess. It's Grey. He's doing the pushing.'

'Pushing for what? He can't get Rollo voted off the board. We own the majority shareholding.'

'The rights issue is imminent. Next week, in fact. He wants the launch party to go ahead.'

'What if we don't have Rollo back?'

'He says the company isn't just Rollo and we should go ahead, even if the matter does become public.'

'Why wasn't I at this meeting?' Fee's voice had sharpened.

'It's in the rules,' said Roddy apologetically. 'Where one director is known to have a strong personal interest, he or she can be excluded from any particular meeting that affects that personal interest.'

Fee dragged her mind back from outrage and panic. This was a business matter. She would need friends on the board if matters got worse. She believed she had those friends already, but she must be careful now not to antagonise anyone, nor to behave unreasonably.

'Have you been authorised to tell me this?' she asked.

'No,' said Roddy.

Fee looked at him. She had that creamy post-coital sheen to her that Roddy found intoxicating. It was something to tame such a monster, if only transiently, and Fee Cambridge was undoubtedly a monster.

'If anything has happened to Rollo,' said Fee deliberately, 'I inherit his holding. Your actions won't be forgotten.'

Roddy believed her. She was a cold-blooded sexual fanatic in his opinion, but not without honour.

9

They prepared him for combat by giving him a short sword and targe. After some time spent familiarising himself with these antique weapons, Rollo was led to his cage and told to get into it. All the cages were lined up, and each one had an armed man inside. The women had no fear of the armed men. The painmakers they controlled were infinitely more effective weapons.

All the women were there. Rollo saw Melissa and the girl so like her that he had mentally tagged her Melissa-twin. There was Felicia and Jye. There were the others.

The queen walked among the caged men. 'Do you like your cages?' she enquired sweetly. She stopped by one man. Whether it was the weapons in his hands or some last flicker of resistance, Rollo didn't know. But he refused to answer.

The queen stood waiting. Suddenly the man gasped and doubled sharply. 'No,' he said hoarsely.

It was Peto. Despite his servile behaviour, it had been decided that he should be treated like the other men. Plainly this did not please him.

'Then you have a chance to escape them. This combat we are arranging – your suggestion, I think. Each man will fight another. Then the three winners will fight each other. That way we will have a clear victor. He will be allowed to go free.'

'How can we believe you?' shouted a man.

'Why shouldn't you?' returned the queen. 'What difference does it make to you, anyway? I think you will fight if we say so.'

'We have no quarrel with each other,' said another man.

'Yet you will fight.'

'How will you determine the winner?' asked another man.

'Ah,' said the queen. 'That I haven't decided. It's so difficult. If you bore me, I may make you fight to the death. If you give me a good show, I might just announce the winner when a clear superiority has been established.'

'If we fight to the death,' said one man bitterly, 'you will release a multiple murderer and leave yourself with no playthings.'

'Playthings can be replaced.'

'The police will catch you, you'll see.'

'They haven't suspected us of anything yet.' The queen was smiling.

'But if you release one of us as you have promised . . .'

The queen interrupted. 'No one knows who we are or where we are. Some of us lead double lives. We know people and can influence them. Moreover, we are capable of pursuing one who has been among us. We can bring his new-found freedom to an abrupt end. No, I do not think that visiting the police will help. Once free of us, you had better stay away and never think of us again. We will not exist. Do not call us from the shadows of that seeming non-existence, or we will draw you in to us as easily as we did the first time.'

Rollo said nothing. He was sickened. He had no desire to fight with these other men. They were derelicts, he had guessed as much, though young still and having some strength.

Kindness was not an intrinsic part of his character, but he did not indulge in gratuitous cruelty either. He reckoned he had a fair chance of winning, despite a month's dragging imprisonment. He had exercised his body when he could, and the reduction in his food had given him a whippy, tensile quality.

He was bruised and in pain, of course. Just because he had hidden the effects of his probings into his own body, it didn't mean that the wounds were any the less. He was stiff and sore. It still made him feel sick to think of his fingers digging in the red bloody meat of his own flesh.

217

In a simple 'us or them' situation, he would fight for himself to the end. There was no problem there. But this wasn't that sort of simple situation. He would be fighting men as desperate as himself to be free, innocent of anger against them, for the crowing delight of some blood-thirsty women. Pain-thirsty women. He could imagine what the cult queen would be having done to herself while the men fought and struggled in the arena.

He didn't want to do it. He would be jerking like a puppet. He didn't want to do it. He would have little choice, however. He may have removed his implants, all except the one, but if he failed to respond to the pricks and spurs of the painmakers, they would discover soon enough what he had done, and remedy the situation.

He lay in his cage in misery. He knew that misery was debilitating and he should not give way to it. But he had spent the better part of a month trying to work out the angles, keeping up a resistance in his mind, a refusal to bow to the women. A refusal of the mind was all that he had succeeded in, for the women had made his body bow at will.

He closed his eyes and imagined his wife. She was sly, amused, wicked, inventive, wholly original – and his.

He imagined their comfortable home, with the madness and anarchy of the jungle caressing its walls and domes.

He imagined a drink in his hand, something to watch on the screen, a business problem to resolve.

He imagined cool silken thighs, the welcoming embrace of the black velvet cunt, the slow giddy rise to pleasure's peak . . .

'Rollo Cambridge.'

He opened his eyes. An anger so intense he couldn't speak passed through him. Not even his dreams were sacred. There was nothing left to him. He was stripped. He might as well die, using his own sword.

'Rollo Cambridge. It is, isn't it?'

He rolled his head sideways and looked into the face of his tormentor, wishing her dead.

* * *

'Who disturbed the pets last night?' Sister Grace's voice was gentle.

The girls were playing a ball game together in the outer court. They stopped and came up to the senior sister.

'Disturbed the pets?'

'How, sister?'

'What do you mean?'

Their voices came innocent and uncharged. Sister Grace said: 'Children, someone went into the pets' quarters and said something. They were asleep and didn't hear clearly. It might have been – though this hardly sounds credible – the name Rollo Cambridge.'

Two of the girls hadn't heard of him. Others knew he was a businessman. 'He's Zoo, isn't he?' Jessamine said.

'Sister Grace,' said Sandrina. 'May I speak with you in private?'

Grace led the way to her office, a cool room painted in white with green plants around to soften and enrich the atmosphere.

'What do you have to tell me?' asked Grace.

'Sister,' Sandrina began. She was flushed, hot with confusion. 'It may have been me.'

'May?'

'I find this hard to say. I have had an adolescent passion for this man, whom I have never met in the flesh, for several months. While my own man was treating me badly, I fantasised about this other man, who is very good looking and very rich. I don't always find my living easy to earn.' Sandrina paused and swallowed. 'I became very disturbed. I was unhappy. The feelings that made me reassess my life and come eventually to you also disturbed my sleep. I was told that I sleep-walked several times. I made the decision to come here and I thought that that had eased my mind, and that the sleepwalking was over. But last night I woke, sweating and afraid, with this man's name in my mind. It was as though he had the power to call me from my safe haven among you, and force me back into a life I hated. It was a nightmare. I had no knowledge of sleepwalking.' Sandrina gazed earnestly at Sister Grace, her eyes bright with tears. 'But the coincidence is too great.'

Sister Grace rose and began to pace softly to and fro. Sandrina stood with her head hung and waited. She had prepared this story to cover herself and was gratified at how she had put it over.

Yet part of her was sorry. These were not bad people. There was peace to be found here among them. It was a shame she had to lie and deceive when she could have relaxed and opened herself to new ideas, in case they provided the answer to her condition.

There was truth in her invention of nightmare, that Rollo had called her from this seclusion.

Grace said: 'We must rid you of this baleful influence. The question is how.'

'It shall be as you wish, sister,' said Sandrina. 'As you think best.'

'Tomorrow,' said Sister Grace, 'the pets enter the next phase of their life. We hold our rally when we call upon all our sympathisers in the town to show themselves in a massive statement concerning the rightness of our cause. The pets will make their total commitment then, in front of what we hope will be thousands of people.'

Sandrina felt two neatly opposing emotions. She wanted the rally to be a success. Yet she felt the pets' actions were a deliberate attempt to appeal to the most ghoulish and salacious aspects of human nature. People would be coming to see the men operated on. It was a guaranteed crowd-puller.

'Yes, sister,' she said humbly.

'We have promised the pets one last taste of what they are giving up for ever. We do this so that they know what it is they enter into. Let no one think we use force. This is a free decision.'

'Yes, sister.' Sandrina was careful to keep up her meekness.

'You shall supply the pets' final meal.'

Sandrina lifted her face. Her mouth fell open. She stared at Sister Grace. 'Me?' she faltered.

'They will confirm in themselves their desire to abandon such vile practices,' said Sister Grace. 'And so will you.'

'How many of the pets?' whispered Sandrina. She was genuinely shocked. She could feel the blood draining from her skin.

'Five,' said Sister Grace. 'It will not be a pleasant experience, but no doubt you will all be the better for it. I think you will not sleepwalk after this, sister.'

Richelle had been examining the body of the man in the cage for some time before she spoke to him. He wore leather briefs, the rest of him being quite naked.

She saw the broad gleaming chest, the muscles, the sinewy thighs, the whole masculine power and grace of the man as he lay apparently sleeping.

It was anathema to her. He reminded her of a lion, even to his golden mane, and she would have preferred to make contact with the beast than the man.

She called his name.

She saw the muscles in his face tighten. She called his name a second time. His head rolled over and he looked at her.

The blue eyes were startling and vivid, wholly unexpected. She had seen him on the screen in news reports, but had thought the extreme blue of his eyes was part of some flattering touching-up process. Now she saw him alive, in the flesh, and a cold wash of terror went over her.

The man had an aura of power undiminished by his humiliating circumstances. Moreover, he was nakedly furious and his fury was directed at her. She had never felt such an intensity of concentrated anger. She felt weak with it.

'Don't gloat over me, you callous bitch,' he hissed.

She was shocked at the quality of his resistance after all this time. Shocked and pleased. This was no limp and broken creature she had to bring out. Here was the man himself in all his arrogant beastliness.

'I'm a friend,' she muttered.

'Come closer so I can spit on you,' said Rollo.

'You don't understand. I'm here to help you.'

Rollo was amazed. They really thought they could catch him twice. He also knew he must get himself under control.

He was being far too revealing to this bitch-sister. She had caught him at such a vulnerable moment he had been unable to hide his true feelings. Had she used the painmakers he would have jumped back into line fast enough, but because she left him he let his anger feed and burn and grow.

What hurt especially was the raw beauty of her appearance. She had vast hazel eyes, dark and thickly-lashed. Her brows arched in a thin, sweet line, achingly beautiful. Her lips begged to be kissed. Her dark hair, a rich deep coppery red, was short and cap-like over her head, gleaming with health. It was cut so feathers curled provocatively at her ears, on her broad brow, at her neck.

'Damn you,' she said. 'Fee sent me.'

It was worse than a painmaker. He was stabbed so sharply he couldn't breathe. The pain flooded outwards through his body. His heart tumbled frantically.

Slowly his pulse steadied and his breathing calmed. Just to hear Fee's name on someone's lips had done this to him.

He felt the sweat rolling down his body. He clenched his muscles and stared at the ceiling of his cage. This refinement of torture was something he must get used to, must develop protection against.

He looked at the woman again. 'Go away, little girl,' he said venomously. 'Play with someone else. I have to rest so that I can be ready for tomorrow.'

'Why won't you believe me?' She felt desperate.

Rollo closed his eyes, willing himself not to hear. If Fee was involved, the police would be here, not this lone girl. What she said was a nonsense.

He remembered how they had failed to believe him when he said who he was. They claimed, and he had no way of checking it, that no account of his disappearance had been on the news on screen. He was hardly giving himself a false importance by realising he would be big news if he vanished into thin air.

TransFlow and the share issue was something he didn't think about. It was too bitter that he should be snatched at such a crucial time. He didn't know the date exactly, but the flotation must be imminent. He could hardly imagine how the board must be handling his disappearance.

Fee would do what was right. What was the phrase? She would keep his name over his stall and his straw fresh. He reckoned Fee would do that forever, until she was given sight of his corpse.

That might be very soon. Things were not looking good.

Richelle abandoned her attempt to speak to Rollo. She must be attracting attention staying here so long, and she was new enough to be watched. She moved on to another cage and squatted, watching the man inside.

He smiled ingratiatingly. Then he rolled over and slipped down his leather gladiator's briefs.

For a moment, Richelle thought he was offering her an insult, showing his bottom to her. Then she realised he was obeying an older tradition. It was the gesture of appeasement, the acknowledgement of superiority.

She must leave this very evening and get the police. She couldn't get Rollo out, that was obvious. She had arrived just in time. These terrible women were planning to make their captives fight tomorrow. She only had a few hours left to do what must be done.

She knew what she had achieved. These women were definitely criminal, as well as being sexually perverted. They would receive no sympathy from the population at large. Meanwhile, the police would be able to call off their planned raid on the rally tomorrow. That would keep temperatures down and avoid an unpleasant load of trouble. She had been astonished, coming back to the town from the Zoo, at how very nasty the talk was.

They certainly hated the Zoo. Fee must come with her after this and walk among the people, suitably disguised, and see what damage the Zoo parties were doing. The revelations were coming thick and fast. It was dramatic journalism, even though she didn't believe the half of it. Meanwhile, feeling was being whipped up to a frenzy. The New Moralists must be lapping it up. Each revelation, true or false, was adding another thousand people to their rally tomorrow. The whole town would be turning out, partly to see what sexual grotesquerie was going to be practised on

223

these so-called volunteer men, and partly to express outrage at a week of smut in the gutter press.

A meeting of the sisters was called. Richelle attended with suitably subdued mien. She had been noticed talking to the prisoners and was reprimanded. She must be very careful.

The queen sat on her throne. The cult members sat round in a semicircle of devotion.

The queen spoke.

'We have a new sister among us,' she said. 'I wish the new sister to come here and kiss me, as is my right.'

Richelle rose in some confusion and went up to the throne. She hesitated, unsure what to do. The queen hadn't stood up.

'Kneel, sister,' she said quietly.

Richelle knelt. The queen opened her legs. Her silver robe came apart. Richelle drew her breath sharply. She could see clear up to the queen's vulva.

'Kiss me, pretty maid,' said the queen. She laid a hand on Richelle's head and stroked her feathery cap of hair.

Richelle bent her head. The knees parted. She saw the hair, thick and black, curling over the secret place. She put out her tongue. It was hot, very hot, here between the queen's thighs. Her tongue touched the central fissure. She pushed the hair aside. She was assailed by musk. The queen exerted a pressure on her head and she sank into the warm, wet, female pit and began to suck.

Several moments passed. The queen adjusted her posture. Then she began to speak again.

'Many of you will have heard that the New Moralists are holding a mass rally tomorrow. I thought you might like to attend, but not because you care for this New Morality of theirs which is old, old as history and as useless. No, I thought you might like to attend because they promise some very special entertainment. I gather some men have presented themselves for the knife.'

Somone tittered.

'Or some such thing,' said the queen carelessly.

Richelle burned. She enjoyed women very much, but this

was no spontaneous eruption of joy. To be ordered to perform this service, to have to do it publicly, was very dreadful to her.

'In order that you, my dear ones, should have the pleasure, if pleasure there be . . .' The queen was positively purring. Richelle forced herself to perform her function well. Her tongue snaked into the queen's pussy and probed there.

'We must bring forward the combat. Our gladiators must perform tonight. Then they can rest and lick their wounds ready for the second round in a day or so's time.'

'I thought they were going to fight to the death.' Jye's voice was icy.

'Maybe they will, Jye sweetheart. But we should not tell them so at this stage, I think. Just before the contest will be soon enough. Let it be in two hours.'

The queen stopped. Richelle had faltered. The queen tapped her shoulder. 'Sister,' she said silkily, 'why do you hesitate?'

Richelle drew her head back. Her face was red. 'The honour is so great, sister,' she said. 'Forgive me my momentary lapse.' Once more her tongue touched the erect pert little clitoris.

She had been brought by a private car, blindfolded and ignorant as to her destination. The building had no windows, and gave the impression of being sunk in the ground. The cellars were old, of another period in time altogether, dating from long before the invention of chemoconcrete.

Richelle knew she had to get out and find help so swiftly that the women didn't smell a rat, fold their tents and vanish. The men were going to fight the first round in less than two hours. The arena was being sanded and prepared. Benches were placed about it so the sisters could sit and watch, to enjoy the men fighting each other. It was no more than a large room, low-ceilinged and oppressive in its ancient stone. The atmosphere was dank and unpleasant. Only the more modern rooms felt dry and truly warm.

She couldn't imagine where any such building might be. She knew the town well, having worked as a journalist for years in it, yet this struck no chord. The outside must be cladded in more modern building materials. She could not forget such a building as this.

She felt desperate. Time was so short. Fee had not been able to set up an implant as she had done with Sandrina: they would have had to sacrifice another twenty-four hours.

Fee was pressured partly by the problems at TransFlow. Richelle couldn't think how they were holding back the information that Rollo might not be alive and well and in full flow as chief executive. Not a few people must know the truth, and it said something for their organisation that no one, as yet, had leaked it to an avid press.

Maybe they had, thought Richelle cynically. She was alive to the market consequences of Rollo's disappearance. Maybe the various editors did know the truth, but were being compelled by the government to keep quiet.

It was not a line they could follow indefinitely. The news must break, unless Rollo was returned to the fold.

Fee had been panic-stricken at the thought of Rollo being castrated in public. Now she half-thought he might be here, with the Sisters of Pain, wherever 'here' was. She was just desperate anyway to have him home. In her queer way she loved him; Richelle acknowledged that.

Perhaps she could escape during the fighting. There would be three contests as the six men were pitted against each other in pairs. The three winners would be allowed to rest for a day or so while the sisters enjoyed whatever the New Moralists' rally would bring on the morrow, before returning to their own personal, nasty concerns.

Leaving during the fighting might be easy, because the sisters would be distracted. But would it be too late? Rollo might be killed, and so might some of these other poor men. She had a duty to all of them, not just to her lover's husband.

For a moment, things had gone quiet. Most of the women were in the clubroom resting, reading or wearing music hoods. They had a big evening ahead of them and a big day following on. Richelle found the girl Mamie, her own ex-lover, and spoke to her.

Mamie was a tall thin girl, one who had never learned the art of being graceful. She carried with her an habitually apologetic air and her large, dark eyes would blink nervously if she was spoken to sharply.

In bed, she had proved to be a spiteful and enterprising lover. The little-girl-lost act was carried on at all times, but she enjoyed inflicting minor pains. She had serviced Richelle so ruthlessly at times that it was worth the occasional bite or scratch, but in the end the lack of emotional warmth and intellectual fire had brought the relationship to a close, even though the sexual fires had remained stoked.

Even now, Richelle felt a pang of lust for the angular malicious brat. She had been exciting, gobbing hard at her vulva and tweaking fiercely on her clitoris. She should have been happy here with the Sisters of Pain, but it was not in her to be satisfied. She had the nature that spoiled what it liked, and now her warped personality had turned her against these her soul-sisters in sadism.

It had pleased her to tell Richelle about the sisters. She lacked intelligence and never saw the consequences of her actions, frequently blaming those who turned against her as cruel themselves. As far as she was concerned, she was always meaning well, acting innocently. She had told Richelle she wanted to leave the sisters, and Richelle must help her. This was because the sisters made threats against those who wished to leave the sect. There was nothing explicit. You just knew membership was for life.

She treated Richelle as all-powerful. Indeed, the journalist was considerably older than Mamie, though less experienced because less promiscuous. Mamie demanded that Richelle get her out, and was quite happy to get Richelle in in order to accomplish her own escape.

She had been with the sisters for a year. She was trusted, as much as anyone ever trusts a malign child, for her mind had not moved on when her body matured. She had told

Richelle about the men imprisoned and Richelle, used to her lying, and knowing Mamie wanted her help, had not believed her. She had questioned Mamie about the men, what they looked like, what their names were, but Mamie refused to tell her any more. She could sense when Richelle's interest sharpened. She would use that interest to serve herself. She wanted to suck Richelle in.

Richelle took a duo music hood and placed it on Mamie and herself. She turned the volume very low. No sound escaped and they could talk safely.

'Mamie,' she said gently. It was always difficult to get what one wanted from the girl. Once her dim, cunning mind had grasped what was wanted, she would go out of her way to prevent it.

'Kiss me, big lady,' said Mamie. Richelle obliged.

'Darling,' she began again.

'When are we going to escape, big sister? Will you enjoy the men going bim-bam, snicker-snack with their swords?' Mamie tittered.

'Honey-child, we'll escape soon. But first clever Mamie must show big sister the door to outside, so that when the time comes, I'll know which way to go.'

'I'll show you tomorrow.' Mamie always did this, exploring how urgent any request was by blocking it in different ways.

'Tomorrow we'll be busy. Kiss me, sweet one.'

They kissed lovingly. Mamie pinched Richelle's breast.

'Show me the door,' murmured Richelle, 'and we'll play spank-sisters.'

'Play spank-sisters first.'

'No, no, no. First Mamie does what big sister wants, then big sister does what Mamie wants.'

Mamie gave way abruptly. 'Did I tell you,' she said cheerfully on their way along a corridor, 'what Sister Felicia did to the silly man?'

'No. What was that, Mamie-sister?'

Mamie giggled. 'She let him out of his cage. She said she was going to help him. Then she let him fall into the mud pit. He nearly drowned. We made him beg.' She broke into a high peal of hysterical laughter. Richelle found her blood ran cold.

'Just the one man?' she queried gently. 'Or did you play such a good game with all of them?'

'All of them at different times. It was so funny. We hid in the dark. Were they surprised! Then they cried and begged when they thought they might die.'

'What a funny game,' said Richelle feeling sick. No wonder Rollo had rejected her advances. He had assumed she was up to another malicious trick.

'Here's the door,' said Mamie.

Richelle stared at it in dismay. It was large and strong-looking. 'Can Mamie open it?'

'My man-tickler opens it.'

'Your man-tickler?'

Mamie leant in confidentially. Richelle wondered how she could have enjoyed the horrid creature. She had to prevent herself from shuddering now. 'I have a little friend,' Mamie murmured. 'If a man doesn't do what I say, I tickle him. It has a control for the door as well.'

Richelle understood. She hadn't been issued with a control for the painmakers yet. Therefore she couldn't open the door.

'What's outside?' she asked. 'Can Mamie tell me?'

'Spank-sisters,' said Mamie cordially.

Richelle gritted her teeth. She plastered a smile on her face. 'If Mamie won't tell big sister what's outside, she'll get spanked.'

'Won't tell, won't tell.'

Richelle pulled the girl's baggy shorts down. She bent her over sharply and, without any attempt to tease, hit her as hard as she could on her bottom. She spanked with breathless urgency, using all her strength. After one shocked moment, the girl over her knee began to howl and wriggle.

Richelle spanked savagely on. Then she rammed two fingers straight into Mamie's cunt.

'Is that nice?' she hissed. At the same time she felt something small and hard.

'You hurt me,' sobbed Mamie. 'Now I hurt you.'

'No,' said Richelle brutally. She pinched Mamie hard on her clitoris. The girl jerked and fell off her lap. Richelle was left holding a small rectangular flat object.

'What's this, pussycat?' she asked.

'Won't tell you.'

Richelle pinched her thigh.

'Don't hurt me,' wailed Mamie. 'It's my man-tickler. I keep it in my pussy hole so when I want to make a man jump, I have to play with my pussy bits.'

The girl needed therapy. She hadn't been as bad as this when she and Richelle had been lovers. The Sisters of Pain had taken Mamie down a dark road, and this vicious creature was their doing.

Richelle looked at the time. 'Nearly fighty time,' she cooed, her mind running rapidly. 'Big sister can put your man-tickler back during the fight. Won't that be fun?'

'We aren't allowed to use them during the fight,' sniffed Mamie. 'Only the queen can use hers then.'

'So no harm big sister has Mamie's. Mamie will like to have her pussy hole played with, yes?'

'Big sister mustn't hurt Mamie.' The girl was sulky.

'No more spank-sisters,' said Richelle. She turned and opened the door.

She gazed out at a totally empty level plain. She had never seen anywhere like it. The grass stretched apparently for miles, its silvery, undulating movement showing how the wind blew.

She stepped outside. For a moment her mind was so frozen she couldn't even see the road. Then she saw the cars parked against the building. The road went round the far side to where she couldn't see it.

Mamie was calling urgently. Richelle ignored her and ran to the corner.

She could now see the access road to this strange squat blind building, set in the middle of nowhere. The broad pale track disappeared over the crest of a nearby hill.

She came back into the building thinking furiously. She hoped the opening door had not set off any security alarms. She rather thought not. The building was singularly backward in the fixtures and fittings. There appeared to be few electronics around, and electricity was used at its most basic level, for lighting, warmth and doorlocking.

She didn't know what to do. The fighting was imminent. She couldn't get away and find help in time. They were miles from the town. It hardly seemed credible.

There was nothing to stop the town people from coming out of the town, but there was nothing to make them do so, either. The town included magnificent parks, water avenues, pools, rivers, woods and spacious plazas in its design. Out here was a ghastly featureless emptiness. The barrier was mental; townspeople didn't want to leave the town. It was the sisters' ingenuity to capitalise on this.

Richelle cudgelled her brains. To one side of the town lay the folding jungly hills that hid the Zoo. To another lay the remains of the old city, a sordid decaying ruin where human scavengers carried out a kind of sub-life. Long ago, sociologists had decided it was better to leave these half-people and criminals in their vile nest. All societies produced disorderly and pathological types. The very decency and crime-free order of the town relied upon the most bizarre elements of humanity having somewhere else to go. The city was the town's human sewer.

The rest was just the rest. Nothingness. Open veldt, woodland and wild animals all left in peace except for the occasional starlane, the overhead roadway used by Connet cars going from one town to another.

She must attack the queen and take her hostage. She must make the women abandon their man-ticklers. Then the men could walk out and be free.

She needed a weapon, a knife. She felt terrible. She was not a violent woman.

The preparation for the pets' final pleasure, if pleasure it was, was horrible. The girls undressed Sandrina and bathed her. Their hands went everywhere, all over her body, and all the time they laughed and sniggered at what she was going to have to do.

231

Having bathed her in aromatic oils, they manicured her and massaged her gently till her body was loose and relaxed.

'Now you must be prepared for the nasties to come,' one of them said. She took a man-hater and began to insert it into Sandrina's sex.

Nothing had made her lose her embarrassment at having women see her naked and touch her body. This invasion of her sex, of her most private place, was an agony of mortification.

'You don't have to do this,' she said, squirming.

Soft hands held her and trapped her. They pressed at her sex. 'Stop it,' she begged. 'Leave me alone. This isn't fair.'

Abruptly they stopped. Sandrina was released. The girls fell silent. Sandrina lifted her tear-streaked face.

Sister Grace was walking towards her. She stopped, and with great delicacy, eased the man-hater out of Sandrina's body and laid it to one side. She looked at the quivering naked girl.

'I am pleased,' she said in soft, measured tones. 'You have not been with us long but already you have significantly advanced.'

'I don't like it when they touch me,' gasped Sandrina. She was feeling near the end of her tether. She couldn't find Rollo and she was dreading the coming events.

'Quite right,' said Sister Grace. 'We don't want you to like it. That is the point, child. We are weaning you off the compulsion to spoil your lovely body with sex. You don't like the girls. I think that shortly, you will be thankful you need have no more men. Ever. That is the freedom we offer you. That is the prize.'

Sandrina shut her eyes. At the moment, she could hardly think of anything nicer than having her body properly clothed and left in peace. Yet she must have five men. Her lower lip began to tremble.

'Come now,' said Sister Grace. 'Time for your next lesson. Once you have come through this, you will be free. I promise you this.'

They wouldn't let her wear clothes. It was horrible, her

232

nudity among them all. Red in the face and trembling with nerves, Sandrina allowed herself to be led to the pets' quarters. She could think of no way of escape, short of admitting she was an impostor.

She was not absolutely sure she was an impostor any more.

They entered the pets' quarters. The men were sitting around looking nervous themselves. They wore loose-fitting short trousers, nothing else.

Sandrina felt terror and shame. She couldn't ever have liked sex, surely? She couldn't remember liking sex, nor could she remember the men she had wanted.

For a long, terrible moment she thought Sister Grace was going to stay and watch. But then the sister left and she was on her own with the men.

She stared at them like a terrified rabbit. The tension grew. One of them suddenly gave vent to a high-pitched, hysterical giggle. He lurched forward and fastened a sweating hand on one of her breasts. He jabbed his other hand up hard between her thighs.

A dizziness overcame her. Her legs buckled and she began to fall. The men caught her, holding her arms, her head, her legs. The man who had grabbed her first wriggled quickly out of his shorts. Making a snorting noise, he began to burrow urgently between her legs. The others set up an excited chattering and squeaking. They held her long limbs open. A moment later it had begun. She felt the slick little cock enter her pussy. Egged on by the others as if he were a horse running a race, the man began a fumbling rush to climax.

To begin with, the first two men fought with visible feebleness. They struck faint-hearted blows at each other's shields and walked round the fighting arena slowly, as if to spin out the whole process. The queen soon altered that. She began to tickle them up using the painmakers to stimulate their performance. They soon learned that every time they lagged, she would ginger them up unpleasantly.

Inevitably they began to fight in earnest. As they grew

233

tired, their blows grew wilder and their ability to block grew less. A sword struck home twice and the sand was no longer clean.

The men tried to stop. The queen forced them on. Finally, one of the men landed a swinging blow with the flat of his sword on the side of the other's head.

The man who was struck fell to the ground and didn't move. Clearly he was unconscious. The other man was panting and blood-streaked. He turned to the queen and with a gesture of disgust, he threw his sword away.

He stood plainly waiting to be punished. But the queen decided that he was the winner and should be allowed not to kill his opponent. Richelle breathed a sigh of relief. She planned to make her move during Rollo's fight so he would see that she meant what she said. Had the queen ordered a death, however, she would have had to make her move immediately.

Rollo came on next.

Richelle was astonished that the women had not perceived the swan among their ducks. Of the six prisoners, five were flabby, weak-looking men. Rollo Cambridge was like a king among them with his broad golden chest and strong sinewy legs.

The queen was taking refreshment, laughing with her girls. Richelle clutched her knife nervously. One girl crept between the queen's legs. The woman was at ease, amused by what someone had said.

The two men stood ready. Rollo looked calm. His opponent looked frightened. Rollo wouldn't look at him and in a blinding moment of revelation, Richelle thought: he's decided to kill him. That's why he won't look at him. He's going to kill to get his freedom.

Her hand was slippery on the knife. At that moment the queen gave the order to start.

Rollo whirled, his red crest flying. The women gave startled applause. This was what they hoped to see. Rollo advanced on his opponent and struck out savagely. Richelle stood up. The man Rollo was attacking ducked, terrified, holding his shield and sword high in front of him. Rollo knocked the sword out of his hand and picked it up.

There was a moment of stasis. Richelle felt literally frozen with horror. She knew she must act.

Leaving his opponent kneeling in the sand, Rollo walked across the arena till he could face the queen. He lifted the sword in his left hand. He then brought it down hard on his right arm.

There was a shocked gasp. Blood sprung red. Rollo dropped the sword from his left hand and fumbled in the wound. A moment later he threw the last painmaker away.

Ignoring the blood streaming from his gaping wound, Rollo picked up the second sword again. 'Now,' he said, and they all knew he was speaking to the queen, 'I will kill you.'

There was pandemonium. Rollo leapt over the first benches whirling his two swords, blood spurting in a crimson arc from his arm. The women scattered, all reaching for their man-ticklers, the triggers for the painmakers.

Rollo bounded over the remaining space. He lifted his sword high over the queen. She cowered back, raising terrified eyes. Her women fled. The other men were screaming as their painmakers threw them about like rag dolls.

Richelle saw it happen. As if in slow motion, blood rolled, jewel-like, down the muscled column of Rollo's raised upper arm. She saw his set features, his blazing eyes. She saw his face go white, greenish-white. He made a faint cry and staggered. His forehead shone suddenly greasy wet as sweat sprung upon it. His arm faltered and he began to fall.

Richelle ran forward. She came behind the queen and held the knife to her throat. 'Stop hurting the men,' she screamed.

Rollo lay in a faint, blood streaming from his arm. He must have severed something important, a vein or an artery.

The women were stupefied at this new turn of events. Richelle wrenched the queen's head back so that the blade of the knife could clearly be seen against her white throat. 'Tie up his arm,' she shouted. 'Quickly.' She pressed against the queen's throat and heard the woman gurgle.

Someone bound Rollo's arm high up and twisted it tight. The tourniquet held and the dreadful gushing of blood stopped.

'Now,' said Richelle, trying to gain control over her voice so that she exuded authority rather than panic. 'Every woman must take off her control for the pain-makers. Now. I want to see them all.'

Mamie came over. 'You shouldn't do this, big sister,' she said earnestly.

'Shut up, Mamie. I've got my hands full. Collect up the triggers, will you.'

'No chance. The men will hurt us if I do that.'

'Mamie, we're getting out of here,' said Richelle patiently. 'Now do as I say.'

Mamie bent and picked up one of Rollo's swords. She held it out at Richelle. 'What if I say no?'

The queen made a desperate glottal noise deep in her throat as Richelle tightened the knife. Mamie giggled. She pricked Richelle in the shoulder, ignoring the queen's bulging pleading eyes. Then she fell over.

Rollo had his eyes open. He had pulled Mamie's feet from under her. He took the sword from Mamie and sat there, looking white and shaken.

'I'm making the women drop their painmaker triggers,' said Richelle. It was an effort not to let her voice shake. She wasn't cut out for this. 'Then we can get out of this place with all of you.'

'It was just a joke,' said Mamie sourly. 'I'll help collect the ticklers.'

Rollo stood up. He looked very bad. 'Who are you?' he said hoarsely.

'A friend of Fee's. I came here to get you out.'

The queen choked.

'Why not the police?'

'They're looking elsewhere. We couldn't wait. Look, there are cars outside. We'll have to sort out the owners.'

Rollo looked at the women. Each car would have in its computer the DNA code of whoever was allowed to drive it. 'Where are we?' he asked.

'I don't know. Miles from anywhere. Out of the town.'

Mamie handed over the triggers. Rollo counted them. For the first time, Richelle relaxed her hold on the queen. She still kept the knife in place, but with a looser grip.

Richelle raised her voice. 'There are six cars outside. I want the six drivers.'

The women stirred and didn't answer.

Richelle held the knife tight again. 'I mean it,' she cried.

It was Jye who answered. 'Why should we help you, sister, when you betray us?'

'Because I will kill your queen.' Richelle tried hard to sound convincing.

Jye stood up. 'What does that matter now?' she asked bitterly. 'What future has any of us? Death might be preferable.'

The queen went stiff.

Rollo said: 'I will deal with this.' He took one of the triggers. He walked between the women and went back into the arena. There he found the painmaker he had torn from his own arm. He took it to Jye and faced her.

His hand snaked out, his left hand. He grabbed her throat and squeezed. With his weak right hand he then slipped the evil little thing between her legs and into her sex. Her face froze. He held up the trigger. 'The drivers,' he said, 'or you will dance, sister, to the tune you have been playing to these men.'

Ten minutes later, three of the six cars had drivers and were loaded with the men. In Richelle's car, there was the queen as driver, Mamie, Rollo and herself. The other three cars had been rendered undrivable. The women remained locked in the building which was now their prison until the police came for them.

Night had fallen during the combat. The sky was starry and vast, the great plain black. Where the road disappeared, a dull light could be seen in the sky, lights from the distant town. Richelle and Rollo left last to ensure all the men got safely away.

The queen was driving their car. They did not know her name and Richelle did not care to find out. She simply

237

wanted the woman handed over to the police, to have done with her.

She knew she had a story, though she didn't know if she would ever tell it. Her loyalty to Fee came before her need to make money from this particular episode in her life.

Part of her wondered cynically how long her relationship with Fee would last once Rollo was home. She might not like men, but this was no inconsiderable person. In health and strength he must be overwhelming.

They came over the crest of the hill. There before them lay the massive sprawl of the town like a starry sky upturned, dazzling and beautiful. Richelle felt sick with relief. She had hated it in the sisters' citadel. She had hated the violence and the mayhem with every part of her soul.

The queen said: 'It does not suit me to be handed over, tame, to the police.'

'You should have thought of that before you engaged in criminal activity.' Richelle's voice was acid.

The car swung suddenly and violently to their right. The vehicle crashed and bumped over the rough ground. It struck a rock with a terrible blow and stopped dead.

The queen was out in an instant. She tucked up her robe and ran. Within seconds she was lost to sight.

Mamie was crying. Richelle climbed wearily out of the car. The town had seemed enticingly close but it must be several miles away yet.

She couldn't tell what was wrong, but she guessed some vital part had snapped underneath. She opened Rollo's door to speak to him and was horrified when he fell out.

He was unconscious again. His wound was bleeding. The crash must have set it off.

She must replace the tourniquet. She had taken off the first one some time previously, knowing it was dangerous to leave them on for any length of time.

She bent and tore the hem of the robe she wore, the robe given her by the sisters. She tied it as tight as she could around Rollo's upper arm. She didn't have anything suitable to put into the knot so she could screw it tight, but she thought she might have done enough. Now she bound the wound itself over again, throwing away the blood-soaked bandages.

Rollo regained consciousness during all this. He said nothing, but she could see the starlight gleam in his open eyes.

'She made off,' he said faintly.

'Yeah. What the hell,' said Richelle. 'She can never enter a town again anywhere, once we've told our story.'

Rollo closed his eyes. 'Sister,' he said. 'I don't feel so good.'

'Look, I'll leave you here. Mamie can look after you. It'll only take me an hour or so to walk into town and then I'll be back with real help. You'll be fine.'

Rollo opened his eyes again. 'You don't leave me with that dippy bitch,' he said clearly.

'She won't hurt you.'

'You sure about that, sister?'

Well, she wasn't sure. 'I could send her for help,' she said doubtfully.

'That's a much better idea.'

'But she might do nothing. You understand? She might not report us.'

'You both go.' His voice was faint. 'I'll just rest here till you get back.'

Richelle stood up and went round to Mamie. She encouraged the girl out of the car. 'Mamie,' she said softly. 'You see the lights?'

'Yes, big sister. I don't like this.'

'Go to the lights, Mamie. It's the town.'

'I know it's the town. I'm not stupid.'

'Find a policeman. Tell him we're out here. They'll find us if you say we are here.'

'Why can't you come? Why don't you go? Or send the man. I don't like the dark.'

'The man isn't well and he needs my care. If you tell the police, you'll get a big reward.'

'Why?'

'The man is terribly rich and important. He'll pay you lots of money for helping to save him.'

'Does he say that?'

'Of course.'

They went round the car to Rollo.

'Will they pay me money if I tell the police?' asked Mamie.

'I said how important and rich you are,' interrupted Richelle.

'I'm very rich,' said Rollo. 'There'll be lots of money. You be a clever girl and do what we ask.'

'Play spank-sisters first,' said Mamie.

Richelle's heart sank. 'Not now, Mamie,' she said in a kind voice. 'The man is ill and in pain. You tell the police, then he'll give you lots of lovely money.'

Mamie was silent. 'I don't like the dark,' she said obstinately.

'You can't get lost. I'll come with you to the road. All you have to do is to follow it to the town.'

'I'll go in the morning,' said Mamie brightly.

'Now,' said Rollo. 'Or no money.'

The girl sulked silently. 'Then kiss me goodbye,' she burst out suddenly. She sat down and opened her legs.

Rollo was silent. Richelle wanted to scream. She knew exactly what the girl wanted, and she knew that if she gave way on this, Mamie was very likely to do just what they asked. She never did anything without collecting first. Money in the future was one thing. A kiss now was quite another.

She didn't mean kiss however. She meant full-blown oral intercourse. She was lying on the damp grass waiting for Richelle to kiss her pussy, while Rollo lay on the ground beside them.

That was deliberate, of course. The girl had an unerring feel for pain. She would know Richelle didn't want to do this, and Rollo would be both disgusted and in agony. That's why she would enjoy it so much.

'Darling,' said Richelle desperately. 'Of course.'

Mamie had taken her shorts off. She opened her legs wider. She had positioned herself so that the interior light from the wrecked car spilled over her spidery body. Rollo could see all her sex.

240

Mamie's head came up. She looked at Rollo looking up her legs. She reached between them and pulled herself open. 'Oooooh,' she said. 'I like that.'

Richelle bent her head, her hands going instinctively to brush back the hair she no longer had. It had been a sacrifice worth making. No one had recognised her as the feature writer who exposed the cults for what they were.

This sacrifice too was worth making. Rollo's opinion meant nothing to her. Anyway, she was doing this for his sake, if he had the wit to see it.

She thought of Fee. She opened her mouth and put out her tongue. She touched Mamie on the clitoris. The girl sighed and settled. Richelle kissed the open pussy before her.

The first man left her as abruptly as he had entered her. Sandrina felt a spasm of annoyance. She hadn't wanted to have sex with the pets, but now they had embarked upon it she at least expected to be treated properly. The man had stuffed it in, poked it about a bit and then pulled it out. He could as well have been rodding the drains.

She felt irritated, tickled and aroused. She was still being held by the men, but another one had gone between her legs. She felt his fingers in her pussy and she heard him laugh. She blushed suddenly. This was terrible. These men were watching each other fiddling about with her. Then she gasped. Another male organ was going into her.

It was larger than the last one. He was more determined, more controlled. She was squelchy inside and his cock slid easily in and out. As he poked her, someone rubbed her breasts. The men still held her. She felt trapped between them. She began to writhe, and catching them unawares, she managed to pull free and knock the man out of her.

He gave an outraged cry. His cock stuck outwards, stiff and covered with a slimy, sticky membrane, a cocktail of sexual juices.

She felt a vice-like hand on her shoulder. 'Put it in her mouth,' someone said.

They laughed excitedly. 'No,' she said. 'Down below or nowhere.'

'We do what we want,' one of them said. 'It's the rules.'
'And what we want to do is you.'

The cock was in her mouth. She considered biting it. But it was her duty to service the pets. She couldn't remember why she must submit, but submit she must. Her mouth closed over the fat wet thing. She sucked desperately. They had jerked her into a half sitting position and the man was standing, putting his cock in her mouth and jerking his hips to bring himself to climax.

He tasted salty-spunky. Sandrina imagined Rollo. She would do this gladly with Rollo Cambridge. She sucked desperately.

She would do this gladly with Fee Cambridge. Richelle sucked desperately. The bitch would try to hang on as long as possible. The better she sucked, the quicker Mamie would come.

The night wind on the prairie blew. It lifted Rollo's dank hair. It stirred Richelle's robe as she bent to her task. Rollo saw that her rear was partly exposed.

He reached over. Taking care, he slid a finger into the dark slit moving slightly in front of him. He felt Richelle's body heat close reassuringly around him. She jerked slightly but continued to lick the disgusting little girl. He paddled slowly in her pussy and thought how tight it was.

Richelle nibbled Mamie's clitoris. The girl had a very large one, a tiny penis that relished firm treatment. Then Richelle worked down the long fissure, kissing all of the complicated flesh there till she reached Mamie's anus. She kissed the little puckered arse and felt the girl shudder with delight. She kissed back to the pussy hole and put in her tongue. She lapped the melting juices of the aroused girl. She ran her tongue round and simulated penetration. Then she closed her lips tight and sucked hard.

Biting, sucking, probing, kissing and licking, she finally brought Mamie to shuddering climax.

She sat up and leaned back. The thief hand was still under her, cupping her bottom, a stray finger curling into her vulva and penetrating her.

Mamie sat up. 'That was nice,' she announced in a satisfied voice. 'Mamie kiss big sister now to say thank you.'

'Mamie say thank you by walking into town and telling a policeman we are here.'

'But big sister needs kissing.' The voice was primitive and cunning. Richelle felt she was in the company of a snake.

'I'll kiss big sister,' said Rollo from the darkness. 'Mamie go now.'

Mamie burst out laughing. 'Richelle hates men,' she said clearly. 'She hates them worse than Mamie does.'

Richelle stood up. 'We will walk to the road now,' she said gently. She put her arm round the tall, thin, gangling girl. 'Mamie is clever and always right,' she said as they walked away. 'Soon she will have lots of money because this silly man will give it to her.'

'Goody.'

'As long as she tells a policeman straight away and is a good helpful girl.'

'Of course,' said Mamie, suddenly on her dignity. 'I know he's hurt. He needs to be in hospital. I'm not stupid you know.'

'I know,' said Richelle. She stood on tiptoe and kissed the girl's lips with great tenderness. 'I'll see you soon, sweet one. Goodbye for now.'

She crouched at the side of the road and watched Mamie till she could see her no more, the dark moving blur lost against the pale ribbon of the road. She had done the best she could. If no help came within a few hours, she must go herself and leave Rollo in the car.

She knew it was possible to get a fever from untreated wounds. She wondered how long it would take before Rollo's fever started.

The cock emptied into her mouth. Sandrina gulped it down. The men were watching her avidly. She had a feeling they shouldn't be enjoying this. They were due to have discs fitted on the following day, in public.

Number two sighed happily and slowly withdrew his

cock, watching it emerge from between Sandrina's lips. It shone at first, but gradually it shrivelled and softened until it hung limp.

'Turn her over,' someone said. She was limp as they rolled her over. They drew her knees in under her. She felt fingers again, probing her sloppy cunt. They came and went, came and went, as if the next man, number three, wanted to empty her pussy of spunk before he entered it.

Then she realised what he was doing. His fingers entered her again, but now they were somewhere else. She yelped and tried once more to pull away.

They held her fiercely. They had fallen silent. She could feel their excitement. They were very keen for this next thing to happen.

Having prepared her arse with sexual juices, number three now made ready to enter it with his erect cock. He pressed against the little entrance. It had been stretched lately by the horrible things the sisters had done. Sandrina tried to squeeze it shut but inevitably it yielded to the remorseless pressure.

'Rollo,' she said, a tear squeezing from her eye. But no one seemed to hear her.

His cock was all squeezed in now. He drew back slightly and began to fuck her. To bugger her.

It was so hard to remember why she had to do this, why she couldn't object and walk away. It was something to do with Rollo, only he wasn't here, where she needed him.

The man in her – number three, only two to go – was taking his time. They were all enjoying this very much indeed. Sister Grace would be very angry if she knew.

Someone said: 'Let's fuck her other hole too.'

'At the same time?'

'It's not possible.'

'It's worth trying.'

They tried. They had her on her back, on her side with one leg in the air, on her front with both legs up. Then one of the men lay down. His legs were open and wide apart, bent over the edge of the couch. They sat her on his erect cock, sat her so that his cock slid into her arse, forcing her down so that her own weight pinned the invader inside her.

In this position, it was just possible for another man standing in front of her to get the very end of his cock into her pussy. They thought this amazingly clever.

'We should do her mouth at the same time,' said another man.

They bent her head back. The man stood on the couch astride her. He crouched till his cock dropped into her mouth.

For some long minutes the man under her jiggled her up and down, the man in front of her tickled the outside edge of her pussy and the man astride her shafted his cock into her mouth.

The man under her came, jerking awkwardly as excitement at what they were doing overcame his discomfort of position. The two men, one on each side, lifted her so that although her anus was still penetrated from below, now it was only slightly so. This enabled the man in front of her to pump vigorously into her body and eject his own spunk into her. At the same time, she felt her mouth fucked hard by the man standing astride her. He came too and she found herself gagging, for the tilt back of her head made swallowing difficult.

She was released and lay inert for some time. She felt dazed and mentally numb by what had taken place. However, she had had five men; she had done what was required of her.

After some time she sat up. She shook her head and then eased herself off the couch. She stood shakily wondering if she could just walk out. She dearly wanted a shower, and she didn't want anyone outside this awful room to see her in this condition.

A voice penetrated her abstraction. 'What are you doing?' it said. It was a high, whining voice.

'Leaving,' she said thickly. 'I've done my duty.'

There was a high-pitched titter. 'Not yet, sister. You can't go yet.'

'I've had you all. I counted.'

'No one stipulated,' said a crafty voice, 'that we only had you once. None of us is ever going to have a woman

245

again. So sister, your duty isn't done yet. Not by a long chalk.'

'I hate men,' whispered Sandrina.

'You hate men,' said Rollo Cambridge.

Richelle hugged her knees and shivered slightly. 'Not socially. I get on fine with men socially and at work as my colleagues.'

'Sexually.' Rollo's voice was deep and strong and quiet. He didn't sound like a man who would die if he didn't receive immediate medical attention.

'Yes, sexually, I prefer women to men.'

'How is Fee?'

'She's well, but very worried.'

Rollo lay quietly. 'It's been a very strange time,' he observed.

'A month. Have you suffered a lot?'

'A month. Then the rights issue hasn't taken place yet.'

Richelle laughed. 'You Cambridges,' she said. 'Fee's held the fort for you. You don't have to worry.'

'Fee is a woman worth dying for,' said Rollo.

Richelle shivered again. The calm statement out of the night had a chilling intensity. 'I guess she feels the same about you,' she said lightly. 'The public don't know you've disappeared, by the way. Fee's been visiting a smoker daily.'

'A smoker?'

'You had ligament trouble. You had to rest your legs absolutely. You worked from a clinic. You've been there a month now.'

'Time I came home.'

'Yes.'

'Who are you?'

'My name is Richelle Matthews. I'm a features journalist, an investigative writer. I've done a lot of work on these cult groups that have started up lately in the town.'

'So you came in alone to get me out?'

'We thought the New Moralists had you. There is a big police operation planned tomorrow, mostly because of

246

you. Then Mamie told me the Sisters of Pain had men hidden out here. The police said they would deal with tomorrow first. If they didn't find you, they'd follow up this lead. Fee couldn't wait.'

'You belong to these sisters? You feel like them?'

'Don't be stupid. Mamie got me in yesterday.'

'Why?'

'She's an ex-lover. We split and she got entangled with these people. They frightened her and she wanted out. She came to me for help.'

'*They* frightened *her*?'

'She wasn't so bad,' said Richelle defensively. 'They've taken her way too far. She was never this bad before.'

'And what is your motivation, Ms Matthews? Why did you risk yourself to save a hated man?'

'I don't hate you. I just don't want to fuck you.'

'Why did you come for me?'

'I'm a friend of Fee's.'

There was a long silence. 'Not a month ago, you weren't,' said Rollo softly. He reached out his good arm and found her naked rump under the torn hem of her robe.

'Get out of there,' hissed Richelle.

His finger sank inside her pussy. 'I'm trying to get closer to my wife.'

'I'm not your wife, damn you.'

'But my wife's been here, hasn't she?'

He caught her suddenly with his good arm and with surprising strength pulled her down onto his chest. His mouth found hers and holding her tight against him so that she had trouble breathing, he kissed her savagely.

When he released her she backed angrily away. He was so strong and so vulnerable she didn't know how to treat him. She could walk away into the night so easily. It was as though he played with this, driving her away when he needed her.

Hadn't he had enough, this last month? Was his appetite for danger unsatisfied?

Perhaps it was fundamental to the man to push every situation he was in, despite the possible consequences to himself. Perhaps that was what made him what he was.

Her anger evaporated into a grudging admiration.

She said: 'You don't have to drive me away. I'll go if you want me to and get help in case Mamie lets us down. I was staying because you were faint and wounded.'

'I feel better. The car was bumping me about. It's good to lie still and feel cool. I kissed you because my wife had kissed you and I wanted to taste her. I know I should apologise.'

She came to him then. 'You complex bastard,' she said queerly. 'No wonder Fee is like she is about you.'

'Tell me about this police raid tomorrow.'

So she did.

10

Fee spent Friday evening at a director's thrash for Con-Comm. She had been invited as a courtesy, though Con-Comm were divided in their hostility to TransFlow. Some believed that in the prevailing economic climate they had no choice but to accept TransFlow as carriers of their products, reducing their own immediate costs though losing greater profitability in the future. Others thought they might yet win through without TransFlow, and raise the capital needed to build their own infrastructure. Fee had insider reports on the finances of ConComm and knew TransFlow had to prevail. However, she would prefer this new arm of business to be wholehearted and not sulky when it came into TransFlow's grasp.

She set herself to be charming. This despite her husband being missing for a month, a police raid that might recover him in time to save him from public castration due the following day, and, if he were elsewhere, the possibility that he was in the hands of a female group dedicated to the exercise of sadistic practices. Fee excluded this from her mind and did her duty by Trans-Flow. She had a private agenda to follow as well. Simeon Grey's moves against Rollo mattered. She had to block them and counter-attack. She proposed to do that this very night. It was an excellent opportunity to lay the groundwork.

She was very tired when she arrived home late that night. She was behind-hand with her own company, and needed to put in a couple of long weeks with it to get things back under control.

I want this to be over, she thought in desolation. I need this thing to be settled.

She swam up through layers of sleep as insubstantial as gauze. Her body felt strange, stretched, soft, plastic. She crooned a little to herself as the miasma of sleep left her.

It was warm and sunny. She lay bathed in yellow light. Her first thoughts were: *I am a whore.*

It was true. Last night she had admitted men to her body in all ways, continuously, against her personal sexual desires, because she had been told to do so for the profit of others. She had benefited the New Moralists and pandered to her own body.

She roamed around the room she was in, touching things. Then she placed a mirror on the floor and squatted over it.

The hairless lips of her sex wavered soft and slug-like. The flesh darkened at their blunt edges. This provided the contrast with her bright pink inner flesh.

Sandrina reached under herself and opened her lips. She was very moist and loose. She had lost count, but she thought she had had intercourse some twelve or fourteen times the previous night.

Not all of the penetrations had been in the vagina. The men had become very excited about buggering her. Sandrina looked at her little crinkled arsehole.

She teased this open too. It was very soft and easy. She exerted her muscles and made it pout out and suck in.

Now she clenched her pussy muscles. Her clitoris waggled gently. She reached under and touched it.

After a moment she licked the tip of her finger and touched her clitoris again. She squatted dreamily, still naked and sleep-warm, frotting the tiny thing which glistened and stiffened as she became aroused.

Sandrina teased herself more firmly. Her tongue came out between her teeth. She rubbed and tweaked the sensitive member and soon she had her reward.

Her pussy hole vibrated gently. Through the pulsing muscle, liquid dripped. Sandrina sighed and gave way to

250

the delicious ripples of pleasure coursing gently through her. The mirror was clouded. Drips of love juice had settled on it.

She stood up. On a surface by the bed was a drink tube. Making sure it was done up, Sandrina squatted again over the mirror. This time she pouted her little arsehole and then slid the drink tube into her own bottom.

She looked at herself. The tube stuck out of her, bloated and unyielding. She squeezed her arse muscles and watched the tube dance about.

She began to squeeze rhythmically. The tube wobbled. Sandrina strained and slowly the tube began to eject with the force of her contractions. By the time it finally dropped free of her, ejected by her own internal muscular force, she was in orgasm again.

She stood up. At that moment Sister Grace came in with something over her arm. The previous night she had taken Sandrina from the men and brought her here to wash and sleep. Sandrina had been filled, covered with spunk. The men had climaxed in her sex, in her arse, in her ears, in her navel, over her breasts, in the cleft of her bottom, on any part of her body they could use to pleasure their cocks. She was smeared and slimed with their excess and it had taken a long time to cleanse herself.

'How are you this morning?' asked Sister Grace.

'I am well, sister.' Sandrina's voice was low and humble. Inside she felt jumpy and excited. It pleased her to be so secret. Her pussy was tingling pleasantly and she kept flexing her cute little bumhole.

'You have performed an unpleasant duty admirably. This is recognised. Never again will we ask such a thing of you. Meanwhile I bid you wash, dress and breakfast. This is our special day. I have here your robe. It is saffron, sister, the colour of the pure. We bid you join us on the platform.'

'The platform?' Sandrina raised sly eyes.

'You have deserved this honour. Be with us, sister. See the crowd like a sea at our feet. See the men who soiled you last night fitted with their discs before your very eyes. They will never penetrate any other woman.'

Sandrina's voice was still soft. 'Will there be such a crowd?'

'They gather now. There must be several thousand already there. This rally will not be forgotten, little sister. And you too will have your place in it.'

Maslow was in the crowd. He was dismayed by the turnout. He didn't interpret it as a vast move to a higher moral understanding because he could hear what was being said in the crowd.

They were here for two purposes. They wanted to be where everyone else was, where it was all happening. And they wanted to see if the rumours were true, that a dozen men or more were going to have their penises chopped off in public.

The crowd was good-humoured. Vendors moved among them selling food and drink. The sun shone and there was a holiday atmosphere.

The rumours circulated constantly. The sisters would engage in sex on the platform. The sisters would be sealed into chastity belts on the platform. The men were having their balls and their cocks cut off. The men were undergoing sex change operations.

It was around lunchtime that the rumours got uglier. It was very hot. The crowd, having assembled too early, was bored. Maslow heard how the Zoo, to flout how the town felt, was deliberately holding an open-air sex party at the Zoo-gate through which all had to pass to get in or out of the Zoo. They were cocking a snook at the town. They were engaging in licentious sexual practices in sight of those outside.

It seemed to Maslow that it wasn't so much the sex as the intended insult to the town that upset people. He wondered how much of it was true. Probably none of it. The crowd was now so thick it had become almost immovable.

The tension grew. The rally was due to begin at one. It would soon be that time.

They were setting up the platform, getting the chairs ready, testing the speakers. Whatever happened, thought

252

Maslow, it had to be a disappointment after a build-up like this.

Richelle woke feeling cramped and cold in the dawn. The events of the previous evening rushed in on her. Her heart sank when she saw the time. Mamie had let them down. The girl had gone astray. Hours had been lost, and now she herself must walk to the town and get help for Rollo.

Rollo. What state was he in after a night in the open? He had refused to sleep in the car despite a mild danger from wild beasts and despite the cold.

Richelle came out of the car and looked at him.

He still wore his leather briefs, though he had discarded the other trappings of his infamous gladiatorial combat. All but naked, he lay with his sword beside him, its bright blade misted with the dew.

The dew lay on Rollo also. His broad golden chest was pale and shiny with it. His hair was wet with it, darkened from its normal blond. As she looked anxiously at his arm she saw his eyes open, bright and blue.

'You must be very cold and uncomfortable,' she said.

'Freedom makes a comfortable bed,' he said. 'It hasn't been a soft month.'

'How's the arm?'

'Stiff. No worse. Our little friend change her mind, huh?'

'Unless a lion got her.'

'He'd have spat back such a sour morsel.'

'Do you mind waiting while I walk into town?'

'Hold on for a moment. Maybe I'll be able to walk too.'

She watched him stand and move about. She could see it hurt him, but he moved his arm until it could be held in a comfortable and natural position.

They walked across the wet grass to the road. Birds were singing and from far across the broad plain came the bark of some distant creature. When they got to the road Rollo stopped. 'Look at us,' he said gently.

Richelle looked down at her golden robe, the torn hem, the material streaked and muddied; she had no underwear.

Rollo wore only his briefs. 'We're going to cause something of a stir when we arrive in civilisation,' he said.

Richelle took his point. She went back to the car and checked it over. It had belonged to the queen. She had indeed carried spare clothing in it.

There was no underwear, but Richelle was able to put on a dress and look clean and fairly normal. There was nothing for Rollo.

'Look,' he said. 'These leather things are wet and stiff. They're going to rub my thighs as I walk. How about we fashion some kind of shorts for me from what you were wearing?'

He made Richelle help him remove the briefs, saying blandly that he couldn't manage with one hand. She had to crouch in front of him and haul. She saw his sex as it sprang into view, she saw the golden cloud of hair and she determined to ignore it. Gritting her teeth, she helped Rollo step out of his things, feeling his hand on her shoulder as he balanced.

He stood unashamed, naked but for a pair of leather sandals. She saw the neatness of his hips, his tight buttocks, the strength of his upper thighs in relation to the heavy hanging balls and long soft penis nestling against them.

'That's better,' he said. 'Some air, at last.'

She faced him. 'Did they do much to you?' she asked baldly.

His mouth smiled but his eyes were cold. 'They made me fuck,' he said. 'They used the painmakers when I didn't want to play.'

'You only had the one painmaker.'

'I had five. I took the others out earlier.'

The blood emptied from her face as she absorbed the implications of this. She had to admire him. He was one hell of a man.

She knelt again and began to twist the gold cloth of her old robe about his loins. He stood rock steady. Her hands trembled when they came close to his sex.

He put a hand on her head. She looked up. 'It disgusts you, doesn't it?'

'Yes.' She was awkward. Objectively, his sex was lovely. It was just that she didn't want it used on her.

'Always?'

'Almost always.'

'There's nothing wrong with it, Richelle. It doesn't bite.'

She gave up trying not to touch him, then. The back of her hand brushed into his cock, she felt the hair of his groin and the soft baggy swelling of his balls.

'It doesn't look very natural,' she said doubtfully when she had finished. 'You look like some specimen of early man in a loin cloth.'

'It feels more comfortable. Maybe I'll wait on the edge of town while you go in. Now, let's go. You can tell me what's been happening this last month. I could bear to hear some news.'

It was a long, dull and tiring walk. They were both hungry and thirsty. Richelle was uneasily aware that time was running out for her to get the police raid cancelled.

At the town fringes they did as they had agreed. Rollo settled himself as comfortably as he could with his back against a tree. Richelle went on in. She wanted to contact the police, to tell Fee she had her husband back safe and well, and to get medical assistance before Rollo's arm scarred. The wound was certainly clean and uninfected as best she could judge. There was no inflammation, and only local pain and stiffness according to Rollo.

Richelle's first problem was that she had no identification with her beside her own fingerprints. Only the biggest shops and a few vidi booths had direct finger-reading equipment. She carried no credit cards. She intended to go into a shop and ask for help.

Her second problem was that inexplicably, on a Saturday morning, all the shops she came to where shut. Moreover, the streets were peculiarly empty. She couldn't understand it. It gave her a very creepy feeling.

She came to a vidi booth and considered. She could not pay for a call. She was reluctant to call the emergency services because she knew that all emergencies were watched by the press and, after all this time of keeping

Rollo's disappearance secret, she didn't want to blow it by calling out the cavalry.

She called Fee and reversed the charges, but Fee wasn't home, and her answermachine hadn't the authority to accept such calls.

She couldn't go through her newspaper contacts. She considered her friends. She tried one or two but no one was home.

No one was home. The whole damned town wasn't home. What the hell was going on?

Richelle walked into a garden and took some clothing off the line. Not everyone liked their washing dried in a machine; outside, dried washing had a special fragrance and freshness that she enjoyed herself. The garments that she had stolen had been dried over honeysuckle and the perfume impregnated them deliciously.

She had breeks and a tunic over-shirt for Rollo. It might not fit very well, but it was standard male wear, and he would have a passing respectability.

Rollo appeared to be asleep when she got back to him. She was struck afresh by the magnificence of his body. She shook herself irritably. She disliked males. This was an abstract appreciation, no more.

'I've hit a problem,' she said.

He watched her intently.

'There's no one about. The whole place is empty, as far as I went. I can't get through to anyone I know on the vidi, including your wife. I stole these clothes and I suggest you come into the town with me. It seems we're in for a longer walk than I had anticipated.'

Rollo unwound his loin cloth and dressed. The breeks were baggy, having come from a fatter man, but the tunic shirt was strained across Rollo's wide shoulders.

The clothes were a deep green. 'It could have been worse,' said Rollo gravely.

Richelle grinned. 'I avoided the pink ones.'

Together they went into the silent town.

Sandar called Fee early, earlier than was necessary. He had

agreed she could be in on the raid, and he was honouring his promise with evident ill grace.

'Can you be at the Zoo-gate by ten?' he asked aggressively.

'I guess I can make it in three hours,' drawled Fee. She hadn't returned home from the ConComm beano till the early hours. She was very tired.

She bathed and dressed carefully. She would be at the raid headquarters all day, whilst Sandar controlled his men. She must be ready in case she saw Rollo. She chose an all-over, black, close-fitting costume, a spray-on as they were called, though they were no such thing. Only women with the very best and firmest of figures could wear them, the latex garment clinging like a second skin. Fee had the necessary figure and lithe grace.

She strained her hair tightly back and bound it flat to her skull. She was determined to present no soft, fluffy, feminine front to the wretched Sandar.

Rollo. She might see him today.

She wondered how Richelle was getting on.

Sandrina was frightened when she came onto the platform. The crowd had begun to cheer as the women assembled, and the sound and sight beat at her till she felt she saw the doors of hell gape open.

They were there in their thousands. They were a river of people, a flood, and their mouths all gaped as they shouted.

The noise hit her in great waves. She smiled mechanically, deafened and numbed by the blast. She took her seat and felt her legs tremble.

The senior women came out. They held out their arms to the crowd and showered flowers upon them. The noise grew to a terrifying crescendo.

Sister Leesl came forward to speak. She leaned into the microphone. Her voice, magnified but not distorted, carried to every reach of the crowd. They fell silent and began to listen.

Sandrina didn't hear what was said at first. When she

257

had sufficiently recovered from her first shock, she began to take note of what was said.

The sister spoke about the eternal problems of crime and lawlessness, of violence and aggression. She spoke about how the town had emptied most of its crime into the old city, and its sexual decadence into the Zoo. This made the town seem very nice, but the problems remained. Moreover, there was a cycle to these things and the town was in an upswing. Strip shows, feelie bars, houses of pleasure, all were on the increase. With them came corruption in the town hall and in the police force, an increase in crime, both against persons and against property.

Politicians lied about these things. There was a conspiracy of silence. Things were slipping dangerously downhill. Those in authority hid the truth.

The crowd was quiet under the hot sun. A distant buzzing could be heard, but no one took any notice.

Sister Leesl explained that it was a lie that the New Moralists were against men. Men were half the human race. They loved men. They embraced men. They needed men. But as always, purity and moral guardianship had to come from women. This was only to be expected.

Why was so society so bad? Why did it always teeter on the edge of anarchy?

The sister's voice grew thrilling. She was an hypnotic speaker. She could tell people why. She would tell people why. It might be information they didn't like, but let them reflect a little. They would understand. They would see the truth.

She explained that she referred to sex. This would hardly be news to them. What might be news to them was that frequent studies had shown the link between sex and crime. Sex inflamed. Sex blanked the conscience, the best part of a human. They only had to look to the Zoo to see where unbridled sex led.

Fee was watching on a monitor, sitting beside Sandar. 'We're pretty law-abiding in the Zoo,' she said sarcastically. 'The lady's argument is flawed.'

'The lady is a liar,' said Sandar. 'She's making this tripe up. None of this exists.'

Leesl explained that the government liked the population to blind itself with sex because it pacified the political, the democratic instinct. A population engaged in sexual activity didn't argue over new taxes, didn't notice corrupt officials, ignored scandals in high places. She told the hot sweating crowd there was a conspiracy, and it was time it was brought to an end.

'We must smash the conspiracy,' she said earnestly. 'We must end corruption and decadence. We must do this with our own hands.'

The crowd roared approval. Sandar was restless. 'She's inciting the mob,' he said uneasily. 'Does she realise this might get out of hand?'

'I think that's what she wants,' said Fee.

'We must cleanse ourselves first,' said Leesl. 'We women must close our sex against the intrusions of men. Men must give up their power to penetrate.'

The crowd hissed excitedly. This was gripping stuff. They would get to the meat of the rally soon.

Leesl prolonged the introduction as much as she could. Fee found her stomach tightening in anticipation. She could see Sandrina on the platform. The girl wore a curious hood and looked spaced-out. Was she drugged?

When the men came on in a sheepish line, the crowd stood on its feet and roared. It took Leesl five minutes to get peace so that she could be heard.

'They will try to silence us,' she screamed. 'But we will not be silenced. We will not be silent till every male in the land is fitted with a disc. In a sterile tent, totally transparent, you will now see these men given a local anaesthetic and then have a disc implanted in their penises, as they vow never to indulge in penetrative sex again.'

The crowd screamed like an animal. The men dropped their trousers, exhibiting their naked normal sex. The tent ballooned behind them.

'He's not there,' cried Fee. 'He's not there.'

'Take them out,' ordered Sandar. 'Take the men out. Go in now.'

The helibuzz that had loitered at a distance swung into

259

view over the crowd. People ducked in surprise, causing chaos in the tight-packed ranks of humanity. Those on the platform looked up and saw it like a giant insect hovering over them. Leesl pointed at it and screamed, though no one could hear what she said. Her intention was obvious enough.

There were police in riot gear all around the crowd now, on every building top. The noise rose. The helibuzz went in. Men in combat gear dropped from it and grabbed the semi-naked pets. Leesl physically tried to stop one trooper and was pushed aside.

The crowd began to surge in a screaming howling fury onto the platform. Sandrina stood up and looked wildly round her. Leesl was mouthing imprecations at the helibuzz as it took off. The police around the crowd began to fire tear gas.

Into the reducing noise came Leesl's voice once more. 'The Zoo, the Zoo, the Zoo,' she screamed.

The crowd understood. The police were hand in glove with the Zoo. The Zoo was the evil source of sex. The Zoo had the government in its pocket. It was all the fault of those rich promiscuous bastards in the Zoo who had chosen today of all days to flaunt themselves naked in another of their foul parties.

Fee was standing up, staring at the monitors, her mouth gaping open. 'It's a riot,' she said. 'A real riot. Tell them to close the Zoo-gate. For heaven's sake, Sandar, stop this.'

Sandar was talking urgently to his troopers. They had to break up the crowd, isolate its factions, calm it and above all, they had to keep it away from the Zoo and from government buildings.

'Sir,' said a trooper. 'The crowd are coming this way. I think we should evacuate. There's a helibuzz available.'

Sandar didn't argue. It was better to run and avoid feeding the crowd's appetite than to succumb to it. Any success the rioters had at this stage would be fuel to the flames, urging them on to more mayhem. Above all, they must be thwarted.

Fee stuck by his side. They entered the four-seater helibuzz and it took off immediately.

Outside, the anarchy was truly three-dimensional, no longer confined to a screen that could be turned off. Fee felt amazement and a trickle of excitement. Her fear had left her. Rollo was not among those poor men; that was bad, she didn't have him back, but he hadn't been drugged and made stupid all these weeks.

Sandar was trying to control his centre of operations from the helibuzz, and was not getting much luck. The pilot suddenly screamed. The helibuzz went into a steep plunge. Fee felt Sandar's arm like an iron bar across her chest. She had no time for anything but a huge astonishment. So this was the end.

In the crowd, Maslow knew the inevitable somewhat sooner than Sandar. The crowd felt like a huge amorphous beast. Gradually it swamped with violence. Maslow knew they were being incited, knew what was being demanded of them. Knowing also that the police were about to sweep in, he made his move early.

He didn't like the look of Sandrina. She seemed shocked and blank. These damned women had been doing something very terrible to her, that was for sure.

He began to push his way to the front. All around him they yelled incessantly. Over it he heard the helibuzz coming in. He heard Leesl's venomous parting shot. Then all hell broke loose.

The crowd started to turn. Maslow pushed against it, still trying to get to the platform. Leesl was urging them all to go to the Zoo. Maslow used his elbows and then his fists. He was determined to reach Sandrina. It was taking a long time.

The noise of the helibuzz receded. Then it seemed to him, as he struggled and sweated, that it came back, louder than ever.

On the extreme edge of his vision he caught the flash and gout of flame from the crashing helibuzz. His heart lurched within him. The tear gas was reaching him, tangling with his eyes and making him cough. He had lost sight of Sandrina.

The forward sway of the crowd and its reversal as it began to head for the Zoo shook the underpinning of the raised platform, and Sandrina came off it, half-falling, half-jumping. Only her dancer's natural grace and the cushioning effect of the massed bodies stopped her from hurting herself.

She felt bewildered and disoriented. She saw the pillar of fire and wondered if the police were firebombing the crowd. She was crushed and squeezed and caught up by the swirl of people. She felt the onset of claustrophobia as the very air became too thick and hot to breathe.

Then she was choking and coughing. No one would stop and she was carried along helplessly with her eyes streaming. This was the stuff of nightmares. She was crushed. She couldn't breathe. If she stumbled she would go down and be trampled to death.

Her arm hurt terribly. A vice-like hand had closed round it and she was hauled to one side. Someone was fighting right by her, a fist smashed out, and then she was pulled against a man's chest.

'Maslow,' she said, and coughed.

'Here. Let's get out of this.'

He shouldered his way out, using brute strength. He hit people in the belly and kicked their legs in his efforts to break through.

Then he was pushing her down onto her knees. He forced her to crawl. There was a sudden space. He urged her on. The effects of the tear gas diminished. The light, the heat, the crowd all disappeared.

They were in quiet gloom. Maslow was beside her. Sandrina looked at him with huge eyes. 'Where are we? What's happening?'

'The platform collapsed. We've crawled under it,' said Maslow. He grinned in the half light. 'You OK?'

Her face was white and scared. Her saffron dress had been pulled apart so that one breast hung exposed.

'Those people have gone mad,' she whispered.

262

He reached forward and began to tuck the breast back into her clothes. The heavy flesh was cool and resilient in his hand.

'Your sisters drove them that way. Now they've gone to bust up the Zoo. What's been happening to you?'

'They made me screw everyone.'

'*What?*'

'All the pets. All last night. Their final fuck. Over and over, all of them.' Sandrina turned over and presented her rump. She hauled her robe up. 'Here,' she said, fingering her pussy. 'And here.' She touched her arse. 'And here.' She rolled round straddle-legged and brought out both her breasts. 'And here again.' She put a finger in her pussy.

'Now,' she said. 'I want you. Exorcise them for me. Fuck me, Maslow. Please.'

He knelt up and pushed her shoulders so that she fell back. He looked down at her breasts spilling loose. Her legs were wide apart. Outside their cavern, the crowd passed away to find better game. Faint bars of light traversed the gloom. Maslow took out his sex, his whole perfect sex, and thanked heaven those men had been snatched, even though it had precipitated the riot.

He had no doubts about what he was doing. He wanted the girl. This private place, so cool, so calm, amid the violence outside, might have been especially created to encourage intimacy. He slid his sex into the girls ripe soft pussy. He felt himself sucked in and kissed by her inner muscles. She cried out softly with pleasure and strained up to him. He began to fuck. Sandrina removed her helmet.

Sandar hit Fee's seat belt release and his own. He held her with one arm tight round her, so tight it hurt. He opened his side door and fell out, pulling Fee with him.

They crashed through the branches of a tree and hit the ground where the earth was soft. Sandar rolled his body on top of Fee's and a moment later, the blast from the crashed helibuzz rocked them. The heat seared over them. Then it was quiet.

Gradually noise reasserted itself. Fee began to struggle

263

to sit up. She could hardly believe she wasn't seriously hurt in some way.

Sandar restrained her. 'Keep down,' he hissed. 'They'll know you're Zoo. You look Zoo. And I'm in uniform. They'll tear us to bits.'

Fee quivered and obeyed.

'We'll make it into that building,' murmured Sandar. They had crashed outside the park.

'It's locked.' Fee was equally quiet.

Sandar smiled grimly. 'I'm a police chief, sweetheart. I carry a universal key.'

They huddled in the thin bushes, only a yard or so from the thrusting crowd. At last Sandar said: 'Now. Quick. Head down.'

They burst out of the bushes and shot across the empty-ing space. Sandar had triggered the lock and scooped Fee inside before she had even had time to take in the smell of panic and bloodlust that rose from the running, mindless people outside.

They were in the foyer of a large building, an insurance firm or some such. Plants stood around in elegant pots and there was a large, unmanned reception desk.

Sandar led Fee swiftly away from the smoked plastiglass doors. They ducked behind the desk and found themselves in a cool carpeted area.

For the first time, Fee looked at Sandar. 'You saved my life,' she said steadily. 'You are a very fast-thinking man.'

Sandar looked at her. She didn't realise it, of course, but from the moment the helibuzz had gone out of control, his only thought had been to keep her alive. He looked at the long lissom body clad tightly in black. The ice-green eyes, the colour of water spating from a glacier, stared at him. He could see her scar delicately shining, as though ghost powder was caught in the frail snake of flawed skin.

Knowing Fee Cambridge, it probably was.

He wasn't aware of it happening. It was as though a well opened up and he slid inexorably into it. One moment they looked at each other, the next she was in his arms and her mouth was open under his. Her breasts pressed into his chest. She clung to him. His hand went between her legs and he felt what he could not see.

Fee broke the kiss. 'Shouldn't you be working?' she asked.

'I can't do anything. Except stay low so the crowd doesn't eat me.'

'Eat me,' whispered Fee. She released the fixing on her clothes. Her breasts spilled out, long and ripe. Sandar bent his head and she felt the erotic tug as he sucked one dark nipple. A moment later his head went down. His mouth closed over her vulva. She felt the faint roughness of his chin, the rasp of his teeth, and then she felt the powerful probing of his tongue as he entered her Jade Gate.

Rollo and Richelle walked through the deserted town. There were no shops open. No one was home. The streets were stripped bare of people. There were no taxis. When they tried to vidi, no one was home.

'We could call the emergency service,' said Richelle doubtfully. She wasn't keen on her own account, let alone Rollo's.

'No. We've come this far. We'll go on.'

Richelle said: 'I suppose it could be the rally.'

'It was billed as a big thing, huh?'

'They were clever. They have men appearing who have consented to be castrated. At least, that's the rumour. There was this feelie bar manager who got snatched a couple of weeks back. Whoever grabbed him fitted this disc thing round the end of his cock under the foreskin, so he couldn't get it up any more.'

'Can't it be removed?'

'Apparently that's very difficult, but I don't know why. They sealed it to the skin somehow. I'm afraid I found the details pretty grim and didn't go into it all.'

'It was thought I might be one of these poor saps?'

'They might have some brainwashing techniques. We didn't know anything. We could only guess.'

They came to a fountain in a plaza and sat down. After a while Rollo stood and removed his shirt. He proceeded quite calmly with a public wash. Then he joined Richelle. 'That feels better,' he observed. 'I suppose those guys being done was the main attraction.'

'It wasn't as crude as that. But yes, I'm sure they knew what they were doing. The organisers, I mean. I guess the ordinary adherent wouldn't realise how things were being manipulated.'

'Feelings are going to be running high,' said Rollo.

'Yes.'

'And the police are going to interrupt the fun.'

'At some stage. I don't know any details, of course. Maybe they'll call it off when they see you aren't there. Maybe Sandrina will have made contact.'

'Sandrina,' said Rollo and smiled.

'That's how you like them,' said Richelle bitterly. 'Desperate for it with you.'

Rollo looked at her. Richelle met the blue gaze with contempt. Rollo watched her steadily.

She had had time to think about him. He had a whole life waiting for him to step back into. He headed a vast corporation. He had vital business concerns. He talked with government ministers. He was unimaginably rich. The world lay in his palm like a pearl.

She saw herself through him, how small she was, writing stories in newspapers. Yet he was only in his forties. He was a man who might still enter the history books.

'I don't make the rules,' said Rollo.

'They might have been made for you.'

'You believe that?'

She was silent. In truth, she didn't believe his meteoric success was blind luck. She believed he had made his own luck, by cleverness and application.

He was telling her it wasn't his fault if the power groupies fell down and opened their legs in front of him. He had advantages and he used them. It was as simple as that.

'We'd better go on,' she said.

'You find my wife a good fuck?'

She struck him. Having done it, she could hardly credit the action. She had never struck a man.

266

Rollo didn't touch his reddening face. Amusement crinkled his eyes. She had given herself away. Now he knew.

Fee lifted her haunches off the ground and felt the joy of Sandar's tongue penetrating her. A moment later his thumb was in her whilst he fumbled with his trousers with his other hand.

He came forward with his cock erect. It slid into her wet pussy and she bore down on him so that he gasped. She wrapped her legs tightly round him and began to jerk herself off on his cock. It was a moment before he could get control again. Then he grabbed her hips and steadied her, and began to slam into her.

'Do it here,' begged Sandrina. 'That's what the men did. Make it go away.'

She was kneeling with her back to Maslow. He bent to kiss the arse she offered him. Then he touched it. The delicate flesh quivered. He slid a finger in and felt her grip him. He took his rearoused cock and sank it into the tight proffered orifice. He cried out as Sandrina pinched at him. Then he began to fuck her frenziedly, holding her cheeks apart and watching as her long breasts swung into view from under her as he slammed into her body.

It was easy to get erect again. All he had to do was to touch her silky shaven head with his cock. Her skull felt like his cock when it was aroused, hard, covered in satin. He ached to caress it.

They came to the cars first. It seemed that cars littered every place that could be seen, hundreds of them. Here people had come in from the suburbs and then parked and walked to Sunshine Park.

They could hear the crowd now. It made a roar like a stormy sea, like a mass of speeding cars, a kind of growling menace that got louder and louder as they approached.

'Perhaps we'll meet a policeman soon with a communicator,' said Richelle uncertainly.

'Look.'

Rollo's voice had an edge to it. She looked and saw police then, for the first time.

There was no way they could approach. The police were in full riot gear and terrifying to see. Their menace was explicit. Even as they watched, the troopers began to run towards the crowd. Tear gas canisters exploded over them. The crowd heaved like a giant venomous beast and began to disgorge bits of itself. People scattered and started running. The troopers moved in like belligerent sheepdogs and began to shepherd the running people, using their riot sticks and sting guns.

Richelle had her hand on Rollo's arm in shock. 'I don't believe this,' she whispered. 'What's happening here?'

Rollo said: 'We've got to get out. We mustn't get tangled up in this thing.'

Then they heard the crowd baying one word over and over again. The sound swelled in intensity, utterly malign and evil in intent. Rollo stopped, alert. Richelle saw his face blanch and all its muscles tighten.

'Zoo,' the crowd chanted. 'Zoo, Zoo, Zoo, Zoo, Zoo.'

'No,' she said frantically. 'There's no point. Fee's not there. You're wounded. Stop it, Rollo.'

'I'm going home,' he said, and he began to shamble after the running crowd.

The shattered platform structure seemed infinitely safe and quiet. The crowds were all gone, and there was silence in the sun-splashed dusty park, as if nothing had ever taken place.

Sandrina said lazily: 'Maslow?'

'Yes.'

'Nearly there.'

'Where's that?'

'Each place. They used it. You must.'

'Sandrina . . .'

'No. I'm telling you.' She bent over his cock, crooning slightly. She held it in her hands and caressed it. She kissed the damp tip. She licked at it like a lollipop. Then she put her whole head into his groin and gently rubbed.

268

'Sandrina, I don't know if I can make it again.' Though he said this, Maslow didn't sound troubled.

Sandrina laughed. 'I can make you come,' she said. She lowered her head. The cool satin skin touched his belly. Her mouth engulfed his sex. He felt her suck and kiss and tongue him.

He lay back relaxed. His loins stirred pleasantly. It amused him to think that the girl seemed crazier for sex than before she had tangled with the New Moralists. So much for her training.

Rollo and Richelle stood looking at the smoking remains of the crashed helibuzz. 'This is a bad day's work,' said Richelle shakily. 'What has turned these people into such a mob? What's gone on here?'

'The rights issue is scheduled for next week,' murmured Rollo. 'I guess we'd better defer it. The financial houses will be restive and nervy after this.'

'Is that all you can think about?'

'My wife is what I'm thinking about,' said Rollo grimly. He hefted a piece of broken rotor blade. He looked up sightlessly, wondering how to get to the Zoo, how to protect his wife when he didn't know where she was.

Inside the building opposite, Fee had finished with Sandar for the time being. The lean, athletic policeman was good at fucking. She had known he would be, just as she had known that his antagonism masked the fact that he lusted after her. The violent sex had restored her sense of proportion. The shakiness that threatened her after the shock of the riot, followed by the crash of the helibuzz, had been exorcised. The sex refreshed her, as it always did. She felt strong and capable again.

She climbed stairs and found a first floor window. She looked out of it to see what was happening, whether the streets were clearing.

They were. There were only a few scattered people now, walking rather than running in the general direction of the Zoo.

She looked across to the blackened and burnt remains of the helibuzz. Her jaw dropped. She gaped. Her eyes seemed to start from her head. She felt the hair rise on the nape of her neck.

She wheeled sharply and crashed into Sandar. Not seeing him, she caught herself up and ran for the stairs. She hurtled through the large foyer and wrestled briefly with the doors. A moment later she was out in the warm dusty air.

The smell of burnt oil stung her nostrils. She began to run, giant steps, infinitely slow. As she ran down the shallow stairs leading up to the building's doors, she shouted.

It was like a nightmare. For a long time no sound came out of her mouth. Then the tension eased. She heard herself. 'Rollo. Rollo. Rollo.'

He looked up. He saw the slim, black-clad woman with the white face and tightly-bound black hair. He even saw the blazing green eyes.

For a moment he couldn't move. Then he lurched and began to stumble towards Fee. At his side Richelle looked on, astonished. Then she felt a surge of delight and thanks. Fee wasn't in the Zoo under attack. She was here, safe.

'Fee,' shouted Rollo at the top of his voice.

People stopped to stare. Rollo and Fee came together, Fee immediately in Rollo's arms, against his chest. They held their heads back and gazed at each other incredulously. Sandar came up behind Fee, watching them.

'That's Fee Cambridge,' someone shouted. 'She's a Zoo bitch.'

An ominous ripple ran round the small crowd. Fee looked every inch a Zoo woman. No one from the town dressed so slinkily.

Rollo held Fee by the waist, looking into her face. Her hands were on his shoulders as she stared back at him.

Sandar gazed uneasily round the crowd.

'Zoo bitch,' said someone. These stragglers knew they were going to miss all the fun at the Zoo-gate.

'And her stinking trooper. Look, they get personal protection.'

Again that ripple ran round the crowd. It was gelling into a single entity, becoming a tiny version of the mindless riot beast.

270

Richelle felt chilled.

Sandar said: 'Get back into the building. Now. They're turning nasty.'

Fee said: 'Rollo.'

He stroked her face and smiled.

'They're going to do it now,' someone said. 'Look at them. Filthy beasts.'

Sandar said: 'Into the building. Now.' He pulled Fee.

She turned and smiled at him. 'Of course,' she said. She was deeply and utterly happy.

A stone hit her on the chest. She gasped and put a hand up to herself.

Rollo spun on his heels. He stared out at the crowd. One man was laughing, jumping up and down and pointing at what he had done.

In one fluid movement Rollo stooped, picked up the piece of rotor blade and whirled it above his head. The wound in his arm burst. His sleeve fell back and blood streamed down his arm. He let out a blood-curdling cry and ran at Fee's attacker. He hit him so hard the man was lifted off his feet and thrown back into the crowd.

They roared. Sandar pulled out his whip gun and grabbed Fee. 'Back,' he yelled. 'Back.'

The crowd moved forward. Rollo struck two more men, dancing lightly on his feet. He looked over his shoulder, saw Sandar armed and retreating with his wife, and ran to join them.

Richelle was running too. She tripped and stumbled. A stone whizzed over her head. A moment later she felt herself grabbed. Using his left arm, Rollo had swept her up in passing.

Now they all four ran up the steps. Sandar opened the doors with his universal lock. A second later they were inside, the doors locked tight behind them.

The crowd began to hammer futilely against the plasti-glass. Stones richocheted off it. The four inside fled up the stairs and out of sight.

The Zoo-gate gave way under the determined assault. The security alarms screeched and automatic sprinklers soaked the rioters as they surged into the Zoo. They ran along the moving walkways which came to a slow halt.

The rioters slowed to a walk. It had been a long haul on foot from the town and they were getting tired. Now they were in Sin City itself.

They felt curiously cheated. The cool open precincts were made in soft colours. The bubble domes let filtered sunlight through. Some walls were opaque and had works of fine art hung upon them, pictures, rugs, strange woven hangings in subtle colours. Other walls were clear, so that the green of the jungle could be seen as it went about its remote and alien business.

'Why are we here?' asked someone uncertainly.

'I thought they did it on the streets,' said someone else.

'We could smash the shops,' suggested another hopefully. 'Look what's in them.'

This seemed in bad taste. The rioters felt sleepy and relaxed. They were finding it increasingly hard to remember why they had come here.

The damp air had a pleasant smell, a little spicy. Their clothes were wet and uncomfortable. Slowly the riot began to break up and the entity that had been the crowd faded like smoke. They were individual humans again.

They were individual tranquillised humans, did they but know it. The Zoo's defences were subtle and varied. Having soaked the crowd and then pacified it chemically, the temperature now began to fall. Soon people were shivering. To go back outside into the warm sunshine became suddenly most desirable. They didn't know why they were here. The Zoo was OK. It was rich, it was pretty, but that was the beginning and end of it. They were townsfolk and proud to be so.

The crowd broke, wavered, and turned for home.

The board meeting had been successful. Rollo was magnificently in control. The media were handling the riot almost as a non-event, and the rights issue would go ahead as planned.

After the meeting he and Fee travelled back to the Zoo together. 'You going to fill me in?' he asked.

'What about?'

'The reason why you supported the ConComm proposal that we swap a board member. It's giving a lot away, honey.'

Fee sniggered. 'You bet. Only, it was my suggestion to ConComm. I just told TransFlow that it was ConComm's suggestion. I said that when I attended that hospitality night the Friday evening before the riot, before I got you back, they suggested to me informally that they would favour us as franchisees if we agreed to having one of theirs on our board. Actually I suggested it to them as a concession that might appeal to them.'

'I'm with you. But why?'

'Simeon Grey was out of hand while you were away, Rollo. He was making moves to oust you, calling board meetings with me absent, and so on. This way he gets to go to ConComm with no loss to us since he's a pompous old windbag, and we get some talent from them.'

Rollo said: 'I knew you'd look after my interests.'

'And TransFlow's,' purred Fee.

That evening, they went to the Castel d'Amour to watch Sandrina in her new spot. Her shaven head added new drama to her performance. A diamond stud winked in her sex.

They went with Richelle Matthews. Afterwards, the three of them came back to Rollo and Fee's bubble house in the Zoo.

Rollo sat in a chair and watched. His wife was naked, on her back and arched like a bow. Between her straining legs Richelle sucked her into a frenzy.

He came over and yanked the women apart. He pushed Fee onto her side and slid his cock into her wet, aroused sex. Richelle's mouth had prepared her. He would now have her.

He lay on his side at his wife's back. His hips jolted steadily. As he filled her cunt, Fee lay facing Richelle. She kissed her mouth and fondled her breasts while her husband fucked her from behind.

273

He couldn't get enough of Fee. Afterwards, she crouched over Richelle, kissing her pussy and moving up to kiss her mouth and her breasts, then coming down again to kiss her moist open vulva. Even as she did this, Rollo entered her again. She kissed Richelle, bending over her, their breasts mingling, as Rollo pumped into her own endlessly greedy pussy.

Suddenly Rollo pulled out. Before either woman had realised what was happening, he slid his wet cock straight into Richelle's open sex. Gently he began to work her.

She gasped and tried to pull away. Fee laughed and kissed her, sucking her nipples, making her writhe with the ardour of her embraces.

Richelle felt a panic at Rollo's entrance. She had become fascinated with his body, she admitted it. She was enjoying the spice of being loved by Fee while Fee was penetrated by a man. But now his big sex, and he was very big, was in her own private place, her inviolate place, and she was afraid.

Fee calmed her and kissed her. Fee caressed her and fondled her. Her whole body felt rich and honeyed. The manflesh in her was ripe. Her clitoris was stimulated at every stroke. She couldn't resist; her orgasm was coming.

Both Fee and Rollo understood the tremors that shook her body. Rollo pulled out of her and bent his head between her legs. A moment later, he was kissing the tender bruised flesh, nibbling its ridges and valleys, sucking the sweet juices of her lust.

Later, Fee said drowsily: 'I realise this might be a bore, Rollo, but I've let you in for something, I'm afraid. It's a promise I made.'

'What's that?' Rollo's voice was deep and contented. His arm was faintly stiff but otherwise his wound had healed well. He had two beautiful women in bed with him, one eager and versatile, the other enchantingly reluctant. He held a breast in each hand, each belonging to a different woman.

'Sandrina. She joined those dreadful women in case you

were there. I promised her access to your body. You'll have to be nice to her, Rollo. Really nice, I mean, however boring she is.'

Rollo sucked a nipple, wondering idly whose it was. He smiled in the dimness. 'Don't worry about me being bored, sweetheart,' he said. 'I feel I'll never be bored again.'

Richelle sighed. It was a velvety sound. She rubbed her short soft hair all over Rollo's cock, tickling him there. Then she twisted over and began tentatively to lick and kiss the thing she had so disliked.

'I'll always think women are better,' she said, pausing for a moment. 'But I'll grant you men ain't so bad.'

In her mouth, Rollo's cock started to grow.

NEW BOOKS

Coming up from Nexus and Black Lace

The Handmaidens by Aran Ashe
March 1995   Price: £4.99   ISBN: 0 352 32985 8

Aran Ashe, creator of the legendary Lidir books, is back with a brilliant new series of erotic fantasy novels: the Chronicles of Tormunil. In this, the first book, we meet Sianon and Iroise, young and beautiful serving wenches who seem condemned to a future of absolute obedience and self-denial in the sinister Abbey. Help may be at hand in the form of a handsome young traveller – but it's help at a price.

The Governess at St Agatha's by Yolanda Celbridge
March 1995   Price: £4.99   ISBN: 0 352 32986 6

A welcome return for Miss Constance de Comynge, former Cornish governess. Now she's headmistress of St Agatha's, a young ladies' academy where discipline is foremost on the syllabus. Competition is tough for places in the 'Swish Club', a select group whose beautiful members revel in punishing each other – and prominent members of the local gentry.

Lingering Lessons by Sarah Veitch
April 1995   Price: £4.99   ISBN: 0 352 32990 4

Leanne has just inherited an old boarding school, but she has to share it with the mysterious Adam Howard. Only one thing is certain about her new partner: he is a true devotee of corporal punishment. The last thing Leanne expects is to be drawn into his sordid yet exciting world, but the temptation proves irresistible.

The Awakening of Lydia by Philippa Masters
April 1995   Price: £4.99   ISBN: 0 352 33002 3

As the daughter of a district commissioner during the Boer War, Lydia has plenty of opportunity for excitement – and plenty of sex-starved men to pleasure her. But their skills are nothing compared to the voracious sexual appetites of the local tribesmen, who waste no time in taking the stunning sixteen-year-old captive.

Unfinished Business by Sarah Hope-Walker
March 1995   Price: £4.99   ISBN: 0 352 32983 1
Joanne's job as financial analyst for a leading London bank
requires a lot of responsibility and control. Her true, submissive
self has little opportunity to blossom until the suave,
gifted and dominant Nikolai walks into her life. But her happiness
is soon threatened by the return of an equally masterful
old flame.

Nicole's Revenge by Lisette Allen
March 1995   Price: £4.99   ISBN: 0 352 32984 X
It's taken Nicole Chabrier four years' hard work at the Paris
Opera to make something of herself. But when France erupts
into revolution, she has to rely on a dashing stranger to save
her from an angry mob. She is only too happy to use her considerable
charms to repay the favour and to help Jacques gain
revenge on those who wronged him.

Crimson Buccaneer by Cleo Cordell
April 1995   Price: £4.99   ISBN: 0 352 32987 4
Cheated out of her inheritance, Carlotta Mendoza wants revenge;
and with her exquisite looks and feminine wiles, there
is no shortage of men willing to offer her help. She takes to the
seas with a rugged buccaneer and begins systematically boarding,
robbing and sexually humiliating her enemies.

La Basquaise by Angel Strand
April 1995   Price: £4.99   ISBN: 0 352 32988 2
Oruela is a modern young woman of 1920s Biarritz who seeks
to join the bohemian set. Her lover, Jean, is helping her to
achieve her social aspirations. But an unfortunate accident involving
her father brings her under suspicion, and a sinister
game of sexual blackmail throws her life into turmoil . . .

NEXUS BACKLIST

All books are priced £4.99 unless another price is given. If a date is supplied, the book in question will not be available until that month in 1995.

CONTEMPORARY EROTICA

THE ACADEMY	Arabella Knight	
CONDUCT UNBECOMING	Arabella Knight	Jul
CONTOURS OF DARKNESS	Marco Vassi	
THE DEVIL'S ADVOCATE	Anonymous	
DIFFERENT STROKES	Sarah Veitch	Aug
THE DOMINO TATTOO	Cyrian Amberlake	
THE DOMINO ENIGMA	Cyrian Amberlake	
THE DOMINO QUEEN	Cyrian Amberlake	
ELAINE	Stephen Ferris	
EMMA'S SECRET WORLD	Hilary James	
EMMA ENSLAVED	Hilary James	
EMMA'S SECRET DIARIES	Hilary James	
FALLEN ANGELS	Kendal Grahame	
THE FANTASIES OF JOSEPHINE SCOTT	Josephine Scott	
THE GENTLE DEGENERATES	Marco Vassi	
HEART OF DESIRE	Maria del Rey	
HELEN – A MODERN ODALISQUE	Larry Stern	
HIS MISTRESS'S VOICE	G. C. Scott	
HOUSE OF ANGELS	Yvonne Strickland	May
THE HOUSE OF MALDONA	Yolanda Celbridge	
THE IMAGE	Jean de Berg	Jul
THE INSTITUTE	Maria del Rey	
SISTERHOOD OF THE INSTITUTE	Maria del Rey	

EROTIC SCIENCE FICTION

FANTASYWORLD	Larry Stern	
WANTON	Andrea Arven	

ANCIENT & FANTASY SETTINGS

CHAMPIONS OF LOVE	Anonymous	
CHAMPIONS OF PLEASURE	Anonymous	
CHAMPIONS OF DESIRE	Anonymous	
THE CLOAK OF APHRODITE	Kendal Grahame	
THE HANDMAIDENS	Aran Ashe	
THE SLAVE OF LIDIR	Aran Ashe	
THE DUNGEONS OF LIDIR	Aran Ashe	
THE FOREST OF BONDAGE	Aran Ashe	
PLEASURE ISLAND	Aran Ashe	
WITCH QUEEN OF VIXANIA	Morgana Baron	

EDWARDIAN, VICTORIAN & OLDER EROTICA

ANNIE	Evelyn Culber	
ANNIE AND THE SOCIETY	Evelyn Culber	
THE AWAKENING OF LYDIA	Philippa Masters	Apr
BEATRICE	Anonymous	
CHOOSING LOVERS FOR JUSTINE	Aran Ashe	
GARDENS OF DESIRE	Roger Rougiere	
THE LASCIVIOUS MONK	Anonymous	
LURE OF THE MANOR	Barbra Baron	
RETURN TO THE MANOR	Barbra Baron	Jun
MAN WITH A MAID 1	Anonymous	
MAN WITH A MAID 2	Anonymous	
MAN WITH A MAID 3	Anonymous	
MEMOIRS OF A CORNISH GOVERNESS	Yolanda Celbridge	
THE GOVERNESS AT ST AGATHA'S	Yolanda Celbridge	
TIME OF HER LIFE	Josephine Scott	
VIOLETTE	Anonymous	

THE JAZZ AGE

BLUE ANGEL NIGHTS	Margarete von Falkensee	
BLUE ANGEL DAYS	Margarete von Falkensee	

BLUE ANGEL SECRETS	Margarete von Falkensee	
CONFESSIONS OF AN ENGLISH MAID	Anonymous	
PLAISIR D'AMOUR	Anne-Marie Villefranche	
FOLIES D'AMOUR	Anne-Marie Villefranche	
JOIE D'AMOUR	Anne-Marie Villefranche	
MYSTERE D'AMOUR	Anne-Marie Villefranche	
SECRETS D'AMOUR	Anne-Marie Villefranche	
SOUVENIR D'AMOUR	Anne-Marie Villefranche	

SAMPLERS & COLLECTIONS

EROTICON 1	ed. J-P Spencer	
EROTICON 2	ed. J-P Spencer	
EROTICON 3	ed. J-P Spencer	
EROTICON 4	ed. J-P Spencer	
NEW EROTICA 1	ed. Esme Ombreux	
NEW EROTICA 2	ed. Esme Ombreux	
THE FIESTA LETTERS	ed. Chris Lloyd	£4.50

NON-FICTION

HOW TO DRIVE YOUR MAN WILD IN BED	Graham Masterton
HOW TO DRIVE YOUR WOMAN WILD IN BED	Graham Masterton
LETTERS TO LINZI	Linzi Drew
LINZI DREW'S PLEASURE GUIDE	Linzi Drew

Please send me the books I have ticked above.

Name ....

Address ....

....

....

.... Post code ....

Send to: Cash Sales, Nexus Books, 332 Ladbroke Grove, London W10 5AH.

Please enclose a cheque or postal order, made payable to **Nexus Books**, to the value of the books you have ordered plus postage and packing costs as follows:

UK and BFPO – £1.00 for the first book, 50p for each subsequent book.

Overseas (including Republic of Ireland) – £2.00 for the first book, £1.00 for the second book, and 50p for each subsequent book.

If you would prefer to pay by VISA or ACCESS/MASTER-CARD, please write your card number and expiry date here:

....

Please allow up to 28 days for delivery.

Signature ....